BLESSED
ODDS

BLESSED ODDS

Riftborn * Book 2

STEVE McHUGH

Podium

For Keira.

Copyright © 2023 by Steve McHugh

Cover design by Podium Publishing

ISBN: 978-1-0394-1952-0

Published in 2023 by Podium Publishing, ULC
www.podiumaudio.com

Podium

GLOSSARY

SPECIES:

Ancients: The oldest, but not necessarily the most powerful, members of the rift-fused. They ensure that there are checks and balances between rift-fused and humans.

eidolons: Living embodiment of rift power that reside as caretakers of a riftborn's embers. Can change shape to most animals as needed. Are always two for every riftborn's embers.

fiends: Animals that die on Earth close to a tear and are brought back to life from the power of the rift. Come in three kinds: lesser, greater, and elder.

practitioners: Those born inside the rift. Can create constructs along with using the rift to imbue writing and potions with its power.

Primes: The rulers of Inaxia, the capital city of the rift.

primordials: Creatures that live inside the Tempest in the rift.

revenants: Those who died on Earth as human close to a tear and were brought back to life by the power of the rift. There are ten different species of revenant.

rift-fused: Anyone or anything given power by the rift.

rift-walker: Can create tears between the rift and Earth at will.

riftborn: Those who were mortally wounded on Earth as human but were taken into the rift and gifted incredible power. Can move between Earth and the rift using their embers.

GROUPS:

Guilds: Seven groups of powerful rift-fused who ensure that humans and rift-fused live in harmony.

Investigators: Police force of Inaxia.

RCU (Rift-Crime Unit): Multi-nation agency who investigate crimes committed by and against the rift-fused.

Talon: Guild member trained in secret to remove threats to their Guild.

PLACES:

Crow's Perch: Prison city in the rift, run by the Queen of Crows.

embers: The pocket dimension used by riftborn to travel between Earth and the rift, as well as to heal any physical wounds the riftborn has sustained.

Inaxia: Capital city of the rift.

Lawless City: City in the rift that doesn't want to live under Inaxia rule.

Nightvale: Settlement in the rift.

rift: Dimension attached to our own that allows incredible power to flow out from it through tears between dimensions.

Tempest: The maelstrom of power at the north of the rift.

BLESSED
ODDS

CHAPTER ONE

London in the summertime is that awful combination of torrential rain, stifling heat, and unbearable humidity. Usually one right after the other, occasionally all three at the same time. Either way, you spend half of the time feeling like you're walking through treacle.

The sun shone through the windows of the cab as the driver weaved through early-morning traffic, and I tried my best not to be concerned about other people using the road. London roads were more Mad Max–inspired than most other parts of the country, and I'd long since given up driving in the city if I could get away with it.

"Lucas, King's Cross station, now," Ji-hyun had said before hanging up.

I'd called the concierge to get me a taxi, and had been dressed and out of the hotel door a few minutes later. The car had been waiting for me as I stepped outside of my hotel near St Paul's Cathedral. Ji-hyun Han, Nadia (no last name), and I had all been staying in the same hotel, although Ji-hyun and Nadia had left earlier to meet the human detective who was helping us while we were in London.

I got into the black cab and told the driver the destination. Thankfully, there was no conversation, and it meant I could sit back and continue to wake up. I'd been mid-breakfast when the phone call had stopped me from finishing a second cup of coffee.

The possibilities of why Ji-hyun had sounded so urgent rattled through my brain. She wasn't hurt; I was sure of that. She and Nadia were more than able to take care of themselves. It was probably to do with why we were in London, still searching for those blasted vials of the super serum that Callie Mitchell had sent to buyers several months earlier. Dozens of vials of lethal gene-mutating serum sent all around the world. We'd only found nine. The odds weren't exactly in our favour that we'd find the rest before any more of them were used to transform whoever took them into a monster.

Six months earlier, I'd killed Mason—a spoilt, rich brat with delusions of grandeur—and Callie had gone to ground; half a dozen people had used the vial they'd received. They'd all been criminals of various levels and had all been about as pleasant to deal with as having sandpaper rubbed over your genitals. They'd also all died horribly, either because their body hadn't taken well to the drug they'd taken, and they'd essentially melted, or because some rift-fused were there to put them down. But either way, they hadn't been stopped before they'd killed people. Callie had innocent blood on her hands, and she was going to eventually pay for that. But first things first: find the rest of the damn poison.

Ji-hyun had been asked to take over the investigation on behalf of the Rift-Crime Unit, primarily because most of the New York branch where Callie had been were either dead, working for the bad guys, or both. I got the feeling that Ji-hyun accepted more out of a need to punch Callie—and anyone working with her—in the face than anything else.

Our investigations had revealed that a man calling himself *the Crou-pier*—for reasons I'm sure he thought were incredibly clever—had arranged the meeting between Callie and her buyers. Callie had escaped while I'd killed her underling and was . . . who knew where. That left one thread to tug on.

A cyclist took their life into their own hands and cut up the cab, prompting the taxi driver to throw some good old British curse words at the offending rider, who stopped and stuck his middle finger up before continuing on.

"Fuckin' cyclists," the taxi driver said in an east London accent. He was white with a bald head and a few days' worth of stubble. On the back of his left forearm was a tattooed badge of a military unit, although I couldn't have said which one.

I gave a noncommittal grunt; I was just glad no one got hurt. Cyclists in London are part daredevil and part insane-asylum escapee, the degrees of each part dependent on the day and weather conditions. The hotter it got, the less inclined anyone was to be nice to one another.

"You from London?" the driver asked.

"No," I said, steeling myself for the inevitable conversation. "Was born up north, but I spent a lot of time in the city. At some point, my accent sort of merged into one that doesn't sound like I'm from anywhere."

"You're from Yorkshire?" the driver asked with no hostility or mocking in his tone, just a genuine level of curiosity.

"Not exactly," I said, not wanting to get into the whole thing about being born when Yorkshire was just a collection of tribes. The world knew about riftborn and revenants, about how they were created, about our exceptionally long lives, but that didn't mean they were always welcome. Their knowledge of us as a species was relatively new, and fear was still a big part of their reaction to us.

"It's a bit of an everywhere accent, isn't it?" he said.

I nodded. "It's what happens when you move around a lot," I told him. "You from around here, then?"

"Hackney," he said. "Hence the Hammers badge. You a supporter?"

"No," I admitted. "Moved around so much that I never really settled on a team. Always enjoyed going to watch a game, though. Well, most of the time."

"Yeah, not every game can be a blinder," he said with a chuckle. "I take my nippers to them, though. Good time to spend with the kids, and it gives the wife some time off." He laughed at that one.

"She not a fan?"

"She's a fuckin' Man City fan," he said with slight disgust in his voice.

"Must be fun in the house when they play each other," I said with a smile.

"It's hell, mate," he said. "They battered us last time and she didn't let me forget it for weeks. She made me fish and chips that night and spelt out *4–0* on the plate."

I laughed at that.

"It were fuckin' quality, if I'm honest," he said with a laugh of his own. "Hopefully, one day I can repay the favour."

The cab stopped, and I paid, leaving the driver a nice tip for his morning trouble. "Best of luck at the next game," I said.

"Thanks, have a good day, mate," he said, driving off.

I turned around to find Ji-hyun staring at me. Judging by the expression on her face, it was not going to be a good day.

Ji-hyun Han was little over five and a half feet tall, with long brown hair that was, as usual, scooped back into a high ponytail. She wore black boots, jeans, a red T-shirt with a Starfleet badge from *Star Trek* on the left breast. Unlike most redshirts, there was a hundred percent chance that she'd make it back from an away mission.

"What happened?" I ask, looking around for Nadia and feeling concern in my gut.

"Nadia is fine," Ji-hyun said, as if sensing my thoughts. "She's gone with Ravi."

"Okay, so, what was the urgency in getting me here?" I asked. "What's going on?"

"You remember our inside man who has been feeding us information?" she asked.

"Simon Wallace?" I asked. Ex-paratrooper, current criminal, and all round semi-bad guy. He drew the line at innocent people dying because someone turned into a monster and went on a rampage. I actually liked the guy: he was completely honest about what he was and why he did it, and that was always better than people who made excuses because they couldn't outright deal with their life choices.

"That's the one," Ji-hyun said as I followed her across the wide-open space in front of King's Cross train station. "Well, Simon just called and informed us that the Croupier and his people are boarding a train from King's Cross to Edinburgh in an hour and ten minutes."

"That's going to be a very busy train," I said, thinking with concern at what might happen on a speeding train that was packed with commuters, if the Croupier found themselves threatened.

"It's going to be empty," Ji-hyun said with a smile as she stopped and turned to me. "Mostly empty."

"Why?" I asked.

"Because it's not a normal commuter train; it's a rich-person train."

"Is that really a thing?" I asked as she turned and began walking again.

"Sort of," Ji-hyun said. "We'll go see Ravi and he'll explain."

I wordlessly followed Ji-hyun up a nearby street, where she indicated two unmarked police cars. Looks like Ravi had bought backup.

We arrived at the hotel, the name of which I didn't catch or care about, and stepped through a set of automatic double doors into a large, spacious lobby. A rock feature sat in the centre of the large room, in front of three elevators. Lights shone from the base of the feature, illuminating the lower half of the fifty-foot-tall sculpture in a slowly shifting rainbow of colours.

The right of the foyer lead to a restaurant that proudly declared itself to have the *best steak in town*, which I doubted. The restaurant was empty. The right side of the foyer was the check-in, and there were currently half a dozen people queued there.

"You got the medallion on?" Ji-hyun asked.

I fished my Guild badge—a copper-coloured buckler shield made out of hardened stone with silver sword and hammer crossing over it, and a small black raven atop it as if holding the shield—out from under my dark blue plain T-shirt so it was visible to everyone. The badge of the Raven Guild. I was the only member left after everyone else had been murdered, but it still afforded me the same privileges as when the Guild had been full. Every law enforcement agency in the world knew what a Guild badge meant: *give me access and keep your mouth shut.* Not every member of law enforcement was happy about it.

Two plain-clothed officers, obvious to anyone who'd worked with their type before, stood in front of the elevator: a man and woman, just talking to each other as if they weren't there for any particular reason. Both looked over at me and stepped aside when they saw us, passing me a key card.

"For the room," the female officer said.

I thanked them as Ji-hyun pushed the button for the elevator, and the four of us waited in uncomfortable silence. Law enforcement might know what the medallion meant, but that didn't mean they had to like it. There had been members of Guilds in the past who had used that power in unethical ways, and stories grew about how Guilds were a law unto themselves. How we didn't care about human laws. Half the time, we were so busy trying to ensure that either humans didn't kill revenants or vice versa that human laws just became a bureaucratic over-complication.

The elevator eventually arrived, and Ji-hyun and I stepped inside, giving me a moment of relief.

"Police aren't happy we're here?" I asked.

"Don't care," Ji-hyun said with a shrug. "Their boss is okay with it and that's all I care about."

"You left Nadia with Ravi?" I asked.

"She likes him," Ji-hyun said with a sigh, as the elevator door opened, and we both stepped out into a small, windowed foyer with glass and dark-wood doors on either side. I spotted a card reader on the door leading to the rooms. You had to be a guest—or at least have a working card—to get through it.

I scanned the card over the door, and Ji-hyun pulled it open before I could, holding it for me as I stepped through.

"Ta very much," I said with a smile.

"Don't get used to it," Ji-hyun said with a smile of her own.

I followed her the short distance to a hotel room, where she knocked twice and the door opened, revealing Agent Ravi Gill.

Ravi was just over six feet tall with brown skin and a slight Cockney accent. He wore a dark grey suit that I wasn't convinced was standard issue. He'd been our point of call when we'd arrived in London to investigate the missing vials. He worked for the RCU, but due to underfunding and how a lot of people still didn't trust those who had died and returned, the RCU in the UK was only recently given its own autonomy. Before then, it had been merged with an MI5 unit, meaning some of the RCU members were human. It also meant you had to be *really* good at your job. Humans tended to be a bit squishy, especially when it came to having a revenant or fiend barrelling toward you.

Public opinion was still divided on rift-fused—those humans or animals who had died and then been powered by the rift and returned as something more. Some hailed revenants and riftborn as miracles, but others called us demons, devils, and much worse. Certain politicians play on that fear of the unknown, and the politicians in the UK were no different from those anywhere else. Find a scapegoat and make everything their fault.

Thankfully, Ravi been helpful and considerate, and had wanted to catch Callie Mitchell and anyone who had helped her a lot more than he wanted to play political bullshit with us. I liked him. But more importantly, I trusted him to do his job well.

I stepped inside the hotel room, following Ji-hyun as I took in the layout of the room: One king-sized bed, lit by small lamps on either side of it. The bed was messy, the pillows on the floor beside it, the white cotton duvet cover strewn in the corner. The end of the bed had a metal footboard that Nadia was perched on. She was, as always, barefoot, and her chains were wrapped around her, like a comfort blanket.

Apart from the bed, the room had a wooden desk with coffee machine and phone on it. The curtains were open, and light flooded into the room. The room's key card was inserted into the card reader next to the door. The bathroom door was ajar, light spilling out over the dark purple carpet. There were pieces of artwork on the walls of the room and a small HDTV up on the wall opposite the bed.

"Been productive?" I asked Nadia.

Nadia was five feet tall, with short dark hair and olive skin. She wore faded blue jeans and a bright yellow T-shirt. She allowed herself to fall back onto the bed and lay there like she was making a snow-angel in the bed covers.

"She okay?" Ravi asked.

"Define *okay*," Ji-hyun replied.

Nadia let out a slight giggle.

"She's fine," I said. "Nadia, are you fine?"

"Dandy," she said, giving a thumbs-up.

"She's probably seeing a new timeline," I said. "Chained revenants can see multiple threads of their own future. Sometimes, those threads are . . . strange and cause momentary lapses of . . ." I gestured to Nadia, who was now bouncing gently on the bed. 'Well . . . this . . ." I said.

Ravi looked over at Nadia and smiled. "Fair enough," he said, looking back at me. "Sorry to get you up early."

"No bother," I told him. "Ji-hyun said you have a rich person's train and a target."

"Every morning at exactly ten a.m., a train leaves King's Cross and doesn't stop until it reaches Edinburgh," Ravi explained. "It then comes back. Every. Single. Day. It's used by a very select group of people, who I believe are involved with the Croupier. It's where deals are done."

"And who arranged this exclusive train?" I asked.

"I'm looking into that right now," Ravi said. "It went through a committee with the government, but so does a lot of stuff."

"So, some MPs might be involved?" Ji-hyun asked.

"I can neither confirm nor deny that we are currently looking into several sitting members of Parliament," Ravi said as if reading it off a teleprompter.

"You've said that before," I said.

"It could just be a coincidence," Ravi said.

"I don't like coincidences," Ji-hyun said.

"I don't like beetroot," Nadia said, from where she lay on the bed. "You forget you've eaten it, and then you go pee, and bam, you see pink pee and freak out."

Everyone turned to stare at Nadia before pretending like that part of the conversation hadn't happened.

"So, are we sure that this Croupier is on board the train?" Ji-hyun asked.

"No, but Simon says his allies will be," Ravi said. "They could be a source of great information."

"So, why not just stop the train in King's Cross before it leaves?" I asked.

"Because if they don't go quietly, we've got a rift-fused battle in the middle of one of London's busiest train stations. Innocent people would be hurt. I don't think any of us want that."

"So, we need to get on the train and stop it once it's some distance from a populated area," I said.

"That's the plan," Ravi agreed.

"Okay, so, how do we get on?" I asked.

"I assume you'll figure a way," Ravi said.

"How do you guys get on?" Ji-hyun asked.

"You'll have to stop the train, and we'll be there when it's done," Ravi said.

"Let me get this right," I said, leaning up against the edge of the bed. "You want us to board a train with potentially dangerous people on board, stop them, stop the train, and somehow do this *safely*?"

"Can I fight on the roof?" Nadia asked sitting up. "I've never fought on the roof of a train before."

"You do realise that fighting on the roof of a train would be near impossible," Ji-hyun asked.

Nadia waved her arms. "I died. I was reborn. I have chains coming out of me. I can see multiple futures. Which part of fighting on a train is harder than all of those?"

"Everyone has a dream," Ravi said.

"Yes," Nadia almost shouted. "See, Ravi believes in me."

"I'm not sure I'd go that far," Ravi started.

"No need to backtrack," Nadia said, getting to her feet and hugging a clearly confused Ravi. "You believe in me, and that's all that matters."

"Yes, Ravi," I said with a smile. "All Nadia needs is the belief that she can fight on a train roof. Physics be damned."

Nadia clapped. "I'm going to mentally prepare myself." She left the room a moment later, and everyone exchanged a bemused look.

"Are all chained revenants like her?" Ravi asked.

"No," Ji-hyun said. "Some are completely insane."

"Or murderous," I added.

"Or just psychotic," Ji-hyun continued.

"Or all three," I said.

"Those are the fun ones," Ji-hyun said, pointing at me as if I'd said something perfect.

"Can you do this?" Ravi asked, his voice now serious.

"Of course," Ji-hyun said. "I'll go find Nadia and make sure she's not trying to learn how to fly or something."

"No bravado," Ravi said when we were alone. "Our informant got us this information."

"Is Simon still safe?" I asked.

"He's being monitored for now," Ravi said. "There's nothing linking him to anything we're about to do, but we're keeping an eye on him and his family, just in case. So, can you do this?"

"Ravi, we can do this," I said. "I'm not convinced Nadia will be able to have a fight on the train roof, but the rest of it, sure. What's the target's name?"

"Eve Dior," Ravi said. "We know that's not her real name. She's Caucasian, about five-three, maybe nine stone, we have no photos of her. No one has photos of her. Simon wouldn't risk taking any. She terrifies him. He's an ex-paratrooper."

"Scary lady on a train," I said. "We'll deal with her. Bring her in, get you to question her, and hopefully we'll get intel on where the rest of the blasted vials are."

"If we can get her and get intel, we might be able to stop this before more people die," Ravi said.

"Let's hope so," I told him, and left the hotel room, feeling like neither Ravi nor myself believed that.

CHAPTER TWO

King's Cross railway station has had quite a lot of investment put into it over the years, turning it back to something approaching what it would have looked like in its glory days of the nineteenth century. The interior was light now, with the high glass roof an impressive sight. It was a far cry from the drab and dingy setting that it had become in the 1980s. Although, to be fair, quite a lot of England was drab and dingy in the 1980s.

"Where does the train leave from?" I asked, looking around at the crowds of people as we walked through the concourse. They were swiftly discounted as threats, just normal travellers concerned with trying to find out where their own trains arrived or left from.

"Platform eight," Ji-hyun said.

It dawned on me that we were missing a member of our team. "Where's Nadia?"

"Remaining inconspicuous," Ji-hyun said.

As much as the world might know revenants exist, chained revenants are still rare, and people stare. I'd rather they didn't. Nadia would also rather they didn't, but the idea of Nadia remaining anything close to inconspicuous was something I'd never considered was actually possible. "Have you noticed that she's more . . . open with us than she used to be?" I asked.

Ji-hyun nodded. "She was tense when we first met, although that was because she thought one of our allies might kill her. She's a bit freer with her personality now."

"It's nice to see," I said, spotting Nadia at the far end of the station, beyond the ticket machines and station staff. Her chains had been retracted up into her arms, something I knew she wasn't keen on doing for long periods. She said they itched under her skin, like a thousand ants marching over her bones.

Ji-hyun passed me a ticket and we placed them in slots on the dark grey barriers, which opened, allowing us through.

A large white-faced clock with black Roman numerals sat above platform eight; we had fifteen minutes before the train would depart. We couldn't arrive too soon, and we couldn't leave it too late. Neither were good options, but when you have no good options, you go with the one that's less likely to bring down armed guards onto you. And it was almost certain that the train—whether or not firearms were legal in the UK—would have armed guards onboard.

The train was identical in shape to every other train that ran the route from King's Cross to Edinburgh. Instead of the usual red and white, or blue and white, our train was black and silver, although with a bright yellow nose just below the driver's cabin.

A guard walked the length of the train. He was a heavyset man with dark trousers and a midnight blue shirt. He wore a black tie and flat cap, and looked more like something out of a 1950s gangster film than a train guard.

"So, how are we getting on the train?" I asked Ji-hyun.

She shrugged and looked around. "And where's Nadia?"

I followed Ji-hyun's search. "Ah, crap," I said. "Where'd she go?"

"Hi," Nadia said from behind me, causing me to jump a little. She was eating chocolate ice cream in a waffle cone.

I turned around to find her standing there smiling. "Where'd you come from?"

"Ah, there's a shop up there," she said, pointing to the far end of the train platform.

"During your exploring, did you happen to come up with an idea how we get on the train?" Ji-hyun asked.

"We ask," Nadia said, turning around and continuing to eat her ice cream cone as she walked up to the guard, waved at him, and said something I didn't hear.

"I'm going to regret agreeing to this, aren't I?" I said.

"Almost certainly," Ji-hyun agreed.

The guard looked over at Ji-hyun and me, and I wondered what was going to happen next. He was almost certainly armed, although he was also unlikely to start shooting on a train platform in the middle of King's Cross. People tend to notice stuff like that, and I doubted his employers wanted the publicity that would bring.

The guard spoke into his lapel, nodding furiously, before waving Ji-hyun and I over. "You're permitted aboard," he said in a thick Manchester accent, motioning toward one of the doors, which slid open to reveal a small hallway between adjoining train carriages. A large man with pale skin, bald head, and goatee stepped into view, unbuttoned his black suit jacket, and pulled it aside slightly to reveal the holster he wore.

"That was very subtle," Ji-hyun said.

"I barely caught it," I said. "Do it again."

"Get on board," the large man said. He looked like someone had inflated him from the chest up.

"You skipped leg day," Nadia said to the guard as she climbed into the train. There was an immediate beeping sound.

"Metal detectors in the doors," the man said.

"Never skip leg day," Nadia continued, ignoring the large man.

The man growled and Nadia growled back before leaving my sight and entering the carriage proper. Ji-hyun was next and there was no beep. The fact that she was unarmed was a little unusual for her, although technically Ji-hyun was a walking weapon, so additional means to kill people weren't exactly needed.

I was last onto the train, and the guard held out his hands.

"Blades," he said, making it sound like I had no choice in the matter.

I removed the two rift-tempered daggers from the sheaths on my lower back and passed the blue-tinged blades to him. "Don't break them," I said.

"You'll get them back," he said, although I was pretty sure he thought otherwise.

The outer train door closed and a bell sounded twice. A second later, there was a jolt and the train set off.

"You know this is a trap, yes?" Ji-hyun whispered to me.

"Oh, yes," I said. "Either Simon let them know we were coming, or they have someone on the inside who did. But we're here now, so let's try not to get killed."

"Good plan," Ji-hyun said.

The carriage beyond was elegantly decorated in red and gold, and looked like something you might have seen during Victorian times. Instead of row after row of seating, there were only two sets of four seats, one at the far end of the carriage, near another door, and one in the middle. There were three guards in the carriage, two at the end, by the tables, and one stood beside the tables in the centre, next to someone whose back was toward us.

The carriage had a deep red carpet, and it felt cooler than it had on the train platform, the HVACs making a low humming noise as I walked by them.

The person with their back toward us had short dark hair with midnight-blue highlights that occasionally caught the light when they moved. They got up from their seat and turned toward us. The woman was just over five feet tall, with pale skin and half a dozen golden earrings in each ear, several of which were large enough to touch her shoulder. She wore a white blouse, black skirt, and black high-heeled shoes. A platinum Rolex Yacht Master sat on her wrist. A woman with expensive tastes. Or someone who liked everyone to know how much money they had. Maybe both.

"Ah, crap," Ji-hyun said with a loud sigh.

"Ji-hyun," the woman said, her accent a slight mix of French and American, as she crossed her muscular arms over her chest.

"Eve," Ji-hyun said, the word coming out a little harsh.

"You two friends?" Nadia asked.

"We were *much* more than that," Eve said with raised eyebrows.

"You work for psychopaths now?" Ji-hyun asked sharply. "Money always was the most important thing in your life."

"Why don't you wait outside so the adults can talk," Eve said dismissively.

Ji-hyun's eyes widened, and for a second, I thought she might rush toward Eve. So did the guards in the carriage, who all tensed, but no one went for a weapon.

"They're not armed," I said, more to myself than anything else.

"My employer doesn't like guns on the train," Eve said. "Not unless absolutely necessary, anyway. Francis there has a gun, as does the train guard. No need for anyone else to be armed. We don't want to bring attention to ourselves unnecessarily."

"I'll wait outside the carriage," Ji-hyun told me.

I nodded. No point asking if she was okay; she clearly wasn't, and the sly smile on Eve's face told me she was enjoying herself a bit too much.

Nadia walked past me and sat down at the table next to the one Eve had been using. "Nice place you've got," she said, looking out of the tinted windows. "Real private-like."

"My employer values the privacy of his clients," Eve said.

"They must have some real clout if they can get a whole train arranged to travel the country every day," I said, noticing that the guards were now visibly relaxed.

"Come, sit, Mr. Rurik," Eve said.

"You don't skip leg day," Nadia said.

Eve looked over at my companion and smiled. "No, I do not."

Nadia gave her a thumbs-up and went back to looking out of the window.

"A chained revenant as a companion," Eve said, motioning for me to take a seat opposite her. "An unusual thing to see."

"I'm an unusual person," Nadia said without looking back at us.

"So, do you feel like telling me why you invited us onto your lovely train funded by blood money?" I asked.

"That's a very dramatic way of putting it," Eve said with a smirk.

"Your boss, I assume they're your boss, is the Croupier, yes?"

Eve nodded.

"Then they're responsible for Callie Mitchell sending out her poison to the world," I said. "Innocent people have died because of those actions. Also, I'm pretty sure you've killed people. You don't get your own train and a spot on the UK's rail infrastructure without having friends in high places. And you don't get friends in high places when you're someone who brokers deals between criminals, without knowing where the bodies are buried."

"And who put them there," Eve agreed, taking a sip of what appeared to be tea from a white and pink China cup. "Would you like some? It's jasmine black tea."

"I'm good, thanks," I said.

"No," Nadia told her. "It sounds like something I'd hate."

"You're more of a green- or white-tea person?" Eve asked her.

Nadia turned back to her calmly. "No, I just don't drink with people I don't like."

Suppressing a smile, I noticed a flash of irritation on Eve's otherwise-immaculate face. The smile that followed was cold and hard. I wondered if she'd killed people herself. I wondered why Ji-hyun radiated anger at her. Eve did not strike me as a woman who was opposed to getting her hands dirty, even if they were perfectly manicured.

"My boss, as you put it, would like to talk to you," Eve told me. She removed a mobile phone from her pocket and placed it on the table, putting in the six-digit number and tapping the little green phone icon, selecting a number with no name above it, and letting it ring for a few seconds.

"Eve," the man on the other end said.

"Lucas Rurik is here." Eve looked up at me. "He's an interesting man, just like you said."

"He's a killer," the man said. "Aren't you, Lucas. I've read up about you. Final surviving member of the Raven Guild, fought in several wars over the centuries, spent a lot of time in the rift."

"I assume you're the Croupier?" I asked.

"You do not approve of the name?" the man replied. "It's a bit too Bond-villain for my liking, too, but it got used once and it stuck before I could change it. You get used to it."

"I guess murdering a few people will make others take it seriously," I said.

"You would guess correctly, Mr. Rurik," the Croupier said, his voice never changing from its conversational tone.

"So, where did you get that file on me, I wonder?" I asked. The only people I knew who might have anything close to a full working file on my history were the Ancients and those who worked for them.

"Anything can be obtained if you know the right people and the right . . . leverage," the Croupier freely admitted.

"Murder and money," I said with a slight sigh. "You really are a Bond villain."

The man on the end of the phone laughed. I'd been trying to place his accent but was unable to. It mostly sounded like posh English, but occasionally there were hints of American, maybe Canadian. It was an amalgamation of accents that together meant nothing. I got the feeling that was done on purpose.

"I assume I'm allowed on your train for a reason," I said. "Did someone give us up? Do you have people working inside the RCU?"

"Simon Wallace," he said, as if testing the name. "I do not like betrayal. Or at least when someone betrays me. But no, he didn't give you up; we saw you enter the station on the CCTV. We have access to it throughout the station. Eve asked me what I would like to do, and here we are."

"So, why am I here?" I asked. The Croupier really liked the sound of his own voice.

"I wanted to give you a chance, Mr. Rurik," he said, rolling the first R in my surname as if he was testing it out to see how it tasted. "As I said, we know that Simon is an informant for your friend Agent Ravi; we allowed him to leak the information we needed to get you on board. I do not wish to see you and your friends as enemies; in fact, I would hope that our little tête-à-tête—although admittedly not a completely private one—might see you realise the folly of what you're doing."

I looked back at the guards behind me and moved my head slightly to see Ji-hyun stood just beyond the doorway on the opposite end of the carriage. She did not look happy.

"Here's the deal." I told him. "You tell me where Callie sent that poison and you can do whatever the hell you like," I told the Croupier. "I don't care about your profession, I don't care about your allies, and I don't much care that you clearly have a lot more power in government than I would usually be comfortable with. I just want to get that crap off the streets."

There was a clicking sound; it sounded like the Croupier was clicking his tongue against the roof of his mouth. "It's deeply unfortunate that you're predisposed to think that way. You are *not* the good guy in this scenario, Mr. Rurik. There is no good guy. There are just the people who get rich and the people who stand in the way of progress. Pick one."

"It's funny," I said, leaning back in the comfortable black leather chair. "You brought me here to offer me a bribe to look the other way, which means you either didn't read my file or you got the worst summary of all time." I looked behind me at the guards. "You employ mostly humans, don't you? Can't employ too many revenants or riftborn for the most part because you don't want to bring the Guilds down on you; that would take a big old chunk of flesh out of your budget. You'd have to call in favours from your powerful friends, and they might not want to tangle with Guild business either. That might bring the Ancients down on you, too. And then you're just running for the rest of your life."

"Do you have a point?" the Croupier asked.

"It means I really don't think you want me as an enemy," I said. "I don't think you want that light shining on you. You want to stay in the shadows, and right now that's where you get to live your life. So, I'm going to make you a final offer, Mr. Croupier. You tell me what I want to know, and I'll leave you alone. You'll be Ravi's problem, not mine. He has the official power to actually arrest you; I'm only here because I want that damned poison off the streets before more people die. I'm not interested in the politics; I'm not interested in your crime sheet or who you have wrapped around your finger. I don't care."

"Give up an ally, or you'll hunt me down?" The Croupier started the clicking sound again. "An intriguing offer, Mr. Rurik, but unfortunately, my reputation would suffer should I betray my clientele and would, irrevocably harm my business."

I sighed. "It all goes back to money in the end."

"And power," the Croupier said. "Money and power. The two corner-stones of life. My offer to you is take the money and go."

"How much money are we talking about here?"

Nadia's head spun around to look at me, a look of surprise on her face.

"A million pounds," the Croupier said.

I whistled, genuinely impressed; that was a lot more than anyone else had ever tried to pay me to leave them alone.

"I do not want you as an enemy, Mr. Rurik," the Croupier continued. "So, you either take the money or you die where you sit. Your friends too."

"Cash or death," I said, looking up at Eve, who maintained a completely emotionless expression on her immaculately makeup-applied face. I wondered just how much she was there as a figurehead so that the Croupier didn't have to get his own hands dirty. He was probably sat on some porch somewhere, smoking a cigar and drinking an expensive cognac, presumably while listening to whatever music it is evil master-minds listened to.

"Your answer, Mr. Rurik," the Croupier said, sounding irritated for the first time.

"My answer is I'm going to find you, I'm going to end your operation, and I'm going to make you wish you'd never heard of my name," I told him as Nadia beamed beside me. "You had your chance, Mr. Croupier, and now you're going to wish you'd taken my offer. I hope you have more people, because the ones on this train are about to get very broken."

The Croupier laughed; it was an unpleasant noise. "You're going to die today, and if by some miracle you survive, you'll be sent to your embers to heal. You won't be seeing me anytime soon. By the time you return from your embers, it'll be months, possibly years, and only then will I come to find you. You won't see me, though." The call disconnected.

"So," I said to Eve as the level of tension built up in the carriage. "You going to draw first, or do I need to?"

Eve stood, brushed down her suit, and picked up her phone from the table. "You should have taken the money."

"You should have gotten more guards," Nadia said as Eve slowly saun-tered down the carriage toward the group of six guards, who had all now removed various bladed and blunt weapons.

I looked up the other way and spotted Francis. Poor Francis; he was going to get his head kicked in, and his entire posture suggested he had no idea. He thought he was a tough guy. He put his arm inside his jacket and removed his gun.

"That sucks," I said, getting to my feet, looking between the two groups. I was surprised to find that Francis had placed the gun on a nearby table.

"You want the group or the solitary idiot who thinks he can take us with his bare hands?" I asked Nadia.

"Group," she said with excitement, her chains releasing. They grabbed hold of the seat opposite her, pulling her forward and propelling her over the seat and toward the group of guards like a small, giddy missile.

I looked back at Francis, who was bouncing from foot to foot as the sounds of battle raged behind me. "Francis, I don't think this is going to end well for you." I looked beyond him to the metal door of the carriage, which was slowly turning bright orange; apparently, Ji-hyun was locked out. She wouldn't take long to get in, although I feared the festivities might be done by then.

Francis smiled and removed his jacket, rolling his massive shoulders. He placed my two knives beside his jacket and picked up a syringe from the inside pocket, plunging it into his bare arm. Francis screamed as his body tore open as if the thing that he became burst out from inside of him. It covered everything around him in red gore as the eight-foot-tall, pale green and brown lizard-thing stared at me. It looked like someone had taken a crocodile and made it bipedal, with massive black claws where Francis's hands used to be. Each claw tipped hand was large enough to fit over my head. Francis screamed and charged me.

"Well, fuck," I said.

CHAPTER THREE

There are no textbooks that explain how to fight an eight-feet-tall monster crocodile-human hybrid while inside a train moving at a hundred miles per hour.

I turned to smoke the second Francis, the rabid version of Killer Croc, charged me, his jaws snapping over the smoke as I moved behind him. Turning to smoke doesn't hurt, but something biting me with razor-sharp teeth in my smoke form doesn't feel good; it's like an electric shock up my spine.

I re-formed a few feet behind him, and he spun, one arm stretched out to claw me, but I was a few inches back from his reach. His huge tail smashed through one side of the tables on the carriage as Nadia recommenced kicking the crap out of everything that moved at the other end of the train.

Another flail of his arm, as if he wasn't entirely used to the new size or shape of his body, and I darted back toward the rapidly orange-turning metal door. "You going to be long?" I asked.

"Yes," Ji-hyun seethed.

Excellent.

I sprinted toward the creature, turning to smoke as it tried to take hold of my arms, moving under his armpit, and re-forming enough to grab one of my two daggers from the partially broken table and slash across his belly. Francis was faster than anticipated and he backhanded me, sending me spiralling through the air and into one of the windows down the side of the carriage. The glass spider-webbed from the impact and I hit the ground hard.

Turning to smoke is almost impossible when I'm semi-concussed. It takes a level of concentration to keep all of me together when I'm in smoke form, and it's hard to do the more I turn to smoke within a quick period of time. I couldn't keep up the smoke act forever; eventually, it would exhaust me and either let Francis kill me or force me back into my embers, which would leave both Ji-hyun and Nadia down one ally. Neither were acceptable outcomes.

I rolled back to my feet, my rift-tempered dagger in one hand, the otherwise blue blade stained with the dark green blood of the creature Francis had become. On the plus side, there was one less vial of poison in the world.

Francis roared and charged, knocking the wooden table through the window, as I dived to the side. A rush of air entered the carriage as I ducked under Francis's swipe and sliced my dagger along the side of his leg, spinning the blade over in my hand and throwing myself past his grasp, slicing through his massive Achilles tendon.

I continued to roll along the floor as Francis screamed in rage and pain, while thick dark blood pumped over the carpeted floor. His boss was going to be so mad when they got the cleaning bill.

The croc roared again, smashing his massive hands into the fixtures above his head and ripping out the guts of the train above us, bringing it all down on top of me. I turned to smoke, moving through the mass of debris, the huge HVAC system crashing down between where I'd been and where a somewhat smug looking Francis now stood. I re-formed a few feet back as parts of the metal door began to melt away, Ji-hyun's blue flame punching through the holes it left behind.

"Okay, this is the way you want to do this?" I asked, turning to smoke again and billowing up onto the roof of the train. I heard Nadia shout *goddamn it*. If I survived this, she'd probably kill me herself.

I crouched atop the destroyed roof of a train and hoped this wasn't as stupid as it felt. I wanted Francis to take the bait, to jump up onto the roof, his twisted brain telling him to kill me more than any self-preservation.

The front of the train was behind me, a few carriages down, and I risked a look to make sure I wasn't about to get hit by anything, and almost got taken out by part of the HVAC unit that Francis threw up at me like a tennis ball. The unit smashed into the top of the train, gouging it before bouncing down and falling to the side.

There was a screech of metal on metal, and I jumped back into the hole as the train lurched to one side ever so slightly. I allowed myself to fall directly onto Francis, who grabbed me around the throat. I wrapped my hands around his scaly claws and turned to smoke. Holding on to flesh when I activated my power did horrible things to whatever I was holding onto. Mostly, the flesh peels and tears like someone trying to get into a particularly stubborn orange. And it's about as messy.

Francis lost his entire hand, leaving ragged strips of flesh and muscle. He looked down at me with hate in his yellow eyes as blood continued to pump over the floor and as I lay on the ground, re-formed and waiting.

He hadn't taken a step when blue flame engulfed him.

I shot to my feet as the stream of flame stopped, and drove the dagger up into Francis's throat as he screamed in pain. I twisted the blade and pulled it out before stabbing him again in the side of the head when he fell to his knees as the carriage lurched again, this time throwing me against the wall, with Ji-hyun grabbing hold of the nearest table while Nadia anchored herself to the wall beside her, the guards either dead or very much wishing they were.

The sound was all-consuming, as if the entire train was being torn asunder as the side of the carriage slammed into the ground, smashing windows and forcing me to turn to smoke so I wasn't pulled out of the broken carriage as we slid downhill. I re-formed next to Ji-hyun, with both of us holding on to the table that was still bolted to the floor, and wrapping our bodies into the space beneath it.

My brain had no time to take in what was actually happening; all it knew was it was bad, which, considering the circumstances was probably underselling it quite a bit. Another ear-splitting scream of metal and I caught a glimpse of a carriage shooting past one of the broken windows, followed by another jerking motion as the carriage we were in changed direction and spun on its side, suddenly coming to an abrupt stop.

Everything took seconds, but it felt like a lifetime.

"Nadia," I shouted, my ears still ringing.

"I'm good," she shouted. "Actually, that sucked a huge amount of balls, but I'm as good as I could be, considering the circumstances."

"You okay?" Ji-hyun asked me.

I looked down at my body; nothing was broken, although I was going to feel sore later. I felt blood trickle down the side of my face.

"It's not deep," Ji-hyun said, touching my scalp.

Head wounds bleed like crazy, and it's difficult to judge just how bad it is until you can see it, so that was good to hear.

The carriage was still on its side, and I dropped down the six feet from the table and looked over to Nadia, who had wrapped herself in her chains to offer some protection, like a giant cocoon of rift-tempered metal. The metal chains were moving apart to let her free, and while she didn't look happy, she didn't look hurt, either.

"That was a lot less fun than I'd hoped it would have been," Nadia said, stepping over the remains of Francis, who had been bounced around the inside of the carriage, his blood creating the most disgusting Jackson Pollock–like painting ever conceived.

Ji-hyun dropped down beside me. "You took too long to kill him," she said as we stepped out of the broken carriage and found ourselves on the side of a large hill. The driver section and three coaches between us were on their side at the bottom of the hill, and two more carriages were above us, twisted and pulled off the tracks.

The carriage that I'd seen going past us had been the end carriage and was now partially submerged in a nearby lake at the bottom of the hill.

"I think it's fucked," Nadia said.

"Nah, that'll buff right out," I told her. I turned to see Ji-hyun staring at me. "Yes, I took too long to kill him, but honestly, I wasn't expecting to fight a crocodile-man in the middle of a moving train and hoped that if I lured him outside, he'd fall off."

"Instead, he threw the HVAC at you, and here we are," Ji-hyun said with a flourish of her arms.

"I never said it worked out well," I conceded. "Besides, I hoped to be able to question him."

"His head is still in there somewhere," Nadia said, giving me a thumbs-up. "I don't think it's attached to the rest of him, though."

I looked down the train toward the driver's cab. "We need to find Eve."

Ji-hyun's face darkened. "She will be dangerous."

Nadia and I followed Ji-hyun down the slippery hill, the sounds of groaning metal continuing to accompany us. There was a distinct smell of burning as we got closer to the driver's cab, and as someone pulled themselves free from the twisted wreckage, I spotted the flames flicking up from the bottom of the cab.

The man who had pulled himself free was the guard who had been on the train platform. He was covered in blood and tried to get up onto his feet but failed and fell back face first into the dirt.

"Nadia, can you check that he's not got a weapon?" I asked.

"You want me to move him away from the burning wreckage?" Nadia asked.

"If I tell you to use your judgement, you'd throw him back in, wouldn't you?" I asked.

Nadia's smile neither confirmed nor denied such a thing might occur.

"Tie him up," Ji-hyun said. "We need to hand as many of these people to Ravi as possible. We can't be seen to be enacting our own brand of justice here. We're trying to work with the humans, remember?"

"So, we hand over Eve alive, too," I said.

Ji-hyun's face darkened. "Yes," she said eventually, turning away and walking down the hill as Nadia handled the guard.

While Ji-hyun searched the carriages for signs of Eve, I made my way to the driver's cab.

I found a fire extinguisher on the ground and used it on the small fire on the underside of the carriage. With the fire hopefully put out, I kept the extinguisher with me as I reached the driver's cab, which was, thankfully, still the right way up. I climbed the short metal ladder to the cab's dented door and looked inside through the broken window.

There were two people inside the cab; one was clearly a guard, judging from his uniform. He'd been impaled to the cab door with a piece of steel that had been torn off something and shot through the cab window like a javelin. The driver was still in his seat, slumped forward over the console, the lights of which continued to flicker.

The windows to the cab were destroyed, the safety glass covering the floor of the cab itself. I put my head through the hole in the door and looked up to find the orange emergency unlock handle still in its original position. A quick reach up and yank on the handle, and the door made a slight hiss as it unlocked.

I pushed the door aside and stepped into the cab as the entire structure shuddered again. I paused; we did not have long before all of the weight behind the cab gave in to gravity and pushed it further down the hill toward the lake. I unfastened the driver's seat belt and pulled him out of the seat. He was unconscious but breathing, although the large bruise on his head meant he would definitely need hospital treatment sooner rather than later.

Carrying him out of the cab and getting him down to the ground was fairly straightforward, although the four-foot drop from the cab door to soft earth made him moan unpleasantly. We'd made it to the tree line, where Nadia sat with the barely conscious guard, when the cab burst into flames.

"Good timing," Nadia said as the cab began to be slowly pushed toward the lake.

"Where's Ji-hyun?" I asked.

"Second carriage from the front," Nadia shouted as I sprinted across the grass toward the slowly moving train as it inched closer to the water.

I turned to smoke and travelled up through the broken window of the carriage, re-forming myself on the other side.

"Ji-hyun," I shouted into the wreckage-strewn carriage. The roof had collapsed, the HVAC unit inside it falling onto the rows of seats that lined one half of the carriage. I spotted several bodies under it, none of whom were in any position to possibly be alive.

"Over here," Ji-hyun replied from the far side of the carriage, next to a warped frame. Part of the carriage wall and ceiling were missing, and a large piece of a second HVAC unit was jammed inside it, presumably the one that had been thrown at me.

"Eve is stuck under here," Ji-hyun said from behind the HVAC unit.

I ran over and looked down to see that Eve was pinned from the waist down by the HVAC, although technically she was pinned by the chair the unit had landed on and folded like an accordion.

"I think her leg is broken," Ji-hyun said.

"I'm not deaf," Eve snapped. Her face was covered in dirt and blood, and one arm hung at an unpleasant angle.

"Revenant or riftborn?" I asked.

"Flesh revenant," she said. "I can heal fast."

That boded well for what was about to happen. "Heal back limbs?" I asked her.

"You are not cutting my leg off," Eve snapped.

"Just checking," I told her innocently, staggering back when the carriage jolted downhill again, causing the HVAC to shift and Eve to cry out in pain.

"Get this damned thing off me," Eve shouted, although it was less of an order and more of a plea.

"Lucas," Ji-hyun said.

"Okay, well, first of all, Eve, you're under arrest for . . . well, honestly for everything I can think of. Enjoy prison. Secondly, you are stuck there, and between the two of us, we're not strong enough to lift a ton of metal off you. We don't have a horned revenant handy, and even with Nadia's help, I'm not convinced it would matter."

"This is a shit pep talk," Eve said.

The carriage lurched violently to one side and the HVAC shifted a foot, which in turn caused more screaming from Eve as the HVAC moved down her leg.

"The only thing that's keeping your leg from being crushed like a grape is the fact that you're a flesh revenant," I told her. "That's also what's going to get you free."

Flesh revenants could manipulate . . . well, their flesh. They could change their bodies to heal quickly, become stronger, faster, heal, or shape-shift, although they were usually only gifted with one or two of the mass of stuff I'd seen flesh revenants do.

I took hold of one of Eve's arms, and Ji-hyun took the other. "This is not going to feel good," I said.

"Just . . ." Eve started.

"Three," I shouted, and Ji-hyun and I pulled with everything we had. Eve's arm dislocated, and there was a truly horrible sound of tearing, but she was free. And screaming. Her body fought to knit itself back together. And while the sounds that it made to do that were less than pleasant, her torn apart leg was healing—by the time Ji-hyun and I dragged her to the hole in the side of the carriage. As we reached it, Ji-hyun heaved the groaning woman and launched her out of the carriage like a lawn dart.

She shrugged at my look as Eve hit the torn-apart earth face first. "What?" Ji-hyun said. "She's alive, isn't she?"

There were sirens in the distance, and I wondered how I was going to explain everything to Ravi.

Eve spluttered, cradling her left arm against her chest, putting her hand inside her leather jacket, as she got to her unsteady feet. "Thank you," she said.

I looked over at Ji-hyun, who was racing toward me at full speed. She collided with Eve, tackling her in the stomach and taking her off her feet, dragging Eve's supposed hurt arm free, revealing the gun she had in her hand.

"That's not very nice," I said.

"Fuck you," Eve said.

"You first," Ji-hyun told her, and punched her in the face, knocking her out. "We have about thirty seconds before she wakes up."

Ten seconds later, a helicopter appeared in the distance. It didn't take long for it to reach us, landing at the top of the hill, close to the train tracks, and I spotted Ravi and his people looking down at us with a mixture of what I was pretty sure was shock and anger.

"Ta-da," I shouted, waving my arms at the train.

CHAPTER FOUR

It had been two weeks since the train crash, since Eve's arrest. She'd been about as cooperative as I'd expected, but everyone was hopeful that she would eventually see that her boss wasn't coming to save her and that that would make her more cooperative. All I cared about was getting to the Croupier and hopefully using him to find Callie Mitchell.

I'd decided to take a step back and go home to New York, primarily because I wasn't *officially* involved in the investigation, but also because I knew that Ji-hyun—who stayed behind—was more than capable of getting answers without me looking over her shoulder. If I stayed, I'd only start to get more frustrated, and I wanted to look into whether there were other avenues to try and find Callie, or figure out who the Croupier was.

Nadia accompanied me home. Her need to be part of *my chain* meant that she was either my shadow or I didn't see her for several days at a time while whatever other chain of possibilities was followed in the roost of her mind.

I'd spent most of my time back in New York at the Stag and Arrow, a British pub–styled bar run by Bill and his husband George, while I made some calls.

The Stag and Arrow was predominantly a pub for rift-fused, humans who had been changed by the rift, and was one of the few places in Brooklyn where we could go without having to encounter trouble from those who might not always have our best interests at heart. The anti-rift sentiment was something that had been there from the moment humanity had discovered that they were not only not alone but some steps further down the ladder of evolution than they assumed they were. Not that *I* considered us to be the next step in human evolution, but the fact that some humans did was the problem. The idea that we were going to slowly eradicate humanity by assimilating them or killing them was nonsensical, but I learned long ago that you can't argue logic with idiots and bigots.

I liked the Stag and Arrow; I liked Bill and George, and the easy atmosphere. I enjoyed Bill's astonishingly good food and the occasional chat. Both Bill and George were revenants, and when we'd first met, they'd both assumed I was human. When they'd discovered otherwise, they hadn't chastised me for my secrets, and we'd all gotten along just fine.

There had been a good reason for keeping my riftborn nature hidden. My past experiences, having had my entire Guild wiped out, had sent me spiralling to a dark place and the need to get away. There's no better getting away than pretending you're something you're not. Still, that was behind me now, I hoped, and I'd been open to those I worked with about who and what I was.

Bill brought me over a bacon sandwich—not American bacon, which is streaky bacon and should only be used to wrap around roast chicken—but actual rashers of back bacon. A proper British bacon sandwich. Bill calls it the food of the gods, which, considering the number of slices, the size of the doorsteps he calls bread, and the amount of fat it all produces, if you eat too many, you probably get to go see the gods sooner than not.

I sat in one of the booths by the front door and ate my first sandwich while drinking a cup of tea that was strong enough I could probably stand a spoon up in it. Proper tea, as Bill called it.

Bill sat opposite me, placing a plate with his own bacon sandwiches—his containing enough brown sauce that it ran down the side of the inch-thick slices of white crusty bread—and a cup of tea, and proceeded to heap sugar into the cup.

"Calm down there, Willy Wonka," I said after Bill put his fifth spoonful of sugar into his tea.

"Oh, I'm sorry, I didn't remember asking you your opinion about how much sugar to put in tea," he said with a wry smile.

"It's a good job you died and came back as a revenant," I said. "Or that might actually kill you."

Bill laughed and took a large bite of his sandwich.

"How's George?" I asked him.

"Good," he said eventually. "He's dealing with some cases about a revenant gang. Bad people come back and are still bad; who knew? He's trying to keep it out of the news, though, because it's not like humanity needs more excuses to mistrust us."

"And Emily?" I asked as he took another bite.

"She's fine," Bill told me. "Mostly fine."

"What does *mostly fine* mean?" I asked. Special Agent Emily West of the FBI had been turned into a revenant six months earlier and had been having difficulty adjusting to her new life. The FBI had placed her on compassionate leave, which she hated with every fibre of her being because she just wanted to get back to the job. George had taken her with him to help out with several cases, so she was at least busy, if not entirely happy with her situation.

"She's a hooded revenant," he shrugged. "She goes invisible without meaning to. She's finding it hard to control with any degree of accuracy."

"You want me to arrange for someone to talk to her?" I asked.

"You mean you?" Bill replied.

I shook my head. "I'm not the person to advise new revenants on how to use their power. I was thinking Gabriel might know someone. I'm heading up there after I'm done eating your food."

"That might actually be helpful," Bill said. "What about Zita?"

Hooded revenants were all about camouflage, stealth, and keeping out of sight. I knew a few hooded, but they're secretive in nature and aren't usually the people who like to talk about their powers. Zita was rare in that she was quite open and honest with who she was, but she also dabbled in the . . . murkier side of life, and I didn't want to presume that she would enjoy talking to an FBI agent, despite having helped us previously.

"Zita might need Gabriel to convince her," I said.

"He is good at convincing people to do stuff," Bill admitted after having spent several weeks helping Gabriel rebuild his church. He finished off his sandwich and pointed at the medallion around my neck. "You're the only one left; you still wear it, though."

I looked down at the Raven Guild medallion. "I didn't for a long time. But I think it's better to deal with your past than let it fester. The Ravens will return one day. Hopefully. Or not. I don't really know. All I do know is that I'll do my best to hold up what I believe, and if that means that the Ravens die with me, then so be it."

"How goes investigating into who was behind their attack and murder?" Bill asked as he wiped his mouth with a napkin.

"It's not," I said. "Callie Mitchell's vials are more important."

"And how's that going?"

"Ji-hyun is investigating," I told him. "She doesn't need help."

"And you also think that if you go away, the Croupier might think you're no longer involved and screw up."

I smiled. "You have a conniving mind, Bill."

"I'm married to a lawyer," Bill said with a laugh. He drained the rest of his mug of tea and got to his feet. "Just be careful, Lucas; it sounds like this Croupier fellow—stupid name, by the way—might actually be exceptionally dangerous."

"I'm going to see Gabriel and spend a few days seeing friends," I said. "If some bad people want to come find me during that time, I think being with people who can protect themselves, and not around the innocent people who live in my building, would be a good start."

"Glad to hear it," Bill said. "Say hi to Gabriel for me. You know his church is doing well."

I did. The Church of Tempered Souls was the only religion to actively involve rift-fused, and also the only one with actual proof that there was something beyond our daily lives. Not everyone was happy about that. Gabriel's specific church was gaining members by the day.

I left Bill a tip on the table and went home to my flat on the opposite side of Prospect Park. I had a two-bedroom flat on the sixth floor, which afforded me lovely views of the city, and was secretly in the process of buying the whole building with a little help from several other riftborn and revenants I knew. Turns out that when you're thousands of years old, you own some stuff that is worth an astronomical amount of money, which worked out well, because buying anything above the size of a shed in New York City costs exactly that amount.

I wanted to make sure that people from the rift had a place to go when they got back, or if they needed somewhere to come and deal with who they'd become. Not every revenant is welcomed back home after the change, and seeing how riftborn don't come back until a hundred years after the rift takes them, they usually know no one. When I'd returned all those centuries ago, it had been to find the Romans had beaten the Carthaginians and all but destroyed the people I'd called family; I felt lost and alone. It took me a long time to feel anything else.

The cab I'd booked arrived an hour after I'd gotten home, thrown some stuff into a bag, made it back down the stairs to the exit, and said hello to several residents as I walked through the foyer to the early afternoon outside. I'd been told by Gabriel that I was going to be staying at his place in Hamble, which was a short distance from Rochester, which in and of itself was an hour-and-a-half flight from LaGuardia Airport.

I left Nadia a voice message to let her know I was going to Gabriel's, something I'd already told her but felt I should remind her. Chances were that she was already at Gabriel's, as I hadn't seen her for a few days. She did have a tendency to be in places with no previous warning.

The afternoon was turning to early evening by the time we landed, and I took a cab from the airport to Gabriel's church. I did actually have my own car, a dark green Mercedes E 53 AMG coupe, but it was parked in Hamble, which was somewhat short-sighted on my part.

I stood on the sidewalk, gazing up at the large gothic church, its steeple towering high above me. The gargoyles decorating the roof looked down on me as I walked through the garden—which was a beautiful kaleidoscope of colour—in front of the church toward the large, dark brown, wooden door. The roof, gargoyles, windows, doors, and the entire interior of the building had recently been rebuilt from scratch after it'd been burnt down by a traitorous piece of shit from my past, Dan. A lot of local people helped; some came to repot the garden that had been destroyed, some helped with painting or woodwork, but it had been a display of camaraderie that had warmed my old, occasionally frozen heart. The church and Gabriel were part of this community, and they were damned if some jumped-up little prick—the actual words of an eighty-four-year-old great-grandmother—was going to take it from them.

I'm not a fan of religions, any religion; I've seen what they can do to people when the power to influence is used to hurt and abuse. I've been stood across the battlefield from armies full of soldiers who believe that their god, and only their god, will keep them alive. Time and time again, I've seen people commit acts of barbarity because they disagreed over which god was the correct god.

But I've also seen people do good in the name of their deity. I've seen people help others; I've seen them give back to their community. People who didn't care about what someone else believed; they just wanted to do the right thing.

So, while I don't like religion on the whole, especially when used as a weapon, I also know that people need to believe in *something*. Humanity, and those of us who consider ourselves adjacent to that term, have always wanted to believe there's something more. That there are reasons to the chaos of the world.

I sighed.

The door to Gabriel Santiago's church opened, and Gabriel stepped out into the early evening sunshine. He wore jeans, a baby-blue T-shirt, and a charcoal cardigan, with a blue-and-gold clerical band around his bicep. He'd regrown a tidy dark beard but had kept his hair short.

"Lucas," Gabriel said, walking over to hug me.

Gabriel had worked with the RCU and Guilds for a number of years, although he wasn't officially a member of any of the latter. At some point during the years I was away, he'd had himself ordained and become a cleric for the church. I'd been a little surprised at how much the position had suited him, although I shouldn't have been. Gabriel was one of the good ones.

"I'm glad you're here," Gabriel said. "Come in; get some food and drink. Nadia is here."

I smiled. "Of course she is."

"You really should have taken your car back to New York; you wouldn't have needed to fly," Gabriel said as we stepped through the front door.

"If only someone hadn't needed to keep it here," I said sarcastically.

"The church thanks you," Gabriel said with a slight bow of his head, but I caught the smile.

"The church can pay for any gasoline I need, then," I said with a bow of my own head.

"I'm sure we can arrange to get you a full tank of gas," Gabriel said. He didn't believe that churches—any churches—should be exempt from paying tax, and liked to put any money the church made to good use in the local neighbourhood. New play equipment for the parks, new computers for the schools, food drives, things like that.

The interior of the church was one of splendour. After walking under the archway just beyond the front door, there were two areas of eighteen pews, with large stained-glass windows on either side of the cavernous nave. The pulpit at the end of the seating area, next to a separate area for a choir, was where Gabriel—or someone from the community once a week—gave his sermons.

I'd been in the church before it had been firebombed and destroyed, and it had been beautiful then, but it was even more so now. They'd managed to recreate it almost like it had been beforehand but with an extra spot of polish.

"Still no cassock," I said to Gabriel as we walked the aisle between the pews.

"I'm not giving a sermon," Gabriel said. "And it's called a clerical gown. *Cassock* is Christian."

"Okay, still no clerical gown," I said. "I'm beginning to think you don't actually own one. I don't think I've ever seen you wearing it."

"I don't like it, truth be told," Gabriel said. "Makes me feel like my church has a dress code. I want people to be comfortable, but I also want to be comfortable. I only wear the gown when I must."

"Do you have different-coloured ones?" I asked.

Gabriel turned back to me. "Are you mocking me, Lucas Rurik?" Gabriel's voice held a hint of chastisement.

"No," I admitted. "Not at all. Genuine question."

"Yes," Gabriel said. "Purple, orange, red, and blue. Each with gold trim. The blue one in particular is very attractive. Not that you'd know, because you never come to sermon. Heathen."

"Did you just call me a heathen?" I asked as Gabriel laughed and continued walking off.

"Hey," I called after him. "I am not a heathen."

I caught up to Gabriel as he reached his pulpit. He stopped, placed a hand against the dark wood and muttered something.

I bit back the witty and brilliant remark I was going to say. "You okay?" I asked him. I'd seen clerics do a similar thing; it was a tribute to someone who had gone missing or died.

Gabriel looked back at me and forced a smile, before nodding. "I am now. The last six months of rebuilding, of . . . healing, has been difficult. It is good to see you again, my friend, although I doubt you'll be here for long."

"And what makes you say that?" I asked him.

"You follow trouble, Lucas," Gabriel said.

"Isn't that meant to be the other way around?" I asked.

Gabriel shook his head. "No, you follow it. You see trouble, and you involve yourself. You can't help it. It's why you came back to us after so many years away. It's why you couldn't let the deaths of the Ravens go. It's why you never can stay in one place for long. You see trouble. You intervene. It's what makes you, you."

"I'm not sure how to take that," I told him.

"Well, I hope," Gabriel replied. "You refuse to stand by and let injustice happen; you refuse to allow bad things to happen when you have the power to stop it. Unfortunately, both of those traits, while noble, tend to lead to bigger and badder problems. Just be careful. Callie Mitchell and that moron Mason had powerful friends, and now you have powerful enemies. Adding this Croupier to the mix is giving you more enemies. Be careful that they don't overpower you by sheer force of numbers."

"Is this a sermon?" I asked, looking around. "It feels like a sermon."

"Call it what you like. I just want you to not get dead."

I placed a hand on Gabriel's shoulder. "They'd have to be better than me."

"Or lucky," Gabriel countered. "They only have to be lucky once."

I patted Gabriel's shoulder and we continued on through the church. He had a point. A point I didn't really want to talk about. But I did wonder, after removing Mason as a problem and exposing Callie Mitchell and the Croupier, just how many more of Callie's allies were going to come out of the woodwork. I had made myself a target, and sooner or later, someone was going to come and try to hit that target. I just needed to make sure that I was on my best form when that happened. I'd died once before, a long time ago, and I didn't plan on making it easy for anyone to accomplish a second time.

CHAPTER FIVE

The church had a large secret basement deep underground where a group of friends and allies and I had worked together to stop Mason and Callie. It was still there, still well stocked, but with the rebuilding of the church came the partial rebuilding of the house just behind it.

The house was a three-storey affair, made to look like any other town-house in the area. When the church had been destroyed, the fire had caused a lot of damage to the house as well. Now that it was rebuilt, Gabriel used it as his home, but also as a place to offer shelter to those needing it.

The dark blue front door led into a hallway, which branched off to a large kitchen-diner, a pantry, an office, and two large reception rooms. The two floors above consisted of three bedrooms and two bathrooms, and the attic was a small but well-stocked library with comfortable seating. I wasn't certain that seeing all of those burned books when we finally got back into the house to clear it out hadn't hit Gabriel harder than the destroyed church.

There were usually newly born rift-fused staying in the house, and today was no exception. A young woman of no more than twenty sat in the downstairs lounge watching TV, while a second woman who was probably twice her age sat beside her. They ate popcorn while they watched their film.

"Gabriel," they said in almost-unison, getting to their feet to greet him.

"Bethany," Gabriel said to the youngest of the two women.

Both women had dark skin, with short black hair, and multiple earrings in both ears. Bethany wore a pair of white-and-blue Adidas leggings and a blue T-shirt, while the second woman wore a green skirt and white sweater.

"Bethany, Sally, this is Lucas."

Both nodded in my direction; a lot of revenants don't like to shake hands, especially newly born ones. They're not in full control of their abilities, and they can hurt people if they're not careful.

"Pleasure," I said.

"Good to meet you," Sally said. "Gabriel tells us that you help out here."

"On occasion," I said, wondering what else Gabriel had told them.

"Have you seen Nadia?" Gabriel asked.

"The chained revenant?" Bethany asked. "She went upstairs to her room."

Gabriel thanked them both and ushered me out of the lounge.

"They been here long?" I asked Gabriel.

"A few days," he told me. "Mother and daughter. Both in a car accident; both woke up."

"Rare that it's both," I said as we climbed the stairs to the floor above. Nadia's room was the second floor, or third floor depending on if you're American or British, and something I'd never quite managed to get my head around despite having lived in America for several years.

"Only two occupants in the car," Gabriel said as we walked past paintings of landscapes that had been hung on the walls. "Sally's husband came here yesterday, but she wants to be able to control her power before she sees him again."

"What are they?" I asked as we began the second staircase.

"Both are spirit revenants," Gabriel said.

Some people would call spirit revenants necromancers, but that was seen as a dirty word to them. They could communicate with, and use the power of, the dead. To get two of the same type born at the same time in the same accident was . . . unusual.

"I know what you're thinking," Gabriel said, stopping at the top of the stairs and looking down at me.

"What am I thinking, Gabriel?" I asked.

"That something feels wrong about two spirit revenants being born together at the same time."

"Not wrong as such," I said.

"It's unusual," Gabriel said. "But there are more and more of us being born now. Or, at least, more coming to us wanting help when they're born. Most in the past just slunk away to the shadows to deal with what they'd become, or they went home and pretended like nothing happened and people got hurt."

The latter still happened, unfortunately, but I had to admit that Gabriel and similar-minded clerics like him had done a lot over the years to make sure that there were fewer cases slipping through the cracks.

"And Emily?" I asked.

Gabriel heaved a sigh. "She's having difficulties," he admitted. "The FBI won't let her back until they're certain she has her powers under control, but she's finding it difficult to adjust. Her boyfriend left her, her mother called her an abomination to God, and her dad . . . well, happy wife, happy life."

"He's spineless?" I asked, already knowing the answer.

Gabriel nodded. "I was hoping you might talk to her. Maybe take her with you when you next work."

"I'll definitely talk to her, and after that I'll see if she can help out. If she comes with us and hasn't got her head straight, she could get herself hurt. Or someone else."

"It's a catch-22 with her," Gabriel said. "She can't get her powers under control because everything else is spiralling around her, and everything is spiralling around her, in part, because she can't get her powers under control."

"I imagine she still blames herself, yes?"

Gabriel nodded.

We walked along the hallway, and Gabriel knocked on a light green door, to no answer. He tried the door handle and pushed it open slightly. Nadia's room was empty, but the walls were covered in vivid drawings.

"Whoa," I said, stepping into the room and looking at the artwork. They were done in charcoal and chalk and depicted battles from the past, judging by the uses of armoured people on horses. The further along the wall they went, the more modern the battles became. Images of soldiers in various uniforms, pictures of tanks, of aircraft. And finally one of me. Smoke poured from my hands, forming devil-like faces. I felt like I was intruding.

"We should come back," Gabriel said, obviously feeling the same.

He closed the door and I looked down the hallway. "Which one is Emily?"

"The red door," Gabriel said, pointing to the door at the far end of the hallway. "Nadia will probably be in the attic, so once you've finished, come find us. Emily refused counselling with me, by the way."

"Thanks for the info," I told him, and strolled to Emily's door, knocking on it twice.

"Yes?" she asked.

I pushed open the door, unsure of what I was going to find.

Emily West lay on her queen-sized bed, looking across at me as I stood in the doorway.

"Nice hair," I said.

She'd had long blonde hair the last time I'd seen her, although now it was closer to shoulder-length and had been dyed silver.

"Thanks," she said with zero enthusiasm. "New me. New hair."

"Same you," I corrected.

"Haven't you heard?" she asked, sitting up. She wore a dark green over-sized sweater with a picture of Oscar the Grouch on it, and black leggings. She pointed to the picture. "This is me now."

"You live in a garbage can?" I asked.

"That's where the analogy falls down," she admitted.

"Yes, that's where it all goes wrong. Just at that bit." I didn't even try to keep the sarcasm from my voice.

"Why are you here?" she asked, her eyes narrowing in slight annoyance.

"Can I come in?" I asked her.

"Not my building," she said, lying back on the bed and picking up a TV remote.

I stepped into the room and looked around. There was a large ward-robe against the wall opposite the window, with the bed in between them. A chest-of-drawers was next to the door, with a good-sized TV on it. The dark carpet was thick and probably felt amazing in the winter, and the walls—like most of the walls in the house—were the same magnolia paint. Few residents stayed for longer than a couple of weeks. Emily might be the longest, but she'd made no attempts to personalise the space.

"Watching anything good?" I asked, picking up a wooden chair from the desk next to the wardrobe and placing it at the foot of the bed.

"It's one of those police procedural programmes where it's all flash and no substance," she said, turning the TV off. "Why are you here?"

"Because I wanted to make sure you were okay," I told her. "Do I need a different reason than that?"

Emily shrugged.

"I heard you're having some issues with work and life," I said.

"Well, I fucking died and came back a monster, so *that's* a problem," Emily snapped.

"No," I said, slightly forcefully.

"No, what?" Emily asked, the anger in her tone threatening to bubble over. She wanted someone to lash out at, to blame, and right now that person was herself. That had to change if she had any chance of accepting what had happened to her.

"We don't use the word *monster*," I told her. "There are actual monsters out there. We reserve that word for them."

"Do you use the word *self-righteous asshole*?" Emily asked.

"That's two words," I said. "Or three; I'm never sure when things are hyphenated."

"Did you think that you'd come here, make me smile, be all clever, and I'd just be right as rain?" Emily snapped.

"Actually, no," I said. "I thought I'd come here, check you were okay, and try to talk you into having counselling."

Emily let out an exhausted sigh. "Gabriel already tried, and I'll tell you what I told him. No."

"Fair enough," I said, getting to my feet.

"That's it?" she asked.

"Sure," I said. "You want me to smooth your hair and tell you it'll be okay? You want me to click my fingers like Mary Fucking Poppins and tell you things get better? You died. You came back. You've been given a second chance at life, so, if you want to sit up here and do this with it, be my guest. But I assumed you'd want your job back, that you'd want your life back."

"I can't," Emily shouted, almost springing up to a seated position. "My job, my boyfriend, my mom, none of them *want* me. Why shouldn't I be allowed to wallow in self-pity? My entire life has gone to fucking shit."

"So, you want to be angry?" I asked. "You want to rage against someone, against the thing you feel is the most unfair? So, what is that thing? What is it you're so angry about?"

"Everything," she seethed. "I hate that I've become this . . . this . . . *thing*. I hate that the life I built is gone. I hate that people look at me with pity, that my own mother can't stand to look at me, that my dad would rather have an easy life than fight in my corner. That the man I loved wants nothing to do with me because he's afraid of what I am."

"And how many of those things can you change?" I asked.

Emily opened her mouth to reply and quickly closed it.

"None," I said. "Your boyfriend is an asshole. Your mom is a judgemental asshole, and your dad is a spineless asshole. Look, what you're going through sucks. It sucks a lot, and there's no easy solution, but if you want something close to your life again, there are things you can do. If you won't talk to Gabriel, I'm sure he has other people you can talk to."

"We were never much of a *talking* kind of family," Emily said.

"That sounds like a wonderfully healthy way to live," I said. "Back when I was a kid, you dealt with your problems by finding an opposing army and stabbing people. Or bludgeoning them. Or . . . well, you get the idea."

"How is that healthy?" Emily asked.

"It's not," I said. "It fucks you up for years, but they leave that bit out of the history books. No one wants to read how the great warrior had so much trauma that he could only sleep if there were torchlights on all around the camp. Or the leader who pissed himself on his horse when he was faced with certain death at the hands of an angry elephant."

Emily stared at me for several seconds. "Is that you?"

I nodded. "First one was. Long time ago. Never pissed myself on a horse, but then, I've never faced down a rampaging elephant, thankfully."

"But you still kill people?" she asked.

"Those that need it," I said. "I made my peace with what I am. With what I've done. It took a long time, though. We didn't have much in the way of healthy ways to process our issues back then. Drink, drugs, hurting people, hurting yourself, being angry or sad all the time. Depression wasn't so much diagnosed as ignored or hidden as a weakness. Men don't cry and all that utter horseshit. I had friends and we would talk about what we'd done; there were shamans or priests who you'd confess to. Look, I'm not saying I know how you feel, though I've been through the whole *coming back to life and having no family* thing as well. But I know *despair*. I know depression. I know that black dog at your side that won't fuck off and leave you alone. You need people to help. You can't do it alone. I tried after the Ravens died, and I went to a dark place."

Emily stared at me for several seconds. "My brother and sister both reached out to me. They want to make sure I'm okay."

"So, there *are* people who care."

Emily nodded. "A few work colleagues did too."

"You need to talk to someone Emily; *help* isn't a dirty word."

"You left alone," Emily said. "You dropped it all and left your friends."

"Yes," I said. "Even someone as old and wise as I am manages to get it wrong."

Emily laughed, although there was little humour in it. "Old and wise?"

"Oldest and wisest," I said with a smile.

"I'll tell you what: you get Gabriel to come see me, and we'll talk," she said.

I shook my head. "Not going to happen. You go to him. First steps and all that. You show *you* want this." Some people need someone to come to them and ask if they're okay, some people need someone to be there when they fall, and some need to make the first step. Gabriel had tried to go to Emily, and it hadn't worked out. I hoped by getting Emily to go to Gabriel, it would force Emily to engage.

"You're a stubborn man," Emily said.

I bowed my head in thanks. "Coming from one as well versed in such matters, I'll take that as a compliment."

Emily sighed. "Fine, I'll think about it."

"Gabriel and Nadia are in the attic," I said.

"Tiny steps," Emily said.

"No," I said. "Talking to Gabriel isn't a tiny step; it's a massive sod-off leap. Actually admitting you need help and then going to get it is the bravest thing a person can do."

Emily looked over at me but said nothing for several seconds. "Are you expecting me to thank you?"

I shook my head. "That's not why I came to talk to you."

"So, why did you?"

"Because like I told you, I've been where you are. I needed people to help me. Someone was always there for me. Sometimes I didn't want them to be, sometimes I tried to push them away, but that's because I'm a stubborn arse. Sometimes you just need someone to show that they have your back. I don't need thanks for having your back. I'll have it either way."

"I don't get the feeling we were ever particularly close," Emily said. "Why do that?"

"Because you're one of us," I said. "And if there's one thing you should know about this little group we've got going on here, it's that we look out for one another."

Emily nodded thoughtfully. "I'm going to go for a run," she said. "It helps me think."

"Thank you for thinking about it," I said. "Enjoy the run."

I walked away before Emily could say anything else. I'd seen plenty of people where she was. The first step had to be made by them.

I took the stairs to the attic, opening the green door to what was a much larger space than when I'd last been there. The partition that had separated the library from the rest of the attic had been removed, and the whole place had been renovated into one library. The shelves weren't very high, but there were hundreds upon hundreds of books, with each shelving unit having a genre written on a plaque that was attached to it.

In the centre of the room, under a large skylight, was a red circular rug, a large L-shaped black leather sofa that defied physics as to how it was brought up there, three black leather chairs, and a walnut coffee table in between the sofa and chairs. A small kitchen area was off to one side, with mugs, a little fridge, and a proper kettle.

Nadia was sat on one chair, a cup of something hot on the coffee table in front of her, a book in her hands, utterly absorbed.

Gabriel sat in a chair beside her, waiting patiently for Nadia to finish.

Nadia closed the book, placed it carefully on the table, and looked up at me.

"Good book?" I asked, taking a look at the cover, which depicted what appeared to be a Greek soldier with a city in the background.

"It's about the Fall of Troy," she said. "I wish I'd have been there to see it."

"I'm pretty sure it's a lot more fun in your head than it would have been living through it," I said.

Nadia nodded slowly. "Probably. Still would have liked to see it."

"I spoke to Emily," I told Gabriel. "No idea if she will actually talk to you, but I hope she does."

"Me too," Gabriel said, sitting back in the chair. "I'm hoping you both can help me with something."

"I wondered how long it'd be before I got asked to do something," I said. "What do you want?" I asked Gabriel, who got up from his seat, walked over to a bookshelf at the far end of the attic, and removed a piece of art from the wall, revealing a safe behind it. He punched in numbers on a keypad and pulled open the safe door, removing something from it, before returning to Nadia and me.

"While you were gone, I asked Booker to look into this Croupier," Gabriel said, passing me a plain manilla A4 envelope.

I opened the envelope and removed the three pieces of paper from it, almost dropping a photo that was also inside. The photo was of a dead man, a bullet hole in his forehead. A poker chip was placed over each eye. One chip was red-and-white-striped, and one blue-and-white-striped. They both had the letters *VI* written on one side of each of them.

"This is where the name came from," Gabriel said.

"This is the Croupier's work?" I asked, passing the photo to Nadia. "How did Booker get these?"

"I didn't ask," Gabriel said. "Not sure I want to know."

The file was short and gave nothing about the Croupier's name or any details about him. It was photocopied pages of a journal written by a detective in the NYPD over forty years earlier. It mostly stated that the Croupier had friends in high places and was able to commit crimes without detection. The investigation into the murder of the man with the poker chips on his eyes—the identity of whom was not disclosed—was stonewalled.

"Where's the detective who wrote this now?" I asked, continuing through the notes.

"They found him in the Hudson," Gabriel said. "Two days after the last entry on that list. His family had been murdered. Wife, two kids, boy and a girl, nine and thirteen, all three shot in the back of the head. Made to look like the detective killed them, then killed himself."

"What was the name of the detective?" I asked.

"Detective Mark McCathy," Gabriel said as Nadia read the file from beside me. "Ex–Army Ranger, homicide detective, forty-one years old. No record of any previous instances of violence against his family."

"Sounds like Croupier had a NYPD detective and his whole family executed," I said.

Gabriel nodded. "Booker said the man who gave him this info was another NYPD detective and had tried looking into Mark's death at the time, then one day, someone nailed his pet cat to his front door. Left a poker chip in the animal's mouth."

"Bloody hell," I whispered.

"And you blew up his train," Gabriel said. "Killed his people. Probably not going to take that well."

"This intel needs to get to Ji-hyun," I said.

"Already sent," Gabriel told me. "One other thing, though. Booker said that the detective he spoke to give him one more piece of information but was told to not write it down. Mark had a riftborn helping him on the case. Strictly off the books."

"I'm not going to like where this is going, am I?" I asked.

"The riftborn never gave his real name," Gabriel said, sparing no feeling for the concern I was suddenly feeling. "He went by another name. Gunslinger."

Oh, goddamn it.

CHAPTER SIX

W ho's Gunslinger?" Nadia asked. "Is he a bad person?"

"Not exactly," I said. "I don't know what his birth name was, but he died in 1778 in New York City, during the American Revolution. He returned in the same place in 1880. His name is Ezekiel Kimble, and he decided that with his newfound power, he was going to hunt down notorious criminals. He became a US Marshal and developed a name for himself as someone who was quick on the draw and a crack shot with a rifle. Started to call himself Gunslinger. Started to make a lot of money hiring himself out as security on the side. At some point, he realised that making money by being on the winning side was preferable to having ethics and morals."

"And you don't like him?" Nadia asked me.

"*Like* is a strong word when it comes to Ezekiel," I said with a frown. "He's a wealthy man with fingers in a lot of political pies. He also still keeps his hand in patrolling the north of Canada, where he lives, north of Greater Sudbury in Ontario."

"So, what's the problem?" Nadia asked, looking between Gabriel and me.

"He's . . ." Gabriel began.

"He can't be trusted," I completed.

Gabriel pointed at me. "That."

"Why?" Nadia asked.

"He likes to embellish everything about his life, about his exploits. There's some truth to everything, but there's so much grandstanding that you're never sure what's fact or fiction. Also, if he was helping Mark with his investigation, I'm wondering how much was *actual* help and how much was trying to ingratiate himself with people in the NYPD. Or how much was trying to get a bigger payday or a spot on the TV. If this Croupier guy came to Ezekiel and threatened him, Ezekiel would drop Mark like a hot potato."

"He values his own person above all else," Gabriel said. "It's why he was never in a Guild. He tried once and told everyone they didn't fit his style, but the truth is they rejected him."

"Doesn't work well with others," Nadia summarised.

"Works fine with others until he needs to put himself on the line for them," I said. "Then you'll just see a dust cloud in his shape like those old cartoons of Bugs Bunny."

Nadia chuckled for a few seconds. "Sorry, I love those cartoons."

"He used to be one of the Forged," I said.

"I have no idea what that is," Nadia told me.

"They were the RCU before the RCU," I said. "They disbanded back in the late 1920s, when a whole lot of them either died or quit en masse, and . . . well, it's a long story. Basically, the Forged were ended and nothing like them existed for decades."

"And Gunslinger was one of them?" Nadia asked.

I nodded. "He's a good hunter," I said. "It put him in high demand. This was before the humans knew rift-fused were even a thing. He was a bit of a celebrity among those in the know."

"So, have you contacted Ezekiel and asked him about the Croupier?" I asked Gabriel. "I assume Booker didn't want to."

"Booker's words were basically *I'd rather set myself on fire*," Gabriel said. "He used more colourful language. And hand gestures. And it lasted several minutes."

I chuckled. "So, did you do it already?"

"That's where it gets weird," Gabriel said. "He called me first. About an hour after I saw Booker."

"*He* called about the Croupier?" I asked, feeling that pit of unpleasantness in my stomach when something clearly sounded wrong.

"No, about Callie Mitchell," Gabriel said. "Ezekiel said there's some old facility up in the woods, used to be some science types—his words—working there, but they've all left. Said he had an encounter with one of them, name of Callie Mitchell. Was about three months ago. Ezekiel said he didn't think anything of it, but he can't get access to the facility and heard that we were looking for someone by that name. Wanted to know if you'd like to go up and check it out."

"That's a big coincidence," Nadia said.

"Yes, it is," Gabriel said. "But it's not out of the realm of possibility that someone with ears to the ground of so many people's lives would have heard about Callie. He said he'd wanted to call to give his condolences about what we went through six months ago but was unsure how to say anything. Sounds like normal Ezekiel to me."

"Could be a setup," I said.

"Could be," Gabriel said. "But there's also the possibility that this is a lead not only into the Croupier but Callie. We need to pull on this thread anyway."

"You think he'd betray us?" Nadia asked.

"To save his own skin, his reputation, or his livelihood," I said, "in a heartbeat. But if there's any truth in what he's said, like Gabriel says, we need to look into it. Ezekiel might be on the level."

"Right, so Gunslinger is liked but not trusted," Nadia said. "Sounds like this is going to be fun."

"That actually sums him up really well," I said. "He's a showman who can never turn off the show, and a coward who likes to pretend he's not. He can fight, he can shoot, but once someone gets the upper hand, or he *thinks* they're going to get the upper hand, he folds like . . . well, like a bad hand."

"He also loves gambling," Gabriel pointed out.

"Could he be the Croupier?" Nadia asked, clearly now very interested.

"He's not the Croupier," I said. "Ezekiel would have signed his own name at a crime scene by now. He's not capable of subtlety."

"Any chance we can go see this other cop who Booker spoke to?" Nadia asked.

"No," Gabriel said. "He wants nothing to do with this. Mark's entire work on the case was 'confiscated.'"

"Anyone else find finger quotes to be weird?" Nadia asked.

"Yes," I agreed. "So, it's Gunslinger or nothing. Guess we're going to Canada. Again."

"Maybe we'll see more polar bears," Nadia said, suddenly excited.

"We're going less than an hour's drive north of Greater Sudbury," I said. "Probably not a lot of polar bears there."

"Could be that Greater Sudbury is involved in an evil plot," Nadia suggested, removing her phone and starting to tap the screen. "They have an IMAX."

"I don't think that's a sign of evil," Gabriel said.

Nadia nodded and continued to scroll on her phone.

"Driving or flying?" I asked.

"Up to you," Gabriel said. "It's a bit of a drive from the nearest airport, though. Gunslinger lives near Halfway Lake Provincial Park. He's got a big mansion up there, agreed to hunt the park for fiends in return for getting it. He's having some kind of party; you're going to be guests of honour."

There wasn't a single word in that sentence that I liked. "Talk about burying the lead," I said. "He's expecting us?"

Gabriel smiled. "Yeah."

"You are enjoying this a little bit too much," I pointed out.

"Six-hour drive," Nadia said, holding up her phone so I could see the screen. "You want me to drive some of it?"

"No," Gabriel and I said together.

"Wise choice," Nadia said. "You do not want me behind the wheel of anything bigger than one of those toy cars you get for kids, and even with that, I think I could do some serious damage."

"Can I assume Booker and Zita aren't coming?" I asked.

"You can assume correctly," Gabriel said. "Also, Brooke is in Hawaii with her husband, trying to get some time away from everything after what happened. So, you're going to be on your own for this one."

"I think we can manage," Nadia said, getting to her feet and slapping me on the shoulder. "Dream team, right here."

I chuckled.

"Good luck," Gabriel said with a smile of his own.

"Get everything you need," I told Nadia. "We'll leave in a few hours."

She nodded.

I walked back down the stairs with Gabriel, making our way back to the first floor and down to the kitchen.

The front door opened and closed immediately after, with the sounds of someone breathing heavily in the foyer of the house.

Emily walked into the kitchen. She was sweaty, her entire face bathed in it, her hair tied back in a ponytail, her T-shirt soaked through. She opened the fridge and grabbed a bottle of cold water. Gabriel filled her in on the situation as she drank. She looked over at me. "I want to come with you."

"I'm not sure that's a great idea," Gabriel said softly. "You're still learning how your abilities work."

"And there's no better way of learning than doing," Emily countered. She looked between Gabriel and me and let out a long sigh. "Fine, I don't want to talk about it. I don't want to discuss my feelings and my thoughts,

I don't want to talk about my parents, or boyfriend, or anything else. I may want to in the future, but right now I just want to feel useful. That would help me more than anything else. Just let me *do something*. Is this going to be dangerous?"

I shrugged. "Maybe. I certainly don't trust the man we're going to see, and he lies like a British politician, so yeah . . . trying to get information out of him won't be easy."

"That sounds like something I could help with," Emily said with more than a little hope in her voice.

"It's your call, Lucas," Gabriel said, expertly passing the decision to someone else.

"Fine with me," I said. "Two things. One, you're not a cop. You're not an agent. You're a civilian in this instance."

"Got it," Emily said.

"I mean it," I continued. "You're there for guidance and to assist with intel."

"I really do got it," Emily said.

"And two," I said. "You're third in the ladder of people on this mission who gets to decide anything. Not because you're on leave, and not because I don't think you're capable, but because you're not coming with us as an active field agent for the RCU, or FBI, or anyone else. I know you're thinking I'm being an asshole by telling you this, and that's fine, but I'm doing it because you need to hear it."

Emily stared at me and nodded. "You're in charge, don't do anything stupid. Got it."

"We're leaving in an hour or so," I said.

Emily smiled, blinked, and took a deep breath. "Thank you." She hurried out of the room, leaving Gabriel shaking his head.

"You have an issue with this?" I asked.

"A little one," Gabriel said.

"She's a highly trained FBI agent," I told him. "She can handle herself."

"She's also having serious problems coming to terms with what she now is," Gabriel pointed out. "My concern isn't that she can't handle herself; my concern is that she's throwing herself into work as a way to postpone dealing with everything."

"I once went to war instead of dealing with everything," I countered.

"And how well did that work out for you long-term?"

"Not brilliantly," I agreed. "Which is why I don't plan on letting her massacre a bunch of Romans."

"Don't be a smart-ass," Gabriel snapped.

"We'll keep an eye on her," I promised. "She might be right, though; she might just need some time away actually doing something. Not everyone wants to talk, and until she wants to, there's very little we can do."

Gabriel took a deep breath and left me alone in the kitchen, where I made a cup of coffee, took a Danish out of a packet of fresh ones I'd found in the bread bin, and sat down at the small table to eat and spend more than five minutes alone.

My thoughts turned to what I'd gotten myself into, and I figured that no matter what else was going to happen in the next few days, being alone was going to be a commodity that would be in short supply. I'm comfortable in my own company and find a lack of society helps keep my brain from overloading.

I wondered how Ravi and Ji-hyun were getting on. I'd have to call them and get an update.

I had finished eating and was placing the mug and plate in the dishwasher when Emily entered the room. She wore jeans and a moss-green T-shirt, and dark boots, which were probably sensible, given where we were going.

She put a dark blue leather backpack on one of the chairs opposite me. "I'm not entirely used to being the one following orders."

"Yeah, I figured that out," I told her.

"I just want you to know just in case I do overstep my boundaries with anything."

"I'll tell you; don't worry," I said as Nadia appeared behind Emily, a black-and-silver holdall in one hand. "You ready?"

Nadia nodded, placing the bag on the table. "Let's go meet Gunslinger," she said with genuine eagerness.

"Hopefully, I won't be a burden," Emily said.

"Don't," Nadia said, her voice harder than usual. "There are enough people in this world who will put you down without doing it to yourself."

Nadia was coming out of her shell, just like Ji-hyun said. She'd found it difficult to find her place at first but seemed more at ease now. It was good to see.

"You both ready, then?" I asked.

They nodded, and we headed into the hallway toward the front door.

"Be careful," Gabriel said as he came down the stairs.

Upon reaching us, he embraced me fiercely. "I'm serious," he said as he looked between us.

"We'll be fine," I said. "Nadia will make sure of it."

"I will bring them back," Nadia said. "Maybe not all of the pieces will be in the same place, but I'll still bring them back."

Gabriel turned to Nadia. "That is not exactly a great comfort."

Nadia shrugged. "Best I've got," she said before leaving Gabriel and me alone.

"We'll be fine," I repeated.

"Something feels . . . off about this," Gabriel said. "Not about Gunslinger, although I share any reservations when it comes to his involvement, I mean this whole Croupier thing. It feels like a distraction from finding Callie."

I shared Gabriel's reservations. "It's still the best lead we've got to hunting down the vials. Maybe this facility will give us some clue where Callie has gone, or at least where the vials are. If Ezekiel met Callie, it means she's got facilities to use. Hopefully, she's left something we can track her with. Besides, this Croupier knows the buyers, and yes, maybe it's done as a misdirection to keep us busy, but we don't have a lot of leads to go on. You work with what you have. Anything else, and we're just running in circles hoping to find something."

"The Croupier is going to be gunning for you," Gabriel said. "And who knows who else Callie has out there in her pay—you're not exactly her favourite person, Lucas."

"There are always people who want me dead, Gabriel," I pointed out.

"I just . . ." Gabriel paused and took a deep breath, letting it out slowly. "Ever since we learned what she was up to, something about Callie doesn't make sense. Sounds like she's riftborn but has no problems experimenting on the rift-fused. She has no empathy for her own people. She's motivated by something more than just a need to discover answers to the rift."

I knew what he meant; something had felt off from the moment I'd discovered that Callie Mitchell wasn't human. That, in the past, she'd gone by the name *Valentina Ermilova*, which we still didn't know if it was her real name or just another alias. We didn't know anything about her except that she was evil incarnate. It's one of the reasons we'd found it so difficult to actually track her.

"I'll let you know when we arrive," I told Gabriel. "You worry too much."

"Or you don't worry enough?" Gabriel said, the seriousness to his earlier tone melting away. He tossed me a pair of car keys, which I caught in one hand. "Black Toyota RAV4. It's off-road. Because I worry too much."

I left the building and caught up with Nadia and Emily inside the church. Emily was sat on a pew, opposite Nadia, who was sat cross-legged, her eyes closed. "We're taking Gabriel's new car," I said, jingling the keys.

Nadia's eyes opened. "Just checking the chains," she said by way of explanation.

"And?" Emily asked before I could.

"Too much," Nadia said. "Unknown which path we're going on. There is one where we stop to get hot dogs and I drop it inside the car and it rolls around a lot."

"So, we're not stopping for hot dogs," I said.

"Spoilsport," Nadia whispered under her breath.

"Any of those paths where horror befalls us?" Emily asked.

"Loads," Nadia said. "But then, that's normal. Horror, violence, death, injury, they befall us so often in so many ways. Most never happen. Not to us. They're only *possibilities*; there's no one true path except the one we've already been on."

"What does that mean?" Emily asked.

"It means we can only be certain about what has already happened," Nadia said. "I don't tell the future. I only see the possibilities of a future."

"There, don't you feel better?" I asked Emily as we left the church and followed the path outside to a small parking area which contained the exceptionally new and mirror-polished Toyota.

"Not really, no," Emily said.

CHAPTER SEVEN

Six hours of driving in one sitting was not something I would do unless necessary, even as someone who isn't human. We stopped every few hours to stretch our legs, swap between Emily and I driving, and grab something to eat and drink.

Every hour or so, the landscape changed, and we were soon moving beyond built-up cities and freeways and passing through vast woodland as we reached the Canadian border.

We went through without a hitch. The guard saw my Raven medallion and practically shook my hand as we drove through. All humans have heard of the Guilds, and most either understand that we help ensure humans don't become snacks to fiends, or they fear us. Either of those is honestly fine.

We reached Greater Sudbury just as the afternoon became the evening. The summer sun was still high in the sky and would remain so for a few more hours yet. It was a pleasant town, the kind of place that's close enough to a big city to allow the people the chance to experience it should they wish, but far enough away to give them space. I understood the appeal.

Nadia woke up just as we were leaving the town and, after lamenting the fact that she'd missed out on seeing the IMAX, stared out the window. I switched the music—which had been on my phone—to the local radio station, primarily to hear the news, but it was just the usual local radio stuff, and I quickly turned back to listen to the music.

The satnav directed me to the area *Forest Drive*. We drove down a long, winding road for ten minutes, occasionally seeing more signs before the first mansion came to view. Followed quickly by four more as we slowed down.

The mansions were in a long line, all facing the forest. All had long driveways, and trees obscuring most of the buildings, with large black iron gates and fences. Guards stood patrol at the entrance, all of them watching us like hawks as we drove by. Not one of them screamed *hospitality*, which I guessed was probably the point. The buildings were a short distance apart. There were eight in total, each one probably three or four times the size of Gabriel's church. A rich person's getaway.

Ezekiel's mansion was the last one on the small street and, like the others, was hidden away behind iron and trees, only giving you glimpses of what may lie beyond. I stopped the car next to a guard hut. A burly-looking guard in a dark blue uniform with black boots walked over to us. He had a gun on his hip and a radio on his lapel. He was white with an almost-bald head and a thin moustache that looked like someone had drawn it on with a biro. A second guard was still inside the hut.

"How can I help you?" he asked, sounding like he'd very much not like to help us at all.

"Here to see Ezekiel," I said.

"Gunslinger," Nadia said from the back, trying to make the word sound moody and cool.

"Is he expecting you?" the guard asked.

"Yes," I said. "My name is Lucas Rurik. This is Emily and Nadia."

The guard nodded and walked back over to the hut, where the glass partition slid aside and he spoke to the guard inside. He came back a moment later as the massive iron gate began to slowly slide open.

"Enjoy your stay," he said.

We drove up the long driveway, with the mansion at the far end, next to a garage that was bigger than my entire flat. The garage's door was open, revealing a ruby-red Bentley Continental GT inside being washed. A midnight-blue Mercedes G-Wagon and a forest-green Shelby Mustang were parked in front of the steps that led up to the mansion's front door. The entire building was made from pale brick, with four columns at the front, holding up a large portico above it. It was like the architects had seen pictures of British Georgian and Victorian mansions and said, "Copy that."

The garden in front of it was lavish and expansive, with beautiful flowers among the large trees. I stopped the car next to the Mercedes and looked back across the manicured lawn, barely able to even see the street beyond.

"Is this guy serious?" Emily asked.

"Bit ostentatious?" I replied.

"Just a little bit," Emily said, looking up at the dark tiled roof, the large windows on either side of the building that looked down on where we stood, the chocolate-brown door with its golden knocker in the shape of a wreath. The whole thing screamed *look at me, look how rich I am.*

"*Ostentatious* wasn't quite the word I was thinking," Nadia said.

"What were you thinking?" Emily asked her.

"Twattish," Nadia replied without pause.

The front door to the mansion opened and Ezekiel strolled out. He wore a burgundy three-piece suit with polished black shoes and a silver waistcoat. Ezekiel's family were Irish, apparently some of the first to arrive in America, if you believed his stories. He had pale skin and shoulder-length light brown hair that was tied back; he was taller than I was, at probably just over six feet, and had a slim build. He didn't look it, but Ezekiel was all wiry muscle. Gabriel once joked that Ezekiel was so good at hunting because nothing would want to eat him.

Ezekiel wore rings on most fingers, some of which glinted as the sunlight caught them. He was clean-shaven and hadn't aged much in the few decades since I'd last seen him. Contrary to urban myth, riftborn do age, just much slower than humans.

After practically skipping down the stairs to greet us, Ezekiel shook Emily's hand with the warmth of someone who has known you their whole life. He went to shake Nadia's, who shook her head. Ezekiel left his hand there for a second longer than was probably comfortable before retracting it and nodding as if nothing had happened.

"Lucas," Ezekiel said, extending his arms as if he were about to give me a bear hug.

"Ezekiel," I said bracing myself for the hug, but he just stood and looked at me.

"I go by Zeke," he said. "Or Gunslinger, your choice."

"Zeke," I said, and noticed the slight disappointment on his face. Too bad, I'm not calling someone Gunslinger; it sounded like a men's aftershave.

Zeke smiled and hugged me, slapping me on the back of the shoulder and pointing to his house. "I'll get my people to bring your bags; come see my home."

"Aren't you having a party?" Emily asked.

"Tomorrow," Zeke said as we followed him up the stairs. "Tonight we'll go to the facility so you can look around. That's why you're here, yes?"

"What did Gabriel tell you?" I asked as we reached the front door.

"Not much," Zeke said. "I'd heard people in the know were looking for Callie a while ago though RCU agents' info. The RCU think that Callie Mitchell is involved in some shady stuff. I did a little digging and found out that she's experimenting on our kind. I didn't know about your involvement until I called Gabriel about the facility, which I only found a few days ago. I was hunting a fiend in the forest and came across it. Gabriel also mentioned that you're looking for a man who calls himself the Croupier."

"You heard of him?" I asked. I'd hoped that we could move things along, to get the intel Zeke knew, but that wasn't how he worked. Threats or flattery had worked in the past, but I'd save those hands until I needed them.

"Some," Zeke said, surprisingly serious. He smiled and pushed open the door. "But first, let's get you settled."

The foyer was much more tasteful than I'd imagined it would be. Polished wooden floors led to a staircase that spiralled around to the floor above. There were three doors in front of me, one to the left and right, and one just slightly off centre. All were painted white, with the left leading to a reception area with dark blue upholstered chairs and a large grey couch. The right had a long walnut-wood dining table with seating for at least twelve people. There were paintings of landscapes on the walls of both rooms. The third door, beside which sat a large grandfather clock, was shut.

"This way," Zeke said, leading Emily, Nadia, and me to it, pushing it open and revealing a massive function room. It was easily forty feet long and thirty feet wide, with high ceilings painted to form a large mural of the rift landscape. The wooden floor was partially covered in a huge red-and-cream rug, and there were floor-to-ceiling windows down one side, with the dark red curtains tied back, allowing in a huge amount of natural light. On the opposite wall were a multitude of frames, plaques, and pieces of artwork. The centre of the wall was a fifteen-foot-high oil painting of Zeke holding a sword in one hand and a musket rifle in the other as the city behind him burned.

"New York," Zeke said as I stared at the painting, thinking it the most self-centred thing I'd ever seen.

"This one says *For Capturing the Chesapeake Gang*," Emily said. "1892. It's signed by President Harrison."

"I did some work for the government," Zeke said, not even bothering to hide his pride at his accomplishments. And to be honest, why should he? He did a lot of great work and helped a lot of people; it wasn't until he realised he could also become exceptionally rich by working with the right kind of people that he stopped trying to help unless it helped him.

"A great man," Zeke said.

I walked over to the windows and looked out on the garden at the side of Zeke's property. An American flag flew proudly just outside of the window. But beyond that, it was mostly open land until you hit the fifty-foot-high red brick wall that signified the boundary, and I spotted two large structures closer to the rear of the building.

"What are the buildings back there?" I asked.

"Olympic-sized swimming pool," Zeke said. "And the other is just a two-storey office I had built. I like to separate my work and home life."

"You married?" I asked him. "Again, I mean." Last I heard, Zeke was on wife number six, or maybe seven. He married at least one of them twice.

"Not since Catherine died ten years back," Zeke said, and for the first time the bluster vanished, replaced with the man. A man who missed his wife. I felt a pang of sympathy for him right there, although I was pretty sure Zeke would manage to smother it before long. "But I have my children and grandchildren," Zeke said. "Even a few great-grandchildren. They're all coming tomorrow."

"I didn't think riftborn could have children on Earth," Nadia said.

"Ah, Catherine had four kids when we met. They're in their late forties and fifties now, with kids of their own." Zeke said proudly. "Grandkids of their own, too. Despite having married so many times, Catherine was the first I ever had a family with." The warmth in his voice was back, the pride in his eyes at the mention of his family.

"I think I met a few of them back in the 1980s," I said. "Two of them, I think. Boy and girl. They were both in their mid-teens at the time."

"Yeah, Jason and Lisa," Zeke said. "They were the middle two. Nicole is the youngest, and Eric the oldest."

"If this party is a private event, we can come back," Emily offered.

"Never," Zeke said firmly. "I have nearly fifty people—mostly family—turning up tomorrow. Catering, too. And some business associates."

"Business associates?" Emily asked.

"Yes, they insisted," Zeke said. "I tried to put them off, but I have a portfolio to attend to and investments to discuss. I figured I'd invite them, let them get drunk, and maybe come out of the meeting a happier group." Zeke laughed at his own idea.

The tour of the rest of the building was done at a quicker pace; the huge kitchen with attached dining area, and doors that led out onto a large piece of decking overlooking the lawn, tennis courts, basketball court, and a good-sized hedge maze. The study, the library, and other rooms all merged into one. The upstairs with two bedrooms on one floor, each with its own en suite, and five bedrooms on the floor above, again with en suite, and then an attic with two more bedrooms. A nine-bedroom house. I hoped not everyone was going to be staying, or they'd have to share rooms.

The bedrooms were all decorated in a similar fashion; king-sized bed, a comfortable-looking armchair, old wooden furniture that consisted of a wardrobe, chest of drawers, and two bedside cabinets. Each room had a slightly different colour scheme, though, with the bedding matching the thick rug on the floor.

"I'm afraid that the ladies will have to share," Zeke said.

"I think we'll manage," Emily said.

"We can braid one another's hair and gossip," Nadia said with glee.

"No," Emily said with a sigh, entering the light-blue-decorated room after Nadia.

"And this one is yours," Zeke said, holding open the door to a room with a green scheme. My bag was already on the bed.

"This is a lot of house just for you," I said.

"Ah, I'm only here a few months of the year," Zeke told me. "And usually, it's full of family. I had to get it extended to add the extra bedrooms in the attic. People aren't all staying this time, thankfully; otherwise, we wouldn't have the space. I'll leave you to unpack. We'll head to the facility later."

Zeke shut the door, leaving me alone to go through my bag. I got the feeling it was going to be a long few days.

CHAPTER EIGHT

I didn't bother unpacking, just put the bag in the wardrobe, before lying down on the comfortable bed. There was air conditioning in the entire house so, while it was still hot and sticky outside, it was relatively pleasant inside.

Someone had placed a bowl of potpourri next to the large HDTV that was on top of the chest of drawers. The potpourri gave a pleasant scent of flowers without being overpowering.

I switched on the TV and scrolled through the myriad of channels, finding the BBC and turning the volume up. A Member of Parliament that the accompanying graphic told me was called Jacob Smythe was joined by several other people on a panel.

I didn't hear what he said originally as the chorus of cheers and boos from the studio audience drowned him out, but the female presenter asked them for quiet and allowed Jacob to continue.

"Look, I'm not saying that all riftborn are bad people," he began.

I rolled my eyes; I knew where this was going.

"But while revenants come back immediately, and we can see and hunt fiends, riftborn can be living within the rift itself for centuries. They could be coming here, having been warriors, pirates, marauders, murderers; we simply don't know. All I'm suggesting is that riftborn need to inform us when they are on Earth, so that they can be . . ."

"Tagged," a different male panellist shouted. "Because in your eyes, they're just criminals."

"No," Jacob said, clearly irritated. "Because they could be a danger to humans. To all of us. We simply don't know. We can't have them coming and going as they please without informing the authorities, and we can't trust the RCU or the Guilds to inform us. The rift-fused need to come under human laws when they are on Earth."

There was clapping, shouting, and I got bored and turned the TV over. There were always people like Jacob. Always people who wanted to make the rift-fused into the bad guys, although singling out the riftborn was new.

I remained on the bed for an hour or so, just relaxing while flicking through the TV channels, until there was a knock at my door. I opened it to a young woman in a black shirt and white blouse.

"Dinner is ready," the woman told me.

"Thank you," I said, following her toward the stairs. "What's it like working here?"

"Zeke's a good boss," she told me without looking back. "A good man, too. You known him long?"

"A long time," I told her. "He's made some very good choices in life to be this affluent."

"He works with a lot of people," she told me. "He's in great demand. He usually lives in New York; he has a penthouse in Manhattan."

"I didn't know that," I said. "I'm sorry I didn't ask your name."

"Rose," she said, looking back at me.

"I'm Lucas," I told her.

"It's a pleasure to meet you, Lucas," she said. "Zeke told me that you and your friends will be joining him out in the field tonight. You must be very excited."

"Beside myself," I said trying to keep the sarcasm out of my voice as we reached the bottom of the staircase.

Rose stopped and turned back to me. "I have worked for Zeke for a few years now, both here and in Manhattan. I know him pretty well, and this is the first time I've seen him afraid. I know that he is boisterous, I know that he is full of bluster like a hurricane of personality, but he is scared of something. I like Zeke. I do not wish for anything ill to befall him."

"You don't have any idea what he's afraid of?" I asked.

Rose shook her head. "Maybe I'm reading too much into it, but it's like there's something weighing on him."

"I'll keep an eye on him," I said. "What are his family like? You met them before?"

"Good people," Rose said, looking around. "Mostly."

"Anything else?" I asked. "Between you and me? Just so I know who to look out for?"

Rose shook her head, as if realising she was perilously close to gossiping with someone she didn't know. "You'll figure it out soon enough." Rose motioned to the door beside her. "Zeke is waiting for you."

"Thank you," I said, opening the door and entering the dining room that was adjacent to the front door.

Emily and Nadia were already seated at the table, next to one another, with Zeke sat at the head beside them. "Lucas, come join us," Zeke exclaimed, raising a bottle of wine.

"Red or white?" I asked, sitting down.

"Whichever you wish," Zeke said.

"We're going out later," I reminded him.

"Alcohol doesn't last long in our systems," he said.

That was true; my body burned off alcohol almost as fast as I drank it, which was why I never drank to get drunk. "Red," I said. "A small glass."

"Safety first," Zeke said with a laugh before pouring the glass.

"You have some lovely staff working for you," Emily said.

"They're a great bunch," Zeke said. "They come with me from Manhattan."

"So I hear," I said taking a sip of the admittedly excellent wine.

"Ah, Rose spoke to you," Zeke said, not sounding like he minded. "Lovely girl; always helpful. I think my grandson, Cory, has a thing for her. I don't think she's interested, though."

The first course was brought through by staff, who placed the blue-and-white china plates of various smoked meats and pieces bread in front of us before leaving.

"A small starter," Zeke said. "Oh, I didn't ask if you were vegetarian."

The three of us shook our heads. "I didn't use to be able to eat dairy," Emily said. "Apparently, that goes away when you die and come back."

"You're a newborn," Zeke exclaimed with a clap of his hands. "Ah, welcome! You're having difficulties getting used to it, I assume?"

There was a silence for a moment while Emily took a bite of the smoked meat and bread, dripping the bread in some olive oil as if she was buying for time. "It's been an . . . adjustment," she said eventually.

"When I first came back, I woke up in the rift," Zeke said. "All riftborn wake up in roughly the same place, a set of caves just outside of the capital city of Inaxia. Beautiful city, as I'm sure Lucas can verify. I thought I'd been captured by the British and demanded to see King George. Got a lot of funny looks from the people who work there helping the newbies. Do you go back often, Lucas?"

"To Inaxia?" I asked. "Not been back for about seven years, maybe a little longer."

"Do you miss it?" Emily asked, curiously.

I nodded. "It's a strange and vibrant city, full of colour, sounds, smells, and people. People from all ages, from all walks of life. People who used to be kings and queens, now running bars or working as merchants. Who-ever you were in this life matters little in the rift. You're a newbie, as Zeke said; your skills help you, not your wealth. Not the influence you had before the rift took you."

"Too true," Zeke said. "It's been about ten years since I went back. Just after Catherine died. I loved it. Always have. Spent a year there, just living and working in the city, helping merchants do their runs between the city and the Lawless."

"The Lawless?" Emily asked.

"Ah, you don't know about them?" Zeke asked, as he finished his bread and licked his fingers clean of any oil. "What about you, Nadia?"

"I've heard of them," Nadia said, who a hundred percent was more interested in finishing her food.

"The Lawless are villages or towns that are full people who have either been banished from Inaxia, or left of their own volition," Zeke said. "Those who are banished are never allowed to step foot in Inaxia again, so those who left of their own accord become merchants who travel between the Lawless cities and Inaxia. They usually have caravans with them, with armed guards. The rift is a dangerous place, and not everyone who had been exiled decides they want to live under the rule of the Lawless."

"The Lawless have rules?" Emily asked.

"Of course," Zeke said. "I understand it must sound weird to be both lawless and have laws, but it's true. They're called Lawless because they don't live by the laws of Inaxia, I believe it was originally meant to be a derogatory term coined by Inaxia, but the people took it as their own. They have their own laws. There are some Lawless cities that are dark, unpleasant places, but most are simply trying to get by without Inaxia's influence or interference. They're good people who didn't necessarily always do good things, or ran afoul of the wrong people."

"Inaxia is a democracy," I explained. "But it's not entirely free. You live by the laws of Inaxia, or you leave. And a lot of people choose to leave. There are multiple cities in the rift, most of whom have close ties to Inaxia or one of the people who run it. The Lawless have no ties to any of those people. Like Zeke said, the rift is a harsh place, a dangerous place. Inaxia can be just as harsh and dangerous, should you make a wrong decision."

We discussed the rift, Inaxia, and matters related to them for a while as we ate beautifully prepared mushroom-and-chicken ravioli and chocolate cheesecake, and when we were done, we retired to the drawing room by a large log fire, which, considering the weather, certainly didn't need to be on.

The darkness during the summer is a slow, gradual thing, unlike in winter where it happens quickly with no meandering. The large clock over the fireplace said that it was eleven p.m. when the four of us got ready for our evening's excursion.

I went back to my room, changing out of my T-shirt and jeans and into some thicker black combat trousers and a dark grey jumper. I put on the sheath for my two rift-tempered blades, and placed the two daggers at the small of my back before putting on a dark green jacket, then left the room to find Nadia and Emily in the hallway, waiting for me.

They'd both changed into dark combat trousers, boots, and thick hooded tops. Emily had a holster against her hip with a revolver in it, and Nadia carried a duffle bag with, I assumed, any number of weapons she'd decided to bring with her.

"You ready?" Emily asked.

I nodded. "Keeps your eyes peeled out there. No telling what we might be walking into."

"What do you see?" Emily asked Nadia.

"The chains say a lot," Nadia said. "Pain, suffering, possibly worse. But there's no betrayal in there. None I've seen. I'm not saying he won't betray us; I'm just saying I didn't see it."

"Hope for the best, plan for the worst," I said.

As we entered the drawing room, Zeke got to his feet and stretched. "Are you ready?" he asked. He'd already gotten changed into forest-green combat trousers, big dark brown boots, and a black jumper. He picked up a charcoal jacket that had been over the arm of the chair he'd been sat in, and put it on. "We could be out a while."

The three of us followed Zeke out of the house and down the steps to the garage. He removed his phone from his pocket and tapped something, the double-sized garage doors slowly moving up to reveal the G-Wagon inside.

"So, this facility," I said. "How long have you known about it?"

"Years," Zeke said. "Never knew what they did. It was always heavily guarded, and they didn't seem like the friendliest bunch." Zeke walked around to the rear of the vehicle, and opened the boot to reveal a large black fabric bag and a small silver briefcase. He opened the case first, revealing several boxes of bullets. ".405 Winchester rifle cartridge. They're for a Winchester 1895 rifle."

"Pretty," Nadia said.

I opened one of the boxes and lifted out a few of the cartridges. They looked perfectly normal. "These aren't going to kill any fiends we might run into," I pointed out.

"Hopefully, we won't need to kill anything," Zeke said, and unzipped the duffle bag and removed a wooden box, opening it to reveal two Colt Peacemakers. They glowed a faint purple.

"Rift-tempered guns," I said. Rift-tempering a gun is easy; it's the ammo that's the hard bit. Rift-tempering ammo tends to explode it, and putting normal ammo in a rift-tempered gun will either imbue the ammo with some of that power, or it'll do absolutely nothing. It's why most people don't bother with guns in the rift; they're temperamental and you do not want to have a useless weapon when facing down a fiend.

Zeke closed the box. "They work one in two," he said, removing a sheathed sword and drawing it out slightly for me to see the purple-tinged blade. "This is for when they don't. A silver handled cuttoe. The sword of George Washington, although his was made with ivory, too." Zeke replaced the sword and zipped up the duffle bag.

The four of us climbed into the car and Zeke started the engine.

"You never finished answering," Emily said from the rear passenger-side seat. "About the facility."

"Ah, well," Zeke said as we set off. "I met Callie and some fellow called Mason a few years back. He came across as this arrogant rich guy who thought he was better than everyone else. And lo and behold, a few months back, his face is plastered all over the TV as he'd done a bunch of crimes and gotten himself killed in the process. Well, something felt off about that, and it sat with me for a few months.

"So, when I came back, I went to the facility. Lots of people shutting it down; met Callie again. She said something about moving out, that the facility was government property now. Didn't say where she was going, and I've done enough messing around with governments to know to keep my nose out of their business.

"But something was still not right. There was an itch I couldn't shake. So, I called Gabriel, asked him if he'd run into Callie and Mason. He told me Mason was dead and that Callie was on the run for crimes against . . . well, everyone. I told him about the facility, and here you are."

The drive was comfortable, but Zeke was more cautious than I thought he would be behind the wheel of the car, and after driving down a main road for several miles, we turned off, going east of Greater Sudbury, through dense woodland.

"How far to the facility?" I asked.

"About ten minutes," Zeke said. "Lots of fiends around these parts. More than usual, I think. I'm beginning to wonder if there are more tears occurring than before."

Fiends were still just animals, albeit animals with incredible strength, and a need to hunt their prey that could border on bloodlust. Herbivore or carnivore when they were alive, it didn't matter to a fiend. Fiends fed on blood and flesh, and they didn't much care where they got either.

"You're not the first to make that suggestion," I said, thinking back to Gabriel suggesting that there were more revenants, or at least more coming to him.

"How do you know where to hunt the fiends?" Nadia asked. "Lucas says you're an excellent tracker."

"I sure am," Zeke said proudly. "I've got motion sensors linked to cameras all over the forest where I live, right up to the lake. Work smarter, not harder."

As we got further into the woods, the road opened up and we eventually arrived at a large clearing next to the beginning of a road that went up toward a military checkpoint in front of a large set of chain-link gates. There were two watchtowers, one on either end of the perimeter.

"That is not a small facility," I said.

"Never said it was small," Zeke said. "We'll walk from here."

The G-Wagon stopped, and Zeke got out of the car, leaving the headlights on, illuminating the checkpoint. I followed him, looking through the light to the front of the facility that had seen better days. Parts of the chain-link were broken, and the barrier that stopped people from entering was broken off.

"What happened here?" Emily asked as she got out of the car and joined us.

"Nothing good," Nadia said.

Zeke passed me the 1895 rift-tempered Winchester rifle, which had an ammo holder on the side of the stock and had already been filled with eight cartridges. "It's already got a full five rounds loaded."

I lifted the rifle and looked down the barrel. It was well made and well maintained, and I had no doubt that it would make a whole lot of fiends think twice. So long as the rift-tempering held and transferred to the cartridges. I'm not really much of a gun guy, having lived for well over a thousand years before they were anything I needed to be concerned with, but I had to admit they had their uses in the hunting-large-dangerous-fiends department.

"You two take what you need," Zeke said, motioning to the weapons.

"I have everything," Nadia said, lifting a rift-tempered, silenced MP5 out of her bag and putting on a holster for more magazines.

Emily took a bolt action-rifle, the barrel glowing blue, and checked it over as I walked a short distance up the hill.

"You okay?" Zeke asked from beside me.

"I don't know," I said. "You have no idea what went on in here?"

Zeke shook his head. "I'm not sure I want to know. I'm not sure I wanted to know back then, either. If I knew, I might have to do something, and . . . well, sometimes it's better not knowing."

I didn't bother with a rebuttal. He wasn't necessarily wrong.

When Nadia and Emily joined us, we walked up the slight hill toward the checkpoint, all of us ready for whatever we might face. I noticed that Emily kept back from the rest of us, her rifle over her shoulder, her pistol in her hands. I wondered if she was keeping an eye on Zeke as well as the surrounding area.

We reached the checkpoint, which was in even more of a mess than I'd first thought. The glass windows of the small office for the guards were shattered, the glass covering the ground, some of which had patches of blood.

The large gate to the facility was ajar, and I pushed it open with more than a little trepidation as it squealed in the darkness.

Once beyond the checkpoint, we remained low and silent, just in case something wanted to check on the new visitors.

The interior of the facility consisted of one large building in the middle and two smaller ones on either side.

"I think they're barracks," Zeke said. "When I was here, I saw soldiers coming and going from them."

"You want to go check?" I asked.

"Not really," Zeke said.

"There's a chunk of the roof missing from that one," Nadia said, pointing across the facility to one of the small buildings.

We moved across as one group, stopping by the first of the smaller buildings, and pushing open the door, revealing rows of bunk beds and footlockers.

The second building was the partially broken one. Part of the front wall had collapsed, as if something had jumped through it and taken the architecture with it. Roof beams jutted out of the hole like broken bones through skin.

"You okay?" I asked as Zeke sniffed the air.

"Dead . . . something," he said. "Does not smell good."

I pushed open the remains of the door with the butt of the Winchester, feeling my eyes water from the stench. "Goddamn it," I snapped.

I took a deep breath and opened the door again, almost immediately finding the cause. "Deer," I said. "Stag, more accurately. Its head is over there, and the rest of it is on the other side of the building."

I walked into what was a large washroom, although the showers and sinks had been tossed around the place. Emily removed a flashlight and moved the light over the remains of the deer. It had massive gouge marks along its rump and down its ribs. It had been disembowelled and there had been big chunks of it torn away, presumably to eat. One leg was missing too. There had been quite a feast.

"Fiend?" Emily asked.

"I bloody well hope so," I said

"The fiend ate and ran," Zeke said. "Didn't eat the whole deer, though, which is weird. Something disturbed it."

"Hunter, maybe?" Nadia asked.

"No," I said. "A human disturbing a feasting fiend is going to get turned into a paste. Bear, maybe. Something to give it pause."

"A really big bear, then," Zeke said.

We moved outside and crossed in front of the largest building, checking out the other two smaller facilities, which turned out to be a kitchen and large mess room, neither of which were anything concerning.

The four of us returned to the front of the main building. The door was busted open, the keypad torn off. There were bloody smears on the glass panels of the door.

"Either something has broken in here—" Emily said.

"Or they left something and it broke out," Nadia said.

"Either way, if it's a fiend, it needs putting down," I said. "Ready?"

Everyone nodded and I pushed open the bloody door.

CHAPTER NINE

The immediate interior of the building consisted of a foyer with a long hallway behind it, where I could see a set of stairs that went up to the floor above. There was a door on either side of the foyer, and there was nothing inside the foyer itself. No furniture, no art on the walls, just sterile white walls and black tiled floor. The room was in total darkness, with only our flashlights and the moonlight from outside offering any illumination. This was not designed to be a welcoming place.

"I smell blood," Zeke said, pushing open the door closest to him and looking inside. "Nothing."

I walked over to the door on the opposite side of the room and opened it. It was full of office supplies; pens and paper adorned two large metal shelving units. I closed the door.

"Nothing here, either," I told everyone.

Zeke and Emily took point, and I hung back with Nadia.

Zeke paused at the base of the stairs and motioned upward.

I nodded.

Emily went first, keeping her body low as we followed. She paused at the top, looked back down at us, and shook her head.

We reached her a second later, and I got what Emily had meant. The room, which was easily big enough to have fit an Olympic-sized swimming pool, was empty. The windows were taped up, with loose strands fraying and letting through meagre amounts of light.

"This is a bit weird," I said.

Nadia stood still, her chains rattling around her as the rest of us took a step back. It was like they were snaking out, trying to seize something . . . or to defend her from something. Neither proposition sounded good for Nadia.

It lasted only a few seconds before Nadia rocked back and forth a few times and opened her eyes.

"You okay?" I asked.

"I get no indication that this room was ever used for anything," Nadia said. "I would expect there to be some kind of residual energy if Callie and her friends had been using rift energy. But there's nothing here, except for us four, obviously."

We all made our way back downstairs and continued on along the hallway, finding only one room with a small kitchen, a mess room, and one that was a bathroom. At the far end of the hallway was a slightly open metal shutter that Zeke pushed up so we could all continue on into a large warehouse. There were crates and boxes full of food, water, medical and engineering supplies. A forklift sat abandoned at the far end of the warehouse next to a metal grate that sat the length and height of the room.

"Okay, so, there's nothing here," Emily said as everyone started to look around.

I walked to the far end of the room and pushed the button to open the warehouse doors, but there was no power.

"Found something," Zeke called out from the far side of the warehouse.

The rest of us walked over to where Zeke was at the side of the warehouse behind several large wooden crates that obscured him from view.

"You found a door," Nadia said. "Well done."

The metal door was closed, and the number pad that was beside it had been busted.

"Everyone ready?" Zeke asked.

We nodded in response and he pushed open the door, which led to a small room with a set of stairs leading down into darkness.

"That bodes well," I said, using my flashlight to see if I could see anything down the staircase.

"I'll go first," Zeke said, and descended the stairs.

Emily looked down at her hands and back to me. "I need to get comfortable with this sooner or later." She activated her power and a dark bone-like armour slid over her body, covering everything up to her eyes, which turned bright green like a night-vision camera. In their transformed form, a hooded revenant was about concealment and stealth, but they also had one dangerous weapon. On the side of each hand, by the little finger, was a raptor-like talon. It was thick enough and sharp enough to be used to climb rock-faces, but I'd also seen them used as weapons with deadly efficiency.

Can you hear me? Emily asked, her voice bouncing around in my head.

Hooded revenants were masters of stealth, and part of that meant she couldn't talk while the armour was activated.

"I hear you," I told her.

Emily's body flickered and suddenly it was as if she wasn't there. Camouflage was a big part of the hooded revenant's repertoire; it wasn't that she was invisible, but it was as if light bent around her. If you stared really hard, you could just make out a shape. When hooded revenants moved, you could tell that there was someone there, but for staying in one place and being unseen, there were few better.

Nadia and Emily took the stairs, Emily's camouflage flickering the whole way. I understood why she was reluctant to use it; it quite literally showed you to be something other than human, and while knowing you weren't human was one thing, seeing it was always something else entirely.

I followed behind and the group of us were quickly at the end of the stairs as Zeke found a powered-up door that had been jammed almost shut.

"You okay with this?" Zeke asked.

I nodded, turned to smoke, and drifted through the gap, re-forming in a small, empty room with glass windows all around it, a walkway leading from the centre of it, and a door on either side. "Give me a second," I said as I pulled the large metal crates away from the door.

The walkway beyond also had glass windows on either side of it, looking down on one of two large rooms on either side. One of the rooms had dozens of beanbag chairs and a floor-to-ceiling video system on the wall, although someone had thrown an actual chair into one of the screens that made up the large monitor. The opposite side looked identical to the first, although the beanbag chairs had been destroyed, their contents covering the floor.

"What is this place?" Emily asked from beside me.

"I have no idea," I said.

The second I opened the door leading to the room with the destroyed beanbags, the metallic smell of blood hit my nose. I stepped inside and walked down the staircase, and knew something was exceptionally wrong. I reached the bottom, and on the wall just below where I'd been standing with everyone was writing. It covered the six-foot-high wall, although it was just one word over and over again in various sizes, some of which was in blood: BLESSED.

What the word meant and why someone had felt the need to cover the wall in the single-worded graffiti was anyone's guess, but I'd never been in a building where someone had written on the walls in blood and everything turned out to be perfectly fine.

I went to find Emily and Nadia, who had gone down to the other side of the walk with the smashed screen.

"That room has a wall filled with blood writing," I said. "And it's much colder in here than out there."

"Yeah, that might explain why we didn't smell that," Emily said.

"Dead guy," Nadia said, pointing to the corpse on the ground, buried under a dozen beanbag chairs.

Emily had turned back into her human form.

Nadia pushed away the beanbags to reveal a very dead and very naked man. His throat had been cut from ear to ear.

"What the hell happened here?" I asked rhetorically.

"Wait, did you say you found writing on the wall?" Emily asked.

The three of us made our way back to the bloody writing, this time joined by Zeke, who had seemingly gotten fed up of being left in the small room as lookout.

"Who, or what, are the *Blessed*?" Nadia asked as she stared at the wall. "And why write it in blood?"

"That is an excellent series of questions," I admitted, although the word *Blessed* stirred a memory I couldn't quite grasp ahold of.

"Nothing good happens from finding writing in blood," Emily said.

"Nothing good comes from finding writing in blood and a dead body," Nadia said.

The four of us left the room and went back up to the walkway, using it to get across to a door on the other side that was thankfully already open.

"So," Emily started as we entered a large room with two doors on either side and another door in front. There was no indication where any of the doors went, nor what we might find behind them. "This facility had a dead body, bloody writing on the walls, and absolutely not a living soul around."

"I'm going to go with *serial killer*," Nadia said. "Maybe a cult."

Zeke had been oddly quiet during our time delving into the facility of death-and-blood-based literary endeavour.

"You been in here before?" I asked Zeke.

"No," he said. "I had no idea any of this was here."

Nadia tried the door directly in front of us, which led to a huge open area with half a dozen self-contained offices along each wall and benches and tables in between. At the far end was a set of stairs leading up to an office that looked down on everything else. The offices were all but destroyed, and a fire had been started in the corner that had seen the flames scorch the walls before something or someone had put it out.

Before we moved into the room, I checked all of the other doors. The two on the left of the entrance led to a guard station, complete with armoury that had been emptied out, and a changing area for the workers, including lockers and showers.

Emily opened the doors on the left, which revealed a second guard station and a set of stairs that went down. There were blinking red lights on the ceiling of the stairwell, making everything look a lot more menacing than I'd hoped they were meant to.

"Tunnel or office?" I asked.

"Tunnel," Nadia said, and set off first, with the rest of us following.

We paused at the bottom of the tunnel as the red lights around a large metal door blinked in unison. The door was, like most of them had been when we'd entered, partially ajar. It was almost like someone had wanted us to get this far into the facility.

I looked through the gap in the door, and my eyes adjusted to the meagre light below and made out nothing that was going to attack.

"Gentlemen first," Emily said, motioning to the darkness.

"How generous," I said, and she smirked.

I pushed open the door with an horrific squeal, revealing a hallway beyond that ended only a few feet in as it became a large tunnel that had been bored into the rock under the facility. Several torches were attached to a charging station on the wall next to where the hallway and tunnel met. I picked up a torch and turned it on, illuminating our surroundings. I guess it was too much to hope for actual lighting, so the torch was going to have to do.

I took a few steps into the tunnel as Emily, Nadia, and Zeke followed, each of them grabbing their own torch, until the combined light from all four of us was capable of ensuring there were no surprises. Hopefully.

I took point down the tunnel, and we remained in silence as we moved. It took several minutes to walk the distance of the tunnel, until it opened out to a large cavern with fire pits around the edge and a wooden deck in the middle with a plinth on top of it. With several rows of benches in front of it, and a dark red rug that sat between the benches and the deck, the whole thing looked more than a little church-like.

A hissing sound took my attention, and the braziers ignited all around us.

"Found the switch," Emily said, pointing to the wall while my heart stopped pounding against my chest.

"What is this?" Nadia asked, walking over to the deck and climbing the steps, standing in front of the plinth and picking up a sheet of paper. "It says *The Blessed will prepare for the reckoning of those who banished us.* What does that mean?"

I had no idea but it still rang a bell with me.

I looked around the cavern; there was a large tunnel in the far corner, although no lights had come on down there. One ominous place at a time.

"There's a door here," Emily said.

I ran over to the wooden door as Emily pushed it open, revealing a large metal prison inside, divided into four smaller cells. Two of the cells had old men inside, but it was obvious that they were dead.

Emily removed a set of keys from a hook on the wall and opened the closest cage. "No idea how he died," she said as she patted him down. "Nothing on him; no way to know who he is. I'd guess he's been here a while, though. Few days *at least*."

Nadia poked her head through the open doorway. "You might want to see this," she said.

Emily and I followed her back out into the main cavern and around the back of the deck, where there was another door. We stepped into the brightly lit hallway beyond and through a large metal door at the end. This room looked like a laboratory and was full of cold storage, computers, microscopes, and machines.

"Those fridges have blood in them," Nadia said. "A lot of blood. All named and dated."

"This doesn't seem like any serial killer I've ever read about," Emily said.

"Those freezers have something else," Nadia said, pointing to the large industrial freezers at the far end of the room. "It's the vials of Callie Mitchell's poison."

"My god, what was she doing here?" Zeke asked.

I practically sprinted over and pulled open a freezer, and there they were, dozens and dozens of tiny vials of purple poison. Questions raced through my mind: *Why were they here? How did they get here? Was this an extra batch? Was Callie working out of this secret place? Was this the only place they were sent to? Why did she leave them behind?* I forced my mind to calm and took a deep breath.

"Twenty-four doses," Nadia said. "Not the whole shipment, but quite a lot of it."

"Why would they be here?" Emily asked. "Callie sold them to the Croupier, who in turn was going to sell them to who knows who."

I didn't have an answer to that. The whole thing was utterly bizarre. I picked up one vial and turned it over in my hand. It was infused with the power of the rift, although I had no idea how Callie had managed it. Or even why she'd want to, but if she'd made it once, she could make it again. We still needed to find her, we still needed to stop her, and the Croupier was still the best way to do that, but finding so much of her . . . *evil shit* was going some way toward making the world a safer place.

"We need to get hold of Gabriel," I said. "The RCU need to get here and catalogue it all and then destroy it."

"The FBI's rift-crime liaison need to be informed too," Emily said.

"Can we trust them?" Nadia asked the question I was already thinking.

"Why not?" Emily asked. "I'm a member of them."

"There were people in the FBI who weren't on our side last time," I said.

"Besides," Nadia said, "humans want to *know* stuff. They want to know how things work, especially when it comes to things they can't control. They don't really understand the rift, no one does, even the people who live there aren't immune to its secrets, but humans would really like to be able to use the rift bypassing those people who have control over it."

"You're suggesting that people in the FBI might take some of these vials and use them as weapons for . . ." Emily paused. "Yeah, okay, I hear it now."

"The FBI, and anyone else involved with human affairs, might well have good intentions, but they have people higher up that they answer to," I said. "Right now, I'm not sure that we can risk handing them a weapon. Or at least so much of a weapon."

"Can it be reverse-engineered?" Emily asked.

"No," Nadia said. "They'd need access to the rift to do it, and that means getting a riftborn on their books; that means the Ancients will start looking into them."

"And that means Guilds," Emily said with a sigh.

"Back in the 1960s, a prominent member of the CIA turned out to be a riftborn who wanted to use the energy of the Tempest inside the rift to increase his own power," Zeke said. "It did not end well for him."

"The Ancients had him killed," Nadia said.

"I remember being told about it," Emily said. "Nothing was done, because riftborn aren't meant to hold human office. No politicians, no heads of security services. Okay, so we could still give them *some* of it. They can't reverse-engineer it, but it could help us identify anyone working against us."

I turned back to the vials and noticed that while they were in batches of six, there was one tray that only had two. "Some of this has been used," I said.

"Used on who?" Emily asked.

"Who or whom?" Nadia questioned.

"Is this really the time for that conversation?" Emily asked her.

Nadia shrugged as an alarm went off all around us; there were a loud click and a hiss of air from somewhere close by.

"Absolutely nothing good is coming from that noise," Emily said.

Zeke ran over to the large door and pushed it open. He looked back at us, and for a moment, I thought he might run, but he stayed there, weapon drawn at the doorway.

A roar coming from the dark tunnel followed the alarm.

"This doesn't sound like something we want to meet," Emily said.

We all ran back toward Zeke, but he closed the door. "We can't let it out," he said before anyone could start screaming at him. "Whatever it is, if it gets into a populated area, all hell will break loose."

"Bollocks," I said. I hate it when people being right puts me in mortal danger.

CHAPTER TEN

The fiend crawled out of a large tunnel and sat there, staring at the four of us. It was a bear. Or it had been before it had died and been infused with power from the rift. It still had the basic black bear shape, but it was five times the size of any black bear I'd ever seen.

The fiend's head had two huge spikes on the back of it, with more spines running down its back. They looked sharp. Because of course a bear needed even more ways to kill and maim. It turned its head, letting me get a good look at it as the moonlight caught it. Its jaw was covered in some kind of bone armour. It moved further onto the platform and I saw the same armour covered the back of its paws, too. There was a huge gash along its stomach; something with claws of its own had tried to tear through the mass of muscle and fur. Something pulsated through the creature and it shivered.

A greater fiend . . . but one that had been modified. Callie Mitchell again.

I looked over at Zeke, whose eyes were wide, watching the monstrous form before us. He took a step back, creating a rustling noise, and the bear's head snapped toward us.

I shot it through the eye with the Winchester, firing all five shots in quick succession, all hitting the side of the skull, with the final one taking off a part of the creature's jaw.

Nadia and Emily opened fire too, and the cacophony of noise inside the cavern was going to ensure my ears would ring for a while after we finished.

"Zeke, now is not the time to freeze up," I said, slapping him on the shoulder as I reloaded the rifle.

Zeke continued to stare for several seconds as a second black bear entered the cavern, this one even bigger than the first, but where there should be fur on its back and flank, there was a beetle-like exoskeleton that was bright yellow with black spots, and it had grown two extra arms. This definitely wasn't like any greater fiend I'd ever seen before.

The larger bear looked around the cavern as if surprised to see us all, settled on Zeke, and charged him. That appeared to wake Zeke from his stupor, and he drew his pistols, unloading on the large bear as it roared in defiance and launched itself down onto the ground in front of us, shaking the floor with the impact.

Emily and Nadia continued the attack on the smaller bear, with Nadia's chains being used as a whirlwind of death as she spun them around in front of her as if she were twirling exceptionally lethal batons.

Emily vanished from view as Zeke continued to backpedal but kept shooting at the larger creature, maybe one in two bullets maintaining any kind of charge.

The first bear, now missing a portion of its head and bleeding from several bullet holes in its legs and torso, charged Nadia, but Emily appeared on the back of the fiend's neck and began to slice into the side of its throat.

Lesser fiends aren't particularly difficult to kill, but greater fiends . . . well, you need to take the whole head or ruin the body so badly it can't maintain itself. And the bear had a really big body.

Zeke flung himself out of the path of the rampaging larger bear just before it hit him, putting some distance between it and him. The bear couldn't stop in time and slammed into the metal door, bending it. I fired twice more into the flank of the bear, trying to damage it enough to slow it down, but the creature turned toward me with nothing but murder in its eyes. That's not anthropomorphism, either. Greater fiends aren't quite animals anymore; there's an intelligence, a cunning and meanness, that just isn't found in most animals.

But as I locked eyes with the creature, I realised that this thing wasn't an animal at all. This thing wasn't a fiend. There was a human in there. Or what was left of a human. The momentary lapse in concentration allowed it to hit me with one paw, sending me spiralling across the cavern. I hit the wall hard, the air rushing out of me, and crashed to the stone floor, wishing I was elsewhere.

Zeke got back to his feet and started to open fire, moving toward the creature with every shot. The bullets hit the hardened armour that covered its body and did little to no damage that I could see.

I forced myself back to my feet in time to see the creature catch Zeke with one paw, knocking him across the cavern close to me. Zeke's head hit stone and he dropped to the floor, dazed, as the creature charged him.

I turned to smoke, rushed across the cavern, and re-formed, connecting a punch with the jaw of the creature and sending it flying back across the cavern. My hand throbbed from the impact, and I wasn't going to be doing that again anytime soon, but the human hybrid slammed into the bear fiend, taking them both off their feet. In a panic, the greater fiend thrashed around, catching the larger creature across the soft belly. The creature screamed an all-too-human sound, making both Emily and Nadia take a step back.

"You've never done that before," Nadia said as she ran over.

"I don't like doing it, because it hurts and it leaves me vulnerable," I said. Putting all of my power into one punch, or kick, is a good way to put some distance between myself and whatever was currently trying to kill me. It was risky, but when it worked, it was pretty effective.

The creature, not bleeding badly across its stomach, turned and ran, leaving an exceptionally angry and badly hurt greater fiend for us to deal with.

Nadia, Emily, and I fired whatever bullets we had left into the open mouth of the charging fiend, and I was glad to see a rift-tempered bullet strike home, removing a part of the beast's jaw. I turned to smoke as the greater fiend reached me. The fiend couldn't stop in time and smashed head first into the rock behind me.

I re-formed, dropping the rifle, drawing my two rift-tempered blades as the greater fiend swiped one paw toward me. It was the size of my skull and, had it hit, I would have been, at best, seriously hurt. I drove one blade up to meet the limb, slicing through it at the joint.

The fiend roared in pain and rage as its paw fell onto the ground behind me while I sprinted forward, slashing one dagger across its exposed ribcage, almost in the exact place of the gouge that something else had already done. The dagger sliced through the beast with no resistance, but the bear tried to shift around to bite me before realising it was missing part of its head, and I drove a dagger up under what remained of its jaw, stabbing the second one into its eye socket. Both blades punctured the fiend's brain, but it thrashed at me as Nadia's chains punctured the side of the creature's ribcage.

The bullet hit the greater fiend between the eyes, and I turned to smoke, moving away as Zeke strolled toward the dying fiend, unloading both pistols directly into its head, until all that remained was a smoking ruin.

I re-formed, removing the two daggers and wiping them on the fur of the greater fiend.

"You saved my life," Zeke said. He had a large bruise on the side of his face, and he was going to feel sore, but otherwise, he appeared to be okay.

I patted him on the shoulder as I stared at the dissolving remains of the greater fiend.

"What was that other thing?" Emily asked.

"Let's go find out," I said, and set off down the dark tunnel with everyone else following.

It didn't take long for the tunnel to open out into a large chamber with a dozen large pens at one end. There were more bears inside two of the pens, but when someone had released them all, they'd decided it was better to fight one another than do anything else. Both were missing large parts of their heads, and both started to dissolve almost the moment we entered the chamber.

There was blood all over the floor of the chamber, and it was impossible to tell what belonged to the two greater fiends and what belonged to the creature that had fled this way.

There was an open metal door next to a large glass window that had been scratched and gored, but remained intact. Beyond it were a viewing area and several computers. A quick search inside showed that all of them had been torn apart, their hard drives missing.

Nadia walked in, saw the large red button next to the door, and pressed it before anyone could stop her. There was a groaning sound as a metal wall slid down the tunnel entrance, blocking the tunnel from the chamber.

"Where did the other thing go?" Emily asked as Nadia pressed the button again, making the wall retract into the ceiling of the tunnel.

"There's a door over there," Zeke said, pointing across the chamber to the door in question.

The four of us went to investigate and stopped at the perfectly normal-sized door.

"That thing couldn't fit through here," Emily said.

"Where there's a will, there's a way," Nadia said, pointing to the bloodstains on the dark rock ground.

"That can't possibly be good," Emily pointed out as I pushed open the reinforced door with my foot, revealing a small room with only a small lift inside, beside a ladder.

"They became human," Zeke said.

"More of Callie's experiments," I said. "The last time I found one of Callie's experiments who'd tried to turn from a monster back to human, they'd quite literally unravelled."

"This must be a more stable batch of what she was working on," Emily said.

"I'll look around down here," Zeke said. "Just in case they left something when they ran."

"I'll stay with him," Nadia said. "Two sets of eyes and all that."

I turned to smoke and billowed up the shaft, ignoring the lift as I reached the very top, where there was an open hatch. I re-formed outside on top of a hill overlooking the facility. There was blood on the floor.

It took Emily a short time to join me, the sound of the lift as it moved up toward the exit rumbling around the area. She stepped off beside me, and the lift automatically began to go down again.

"I guess the elevator is for exit only," she said. "No button here to call it."

I searched the wilderness around us and found tyre tracks on the ground a few metres away from a pool of blood. "So, either they drove away—" I said.

"Or someone was waiting for them," Emily said.

"The question is, were they waiting for us?" I asked.

"You think we were set up?" Emily asked.

I shrugged. "They might have been using the place as a base; maybe they managed to get in and found some vials, tried one, turned into a damn monster. We need to get the vials away from here."

The sound of the lift coming back up toward us broke the silence of the night.

"We found something interesting," Nadia said, stepping off the lift the moment it stopped. She placed a black rucksack on the ground and passed me a wallet.

"They dropped their ID?" I asked, opening the leather wallet and fishing out a driving licence.

"Neil Manor," I said. "Forty-two. Zeke, any chance you know him?"

Zeke shook his head. "Sorry. I can ask the local sheriff; they owe me a favour."

"We don't want to scare anyone away," Emily said. "Don't mention any of this."

"What about contacting the RCU?" Nadia asked.

"We leave it for now," I said. "We go down there, grab every vial we can, and make sure none are able to get out."

"Already done," Nadia said, pointing to the rucksack.

"Is that all of them?" I asked, looking at the dozens of vials in the bag.

"Every one I could find," Nadia said.

"How much of a bad idea is burning this place to the ground?" Emily asked.

"No idea what else might be down there," Zeke said. "If they have something toxic and it gets out, we could bring a lot of trouble on the area."

"We lock it down," I said, closing the hatch as the elevator rumbled back down. "We can't let anyone get in here. Can't contact the local RCU because we don't know any of them."

"I'll go call Gabriel; maybe he can send some people here to help out," Emily said.

"No FBI," I told her. "Not until we know what's actually going on here."

"I know," Emily said. "Keep this in-house for now."

"So, do we hunt for this Neil now?" Zeke asked.

"The morning," I said, looking at my watch. It was just after two a.m. "We all need to rest after that; besides, let him stew. We get his address and hit him early."

"What if he ran?" Zeke asked.

"Risk we have to take," I said. "If he runs, we find him. But we go to his house now, he has the advantage. If there are more like him, we might bring down something bad on us or innocent people around us. During the day, people are out, at work, at school. Less likelihood he's got humans to use, less likelihood he can hide."

We stayed out for another hour before going back to Zeke's mansion, leaving Zeke to sit up while the rest of us went to get some deserved sleep. I showered, discovered that my clothes were muddy and had some fiend blood on them but nothing a good wash wouldn't sort out, and immediately fell asleep.

Upon waking, I got up, got dressed, and found Emily and Nadia in their room.

Nadia sat on a chair, her eyes rolled back in her head, looking up at the ceiling.

"Do you ever get used to that?" Emily asked.

I moved my hand from side to side. "Not completely, but then I don't think she does, either."

Nadia's head lolled forward, and she remained still for a few seconds before looking up at us. "Something weird."

"What is it?" I asked her.

"There's a gap in the chain," Nadia said. "In one of the chains, anyway. So many options, but the one with the gap feels strongest."

"What does that mean?" Emily asked, looking between us.

"Either the chain can't decide what happens during the gap and it's all foggy," Nadia said, "or someone who's linked to my chain has caused it to go foggy."

"You mean me," I said.

Nadia nodded. "The chain doesn't know what happens because there's a break in it. You're not around when it happens."

"Good to know," I said.

"Does that mean you're going to get hurt?" Emily asked, a little panic in her voice.

"No," Nadia said. "It means I'm not with him when whatever is meant to happen then happens. Or possibly happens. Or didn't happen but could have. The chains don't give me a full picture. They give me snapshots of what might possibly be the full picture. With Lucas being wrapped up in my chain, it means that he could be elsewhere. He could be dead, but having met Lucas, I find that doubtful. The last time it happened was when he went to the rift."

"How long is the gap?" I asked.

Nadia shrugged. "Months, years, weeks. No way to know. At least a week, as I've been away from Lucas for days at a time and the chain has never fogged."

"I guess that's a problem we'll deal with later, then. I'll see you both at the car shortly." I left the room, and Emily caught up to me in the hallway.

"Hey, how can you be so calm about the fact you might be forced back to the rift, or killed, or incapacitated?" Emily asked.

"Or I could just be somewhere Nadia isn't," I said. "I could be stuck here, helping find this fiend, or you could, and I could be back in London. There are a million things that mean that Nadia won't be with me for an extended period of time."

"Don't you find it odd that her chain is somehow connected to you so completely?"

I shrugged. "It happens with chained revenants. Usually, they see it as a sign of some kind of deep emotional connection and try to figure out why, or it means they need to kill that person, or protect that person, or something along those lines. Nadia knows it's not to kill me, and it's not that we're in some long-lost love, so I assume she thinks it's to protect me."

"You're capable of protecting yourself," Emily said.

"I know, but if she believes that her chains want her to be at a certain point in time with me, then there's no point in trying to stop her," I said. "She's going to be there whether I agree to it or not."

"She's very calm about you not being around, then," Emily said, looking back at the door to her room.

"She's calm about things she has no control over," I said. "Chained revenants either deal with the fact that sometimes things are out of their control, or they try to see all of the chains at once and drive themselves insane in the process. She might well be the most mentally healthy chained revenant I've ever met."

"Is it wrong to say that I'm glad I didn't turn into one of them?" Emily said.

I shook my head. "Not at all. There are several types of revenant that I think do a lot of damage mentally to the person. The humans think that becoming a revenant is a second chance at life, but sometimes it's just a new way to get hurt all over again."

There was a clang down the stairs and several raised voices, so I left Emily to get ready and descended the staircase, finding the front of the house full of people, mostly bringing stuff into the building.

"Catering," a tall, bald man shouted. "I need the catering." He spotted me as I stepped off the bottom step. "You there."

I pointed to me.

"Yes, do I have to do everything myself?" he snapped. "Bring me the rest of the food; the chef and his team need to start preparing."

"I don't work here," I said. "I'm a guest."

The man huffed and strolled out of the front door.

I found Zeke in his study, sat at his desk, looking at something on the computer. He glanced up at me as I entered, and smiled. "Morning," he said.

"You're having a lot done in one day," I said.

"I've been assured that the setup will only take a few hours," Zeke said. "I considered cancelling, but honestly, I don't want to have to explain about what we found."

"I'm heading to Greater Sudbury with Nadia and Emily," I said. "Did you get an address?"

Zeke opened his desk drawer and removed a small blue Post-it note, passing it to me. "The name and address for Neil Manor. He lives alone. I think I managed to make sure the police stay away."

"You think?" I asked.

"I can only do so much," Zeke said sadly. "Are you three going to be okay by yourselves?"

I nodded. "We'll be fine. You okay?"

Zeke moved his hand from side to side. "You saved my life. Or, at least, you saved me from an injury serious enough to dump me in my embers. I will repay you for that one day."

I waved it away. "See to your family. Make sure none of them leave this area; there's no way of knowing if they released fiends into the wilderness or something equally stupid. We'll ask Neil and find out what he knows."

"Will do," Zeke said. "My cameras are still around the neighbouring area, so if one turns up, I'll let you know. I guess this is going to make a good story for my next book, if nothing else."

"Your book?"

"You didn't know?" Zeke asked, walking over to a bookshelf and removing a hardback, passing it to me.

"*Hunting the Fiend*," I said, reading the blood-red title on the black-and-white cover.

"It's my third one," Zeke said.

I turned the book over and read the back cover: *True Stories from a Master Hunter of Monsters.*

"I'm working on my fourth right now," Zeke said. "They're bestsellers. Sold millions worldwide. You can keep that one if you like; I'll sign it for you."

I passed it back to him. "Sign it, Zeke. I'll leave it with you until I go." I genuinely wanted to read it, mostly because I wanted to find out just how much he wrote was utter nonsense, but there was a part of me that was also interested in what he'd been up to.

"Wait, take my car," Zeke said, removing the keys from his pocket and tossing them over to me. "It's loaded and ready to go. Enough weapons in there to declare war on a small country."

"Good luck with the party prep," I said.

"You're all guests tonight, so be careful and try to come back in one piece," Zeke said with a tight smile.

I left the mansion, dodging catering people as I made my way down the steps and across the driveway to the G-Wagon, to find Emily and Nadia stood behind it.

"Rose told us to meet you here," Emily said.

Nadia sat in the back seat behind Emily as I drove, using the car satnav to make sure I didn't get lost on unfamiliar roads. The sounds of the radio were all that could be heard during the drive, all three of us seemingly having things on our mind.

"You think the three of us will be able to take on that monster?" Emily asked after half an hour of listening to the radio station playing seventies and eighties rock music.

"Oh, yes," I said. "Neil isn't going to know what's hit him."

CHAPTER ELEVEN

I got out of the car and stood on the grass verge next to the tree, looking over at the two-storey brick detached house that looked identical to every other house on the street. Two large windows on the top floor and one on the bottom, a wooden door painted dark blue, a good-sized front lawn that was kept tidy. Some flowers to add colour. It was all very neat and tidy, and looked like somewhere you'd want to raise kids.

The house had a single-car garage, the door of which was painted white, and a short tarmac driveway.

"Doesn't exactly scream *house of a psychotic monster*," Emily said.

"Is your FBI-sense tingling?" Nadia asked.

"I'm not sure that's the official name for it," Emily said.

I had my two daggers against the small of my back, but I went to the boot of the car, opened it, and let Emily choose whatever she needed. I didn't bother with the Winchester. There was no telling when it would or wouldn't work.

"I'm pretty sure I don't need a gun," Nadia said, her chains flicking out as if proving her point.

Once suitably armed and ready for war—Emily had selected a Remington shotgun and already had her Glock on her hip—the three of us walked over to Neil's front door.

We crossed the lawn, and Emily knocked on the door, as there was no doorbell. We all took a step to the side of the door, but there was no answer. She waited until the count of ten and knocked again.

"Out shopping?" I asked.

"Maybe they can't hear us because they're in the bath," Nadia suggested.

"Or that," I said. Maybe they had already run. I hoped not, as I'd rather not have to hunt them down.

Emily knocked again. Still no answer.

I had an itch on the back of my neck. When you've been alive as long as I have and/or had as many people try to kill you as I have, you tend to listen to those gut instincts that tell you something is wrong on a deep level.

Nadia knocked for a third time. No answer again.

I looked through the set of windows beside me, to discover the curtains were pulled shut, so I continued to the end of the house and peered down the short alleyway that ran alongside the building to where I assumed there was a back garden. A tall wooden gate and fence separated me from being able to see what was going on back there. I made my way to the gate and turned the hoop-shaped handle. The gate wasn't locked and opened freely.

The back garden was overgrown, with a single paving-stone path leading to a large metal shed that looked like it had seen better days. I took a stroll through the jungle to find that it was locked, a large padlock keeping anyone from getting inside. The lock was new.

I retraced my steps through the lawn and knocked on the rear door of the house. No answer. I tried the handle and found it locked, so I peered through the window into the darkness of the room beyond. It looked like a normal dining room, with a large table and several chairs.

I took a moment to look through the window of the room next to it and found a large kitchen, also empty. I returned to the front of the house, where Nadia and Emily were still waiting.

Nadia leaned up against the front door, which suddenly opened. "Oh, dear," she said, faking surprise and practically jumping back from the ajar door. "The door, it just opened."

"Like magic?" I asked.

Nadia pointed at me. "Yeah, like magic."

"You know this is called *breaking and entering*," Emily said, dampening our enthusiasm.

"I think this is just *entering*," I said. "I didn't break anything."

"I'm not sure a judge is going to care much," Emily replied as I reached the door at the same time as her, and we shared a slight nod before entering the building with no idea of what we were going to find.

Before we could step inside, a police car pulled up at the curb. I inwardly cursed whoever had given me bad luck for the day.

"That probably isn't brilliant," Nadia said.

"I'll go talk to them," Emily said. "Let them know there's an FBI agent here."

"Did you bring your ID with you?" I asked.

"I did not," Emily said. "I was advised to leave it with Gabriel."

"Good luck," Nadia said, and stepped into the house.

I wondered how the police would react when they discovered she didn't have her badge and was technically meant to be on personal leave.

I stepped into the house before the police could shout something. There was a door on either side of a short hallway, and no furniture or pictures on the walls. There was nothing to show that anyone lived there at all. There was, however, the smell of stale air, as if no one had opened a window to let in any freshness for some time.

"I'm out here," Nadia shouted from somewhere to the rear of the house.

"I'll check upstairs," I called back.

As I reached the summit of the stairs, there was a distinct smell, not a good one.

The floor had three doors, two bedrooms and a bathroom, the latter of which was closest, but the smell wasn't coming from there. I continued down the L-shaped hallway, trying to figure out where the stench was coming from. I wasn't worried about any gas biological weapons—they don't work on me—but that didn't mean the stink wasn't having an unpleasant effect on my nasal cavity.

All three doors on the floor had seen better days, with the white paint peeling off, the remains of which were scattered across the dark carpet. I pushed open the closest door with my foot and found an empty room big enough for a bed and some furniture, had anyone wished to decorate; it was empty except for the plastic sheeting that covered every surface. The second room was similar—minus the plastic sheeting.

The last door opened slowly, snagging on the carpet. I stepped into the room, which was large and had windows down one end and a built-in closet against the opposite wall. The room had blackout curtains, which were closed. I tried the light switch, but there was no lightbulb. The smell in the room was stronger than anywhere else, and as I crossed the room, I stepped on something that crunched beneath my boot.

I ignored it for a moment and pulled open the curtains, revealing Emily and the two police officers—a man and a woman—who were listening as she presumably tried to explain our activities. The windows were nailed shut, and as I turned around, something exploded out of the ceiling, smashing into me, and threw me through the windows.

I hit the ground hard and rolled over, landing at the feet of the female police officer, who stared at me in a mixture of horror and outright confusion. I showed her my medallion and pointed over toward the house as my powers of speech tried to catch up to my brain.

The remains of the window were torn to pieces as an eight-foot-tall fiend rushed through them, landing on the ground with a thud and creating a small crater in the process. It must have been hiding in the loft. Maybe that's what the smell was. The creature certainly didn't smell good.

The police officers drew their weapons, pointing them at the fiend. It looked like a cross between a bear and a scorpion. It had two legs and six arms, each one with a pincer at the end, each one the size of my head. The creature had the head of a large bear and was covered in black fur, except for the armour on its back and flanks. Only this time, it also had a long tail with a scorpion stinger on the end that was the same length as my arm. The worst part—although that was subjective, considering the whole thing was the worst part—was the human face. Neil Manor.

How he'd changed into a slightly different variation to what he'd been back in the facility, I didn't know. All I knew was that whatever he'd been during the fight in that chamber, he hadn't had a scorpion's stinger and pincers. Neither of those things were going to make this easier.

"You guys are going to need bigger guns," I told them.

The police opened fire before I could get back to my feet, the bullets impacting with the flesh of the human-fiend but doing nothing to stop it as it bounded toward us with speed that should have been impossible for a creature of its size and density.

I grabbed the female officer beside me and practically threw her over the front of the car as the creature smashed into the tree directly behind where she'd been standing.

"Sorry," I shouted as she got back to her feet. She waved my words away and shouted into her radio for backup. I really hoped help included some kind of military helicopter. Or a tank.

"Any chance you have any rift-fused on staff?" I asked, hoping she'd say yes.

"Gunslinger," the officer said.

"We're on our own, then," I told her. I drew my blades and charged toward the human-fiend, ducking under the swipe from two sets of pincers and narrowly avoiding the sting on its tail as I drew the blades across the skin around one pincer. The wound bubbled and hissed, and the creature screamed, kicked me in the chest, and sent me flying back. I crashed into the police car's windscreen.

I rolled off the side of the car just as the stinger slammed into the hood, all but ruining the vehicle as it tore into the engine block.

The creature reared its stinger back for a second strike, and I turned to smoke, rushing forward and putting power into forming my fist first. I struck the creature in the chest and catapulted it back across the lawn into the house, taking out part of the downstairs window as the rest of my body formed.

"Holy shit," Emily said from beside me as I staggered forward, placing my hand on the police car to keep from falling over.

Nadia left the house at the exact moment the fiend had slammed into it.

Sirens filled the air as half a dozen police cars screamed up the road toward us.

"What do we do?" the male officer who was already there asked.

"Stay out of our way," I said. "Keep anyone from getting killed. If you have anything that is rift-tempered, use it; otherwise, try really hard not to get hurt."

"That's it?" the female cop asked.

"We're experts," Nadia said, leaning over to me and whispering, "We are right?"

I shrugged. "We're as good as it gets right now."

The front door of the house was obliterated as the creature smashed its way back through the structure.

"Do we have a plan?" Emily asked as a roar left the creature's mouth.

"Kill it," I said.

With the daggers in my hands, I turned to smoke and flew toward the hybrid, re-forming and slashing at the right leg of the creature, drawing a scream of pain as the blade bit through flesh and muscle.

Nadia's chains slammed into the joints of the creature's arms, punching through the skin and wrapping around one of the arms. There was a popping noise and another scream as the arm was removed from the creature.

I used the moment where it was distracted to drive one blade into the side of its stomach and tear across, opening a large wound. Thick black blood bubbled out of it, spilling over the ground.

Police swarmed over the lawn behind us, and despite the two cops who had been there when we all shouted at them to get back, several of them started screaming orders at us.

"How is that helping?" I shouted back, avoiding one pincer of the creature as Emily dragged one of the officers out of the way of what would have been a fatal stab of the creature's stinger.

The remaining five officers froze in place, shotguns and revolvers in hand, as the ground beneath our feet shook and a moment later erupted up in a storm of mud and rock, flinging anyone close to the epicentre across the lawn.

I blocked a swipe from the scorpion-bear, but the blow was strong enough to send me flying back into the house, only able to watch as the creature grabbed Nadia's chains. Her chains sliced through the pincers, but the creature had enough purchase to swing her around and let go, sending her sailing over the edge of the lawn and into the garden of a neighbour a few doors down.

Emily scrambled to her feet as the second hybrid-fiend climbed out of the hole it had created. It had hairless pink skin over its torso and face, the latter of which looked almost human except for the huge bat-like ears and elongated front teeth that jutted out and down past its jaw. There was a long red scar across its stomach. Its arms were enormous and covered in some kind of stone-like armour, each one tipped with five two-feet-long claws. It turned toward the police, showing the stone armour that ran down its spine toward legs that were stubby and almost human-looking, not the feet that were much too large for them. It had tiny wings, too, barely able to do anything but flap uselessly.

The scorpion-bear turned and charged back into the house, throwing pieces of masonry and wood at me as I scrambled down the remains of the hallway, trying to steer the fight away from everyone else, who were now occupied with the mole-bat thing.

I caught a glimpse of the mole-bat skewer a police officer in the chest, and knew that he wouldn't be the first victim of what was happening there today.

I grabbed a large piece of brick and sprang to my feet, racing through the house and ignoring the sounds of crashing behind me. Reaching the kitchen, I threw the brick through the window of the back door, shattering it, before turning to smoke and billowing to the outside, where I re-formed myself in the middle of the garden.

The shed door at the rear of the garden was open, but I didn't have time to go searching now. I turned, both daggers drawn, and waited for the creature. I didn't have to wait long, as it tore through the rear of the house, raining pieces of it across the back garden.

The fiend-hybrid stopped and stared at me. "Can't run forever," it said. Its voice was all wrong, as if someone were making words from dragging their nails down a chalkboard.

I took a step toward the creature, exhaled, and put myself into a fight-ing stance. There would be no talking, no witty comebacks. I was going to kill it. I sheathed my daggers.

The fiend-hybrid screamed and charged, its tail snipping out toward my stomach. I stepped to the side at the last second and grabbed hold of the stinger before turning to smoke. To say that it was gruesome would have been an understatement.

The entire stinger was ripped apart as I tore large chunks from it. I re-formed, drew my daggers, and plunged one into the joint where the tail met the spine. I twisted the dagger to the side and ripped it up as I rolled to the side to get away from the retaliatory swipe from the creature.

Blood flowed like a geyser from the massive wounds inflicted on the hybrid-fiend's tail and stinger; apparently, I'd hit at least one artery.

The creature took a step back and I dashed in again, slashing across arms, driving the creature back across the garden with every step. It couldn't defend itself from the speed of the attacks; every time I cut in one place, I was already moving to cut elsewhere. The screams that left its mouth became weaker.

The hybrid-fiend flailed at me, its entire body covered in a myriad of wounds. It staggered and I walked toward the creature, which tried to slap me away with one pincer, and I ducked under it to drive both blades into its elbow, twisting them and tearing them free. I ignored the scream and plunged both daggers into a kidney of the creature, tearing one blade up toward its ribcage, the other to the side.

Apart from being incredibly strong, the creature itself wasn't any more powerful than any other fiend I'd ever faced. Certainly not greater-fiend territory. I wondered about why Mason *had* been so damn powerful when he'd taken the drug, but seeing how he was dead, that was going to be a difficult thing to ask him. Even the creature on the train in England had been a harder fight; it was something to look into.

I walked over to the now-kneeling fiend-hybrid version of Neil Manor and drove one dagger into the side of its head, killing it instantly. It began dissolving as I ran back toward the house, taking the path around the side of the building as the sounds of fighting increased.

There were three police officers at the side of the front lawn, one of which was lying back against the fence. He was covered in blood, while the other two tried to stop the bleeding. Three other officers were injured and had been dragged away to an ambulance at the opposite end of the street. Several more officers, some in what appeared to be tactical gear, stood close to the road, guns ready. No one was firing, presumably because they'd learned it did fuck-all to the thing everyone was trying to kill. I understood the need to keep rift-tempered weapons away from human hands, but maybe allowing people to defend themselves was a better idea than what was currently available to them.

Nadia was going toe-to-toe with the hybrid-bat while trying to stop it from going after the easier prey of the humans. Emily appeared out of the tree next to the fiend as she dropped down onto its head, removing her camouflage in the process, and driving the two talons on her hands into the side of the mole-bat's head.

The creature let out an ear-splitting shriek that caused everyone to clamp their hands over their ears. Emily leapt off the creature and sped away, reapplying her camouflage as the fiend-hybrid focussed on me.

The mole-bat half-ran, half-trotted toward me. It leapt into the air and dove at the ground, its massive claws making short work of the earth as it dug quickly enough that its entire torso was gone in moments. Before its legs could vanish too and make tracking its next attack a headache I could do without, chains wrapped around its legs and yanked.

It tried to get away from Nadia's chains, but the chains were wrapped tight, and every movement just made them constrict tighter, like a metal python with its prey. Blood began to pour from the limb as the chains cut into the leg, and the mole-bat exploded out of the ground. The look of determination on Nadia's face made me wonder what would give first, her chains or the limb of the creature.

It was the limb.

The second I'd seen the creature return out of the ground, I was already running toward it, my daggers out, ready to engage, but as the limb tore free from it, I changed direction. There was a shimmer in the air close to where the creature began to fall, and Emily appeared, slashing across the nose and face of the hybrid, and it cried out in pain. It flailed at Emily, catching her across the shoulder with one giant claw, causing her to spin away, trailing blood. She hit the side of a police car.

Nadia's chains released, and she continued to whip them toward the creature, taking huge chunks of flesh from its torso with every hit. But one chain hit the stone armour on the back of the creature's arm, and it quickly grabbed the chain, trying to throw her across the lawn. She wrapped the second chain around the shoulder of the creature, and the second it threw her, she tightened it, practically degloving the monster's arm, although it left the stone armour around the forearm of the creature intact.

The creature turned to Nadia, trying to catch her with his good arm, but she was moving around to the side, keeping enough distance between them that it couldn't reach her.

The second the creature's back faced me, I rushed forward, stabbing it in the back over and over, but it dodged to the side, catching me in the arm. I hit the floor, trying to roll with the blow, but the mole-bat tried desperately to stamp down on me with its tiny feet. A piece of chain punctured the head of the creature, and I took the moment to drive both my daggers into its skull.

The creature collapsed with a whimper.

"Everyone okay?" I shouted.

"Sore," Emily shouted back as she moved gingerly across the garden from where she'd been thrown.

"Awesome," Nadia said with a big grin on her face.

I looked over at the paramedics tending to the wounded officer, and I hoped they were going to be okay.

"Are we meant to arrest it?" the female officer who had been part of the team first on the scene asked me.

"You have the right to remain silent," I told the dissolving fiend-hybrid. "You have the right to turn to goo. You have the right to be scooped up and placed in a Tupperware box."

"If you do not understand your rights, I don't care," Nadia said. "Because you're dead."

The officer nodded slightly; like most of everyone else who had been there, she was covered in black blood from the creature. She looked down at her uniform, and her eyes went wide.

"It's not toxic," I said. "I've killed enough fiends."

She nodded, although I wasn't sure she was listening at that point.

Nadia helped me to my feet.

"We're not done here," I said. "They were hiding in the attic, I think."

"Apart from Neil, do we know who *they* were?" Emily asked.

"No," I said. "Let's go find out."

CHAPTER TWELVE

I left Emily and the officers to search the building, mostly so I could sit down for a few minutes and have a drink of water that one of them had passed me.

"The mole-bat was stronger than the other one," I said to Nadia, who sat beside me, the pair of us leaning up against the tree at the front of the house.

"And Mason was stronger than both, you say?" she asked. "Maybe different people have different reactions? Or maybe this is a weaker dosage?"

"Also, Mason didn't really turn into an animal," I said. "But the first one of these I saw was some kind of deer hybrid thing. Maybe two types of drugs?"

Several more police officers arrived, working with those who hadn't gone into the building to put up a cordon around the crime scene.

Emily appeared at the doorway and beckoned Nadia and me over.

"Find something interesting?" I asked.

"Yes," Emily said with about as much of a smile as anyone was going to be giving after the morning we'd all had.

We followed her through the partially destroyed floor of the house to the back garden. "That shed has a tunnel in it," she said.

I walked up the garden path, the dead monster now completely dissolved.

We reached the shed and found the ladder going down into a well-lit tunnel. A large rug had been pushed to one side, having once been used to conceal the trapdoor down into the tunnel.

Nadia poked the rug with her booted foot.

"I once had a rug burst into flame," Nadia said casually. "Actual rug in someone's house, and it just exploded. Some practitioners had decided to create a bomb out of rift energy."

"Practitioner?" Emily asked.

"They're people born in the rift," I said. "Actually born there, not from here. They're very rare, and they don't so much have powers like the rift-fused, but they can pull rift energy through into this world and do . . . stuff with it."

"Not the *Blessed*?" Emily asked.

"Project Blessed," I said, the memory suddenly returning. "That was something Callie Mitchell wrote about. Something to do with building an army; we never got more details than that."

"So, this could be something to do with that," Emily suggested.

I shrugged. "More questions than answers at the moment."

"There's more," Emily said.

"It's bad, isn't it?" I said. "It's always bad."

Emily's smile returned. "We have an accomplice."

"And they haven't turned into a grotesque monster?" Nadia asked. "This really might be our lucky day."

"I wouldn't go that far," Emily said. "You're going to want to see this."

Nadia twitched and looked down at the hole. "Nothing good comes out of this."

My eyes adjusted to the meagre light below.

"Gentlemen first," Emily said, motioning to the darkness between us.

"How generous," I said, and she smirked. I sat down, my legs dangling over the edge, half-expecting something to grab my leg as I swung onto the ladder and began the climb down.

The ladder was fifty feet long, and the smell of stale air combined with something cloyingly sweet made the last twenty of those feet an exercise in unpleasantness.

We reached the bottom, walked a short distance to a large metal door, and Emily pushed it open, revealing a large room which was clearly where people were living. It was spacious enough for beds, a small kitchen area, even a TV, although it was currently off. There were wooden wardrobes, too, and a door to the side that was open far enough to show me the toilet.

The two uniformed officers inside the room both looked quite ill. Neither of them even glanced toward the bathroom area, and the second Emily told them they could go, I swore I saw little puffs of animated smoke in their wake, Road Runner style.

"He's in there," Emily said. "It's not pretty."

"I'm partially covered in the insides of two monsters," I said. "Whatever it is it . . ."

The door opened, revealing the thing inside.

"Holy fuck on a stick," Nadia shouted.

The thing was clearly a human male, except he had one human arm and one long arm covered in what looked like a bright yellow beetle carapace, and black mandibles that jutted out of his jaw. His skin was, along with being bright blue and green, snake-like, and his legs were partially fused together. He was mid-transformation, his blond hair covering the floor around him, leaving only clumps behind.

I crouched down to look at him in the eyes, which were like black pools. "Bad day at the office?" I asked.

"Help me," he said, the mandibles clicking, his eyes pleading as best they could.

"Good to know your speech is okay," I told him. "I'll tell you what: you answer our questions and I'll help you."

He looked hopeful at that. "Really?"

I nodded. "Sure."

"Does it hurt?" Emily asked.

He shook his head.

"You sure? Because that looks like it hurt a whole lot," Nadia said.

I looked up at Nadia. "How does that help?"

"Scientific minds need to know," Nadia said with a shrug.

"What's your name?" I asked him, not wanting the conversation to be derailed, which was always a possibility when Nadia was involved.

"Danny," he said.

"Your friends upstairs?" Emily asked. "One was Neil Manor, yes."

"Mary and Neil," Danny told us. "They're dead, yes?"

I nodded again. "You want to tell us what happened? You were at the facility. Tried to kill us. Or Neil did."

"Was just meant to be you," Danny said, pointing a truly horrific finger in my direction.

"Neil had changed from when we fought," I said. "He had a scorpion tail now."

"Neil got hurt," he said. "He took a larger dose, so much more than he was meant to. We all did. Knew you were coming for us; wanted to be ready. Neil was in the loft when you arrived; had to wait to complete the transformation."

"We found a lot of writing in blood at the facility," Emily said. "The Blessed. What or who are they?"

"They're people who want the rift to return to its rightful owners," Danny said, pride in his voice for the first time.

"And they would be?" I asked.

"Those born there," he said, keeping his eyes on me.

"Practitioners," I said. "The Blessed are practitioners?"

Danny nodded. "Originally, yes."

"You're not a practitioner," I told him. "You're human."

Danny nodded again.

"How'd you get mixed up in the political machinations of a group of people from the rift?" I asked him.

"Just doing the right thing," he said.

"And that means?" Emily asked.

"You're Lucas Rurik," Danny said to me, ignoring Emily. "That's your name, yes?"

"It is," I told him.

"You're the reason we're here," Danny said.

"That doesn't really make much sense," I said, standing upright and sighing. "I'm no one particularly special."

"The Croupier thinks differently," Danny said, showing me the tattoo of two dice on his good wrist.

"You work for him?" Emily asked.

Danny nodded.

"I think we're going to need more than that," I told him.

"The Croupier has people all over the world who work for him," Danny said. "A network of those who are loyal to his cause."

"And what is his cause?" I asked before I could stop myself.

"Power," Danny said. "Mary, Neil, and I had worked for him for five years. We were just eyes and ears in this part of the world, low-level people doing low-level stuff. Mary was a cop in Chicago. Neil was a paramedic in Toronto."

"And you?" Emily asked.

"I was the aide to a US Congressman," Danny said proudly. "I'm not going to tell you who it was; he didn't know about the Croupier. All of us just kept our eyes open, reported whatever we needed to, and looked the other way on anything the Croupier wanted us to ignore."

"Drugs?" Nadia asked.

"Drugs, guns, women, men, a host of stuff," Danny said.

"That where the vials of drugs came from?" Emily asked.

"We were asked to keep them safe," Danny said. "That we would be asked to ship them to destinations given to us. Then we got a call to say that we were to create a disturbance. To take the drugs ourselves, to change.

"We weren't really sure how to do it. We knew we needed to create a fuss, but none of us had ever taken a vial before, so we went into the woods to an old cabin. We each took one vial. It was . . . amazing. The power you feel inside you. Once you take a vial, you can change repeatedly, but the effect lessens with every change; you become weaker and weaker until you have to take a second vial. It's addictive. That power, that level of intensity. Is that how you feel all the time?"

"Yes," Nadia said completely deadpan. "I am constantly in a state of wonder and euphoria."

"Who told you I was going to be at the facility?" I asked.

"The Croupier," Danny said.

"And how did he know?" Nadia asked.

Danny said nothing.

"Zeke," I guessed. "Zeke was meant to just take me, wasn't he? That's why Neil was surprised to see all of us, it's why he tried to kill Zeke, he knew you'd been betrayed."

Danny nodded.

I remained silent, not wishing to open my mouth, and let the bubbling disappointment at the revelation turn to anger. I had no idea why Zeke changed the plan or why he would want to betray me in the first place, but when I saw him next, I was going to make sure to get the answers I wanted.

"Callie Mitchell," Emily said.

"She was here a few months ago," Danny admitted. "Stayed at the facility for a while, moved on. No idea where, no idea how. She was just gone one day, as was everyone else working there. There's a room further into the facility where a lot of people were killed. We were left with the run of the place. We tried to get control of our powers; we fought some of the fiends that were down there. The Croupier wanted us to keep the place going in case it was needed again. He said we were an important part of the plan."

"What plan?" I asked.

"I don't know," Danny said.

"So, the Croupier told you to kill me," I said. "Any idea why, or do you just do whatever he asks?"

"He said you were working for your masters, working against the Blessed, working to undermine us, to stop us from helping those who needed it," Danny said in one long stream of consciousness.

"Our masters?" I asked.

"The Ancients," Danny said.

"You think the Ancients are my masters?" I asked him, genuinely curious as to why he would believe that.

"Of course," he said. "Don't try to deny it."

"I couldn't even pick most of the Ancients out of a crowd of people," I said with a chuckle. "But you believe what you want. How well do you know Zeke?"

"Not very," Danny said. "He was at the facility a few times. He spoke to us once or twice; we were told that he would do what he was told and not to worry about him."

"Why?" Emily asked.

"Ask him," Danny said.

"Oh, I will," I told him. "What's the Croupier's real name?"

"No idea," Danny said.

"How do I find him?" I asked.

"You don't," he said. "He contacts you. And even if I knew how to contact him, I wouldn't tell you."

"Loyalty in criminal empires is quite the thing," Emily said.

"Freedom fighters," Danny snapped.

I laughed. "At best, you're a cult."

"You said he's after something in the rift," Emily said as Danny glared at us both. "He's helping these . . . Blessed? The people who want what they think they're owed?"

"We're all helping them," Danny said.

"Why can't he just go to the rift and help there?" Nadia asked. "Unless he's can't. Which would mean he wasn't riftborn."

Danny spat onto the floor. "That name is tainted."

"Riftborn?" I asked. "Why?"

"Because you were *not* born in the rift," Danny said, genuinely angry. "The practitioners are the *true* riftborn."

I closed my eyes and sighed. I'd heard arguments before in a similar fashion, heard people say that the riftborn stole the name from those who were rightfully born in the rift, but the riftborn were around for centuries before the first person actually born inside the rift was even conceived. Some people took me existing as an affront to what they believed they were owed. Honestly, I didn't care what they called me. If they wanted to be known as riftborn, let them.

But it wasn't really about a name. It was, as always, about power. They'd wanted more control, more say in what happened in the rift, about what happened to *all* of those who lived in the rift. They believed they had a given right to be in charge of the entire rift and everyone who lived there, that they *deserved* it. They wanted to be royalty where none such existed. They wanted to be bowed to, to have statues built of them, to have people worship them as something special. To be considered above everyone else. And frankly, that entire train of thought could get into the fucking sea.

There had been an attempted coup which had ended how the vast majority of coups ended, with those doing the attacking being thrown to the wolves, while those in charge are dealt with quietly.

Danny let out a long moan of pain, and the arm that had already turned began to dissolve, leaving dark blue gunk all over the floor.

"Jesus Christ," Emily said, turning away.

"Go take some air," I told her. "Nadia, make sure she gets out of here okay."

"I'm fine," Emily said defiantly.

"There's nothing wrong with taking a break," Nadia said softly. "The cops probably want to talk to someone they think is in charge, and right now that's apparently you."

"I can't be in charge," Emily said.

"They don't know that," Nadia told her with a cheeky grin.

Nadia led Emily of out of the room, and I sat down on the floor, stretching my legs out as Danny came to terms with the fact that he had one less limb.

"What's going to happen to me?" he asked, terrified.

"I don't know," I admitted. "Either you'll start to dissolve and all of you will, or just the bits that aren't human will and the rest will bleed out. Your arm hasn't totally gone, just from the forearm down, so that leads me to believe that eventually, everything that's changed will go, and you'll probably die from blood loss or go into shock."

"I don't want to die like that," Danny told me.

"Well, you fucked around with some serious shit, Danny," I said. "My cup of sympathy doesn't exactly overflow."

"We didn't know that the more you transform, the weaker you become," Danny said. "There must be something you can do."

"I can put you in a Tupperware box next to your friend when you're done," I told him.

"How the fuck is that helpful?" Danny practically screamed.

"You murdered someone," I said. "Tried to kill my friends and me. You're working for a man who has slaughtered countless people, and a woman who is developing a drug that will turn people into monsters. I'm not trying to be helpful." I removed one of the daggers from its sheath.

Danny stared at the blade and licked his lips. "You're going to end it for me?"

I looked up at Danny, at the monster he'd turned himself into, at the pleading in his eyes, at the pain in his face. "How many members are there helping the Blessed on Earth?"

Danny took a deep breath and shook his head.

I got to my feet. "Enjoy your last few hours of dying alone, in pain, on the floor." I turned to walk away.

"We have cells all over the place. Just three or four people at a time." Danny gasped. "Six in America, four in Canada, another three in the UK. Europe, South America, Africa, Asia. The Croupier has spent decades building up the group. Calls us the Blessed Attendants, tells us we're helping to free people. Tells us that we can become revenants . . . that we'll get to live forever in the rift."

"That's not how it works," I told him sadly. "There's no way to ensure anyone goes to the rift. No way to tell who does or doesn't become a revenant. You were lied to. All of you. You're here because the Croupier needs bodies to help him. Needs intel. You're disposable."

Danny stared at me for several seconds, his mandibles clicking.

"I don't want to die alone on the floor like this," Danny said.

I nodded and sighed. "I get that, Danny. You were sold a bill of goods that just doesn't exist. I'm gonna go ahead and guess you weren't the first nor the last."

"What's the rift really like?" he asked me.

"It's magical," I said honestly. "Amazing, terrifying, and everything in between. It's a place like no other, but a place that will chew you up and spit you out if you screw up. It's not some paradise where people get to live the rest of their lives with everything they ever wanted; it's just another step in life. A life that's different to this one but still life. And after that . . . well, no one knows. There are people in the rift who were kings and queens on Earth and now they're fishermen, or guards, or they make baskets. Your status here means little there; it's all about what you can offer, what you're *good at*. Some people don't like that loss in status; some people try to do something about it, and they're not usually there long."

"I was always told it was like something out of a Disney film," Danny said.

"Never had any bird land on me while singing to them," I said. "Not unless you want to lose an eye."

"I'm not going to go there, am I?"

I shook my head. "Only way to make sure a fiend is dead is to use a rift-tempered blade. You're part fiend, Danny. So, I'm not sure what the hell is going to happen to you, but it might just be that I kill you and you come back a full-on greater fiend. I'm not sure you'd want that."

"I almost was that," Danny said. "You maintain your human intelligence while you're transformed, but it's like there's something there pushing at it, trying to get you to take that step further. To hunt. To feed."

"Mason had a vial that was made with elder-fiend blood, or DNA, or something," I said. "Callie made a whole batch of them with elder-fiend DNA and then made a second batch with greater-fiend DNA, which is much easier to come by. Maybe it still has some elder in it, but it's diluted."

"I don't understand," Danny said.

"Callie made two batches of the drug," I said. "She didn't tell Mason about one batch and kept the good stuff for herself. It sounds like she was at the facility to create a more-stable version of the worse drug, the one she gave you. Didn't tell you about any drawbacks. Probably didn't think you were important enough."

"We were meant to die?" Danny asked.

I nodded. "Probably. Mason took one of the good batch, turned into a sort of hybrid elder-fiend, but yours was diluted. Probably made from greater fiends spliced together; it's why you're part one thing and part another. Funny thing is, that it doesn't seem to work brilliantly. My guess is that this is a better batch than the original, as they came apart the second they tried to turn back to human. This is more stable, but not perfected. Any idea why she's so keen on making more of this shit?"

Danny shook his head.

"No, I didn't think you'd know," I said with a sigh.

"We took inferior product?" Danny asked, although it sounded like he was more talking to himself at this point.

I nodded. "I'm going to bet on it, yes."

Danny nodded. "We were keeping a journal for the Croupier about how it affected us. Neil started taking too much of the drug; he longed for it, *needed it*. He started to lose his grip on his sanity. Started to write *Blessed* all over the facility."

"I saw," I said. "Some of it was in blood."

"His blood," Danny said.

"Where are the journals?" I asked, looking around.

"In the footlockers at the end of the beds."

He let out another howl of pain, and more of his arm dissolved as very human blood started to flow out of what remained. It wasn't enough to kill him, but it wouldn't be long before that blood loss would make him loose consciousness.

"Please," Danny said softly. "I don't want to die like this."

I drew a dagger. "Close your eyes, Danny."

He did as I asked, muttering the Lord's Prayer to himself as I drove the blade into his heart. He gasped once and slumped forward, his body beginning to dissolve.

CHAPTER THIRTEEN

I found the journals in the footlockers exactly where Danny said they would be and left the room, exiting the tunnel and returning to the back garden of the Blessed safe house.

There were more personnel than there had been when I'd descended into the tunnels, and at least a few of them were giving me distrustful glances. I carried the three journals in my hand as if nothing was amiss. Confidence is key when you want people to leave you alone. Although visibly carrying weapons also helps.

I met Emily and Nadia at the front of the building, which now had a large van on the lawn with RCU written on it in huge yellow letters and a second, equal-sized Canadian Security Intelligence Service van parked beside it.

"That is spectacularly covert," I said, pointing to the vehicles.

"I guess they ran out of sirens and big flashing lights to stick on top," Nadia said.

Emily sighed. "You know I have to work with these guys, yes?"

"And how happy are they that you're here?" Nadia asked her.

"My FBI supervisor has left several messages," Emily said. "I'm going to need to call her back. I assume the CSIS contacted them when they discovered I was here. Hopefully, they just want to know what happened."

"No, they want someone to blame," I said. "And the people to blame are all dead. Unless they want to scrape that goo off the front lawn and yell at it for a bit, they're going to have to find a scapegoat."

"The FBI isn't going to try to blame us for what happened here," Emily said, grabbing me by the arm and pulling me across the lawn, away from prying ears.

"Are we absconding?" Nadia asked. "I do enjoy a good abscond."

"We are not absconding," Emily said. "I want to know where Danny is."

"Where I left him dissolving on the ground," I said.

"Did you kill him?" Emily asked.

I nodded.

"You murdered a suspect in our custody," Emily said through clenched teeth. "I know you Guild guys do things differently, but humans don't . . ."

"You're not human," Nadia said, kindly but firmly.

Emily's mouth dropped open for a moment. She closed her eyes and took a deep breath.

"I didn't murder him," I said. "I put him out of his misery. Although I'm not above murdering people who need it, Danny was just an idiot who got used and spat out by Callie and the Croupier. Led to believe they were helping the Blessed. Called them Blessed Attendants. Like most cult members, they're abused, indoctrinated, and led to believe that it's all perfectly normal and anyone who says otherwise isn't to be trusted. He was in agony. And frankly, while I wasn't predisposed to be all that nice to someone who wanted to kill me, no one deserves to suffer like that. Humans put animals out of their misery but tell other humans to just grin and bear it. Fuck that. I'm not human, I haven't been for thousands of years, and frankly, your position on death and pain is just backwards." I realised I'd started to raise my voice. It was a topic that angered me.

"Okay," Emily said, looking around.

"Sorry," I said. "He died quickly. And when I meet the Croupier, I'm going to ensure that whatever pain Danny went through is going to be delivered to the bastard who caused it."

"And Ezekiel?" Emily asked.

"I'm going to go find him," I told her, purposefully keeping my voice neutral. The fact that he was seemingly meant to betray me made me angry, but he hadn't gone through with it. I wanted to give him the chance to explain himself. And if that explanation wasn't in keeping with what I expected, he wouldn't be shown any mercy.

I removed my phone from my pocket and stared at it, deciding whether or not to give Zeke a heads-up that we needed to talk. I sighed and called Gabriel.

"Hey," Gabriel said. "Everything okay?"

"Did you get the CSIS and RCU sent here?" I asked him. "Also, hi too."

"Nadia said you might need the RCU," Gabriel said. "I still have people who owe me some favours, so I called the nearest Canadian branch. Not sure about the CSIS; I have no reason to ever speak to them."

"I think Zeke was meant to set us up," I said. "I think he changed his mind for some reason. I don't know if that change is permanent, or if I'm going to go back to his mansion and he's going to try to kill me. Or maybe his whole guest list is just Croupier-approved friends, in which case everyone might try to kill me."

"There's a lake near his mansion," Gabriel said. "I remember Zeke telling me about it. At length. How about you meet him there? Tell him you'll see him after dark; it gives you a few hours to get there, scope the place out. Make sure he's not sending anyone to ambush you."

I smiled. "That was pretty much exactly what I was considering doing."

"Well, great minds and all that," Gabriel said. "Let me know what happens."

I ended the call and rejoined Nadia and Emily, informing them both of my plan.

"You want us to come with you?" Nadia asked.

I shook my head. "Not right now. Can you both stay here? Emily, I'm going to put you in charge of talking to the CSIS and RCU. You've worked in human police forces; you're better suited than anyone. Nadia can help." I passed them two of the journals. "See what you can find in there. I'll take one and give it a read too."

"We'll make sure those vials do not end up in the hands of anyone who shouldn't have them," Nadia said.

"Where'd you put them?" I asked.

"Trunk of the car we came in," Emily said.

"They're in my duffle bag of weapons," Nadia confirmed.

I opened my mouth to ask if they'd both lost their minds, but honestly couldn't think of a better place right now. They needed to be destroyed properly, so until then, the boot of a car was as good as anywhere else.

"I called Gabriel about the RCU," Emily said. "Didn't expect them to arrive so quickly. Not with Canadian security services."

"Let's go find out why," I said, and walked across the lawn to find two men talking to one another, one with *RCU* emblazoned on their jacket and one with *CSIS*. They were both taller than me, with broad shoulders, pale skin, and short hair. The main difference was that the RCU agent had a large bushy beard and the CSIS one didn't.

"Hey," I said. "My name is Lucas Rurik, and I'm with the Raven Guild."

"You going to tell us what happened?" the CSIS man asked.

"No," I said, turning to the RCU agent. "Gabriel called?"

He nodded.

"I'm putting Emily West in charge," I said, stopping both men before they argued. "Not in the investigation, that's all yours, but in informing you what happened here. She's currently on leave from the FBI's rift-fused task force. The other lady who is currently waving at us is Nadia. She's probably not going to help in any way, shape, or form."

"We'll take statements and get a timeline of events," the RCU agent asked.

"Who contacted you and told you to be here?" I asked the CSIS agent.

"Anonymous phone call two hours ago," he said. "We had to come from Toronto. We flew in; there's a private airfield just outside of Greater Sudbury. We work jointly with the RCU in Canada; there's too much space to cover and not enough people to cover it."

"Sounds fair," I said. "I hope you both enjoy the absolute mess you're about to walk in on."

I rejoined Nadia and Emily, opened the Maps app on my phone, and took a screenshot of the area I needed and sent it to Emily's phone. "Meet me there at eleven."

"Why?" Emily asked, looking at the picture

"Zeke has answers and he's going to give them to me," I said.

"He was meant to take you into that facility alone," Nadia said. "I think there's more going on here than just him deciding not to do the Croupier's bidding. That'd be risky."

"I agree," I said. "But I can't find out if I don't ask."

"I'll get a car from the RCU or CSIS," Emily said.

"Or we'll steal one," Nadia said.

"We're *not* stealing a car," Emily countered.

Nadia mimed locking her lips but knowingly winked.

"We're not stealing a car," Emily repeated.

Nadia winked again.

"Be careful," Emily said to me as Nadia grinned. "Just because he didn't do as the Croupier said doesn't meant he won't try to kill you."

I pulled away from the curb and set off back toward Ezekiel's. It was after midday now, which would give me plenty of time to scope out the lake and ensure I had every scenario covered.

I was slightly concerned that the vehicle I was driving carried a number of potentially lethal serums in the boot, but there wasn't really much I could do about that.

Seeing how I had a wait on my hands, I found a secluded spot just off the highway and pulled over to take a read of the journal.

The journal belonged to Neil, which didn't fill me with hope. People who write in blood on the walls don't usually keep great records of their mental state. But it turned out, for the first few dozen pages, to be an incredibly detailed and useful guide about how he'd gone into this with hope about helping people and had slowly descended into feeling like all riftborn should be murdered. There were several pages where he wrote about teachings from people by the name of Matias Sandino and his wife Iola. I'd never heard of either of them, but I took a photo of the page for future reference.

The journal soon became more unhinged, going from detailed notes about how it felt to take Callie Mitchell's drug: *like power flooding my veins as pure sunshine bathed my skin.* To babbling incoherently about how he was going to use his power to get back at his stepdad, about how he was going to make him scream.

The next page detailed what he did to his stepdad and two people who just happened to call at the house in Toronto at the wrong time.

"Fucking hell," I whispered.

That was three days earlier. I continued on through the journal as his mental state deteriorated further. He detailed dreaming of committing murders, drinking their blood, wanting to bathe in it, wanting to . . . The handwriting became scratchy and unreadable, but I got the general idea.

Whatever had remained of Neil after the first few doses of Callie's drug had been burned away by the end. To see someone go from perfectly capable of describing his emotional and physical state to someone who could barely write his name in only a few weeks' worth of pages was terrifying.

The poison didn't just turn people into monsters on a physical scale; it eroded everything that made them human.

I flicked through the last few pages of the journal, the last of which was this morning. He wrote about the attack last night, about wanting to . . . *feast on my innards.* Which was an image I could have done without. He was livid that he'd gotten hurt . . . and there in scrawled handwriting was written how Zeke had betrayed them all. How he would wish he'd never been born, how Neil was going to tear him apart. There weren't even any words on the last page, just drops of blood that had been used to create swirls.

I dropped the journal back onto the passenger seat with a sigh. It was getting on in the afternoon, and Ezekiel's party was either about to start or was already in full swing, depending on how desperate people were for free food and drink. My phone still had reception, which was honestly pretty impressive, considering I was in the middle of nowhere, so I called Emily, who answered on the first ring.

"How's it going?" I asked her.

"About as well as could be expected," she told me. "Lots of questions for us, very few answers from them. Apparently, they received a tip-off about our dead monster friends, but that's as far as it goes. Spoke to my boss who's pissed that I'm involved while officially on vacay."

"Sorry," I said, unable to think of anything else to add.

"It's not your fault," Emily said, sounding resigned to it all. "I'm thinking about taking a lateral move to the RCU. Someone passed me their card."

"They're good people," I said, remembering that Emily had worked with them previously when she'd been with the FBI.

"They are," she agreed.

"How's Nadia?"

"Pissing off anyone with letters on the back of their coat," Emily laughed. "The CSIS kept trying to ask what she saw, and she walked them through the plot of every *Captain America* film without once mentioning any character by name."

I couldn't help but laugh.

"It took them a few minutes to realise what was happening," Emily said. "She'd already done the first film by that point. They're not best pleased."

"I'm wondering what's actually going on here," I said. "I read Neil's journal. You looked at yours yet?"

"Skimmed; it's full of weird cultlike nonsense," Emily said.

I could hear the sounds of raised voices around her.

"Gotta go; Nadia is trying to get several of the agents to listen to her retelling of *Winter Soldier*." Emily hung up as I chuckled to myself before calling Ji-hyun.

"Morning," she said after a few rings.

"How are you doing?" I asked her. "Just wanted to check in."

"Ah, it's great here," Ji-hyun said. "Everyone is super frustrated that the people we got off the train aren't talking. Somehow, Eve's lawyer discovered she was being detained, and now we're having to move her to a specialist facility for people who aren't human. Ravi is slowly losing his mind with frustration, and we've had to change the guard detachment on Simon Wallace because it turned out one of the officers put there had once arrested him for a drugs offence. You?"

"I just had to kill three humans who took the more-stable version of Callie's drug and turned themselves into monsters," I said. "They all wrote journals, and it looks like the drug makes you into a monster in more ways than one. Callie used them as guinea pigs."

"Of course she did," Ji-hyun said.

"I may have to detain Ezekiel," I said.

"What did the stupid prick do now?" Ji-hyun asked me.

"Possibly working with the Croupier," I said. "He was meant to get me killed. Or he turned on the Croupier and stopped them from killing me; I honestly don't know at the moment. I know that Zeke is a self-absorbed poser, but he could have had me killed and he didn't. I don't know if he's still planning on betraying me, or if he's pulling a long con or something."

"And if he does try to betray you?" Ji-hyun asked. She knew the answer, just wanted me to acknowledge it.

"Yeah," I said softly.

"I get that he's a likeable guy," Ji-hyun said. "But if he's playing for the Croupier, he's gone. For good. You don't get to dip your toe in when you're working with people like that."

"I know," I told her, wondering just how much involvement Zeke had had with the murder of the human detective and his family. Had he known?

"Gotta go, Lucas," Ji-hyun said. "Stay safe."

She ended the call, and I sat in silence for several seconds before taking a deep breath, exhaling slowly, and setting off again.

I drove past Zeke's mansion, hearing the music and frivolity well before I reached it. There were a dozen high-end cars on the driveway and several people in expensive-looking suits and dresses milling around outside.

I drove on and stopped the car at a small parking area, getting out and locking it before taking the short walk through the woodland to the lake just beyond.

The water was still, the sunlight bouncing off its surface, giving it a mirror shine. There were a few other people walking around the bank of the lake, most out enjoying the sunshine, although there were a few people running.

I got out my phone and texted Emily and Nadia my exact location. They knew what to do with that information.

There was a large crop of rocks close by, and over the next hour or so, I walked around the area, ensuring there'd be no hidden surprises. Then sat and watched several birds land and take off, flying high across the lake, seemingly not a care in the world. I envied them.

I called Zeke.

"Hey," he said. I couldn't tell if he was happy to hear from me or not.

"We need to talk," I said. "The lake, by your mansion. Eleven p.m. Don't make me come find you, Zeke." I hung up.

I sat on the bank for an hour longer, just watching the dark, calm water before me, before getting to my feet and walking back into the forest. I found what I was looking for a few minutes later. One of Zeke's motion-sensitive cameras. I walked past it as I searched for others. I found four in total, triggering each one several times, before going back to where I'd sat at the lake and retaking my seat. If Zeke was working with people, I wanted them to know exactly where I was. I wasn't about to be ambushed.

I looked up at the moon and sighed. I really did hope I wasn't going to have to kill Zeke.

CHAPTER FOURTEEN

The darkness was well and truly settled in for the night when I heard footsteps behind me through the woodland. I turned to find Zeke, torch in hand, as he walked down the slightly overgrown path. I got up and walked toward the water's edge, looking back at him.

Zeke stood twenty feet away from me. "You know," he said softly.

I nodded. "You going to do something stupid?"

Zeke shook his head. "You going to let me explain?"

I nodded again. "It had better be damn good, Zeke," I warned him. "I'm not in the mood for stupidity or lies."

Zeke kept his hands up and walked over to the bench I'd been sitting on. "I got asked to help a human detective. Mark McCathy. You've heard about this, yes?"

I knew that Zeke could see me in the darkness just fine and nodded.

"He had a wife, two kids," Zeke said. "He was investigating something that looked like it had the involvement of a riftborn or revenant. The name of Croupier turned up more than once. I agreed to go to the rift and talk to some people there. Well, I did just that. And the next thing I know, I'm being kidnapped and dragged to some fort in the middle of nowhere. Kept me there for about a week, beat the shit out of me, threatened me with worse. They told me that if I wanted to live, I had to do exactly what they told me. The Croupier doesn't exist, and if I kept using the name, I wouldn't exist."

"You went back and told Mark that the Croupier didn't exist?" I asked.

"I did," Zeke admitted. "Told him to drop it. Told his superiors, too; tried to get him taken off the case, but nothing worked. One day, I get woken up by some very angry people in ski masks, carrying rift-tempered blades. They tell me they want to show me what happens to people who don't do as they're told."

I remained silent. I wondered if this was like listening to a confession in church; I'd have to ask someone one day.

"So, I get bundled into the back of this shit-heap of a car," Zeke continued. "Taken to Mark's house. Mark is inside; he's bound and gagged, on his knees. A man sat beside him, wore a mask. He patted Mark on the head like he was a dog."

"He was wearing a Talon's mask," Zeke said. "You know, a black mask with a dark grey hood. It had red marks around the eyes and white slashes next to each eyehole. I'll never forget it as long as I live. He looked like a fucking demon sat there in his three-piece suit, his fancy shoes, expensive watch, and that fucking mask from hell. I see that mask in my dreams."

"He's a Talon?" I asked, surprised.

Zeke shook his head. "No, he killed one, took the mask. Wears it to frighten people, but there's more than that. The mask belonged to a riftborn, and it's like the Croupier is wearing it to taunt the riftborn. Like he's wearing it out of spite."

"Go on," I said, putting the information away about the Talon's mask.

"The man working for the Croupier stood, kicking Mark to the ground, took my arm, and led me through the house to the rear room," Zeke said, taking a breath. "There were bodies in there. The wife, kids. All dead. Jesus fucking Christ, those poor kids. There was a camera on the table beside them."

"He took photos?" I asked.

"That's what he said. Photos to ensure that people *knew* what happened to those who crossed him. Each body had a poker chip on their forehead. He took me back to Mark, and some thug shoves a hood over his head, and he's bundled into a car, with me beside him. The Croupier sat up front, being conversational the whole way there. Never once making it feel like he'd just murdered an innocent family."

The sounds of the water of the lake lapping against the bank was all I could hear for several seconds. I didn't want to push Zeke.

"We got out along the Hudson River," Zeke said. "New York in the 1970s was a stain on the rest of the country. People were getting murdered every ten seconds or some shit. The police were just as bad as the criminals, but Mark was different. He wanted to help people; he wanted to make things better. The Croupier made sure no one else ever did."

Zeke let out a long sigh. "The Croupier took the hood off Mark, or had one of his lackeys do it; I don't completely remember. There were five or six others with us, men and women. The Croupier had his people beat Mark. Just absolutely kick the shit out of him unrelentingly. He turned to me, handed me some snub-nose piece of crap revolver, and said, 'You either show your loyalty by showing him mercy, or once they're done with him, you'll be next.' God fucking damn it." The last words were a scream of rage.

"You killed Mark," I said.

"They were pulling his fingernails out with pliers," he said. "They were breaking bones, taking blades to him. They were beating him to death. Torturing him. Telling him what they'd done to his family, over and over. I shot him in the head. Croupier said it would be considered a murder-suicide. I remember laughing at that. How the hell do you cover up all of the injuries that Mark had sustained? But you know what, that's exactly what happened. Murder-suicide. They ruined the lives of a whole family and then the reputation of the cop who they murdered, just to send a message to anyone who dared look into the Croupier. It wasn't the first or last time he did something like that. And he let me live. And he left me alone."

"So long as you kill people for him?" I asked.

"No," Zeke snapped. "So long as I just let his people be. So long as I don't interfere, don't call anyone I know who might interfere. He has people in the RCU, the FBI; hell, even a member of Congress is on his payroll. I don't know who I can and can't trust. Is that FBI agent asking about him working for him to test me? Is it real? Do you have any idea what it's like to live under the constant possibility that people you trust would put a bullet in your head if someone told them to? I murdered a good man to save my own skin and looked the other way for forty years so the Croupier didn't look at me again. I don't want him to ever look my way. And then you manage to piss him off more than anyone has done in fucking years."

"Good," I said.

"Good?" Zeke snapped. "It's not good, Lucas. He told me you were coming. Told me to take you to that facility, to tell you that Callie had been there. Told me to leave you to those fiends, to Neil and his psychotic friends. But I couldn't. I couldn't let a member of a Guild go out like that. But more importantly, I couldn't let someone I liked go out like that. You deserve more than that. You saved my life yesterday."

"So, what happened today when the Croupier found out?" I asked. "I assume he knows."

"He contacted me this morning," Zeke said. "Yelled a lot. I explained that Neil and his idiot friends got involved and it all went to hell. The fiends killed each other before they'd even left the chamber, so only one actually attacked. I fed him a story about how I had to defend myself because Neil had lost his damn mind. I think he bought it."

"But?" I asked.

"But he sent people to my home," Zeke said. "Those three people are with my family right now, and if I don't come back with proof of your death, they're going to start murdering them. My grandson, Cory, he's working with them. The Croupier thought it would be funny to bring one of my own family members into his fold. I need your help."

"Why not ask for my help in the first place?" I asked.

"Because I didn't know if I could *trust* you," Zeke said. "Then you saved my life, and I knew you never would have done that if you'd been sent here as some kind of ridiculous test. I want out, but I don't know how to get out, and I don't know who to trust to help me. Please, Lucas."

"Okay," I said. "If there's anything you're lying to me about, it's going to come back at you in a very unpleasant way."

"I promise," he said. "I didn't know that Neil and his friends were part of the Blessed. They're some kind of cult from the rift."

"I have some questions," I said.

"Anything," Zeke pleaded.

"You think Cory will kill his own family members?" I asked.

"He's not right," Zeke said. "He's . . . not allowed to be left alone with any member of my staff. There's a cruelty inside of him. My son and daughter-in-law, they tried to give him a firm hand, to steer him in the right direction, but he doesn't care. They found that he'd been hunting and torturing squirrels when he was fourteen. Took him to a doctor; the doctor gave him pills. I don't think they help. He's been working for the Croupier, thinks I don't know, but the Croupier likes to remind me whenever I talk to him."

"What's his real name?" I asked.

"No idea," Zeke said with a sigh. "No one knows. He's tied into these Blessed assholes somehow, but I'm not going into the rift to find out more."

"Were you really going to try to kill me?" I asked. "Did you tell the Croupier's people that's what you were going to do?"

Zeke shook his head. "I slipped out of the party; I imagine they're all still looking for me. They have enough hostages that they know I can't be an idiot. Also, when you asked about if Cory would kill his own family members, yes. Yes, he would. The Croupier told me that he'll be the one killing me."

"He's not actually blood, though, right?" I asked.

"No," Zeke said. "Doesn't make it any easier. I raised his father from a young man. I was there when Cory was born. I held him that first day."

"And he's turned into a psychopath," I said.

Zeke got up from his seat and walked over to me. "You're going to help me, though, yes?"

I sat down beside Zeke on the rocky ground. "You want me to go back to your house and remove the people sent there to threaten your family?" I asked.

"If they die at my hand, the Croupier will know and he'll come for my family again," Zeke said. "You need to make it look like I wasn't a part of it. I need to figure out how to extricate myself from his grasp and get my family to safety."

"He help you get rich?" I asked him. "Richer?"

Zeke shook his head. "No."

"Goddamn it, Zeke," I said. "You should have come to me, or Gabriel, or . . . well, or anyone. You should have done it a long time ago. This asshole has been out there killing people for decades, and you just turned a blind eye until he decided to come after you again."

Zeke nodded slowly. "I know."

There was a rustle in the trees behind us, and Zeke sprang to his feet, his hand on his Colt. I looked behind as Emily and Nadia strolled out of the forest.

"Just in case you decided killing Lucas was the better plan," Emily said. "Amazing what these powers do for your senses."

"Hooded revenant," Zeke said. "Do you have a plan?" he asked me as Nadia and Emily stood behind us.

"Yes," I said.

"Am I going to jail?" Zeke asked.

"Almost certainly," I told him. There were nonhuman jails around the globe. Places where abilities were stifled, where rehabilitation was more important than just blanket punishment. The murderers, monsters, and worst of my kind weren't sent to prison; they were executed. Mostly.

"What's the plan?" Emily asked.

"I'm going to call Gabriel and get him to send the RCU people he trusts to Zeke's house," I said. "Zeke is going to stay with you both, and you're going to have a nice journey back to the mansion, where Zeke is going to confess anything and everything he hasn't already. He's going to behave himself." I turned to Zeke. "If you screw around, I'll hunt you down myself."

"I want to help," Zeke said.

"Okay," I said. "Emily, take Zeke back to his party. Zeke, you stay downstairs in the main room. You do not leave that room. You tell anyone who works for the Croupier that I wasn't here but that I'd tripped some camera going back to the party. They're going to start searching for me, hopefully away from too many guests. Emily, you need to stay out of sight."

"That I can do," Emily said.

"When we're done, Zeke, you're going back to Gabriel's church," I said. "Emily and Nadia can go with you too to make sure you're okay. I'll get it cleared with the RCU, although obviously I won't tell them where you actually are, primarily because I don't know who does and doesn't work for the Croupier."

"I'm coming with you," Nadia told me, which I had no issue with.

"The Croupier didn't use riftborn in London," I said. "Is that true here?"

"Two are revenants, one is human," Zeke said. "He hates riftborn. No idea why. He's a practitioner; that's all I know."

"So, that probably means Callie Mitchell isn't riftborn either," I said, following my train of thought. "She's not a revenant; we know that. And if the Croupier refuses to work with riftborn, that means that Callie's a practitioner too?"

Zeke nodded. "You didn't know?"

"I knew the practitioners had believed they'd been overlooked as the rightful rulers of the rift," I said. "There was a big . . . *war* isn't quite the right word, but an attempted coup a while back. Some practitioners tried to kill off the leaders of Inaxia, got caught, some were exiled, and most were executed. I don't know just how much the general public knows about what happened, though, as a lot of it was always shrouded in secrecy, even for the Guilds. I always got the feeling there was a lot more going on than the Primes wanted people to know."

"Croupier is a practitioner working with the Blessed, then," Emily said.

"If he's a practitioner, how is he here?" Nadia asked.

"Riftborn can come and go to the rift as they please to some degree," I said. "We have our embers to act as a sort of barrier to them. Revenants only go to the rift once they've died here. Practitioners are a little different."

"Once on Earth, they can't go back," Zeke said. "Not by any means I've ever heard of."

"They're stuck here?" Emily asked.

"There are only three reasons I can think of for any practitioner to be on Earth," I said. "Money and power, because they're running away from something in the rift, or because they were exiled."

"You think the Croupier was part of that attempted coup?" Nadia said.

I nodded. "He certainly seems to like money and power, but the idea of him being exiled to Earth and really pissed off about it needs to be looked into."

"Do they live forever?" Emily asked. "Can they be killed?"

"Sure, anything can be killed," Zeke said.

"Revenants age slowly, but they still age," I said. "Riftborn have to go back to the rift every century or two to heal up and recharge. We age during that recharge process. It's slow, but we do still age too. Practitioners stop aging completely at the age of about thirty, for the most part. No one knows why; no one knows how. Every hundred years or so, they have to undergo a sort of stasis to renew their body; otherwise, it just starts shutting down. They age decades in a few days; it's how they know it's time to stasis. So long as they do that, they can stay here indefinitely. There are practitioners on Earth who have been around since the time of Babylon."

"So, this Croupier asshole could be thousands of years old?" Emily asked.

"Unfortunately, yes," I said.

"So, you're assuming that the Blessed are in the rift?" Nadia asked.

"As well as here," Emily said.

"And if that's the case, is this Croupier helping the Blessed back in the rift?" Nadia continued. "And if he is, how is he doing it? It's not like he can just open a portal and send through a bunch of stuff."

"I don't know," I admitted.

"I'm glad we're all on the same page of being equally unsure what the hell is going on," Nadia said.

"Zeke," I said. "Tell them everything you haven't already. And behave. Please."

"I will," Zeke said.

"Or I'll cut your hands off," Nadia said with a smile that made Zeke look a little ill.

"How many guests, exactly?" I asked Zeke.

"I don't know," he admitted a little sheepishly. "I have neighbours in there, too, maybe a hundred. Hundred and fifty including staff and the like."

"And three of them are the bad guys," I said. "Great."

Zeke removed his phone from his pocket, tapped the screen a few times while Nadia stood beside him, watching him like a hawk.

"I've sent you pictures," Zeke said.

"Any security in the house?" I asked. "Cameras? Anything they can use to track me?"

"I turned off all of the security on the grounds," Zeke said. "No cameras, no motion sensors. They can't get back into the system without my authorisation. I've also sent you the password. The main office is downstairs, near the back of the building, but there's a secondary camera panel, room at the end of the corridor, next to the stairs. It's behind a painting of a pirate ship."

"You knew I was going to have to help you?" I asked him.

"I really hoped so," Zeke admitted.

"We're not arresting people tonight," I told Emily. "This is a *get in and eliminate the threat*. You okay with that?"

Emily nodded.

"Don't get caught," Zeke said, with more than a little pleading in his voice. "They *will* start killing people."

"We'll do everything we can to keep your family safe; you and I will go look for Cory," Emily said.

"Thank you," Zeke said.

I drove the Jeep back to the mansion and parked up just a little back from it, under the cover of the darkness afforded by the trees. The party was in full swing, and the sounds of revelry could be heard from where I stood.

Nadia and I got out and watched as Zeke continued to drive the Jeep back into the mansion, with a camouflaged Emily in the rear seats. Nadia followed me along the edge of the property wall until we were far enough away from the main gate. "You good to climb?" I asked her.

Nadia's chains grabbed hold of the wall and helped her quickly scale it. I turned to smoke, billowed up and over the wall, and re-formed in the shadows of the trees on the other side. Nadia smiled at me and gave me a thumbs-up. Time to go crash the party.

CHAPTER FIFTEEN

I removed the phone from my pocket and unlocked the screen, tapping the notification of Zeke's message. The first picture was of a white man with short, almost military-style hair, who was almost bursting out of the navy suit he wore. I spotted the tip of a tattoo on his neck and zoomed in on the picture; it appeared to be a tattoo of a skull just peeking out of the collar of his white shirt.

Next photo was of a tall, although slightly less large, man. This one was black, with a similar hairstyle, but also had a thick beard and wore a dark green suit. I wondered if there was some online store catering for muscled henchmen.

The final photo was a woman. She was white, with long red hair with silver streaks that fell over her shoulders. She wore a long silver dress and matching heels. The dress had a slit up one leg that ended at the top of her thigh. I guessed if they were trying to blend into the party, they had to look the part, and all three of them looked like they were there to party. She was muscular and had an eagle tattooed on her shoulder.

There was a fourth picture. A smiling man of about twenty-four in a black suit. He had a clean-shaven face, showing off his chiselled jaw, and blond hair that was tied back in a ponytail. I zoomed in on his eyes and knew that was Cory even without having seen the name in the image header. His eyes were cold, mean. Of the three, he was the one I'd least like to meet on a dark night.

I showed them all to Nadia. "I'll find the woman," she said. "She looks like fun."

"Nadia, we need to be subtle," I said with a sigh, looking over at the annex building, where more people were milling around, enjoying themselves. "Take the annex first; we're not exactly dressed for this, so *try to blend in*."

"I'm great at blending," Nadia said, looking offended. She hid her chains and headed toward the guests while I tried to quash any reservations. I turned to smoke and moved slowly over the grass. Moving slowly sucks over anything more than a few metres. It's hard to maintain my sense of self; it's hard to look inconspicuous. I reached the side of the building and re-formed, crouched down against the wall, and took a moment to catch my breath.

The second time I turned to smoke, it was to move quickly, straight up through the open window, re-forming in the bedroom I was in. I needed to get to the security room and hopefully pinpoint where the targets were.

The bedroom had an open suitcase in it, with several items of clothing strewn about the double bed. I opened the bedroom door as slowly as possible and peered out into the hallway beyond.

The lights were on but the whole floor was empty. I exited the bedroom and set off toward the room at the end. I was about halfway down the corridor when the door to the room I was about to go into opened, and a man and woman—both well dressed, both in their forties, and both wearing wedding rings—practically fell out, giggling and trying very hard to not look like they'd been doing something they shouldn't.

They spotted me and straightened up.

"Hellllooooo," the woman said with what appeared to be a curtsey for reasons only she knew.

"Good evening," I said to them both. "Enjoying the party?"

"Zeke's home is lovely," the man said, and I almost blinked from the alcohol fumes on his breath.

"How long have you both been married?" I asked.

They stared at one another. "Fifteen years," the woman said, raising her hand to show me the huge diamond on her finger. "Kids are at home, and sometimes you just need to . . . you know." She sort of motioned with her head toward the door.

"I understand," I said. "I do need to access that room, however."

"Oh, we're so sorry," the man said. "Come on, dear, let's rejoin the party." He slapped his wife on the butt, and she made a weird snorting, giggling sound that made the man laugh.

I opened the door and stepped into a game room. There was a table in the middle to play card games, a large glass drinks cabinet at one end, and several chairs stacked up in the corner. A large TV sat on the wall next to the drinks cabinet, and the painting of a pirate ship sat on the opposite wall.

I lifted the painting down, propping it up against the wall, revealing a screen which flickered to life and asked for a password. I typed the word in Zeke had provided—*BlackBeard1718*—and the screen vanished, replaced with several commands about cameras and security, as well as a red button that would apparently notify law enforcement. The latter could wait. I was pretty sure that if the police rocked up, it would complicate an already-complex situation.

I tapped the screen to reactivate the cameras and turned as the TV behind me flickered to life with the camera feed.

The TV screen was divided into nine, with ONE OF TEN written at the top. I picked up the TV remote from the side of the poker table and used the buttons to scroll through the camera feed one at a time. The first six were all external and showed very little except for the occasional party-goer. Camera seven was a shot of the entrance to the annex, but I didn't see Nadia—which was probably a good thing—nor any of the bad guys—which was definitely a good thing.

Camera eight was directly outside the back door and showed the woman Nadia was looking for. She was talking on her phone, although there was no sound on the security feed, so I couldn't tell what she was saying. I scrolled to camera nine, and found it to be of the main function room. There were a lot of people in there.

The final screen was of Zeke's office. It must have been situated over the door. Cory was sat in the chair behind the desk. He had a glass of alcohol in one hand and a cigar in the other. A middle-aged man and woman were sat on the ground in front of the desk, their hands tied behind their backs. The man looked like he'd been given a bit of a kicking, considering the swollen eye and cut lip.

There was a gun on the desk. I zoomed in. Glock 17. The grip was red and black, and it more than likely belonged to Zeke. I wondered if he had more weapons that Cory and his friends had gotten into. That might complicate matters.

Cory drank the whiskey and poured himself another while the woman talked to him. Whatever she said pissed Cory off because he grabbed the gun and pointed it at her. At the man, too. There was very little emotion in Cory's face, but he did smile when he sat back down. He was going to be a problem.

Still, out of four targets, I'd found two. That was better than none.

I hoped Cory would stay where he was until Emily and Zeke found him.

I moved toward the door as it opened, and the large white man from Zeke's photos stepped inside, closing it behind him. He had a black steel baton in one gigantic hand and the look of someone who had just found the best present ever.

While the thought to just jump him and get it over with flashed through my mind, I also needed information. I took a few steps back, putting the table between myself and the menacing-looking man.

"Drunk people talk too much," the man said. He had a South African accent and spoke softly, the latter of which I hadn't expected, given his bulk. "The couple you met were really happy to help me find my 'friend.'"

"People who do air quotes with their fingers are really annoying," I told him. "Not going to get your own friends?"

"Whoever kills you gets a bonus," he told me.

"What's the bonus?" I asked, genuinely curious. It's always nice to know what your life is worth.

"More money than you have on you to pay me not to kill you," he said with a smirk.

I whistled, put my hand in my pocket, and removed the bank notes in there. "So, more than fifty bucks?"

The man looked confused. I know it was probably a stereotype, but I got the feeling that being confused was his default state of mind. "Yes, of course. Lots more. You can't pay me only fifty bucks not to kill you. Did you really think I would accept such a low amount?"

I shrugged. "So, you're going to kill me in here?" I asked as he took a step toward me. "Where's the woman and the other guy? I know you said you don't want to share, but what if they hear my long and arduous death screams?"

"They're downstairs and this room is soundproof." He smashed the baton into the wall as if to make his point. "No one will hear you scream."

I wanted to make a joke about *Alien* and how we weren't in space but decided this was neither the time nor place; also, I wasn't sure he would get it.

"What about Cory?" I asked, pointing toward the TV screen.

"Ah, the boy is a special project," the man told me as he continued to walk toward me. "It's unfortunate that you won't be around to see it."

"Did the Croupier tell you who I am?" I asked him.

"Lucas Rurik," the man said. "Ex-Guild member. I'm ex-Recces."

"The peanut-butter things?" I asked.

The man stopped walking, his face becoming contorted with anger. "The South African Special Forces," he snapped. "I think you should take this more seriously."

"Do you fight with peanuts?" I asked him. "Is peanut allergy a big problem over there? That might be considered chemical warfare."

"We do not fight with peanuts," the man screamed. "The words are spelt differently."

Smirking, I threw the TV remote at his head; he dodged it easily, but I'd already turned to smoke. I flew over the table and re-formed just as my fist hit his chest. There wasn't as much power behind the blow as I'd aimed at the fiend, primarily because full power would have resulted in him being torn in half and left me weakened. Even so, it threw him back against the wall with a crunch that sounded like it hurt. His sternum was certainly broken, probably a few ribs. The man slid down the wall, his eyes wide open, leaving a smear of blood where his head had impacted.

Apparently, I'd also broken his skull.

When I crouched down by the man, he opened his eyes, his face twisting, his entire body transforming as horns grew out of his head. I took a knife and drove it up under his chin into his brain. He died instantly.

"I guess you were a revenant," I said, removing the dragger, wiping it on the man's suit, cleaning the blade enough to put it back in its sheath.

Leaving the room, I made my way down the stairs to the lower floor. The back of the house where the woman had been standing was close to the bottom of the stairs. I avoided a group of drunk revellers as they did shots of alcohol out of some giggling woman's cleavage, and pushed open the conservatory door, hoping to find the woman exactly where I'd seen her only a few moments earlier.

I walked down the steps outside of the mansion, looking, but there was no one around. I continued on, stopping at the railing next to a set of steps that led down toward the garden with its tennis court and swimming pool, neither of which appeared to be occupied.

There was a slight noise behind me, and I turned in time to avoid the knife attack from the woman I'd been trying to find. The blade bit into my forearm, cutting across it as I backed away, trying to also not fall over the railing.

"Looking for me?" she asked. Like the dead man from earlier, she had a South African accent; maybe there was an abundance of them in the Croupier's organisation.

"Not specifically," I told her, spotting movement from behind her. "I think she was, though."

Nadia tackled our target from behind, lifting her, both of them careering over the railing to the ground a dozen feet below.

"You okay?" I shouted.

"Find the others," Nadia shouted back.

Nodding, I ran back to the mansion and was almost at the door when two shots rang out from inside the building. I didn't stop and burst through the door as screams began to flood out of the rooms around me.

Heading toward the noise, I collided with a throng of people trying to escape. I turned to smoke, moving over their head as two more gunshots sent guests into a frenzied stampede. I landed next to Zeke's office, kicked in the door, and darted inside just as Zeke and Emily arrived.

The woman from the video was on her knees, her hands tied behind her back. She was weeping over the prone body of the man from the same video. Her husband. He had two bullet holes in his heart.

"No, my boy," Zeke cried out, dropping to his knees by the prone man.

"Are you Cory's mom?" I asked her.

At the mention of his name, her head snapped up toward me. "I'm Rachel. Cory . . . he . . . he . . ."

"I know," I told her. Another gunshot somewhere in the mansion. Cory needed to be found, and quickly. I cut through the cable tie, and she placed her freed hands on the body of her husband.

"Is he . . . " she asked, pleading in her voice that she was wrong.

"I'm sorry," I said. He was dead.

"Maybe he'll come back," Rachel said, hopefully.

Zeke looked up at me and we shared an expression of doubt.

"Your son, where is he?" I asked.

"A maid," Rachel said. "A maid came in, just as Cory shot Jason. He tried to get her to stay, but she ran, he shot at her. Missed. Ran after her."

"I'm coming with you," Zeke said.

"No," I snapped possibly a little more forcefully than I'd considered. "Your grandson is out there, and he'll be gunning for you now. Emily, you get everyone out of here as quickly as you can. Zeke, please help her."

"Please don't kill him," Rachel said.

I blinked, not entirely sure how to respond to that.

"I know what he's done," Rachel said. "But he's still my son. Please. Please try to take him alive."

"I'll try," I said, knowing full well just how unlikely that was going to be.

I left the office, finding that the hallway beyond was now devoid of life. The front door was open, and people were congregating on the drive and running across the lawn. I took the stairs two at a time, reaching the bottom and not slowing down as I ran down the hallway. There was a bullet hole at the end of the hall, next to the window and stairs that continued to the floor above. I moved slower up the stairs and had reached the hallway when a scream cut through the silence.

I hit the next set of stairs at full speed, taking them two at a time, to the floor above. There was a second scream and the sound of flesh impacting flesh.

Of all the doors on the floor, only one was open, and I spotted Cory inside.

"You should have kept your nose out of my business, you little bitch," he snapped, his attention not on me as I barreled into him from behind, throwing him across the room into a set of bookshelves.

I picked up Rose from her prone position on the floor and pushed her out of the room, telling her to go.

"Thank you," she gasped.

Cory was on his knees, reaching for his gun. He fired at me twice, but I'd turned to smoke, the bullets passing through me without causing any long-lasting damage. Still hurt like all hell, though. I re-formed right beside him, grabbed his wrist in one hand, and brought my forehead down on his nose. Once. Twice. Three times, feeling the nose break, the blood flow. I kept hold of his wrist, throwing him. He landed hard, and I kept hold of his wrist, twisting it in an unnatural direction so that Cory finally released his grip on the gun.

I removed the magazine, ejected the round in the chamber, and tossed them to the floor beside me.

"Why kill your dad?" I asked. "Why take them hostage?"

"They found out what I was going to do to good ol' Zeke," Cory snapped. "Found the gun. Tried to stop me."

"So, what's the plan now?" I asked.

Cory rolled away, coming up with a dagger in one hand and a vial in the other.

I threw my own dagger at him. It caught him in the fleshy part of the palm, punching through the opposite side. Cory screamed, let go of the knife, and clutched the now-ruined hand, also dropping the vial onto the floor.

I crushed the vial beneath my boot, lifted Cory's arm in the air, and removed the dagger, kicking his to the far end of the room.

"Hello, Mr. Rurik," a voice I recognised said.

"Where is that coming from?" I asked Cory.

"Phone," he said, gasping with pain.

I picked up his phone, which had landed just under the bed. The hands-free button was already activated. I turned the volume up.

"Hey, Croupier," I said. "Long time no speak. Listen, I'm really sorry about blowing up your train, killing your people, getting others arrested, making your life miserable, and generally just refusing to die. Your boy Cory here was just about to tell me everything he knows."

"Oh, Mr. Rurik," the Croupier said. "You overestimate the value I place on people like Cory. He had a very . . . pronounced set of interests in human physiology. I just allowed him time to pursue those interests in a hands-on manner."

"You trained the little shit to be a serial killer," I said.

"I don't think he's killed enough people to be labelled as such, but that was the ambition. Mostly, he was there to ensure that when the time came, he would do whatever was necessary to remove Gunslinger, should your friend become a problem. Unfortunately for you," the Croupier continued. "You overestimated just how important Cory was to me. Thank you for all you've done, Cory. Good-bye."

I was already running toward the window when the phone exploded.

CHAPTER SIXTEEN

The force of the explosion hit me as I turned to smoke. On the one hand, I now had a very nice hole to leave through; on the other, the shockwave, heat, and force of the blast cut through my smoke form, pushing it apart, making my body scream in pain as I spiralled toward the ground.

I was still vapor when I smashed into the lawn, my entire existence one of pain, my body trying to pull itself back together again while simultaneously feeling like I'd just been put into an exceptionally large, hot blender.

I lay on the ground, my mind scrambled, my body radiating raw agony and heat.

Also, I was a little bit on fire.

Thankfully, I wasn't damaged enough to need the rift—we didn't have time for that.

Someone threw a blanket over me, which I was about to protest, as I wasn't dead, but they started to pat my body down. I wanted to protest that, too, as it fucking well hurt, but my brain and my mouth weren't even close to being on the same page, so I just lay there, allowing people to pat me down, while a long zombie-like noise left my mouth. If I ever wrote a memoir about my life, that bit was being left out.

Emily crouched over me, concern on her face.

"Hey," she said. Maybe. I couldn't hear anything, and my eyesight wasn't brilliant. Apparently, my internal organs and senses were, to put it into medical terms, utterly fucked.

I tapped my mouth with my fingers, and then my ears.

"Don't move," she shouted.

I heard that.

The thing that everyone thinks about me turning into smoke and then re-forming is that I can heal myself in the re-form. That's simply not true. The state of me when I turn to smoke has to be the state I re-form in. I've tried to use the time to heal myself before, and the first time I did, it hurt so badly, I couldn't walk for two days. I've tried a few times since, but it just doesn't work. I'd rather just go to the embers and heal there. I can use the smoke to escape damage—although it still hurts—but not fix damage.

Unfortunately, I wasn't entirely sure I could even willingly open the embers in my current condition. I just had to let my body catch up with itself.

"Ouch," I said after a few seconds, when three paramedics arrived and started talking to me.

"I'm good," I told them, my speech apparently now okay.

"You sure?" Emily asked.

"I can talk, hear, and I don't feel like my entire body is about to combust," I told her. I took her hand and she helped me to sit up.

"What happened up there?" Emily asked.

My head still felt a little fuzzy from the explosion. "Something went boom, and I was almost turned to paste."

"Cory killed his dad," Emily said.

"Tried to kill Rose, too," I said, my blast-addled brain starting to fire. "Spoke to the Croupier, and he activated an explosive in Cory's phone. Rose okay?"

"She got out," Emily said. "Pretty much everyone did. The emergency services found a dead body in a game room."

"That one's mine," I said. "What happened to the woman Nadia was fighting?"

"She's in custody," Emily said.

"Pat her down for explosives, too," I said. "Just in case."

"I'll go let the RCU know," she told me. "They arrived about ten seconds before the house went boom."

"Good for them," I said giving Emily a thumbs-up as she ran off to talk to the RCU. I remained seated on the ground. I wasn't a hundred percent certain that I could stand up and not immediately fall over.

"Did you do this?" someone asked me, their voice full of anger and hurt.

I sat up as Rachel Kimble stared down at me, radiating pain. "No," I told her. "I'm sorry about your husband and son. I tried to stop Cory, but a man he worked for, calls himself the Croupier, he detonated an explosive."

"He was not a good man," Rachel said. "He was dangerous and scary, and my husband and I often argued over how best to deal with him. The police had been to see us several times, and Cory had spent time in Greater Sudbury in recent weeks with new friends."

"Did he tell you the names of any of them?"

Rachel thought for a second. "Neil. He mentioned a Neil. A woman, too . . . I don't remember."

"Mary?" I asked.

Rachel nodded. "Yes, are they involved in this?"

I pushed myself to my feet. It hurt, and I was still a little singed, but I managed it without making a noise like a dying hippo, so I took that as a win.

"Yes," I told her. "They tried to murder a bunch of police officers this morning. They're dead now."

Rachel's entire body crumpled to the ground, crying and screaming. I crouched beside her as she fought to breathe in between the ragged sobs that left her.

"This isn't on you," I told her. "You didn't know. Whatever Cory was, whatever kind of boy he was, he had no chance once these people got their hooks into him. They will be found and punished for their transgressions."

"You'll kill them?" she asked me, pleading. "I can pay you."

"I don't do murder for hire, Mrs. Kimble," I told her firmly.

"Then what use are you?" she snarled at me, stumbling to her feet and moving away.

I took a step after her but spotted the third person in the Croupier's team. He was watching the chaos unfold as he stood by the annex.

He spotted me, turned, and ran, but a gunshot erupted throughout the night air, and a half dozen RCU agents rushed over to the area, guns drawn, waiting for danger.

"It's been dealt with," Ezekiel said as he stepped out of the shadows, holding up his hands. Nadia walked several feet behind him, spotted me, turned, and strolled over as the commotion continued in her wake.

"Hey," she said, sounding incredibly cheerful. "Did I miss the excitement?"

"Mansion blew up," I said. "I was in it at the time."

"You look in one piece," she said, searching the ground as if she might spot a limb.

"I'm good," I said. "Looks like you caught the last of Croupier's people."

"We were watching him from the edge of the property," she said. "Wanted to know what he was going to do."

"Are you okay?" I asked Ezekiel.

"No," he said softly, and walked over to be with his family.

I sat back down on the ground.

"*You* okay?" Nadia asked me, slightly concerned.

"Still feeling the effects of being in the blast radius," I told her. "Body aches still. Probably will for a few hours at least."

Nadia sat beside me. "It's been quite the eventful few days."

"It has," I agreed. "I have to go to the rift."

"I know," she said. "They say that an elephant never forgets, but that's nonsense; it's an elephant. You know who never forgets? Crime bosses. Not ever."

"You have experience of crime bosses?" I asked. "Beyond Mason Barnes?"

"He wasn't a crime boss," Nadia said with a chuckle. "He was a rich boy *playing* at crime boss. My mom, she was Mexican. Born and raised in Tijuana. In the 1980s, she worked for the government in an administration role, something she was doing when she met my father. My father was Colombian. He was also a sicario for a Mexican cartel. I don't remember which one. It doesn't much matter, I don't think. Anyway, they fell in love and decided to elope."

"Your hitman father and government-worker mother ran away together?" I asked.

Nadia nodded. "Because my mother was pregnant with me. Now, it turns out that Mexican cartel leaders don't much like it when you run away from your duties, especially when you do it with a million dollars of money that doesn't belong to you. I was ten when we reached Argentina. We moved a lot, and after so long, I guess my parents just decided that it was safe to stay in one place. I came home from school at the age of fourteen to find my father's head nailed to a wall, and my mother's body which had been similarly dealt with, but they nailed her to a pool table instead. She was in a crucifix pose. She'd been alive when it had happened. Apparently, my father had been made to watch."

There was an anger in Nadia I hadn't heard before, and I didn't want to stop her from whatever reason she was divulging this information to me.

"My father had a friend in Argentina who took me in," Nadia continued. "His name was Anton, and he and his . . . friend, Nestor, raised me. They were also assassins for hire. So, it was an unusual schooling.

"When I was twenty-four years old, I made my way back to Mexico. I hunted down and killed every single person who had helped kill my family. I saved the cartel boss for later. I've genuinely forgotten his name. He pleaded with me. Begged me to let him live, to take his family instead. An eye for an eye. So, I took his eyes. He died hard."

Nadia sat in silence for a few seconds as she breathed slowly in and out.

"You okay?" I asked eventually.

"Yes," Nadia said. "I died eight years later. One of the family members I'd let live killed me in revenge. On a beach in Argentina. I vowed to stop repeating the cycle of vengeance that had been such a part of my life. This Croupier is a just another crime boss; he doesn't forget and he doesn't forgive. And once he's dead, that doesn't mean it's the end of it."

"You're saying that I should just let it go?" I asked.

"No, I'm saying that when you confront him, you need to ensure he doesn't have anyone who can come after you in ten years' time," Nadia said.

"You're worried I'm going to leave one of his people around to come after me?" I asked.

Nadia nodded. "They're a cult. He's working with or for a cult; this whole Blessed nonsense is proof of that. I've been thinking about it. The Croupier is just one piece in a bigger puzzle. Who is he working for? And why? He set up a deal for Callie Mitchell, but why? Beyond money, I mean. And this seems like money was never his main aim."

"I agree," I told her. "I think whatever this Blessed are, they're tangled up in Croupier and Callie, and others. You heard Zeke; there's a Congressman involved, too. We've started something we need to finish. Or I do."

"You know I'm there the whole way," Nadia said. "Just not in the rift."

I knew.

Nadia helped me to my feet as Zeke and Emily walked over.

"The dead guy I shot had a receiver on him," Zeke said. "He set off the explosives that way. Seems like the Croupier had planned for Cory to use those explosives on me, should I ever become an issue."

"You have classy associates," I told him.

Zeke looked embarrassed. "I've spoken to the RCU," he said. "I explained your plan to send me to Gabriel. One of them called him; we had a chat. The RCU are going to take me to Gabriel's church."

"Good," I said. "I'm glad you're taking responsibility."

"Emily and Nadia, I have a favour," I said, removing my medallion and passing it to Nadia. "Take this to London; give it to Ji-hyun. She'll know what to do with it. Zeke, before you get hauled off, arrange a private flight for these two."

"That I can do," Zeke said.

"The place you were taken," I said to Zeke. "The fort in the rift. Where is it?"

"I don't know," Zeke told me. "There's a big city close by, although I don't know what's it's called. I thought about searching for it when I returned to the rift a decade ago, but I wasn't sure that was a stone I wanted to overturn. There was a smell, though, a sweet smell, flowery. It's a moss that grows close to the River of Ghosts, called earthsang moss."

"I know of it," I said, remembering the bright green substance.

"Are you going to tell us what Ji-hyun is going to do with the medallion?" Emily asked.

"I think I prefer the secret more," Nadia said. "It's all clandestine and exciting."

I laughed. "It's a focal point for me to get back from the embers. Like an automatic homing beacon. Wherever that is, I can find it."

"That's so much less exciting than what I had in my head," Nadia said.

"Sorry," I said. "I'm going to the rift. We need intel on the Croupier and the Blessed, I have some friends who might be able to shed light on it. Hopefully, I won't be long."

"Take care of yourself," Emily said, giving me a hug.

Nadia fist-bumped me.

"You might need these," Zeke said, passing me a dozen rift coins, bright and each one about fifty millimetres in diameter.

"Thank you," I said. "I'm sorry about your son. Your grandson, too."

"Me too," Zeke said. "Thank you for making sure it wasn't worse. I'm sorry it took me so long to actually make a stand. I'm sorry . . . I'm just sorry, Lucas. One day I'll be able to repay you for everything you've done for me and my family."

I shook his hand and opened my embers.

CHAPTER SEVENTEEN

The embers are a bit of a weird place. Apart from the fact that every riftborn's is different and that they're tailored exclusively to them, you also have to contend with the fact that everything is covered in a rolling mist. Even so, seeing the shape of Maria—one of my two eidolons who can shapeshift to whatever animal form they wish—walk toward me as a large deer while a small sparrow—presumably my other eidolon, Casimir—perched on her head was one that raised a smile.

The childhood village that my embers resembled was full of people I could only vaguely remember. I couldn't have even told you the blacksmith's name, but there he was, working at the forge without stopping. The forge didn't produce any heat, just more mist.

I felt like the outline of the shadow inside the forge was down to the fact that somewhere in the dark recesses of my memory, the blacksmith that outline portrayed was *meant* to be there. It didn't matter his name, or what he looked like, just that he was where he was meant to be.

The embers are an exceptionally weird place.

"How are you both?" I asked with genuine fondness. They might disagree with me . . . often, sometimes at length, and they might not always be useful, but they are the closest things I have to constant companions.

"Fine," Maria said. "I assume you're here as a stopgap."

It had taken a long time to get used to seeing animals talk. A *really* long time. It was still a little weird, truth be told.

"I need to get to the rift," I said.

Despite the fact that my embers don't join with anyone else's, eidolons were able to communicate with others of their kind.

"Question for you both," I said. "Either of you heard of the Croupier?"

Casimir fluttered over to the wooden fence beside me and transformed into a hawk. "No," he said. "Should we?"

"I don't really know," I admitted. "There's man who calls himself the Croupier who I'm pretty sure has ties to the rift. I'm going to Inaxia to see if I can get answers."

"It's a weird name; maybe someone knows something," Maria agreed.

"He also has connections to a group calling themselves the Blessed," I said.

Maria and Casimir stared at me.

"You've heard of them?"

"How long has it been since you were last in Inaxia?" Maria asked.

"A few years," I guessed. "Why?"

"We've heard whisperings," Maria said. "There's chatter about something to do with that word. I don't know more than that. And that they don't like riftborn."

"I think they're something to do with practitioners," I said.

"That could be bad news," Casimir said. "They've been gaining power in Inaxia over the last few years. There are more and more constructs in the city doing the cleaning, the maintenance work. That kind of thing."

"Is that bad?" I asked.

"Depends on who you talk to," Maria said.

I turned to look at Casimir, who was staring at me as if I may catch fire. "What?" I asked.

"Where's the medallion?" he asked me.

"You know, I don't have to tell you everything," I told him.

"Lucas," Maria said, managing to find a tone that was just the right side of someone's parent about to chastise a child.

"I left it with Emily and Nadia," I told them.

The following few minutes were mostly me being yelled at. By a hawk and a deer. I swear, Snow White never had to put up with this shit.

"You two done?" I asked.

"Maybe," Casimir said.

"Right, when I leave here, I'm going to need to go to a safe zone," I said. "So, Emily and Nadia will take the medallion to London, Ji-hyun will put it in a hotel or a house or something, and I can arrive there when I need to."

"Unless someone grabs it first and you go back into a firestorm," Casimir said.

"Sure," I said. "And if that's the case, I guess I'll have to take care of it then. But I trust Ji-hyun." I couldn't track any other medallions in such a way, although I wished I'd been able to, because I would have found the rest of the Raven Guild medallions in about a week instead of half of them still being missing after a decade.

"What happens if the promise crystal breaks?" Casimir asked.

An old teacher of mine, Neb, had given me the crystal a few months earlier. If it broke, it meant that Neb had called me to her, and I would be immediately transported into the rift. I wasn't entirely sure how it would work if I wasn't with the medallion at the time.

"I'll send word to Neb that I'm in Inaxia," I said, thinking on my feet because, truth be told, I hadn't considered it.

"No one there will know that you're a Raven," Maria said. "You'll have nothing identifying you."

"Good," I said, looking between Casimir and Maria. "Are you both satisfied now?"

"We are," Casimir said. "For the record, it still sounds stupid."

"And for the record, I didn't ask," I told him. "How far to the Inaxia exit?"

"About an hour away," Casimir said, taking off and flying along the misty streets.

"I think I upset him," I said to Maria.

"Emotions and eidolons are odd things," she told me. "He will get over it. Neither of us wish you to put yourself in harm's way, Lucas. Unfortunately, that is one of the things you excel at."

I couldn't deny that.

"Will one of us be accompanying you?" Maria asked.

"I'd like that," I told her. "Also, I don't want to walk through a tear into Inaxia itself. I'd rather not spend hours being interrogated by the guards, diplomats, and administrative people in the city. One of the landing ports against the River Alexander would be useful." When you first arrived in the rift, you usually either ended up in one of three places: a designated landing area manned by guards from Inaxia, in the city of Inaxia, or at a landing area close to another city. The latter may or may not be some distance from the city you want to actually go to. Neb's landing area is a few miles from her settlement of Nightvale far to the north-west of Inaxia.

Eidolons, apart from tending to the embers, can cross over into either the rift or Earth. In the rift, they were unable to change shape but also near-on impervious to harm.

Casimir returned after a few minutes' walk. Possibly. Time was weird in the embers. It went from light to dark, with very little in between, and

I was hurt, which meant that time moved quicker in the embers than it did on Earth or in the rift. I didn't want to be out in the embers during the night-time, as the shadowy figures who were meant to be memories became something else.

At night, the shadows hunted me. They wanted the power that was contained inside of me, and if they caught me out in the open, they might well kill me. At night, you found a building to hide in, and you didn't use your power.

The shadows couldn't pass into a closed building at night-time, just mill around outside them, but if I didn't use my power, they just sniffed around the trail I'd taken, unable to figure out where I actually ended up.

No one seemed to know why they hunted riftborn at night, or even what the shadows really were. The embers held a lot of secrets, even from the riftborn, and the eidolons were either unable or unwilling to divulge anything they knew about them.

"There a problem?" I asked him.

Casimir landed on my shoulder and shook his head. "I want to come with you to Inaxia."

"Sure," I said. "Any reason why?"

"Well, as much as I've made my views on that place known," he said.

"Regularly," Maria muttered.

"You're not a fan," I said, before the pair could continue to verbally spar.

"No, I am not," Casimir said. "But I think you need someone to help you."

"You think you can stay as a bird?" I asked him.

"Any preference?" he asked.

"Your choice," I told him, and he flew away again.

"He's going to pick something big," Maria said.

"So long as it isn't a pterodactyl, I think we'll be okay," I told her. I thought about whether or not an eidolon could actually turn into a dinosaur. I'd never considered it before.

"No," Maria said. "We can't turn into dinosaurs."

I smiled. "Didn't know you could read minds."

"I can't," she admitted. "I've just met you before."

"It would be pretty cool to ride a stegosaurus into Inaxia," I said.

"We could do extinct animals. Maybe a dire wolf, or sabre-tooth tiger, but dinosaurs are too big," Maria said. "We have rules just as much as you do."

"Were the embers around during the time of the dinosaurs?" I wondered more to myself than anyone else. "Was the rift?"

Maria made a shrugging movement, which is a weird thing to see in a deer. "I only came into existence when you first used the embers. We don't hang around, waiting for a riftborn to give us something to do."

"I wonder if I can get some new eidolons," I said. "Ones that don't talk back."

Maria the deer laughed. "Good luck with that."

I smiled, wishing the sky was something more than the mass of grey punctured with blue and yellow. Just once I'd have liked to have seen a clear blue sky. If the darkness was about to descend on my embers, the sky would have been marked with bright red instead of blue and yellow. I was safe, for now.

I stopped walking when I saw Casimir, now a harpy eagle, perched on a fence post beside a large villa. The embers took pieces from my birth home in the area of northern Britain that I'd been born in, and mixed them with the city of Saldae, which was closer to what I actually considered my home.

"You ready?" Casimir asked me.

"I know I said your choice, but would you consider not being something that has the wingspan the size of a fully grown adult?" I asked Casimir. "An eagle is fine, but you're not exactly inconspicuous."

Casimir let out a long, protracted sigh and turned into the same hawk he'd been when I'd arrived. "Better?" he asked.

"Thank you," I said with a slight nod. "You okay with that form?"

Casimir ruffled his feathers, stretched his wings, and hopped from foot to foot. "Yes," he said eventually.

"Take care of yourself, Maria," I told her. "Be back soon."

"Bring the stupid twat back in one piece," Maria said.

"I will," Casimir and I said in unison as Maria walked away laughing.

Casimir landed on my shoulder. "You ready for this?" he asked.

"Let's get it done," I said, and stepped through the threshold of the villa.

Purple and blue crackled all around us as we walked toward the rift tear inside the villa. I placed my hand against the metre-long tear in the middle of a large room, and it immediately tripled in size, growing larger every second.

"You ready?" I asked Casimir.

"I hate this bit," he said as the tear flooded over us.

A second later and I was stood on the banks of a river next to half a dozen soldiers—all wearing red-and-black leather armour that glinted in the sunlight. Of the six, four wore helmets that looked a little ancient Greek in style, with red plumage on top, and two men were without helmets at all. Both of the men had a red sash across their lapel with small golden buttons attached to them. One had three buttons and the other only one, denoting their ranks. Their four helmet-wearing friends had no colour on their armour at all; they were new recruits. All of them had olive skin and, apart from the man with one button on his lapel, short, dark beards.

The four soldiers levelled spears at me but otherwise didn't move.

"You will have to excuse the rudeness," said the man with one button on his lapel. He was clean-shaven, with a scar that ran from his forehead down across his nose and stopped on his cheek.

The second man stood back and watched, letting his captain take control.

I looked around at the landing area. There was a boat waiting on the river that could probably have taken a dozen people at once. The boat master was stood on deck, watching me and the soldiers with a mixture of interest.

"Isn't the port meant to have a small garrison here?" I asked. "Last time I arrived, there were a dozen soldiers, just over there." I pointed across the open field to a small fort. The grass was a mixture of green and orange, and looked like flowers in bloom. The rift messed around with a person's perceptions of what things should look like.

"We are waiting for newcomers," the captain said.

"And you do that on the dock, pointing spears at people who arrive?" I asked, stepping off the tear stone—a six-metre-diameter black stone with purple-and-blue writing all over it that glowed whenever it was activated. Tear stones were only used by riftborn, as we were the only ones to be able to use embers to arrive in the rift. That left me with several questions for the soldiers stood before me.

"We have had trouble here recently," the captain told me.

"Trouble?" I asked. "What kinds of trouble?"

"You are riftborn, yes?" the man with the three buttons on his lapel asked.

"I am," I told him. "And you are?"

"Major Hephaestion," he told me.

Military ranks in the rift were a fluid thing; for a long time, they'd been based on Greek and then Roman military but had started to use more modern terms since the start of the nineteenth century on Earth. They'd taken a while to catch on, and some refused to give up their armour or weapons that they'd been using since birth, but no one seemed to care much.

"Macedonian?" I asked.

Major Hephaestion nodded.

Language in the rift was a little different to back on Earth. Whatever language a person spoke, I could understand it. New languages took a few seconds, but it was the same for everyone. They spoke whatever language they wanted, and everyone else understood. Once I left the rift, I still understood the language. I was fluent in several dozen at the moment and never had to give it a second thought about whether or not I understood a person. The rift gave and took from people, sometimes in equal measure, but the fact that everyone understood one another was one of the benefits of being there.

"So, you're here to ensure I'm not a . . . problem," I said.

"The garrison was attacked," Major Hephaestion told me. "We are still investigating as to why, or by whom, but it's the fifth attack on Inaxia personnel in the last few months."

"Anyone hurt?" I asked.

"Sixteen dead," Major Hephaestion told me. "Mostly revenants."

If you died in the rift, you died. Didn't matter what you were; this was your last life. Game over.

I glanced between the soldiers. A lot of revenants settled to live in their nonhuman form in Inaxia. It was, after all, who they were. The military expected you to stay in human form until necessary. But no matter what form they took, killing sixteen highly trained soldiers was not an easy task for your average bandit or warlord.

"You think I'm part of the attack?" I asked Major Hephaestion.

"We have to check all newcomers," he told me.

"And you're checking boats, too," Casimir said.

"An eidolon," Major Hephaestion said with a slight bow of his head. Eidolons were a common sight in the rift, as most riftborn brought one with them for company more than anything, and they were considered good luck by a lot of people. And revered by more than a few. More so than the riftborn ever were.

"Major," Casimir said. "I wonder if you could stop beating around the bush and actually tell us why you're stopping us from boarding that boat."

"We believe that the river is being used to transport undesirables into the city," Major Hephaestion.

"So, you're guarding this particular part of the riverbank?" I asked.

Major Hephaestion nodded.

I looked beyond him to the boat master, who was no longer bothering to even try and look busy.

"You think this boat has transported undesirables?" I asked.

"Not specifically," Major Hephaestion said.

The vagueness was beginning to annoy me.

"Right, well, I'm going to get on that boat and I'm going to Inaxia," I told them. "If this is an issue, you might want to tell me now."

"No issue at all," Major Hephaestion lied. He was a terrible liar.

Something about the whole situation told me that I would be close to pushing my luck should I decide to try and glean more out of the Major, so I thanked him and his men and walked over to the dock.

"Boat master," I said.

"Philip," he said, in a nondescript accent.

"Philip," I repeated. "Pleasure to meet you. You want to take me to Inaxia."

"If it'll get me away from those idiots, yes," Philip said.

I sat down at the bow of the boat, under a large covering that kept me in the shade as Philip pushed us away from the deck with a giant oar before walking to the stern of the boat and activating the motor, which sent us moving down the river at a reasonable pace.

The boat was well made and had an upper deck, and a cabin below. The cabin had a sign on it saying NO PASSENGERS, and in the rift it's always a good idea to obey signs like that. You never know who . . . or what you'll be angering by not.

The motor, like anything mechanical or motorised in the rift, would have been powered by rift energy itself. The energy itself floods down from the north, where there are huge tears that appear constantly, pumping out energy that eventually forms its own rivers. The rift energy is cultivated, purified by people who know what they're doing, and sold to people like the boat master. It's also used to light specially designed lamps and run the train that moves around the outer edge of the city. It connects everything.

A construct—a bronze, insect-like machine about the side of my head—left the cabin and began to tend to the sail as three more constructs, all identical in size and features, did work around the boat.

"What was that about?"

"They suspect me of being in league with a group of terrorists," he said.

"Terrorists?" I asked, wanting to know more but not wanting to divulge much about why I was there.

"I'm a practitioner," he said, which explained the constructs. You could buy or hire constructs from practitioners, but you ran the risk of A, paying a huge sum, and B, being screwed over by something that may or may not kill you should the practitioner wish it to.

"These terrorists have a name?" I asked. "I'd rather not run into anyone that might cause issues."

"The Blessed," Philip said as the river gradually opened out to be several miles wide. There were a dozen other ships using the river, and occasionally Philip would ring a bell on the stern of the boat and wave at someone.

"They been around long?" I asked him.

"I first heard of them about a hundred years ago, I'd guess," Philip said. "But it was only rumours and whispers of an attack in the city. About a decade ago, their name started to be wider known, crimes would be attributed to them, but it was all rumours."

"And recently?" I asked.

"To my mind, the Blessed were either a nuisance or made up to ensure there was always a good excuse for something awful happening. But that was it. They've graduated to full-on insanity in the last four or five years. Attacking Inaxia garrisons, patrols, even going after people who work for one of the Primes. Bad people."

The Primes were the seven leaders of Inaxia. They were joined by three supposedly neutral Ancients to ensure that arguments were settled without issue. All seven of the Primes had cities of their own in the rift, too, and if you worked for one of them, you had to declare your allegiance by wearing their badge somewhere on your clothing so that it was visible by everyone.

"How long until we reach Inaxia?" I asked.

"A few hours," he said.

"Wake me when we get there," I told him. "I want to use the Locke."

Philip stared at me for a second as if he hadn't expected me to go to sleep, leaving him alone, but I had nothing to fear. Casimir could tear the constructs to pieces, and it's bad form for a boat master to murder their fares. I moved a few of the half dozen pillows that were around me, lay down, and tried to get some rest. It sounded like I was going to need it.

CHAPTER EIGHTEEN

I dreamt of monsters. Of fire and brimstone. Of the kinds of things that some would consider omens, and if I believed in such things—which I don't—I might have been concerned. Even so, I woke up feeling more tired than when I'd gone to sleep.

"I see the city," Casimir said from his perch on a wooden beam close to where I lay.

"How long was I out?" I asked him.

"An hour," he said. "You were moving a lot. Bad dreams?"

"Long day," I said. "Lots of bad things happened in a fairly short period of time."

"It might not help, but I'm pretty sure bad things are going to keep happening."

"You're right," I told him. "That didn't help at all."

Inaxia loomed in the distance. Like most cities in the rift, the city's internal structure was kept in five rings. Guards and the military were in the outer one, merchants next along, living accommodations in the third ring, with schools, libraries, and academia in the second ring, and the power structure in the middle. A lot of farms sat outside of the north and east of the city, and garrisons of varying sizes were placed in strategic places all around the outside.

Inaxia had a hundred-foot-high stone wall, with half a dozen entrances around the wall and several ports to the southeast. We were taking the canal, which meant going into the city itself and having to wait a while for the water to lift us to the port above. The lock took longer to get into the city, but it was a quicker way to actually get further into the city without having to traverse the outer rings.

While, in theory, each ring of the city stayed in its own lane, in practice several of them merged together. Merchants did work in the military ring, and there were people from the academies working all over the place. Apart from those in power, the only other professions that allowed anyone free rein to travel between the rings were the Investigators and medical personnel. Investigators were essentially the police, and they worked outside of the hierarchy of the rest of the city. They went where they were needed, and that meant that they knew a lot of the places that most people didn't frequent. I was in need of one of those people. I just hoped that having not seen her for a long time, she was still around.

The centre of Inaxia was an enormous hill surrounded by a wall that was a few hundred feet higher than the outer walls. On top of the hill was a large complex where the Primes lived. Each Prime had their own lodge and area for their people to live and work. It was called the shield, even though it was no longer circular in shape and hadn't been for hundreds of years.

There were seven spokes coming out of the central ring, each one running until it reached the outer wall. Trains ran around the outer wall, stopping at stations where the spokes and wall met. The whole thing ran on the same substance that powered Philip's ship—rift energy. The trains were a big part of what made Inaxia run. Trains for people, trains for goods. Lifts that took goods up to the high walls. It had long since become a well-oiled machine, although occasionally a Prime overstepped their power and needed to be shown exactly where they should be standing.

When I was an active member of a Guild that had more members than just me, I used to get regular updates about each Prime and how dickish they were being. The consensus was *very* and *regularly*. I doubted that had changed, although I couldn't have said if any of them had been replaced in the years since I last paid any attention.

Most of the Primes in Inaxia followed the same political path. It was the middle of the road. Occasionally, one would want to change something for the betterment of everyone, but they were few and far between. Those interested only in the betterment of themselves were much more common.

Money came in; people lived their lives and, for the most part, were happy. Inaxia actually paid every inhabitant an extra month's wages once a year as a bonus just to make sure that no one got ideas about revolutions or trying to change things. Turns out that a lot of people are more interested in being able to live without money troubles than they are about long-term political change.

"You're thinking about Inaxia," Casimir said.

I nodded. "Been while since I was here last. I'm assuming nothing has changed. Ever. Nothing ever does. Or at least not for a long time. It sounds like these Blessed are trying to disturb the equilibrium."

"You might be a king or queen on Earth, but here you're just the sum of what you're good at," Philip said as one of the constructs climbed down from the sail, beginning to collapse it as whatever passed for an engine on the ship started up again. I hadn't even noticed it had stopped.

"How many kings and queens actually make it here?" I asked.

"Not many," Philip said. "That's what happens when you're in the vast minority. Most the people who come here are commoners. Some are criminals. Some are soldiers. They find their new lot in life quickly. It's surprising how many people who lived hard lives on Earth want to do nothing but farm or fish when they arrive here."

"Practitioners don't have that luxury," I said.

"No, we don't," Philip agreed. "We have to shop around and find out what we're actually good at."

"One of the Primes still a practitioner?" I asked.

Philip nodded.

"And has he said anything about these attacks?" Casimir asked.

"He condemns them in the strongest possible terms," Philip told me. "There was a large rally out to the west a few months back. Lots of people turned up to hear him say the exact right things to the exact right people."

"You think he's lying?" I asked.

"Always," Philip said. "Some politicians want to help people. They take their jobs seriously; they want to try and make everything better for everyone. Some politicians take their job to help themselves and their friends become richer or more powerful. Those people should be drowned the second they show any interest in politics. It's the only way to send a message to future narcissistic, incompetent assholes."

"Little harsh," Casimir said.

"I toned it down a bit," Philip said.

I looked back over at the city. It was considerably closer now, and the ship traffic had increased exponentially in the last few minutes. Most ships were heading north, toward the more prosperous fishing routes, as it was a quicker way to get out into the ocean. I'd been on a fishing boat in the rift once and had never felt so ill in my life.

There were two internal canal locks beside the one we were going to enter. The middle was for ships exiting the city, and the one on the right was for Prime members and their people only. Also Investigators, which had always been a source of much irritation on the part of several Primes, who believed that they alone should be able to use it.

Thankfully, there wasn't a line to use the entry lock, which was big enough to be able to take up to half a dozen boats at a time or one large ship.

"You're nervous," Casimir said. "You think some old grudges will remain?"

I shrugged. "It's a possibility."

The ship entered, and the fifty-foot-high steel doors closed shut behind us, bathing us in darkness before the dim orange lights flickered all around the huge lock. There was a rumble of something coming, like distant thunder, and the water level began to rise.

We'd gone twenty feet in under a minute when I saw the guards stood atop the lock, looking down at us. Presumably wondering what we were doing. Philip wasn't flying the merchants' flag—a set of three gold, silver, and bronze rings, all interlocking—and he wasn't part of the military. Which left private hire, presumably either someone visiting from another city along the river, or someone from Earth.

I remained casual, trying not to do anything which might make the guards twitchy. More than one carried a crossbow, and they'd all be capable of using them.

"Why is it that they're never happy to see anyone coming through this way?" Casimir asked.

"Guards are always the same," Philip said. "Little bit of power and they think they're better than they are."

On Earth, the guards would be called beat cops. And in my experience, they were mostly good at their jobs and wanted to make the city safe, but there were always a few who tried to ingratiate themselves with the Primes, or others who would help them get richer or more powerful. Earth or the rift, some people are still assholes.

The rumbling sound slowly lessened as the water continued to rise, going past a dozen enormous, grated pipes. They were used to drain the water and either pump it back out into the river outside or push it up to the rest of the river above that ran through the city. I'd often wondered if they'd be a viable way to enter the city without being caught, but you'd have to move fast, and if you got caught inside when the water was flowing through, you'd be in serious trouble. The idea of turning into smoke inside a few hundred tonnes of water was not a happy one.

The boat lurched forward, and Philip tossed a line to one of the workers, a huge woman with arms the size of my head. She pulled the rope
toward her, hand over hand, like it was nothing.

The boat bumped against the side of the dock, and I realised for the
first time that the constructs had all gone from the deck.

"Constructs have to be safely stowed away," Philip said.

"That's new to me," I told him.

"I'm not sure that it's an official law," Philip said. "Just . . . a good idea."

I wondered just how many more *good ideas* were in place with regards
to practitioners, and whether the Blessed were making people think that
all practitioners were in league with a terrorist organisation rather than
the actuality that the majority just wanted to live their lives.

"Philip," a tall, thin man with dark skin and a big beard said in a French
accent.

"Investigator Omar," Philip said warmly.

"Dropping off or picking up?" Omar asked.

"Dropping off," Philip said. "Had some trouble with your soldiers."

"Not mine," Investigator Omar said. "Can I ask your name, sir?"

"Lucas Rurik," I told him.

"And your reason for coming to Inaxia?" Investigator Omar continued, his relaxed gaze never wavering from my face.

"I'm here to see a friend of mine. Investigator Torres." I saw the recognition on Omar's face before he nodded.

"She will be at the Investigator main plaza," Investigator Omar said.
"Do you know where that is?"

"About halfway along the city," I said. "I've been here before."

"And your pet?"

"My *name* is Casimir," he said, fluffing himself up. "I am not a pet."

"Your eidolon," Investigator Omar said. "I do apologise. You are
riftborn?"

"I am," I said, noticing a slight tension in his voice. "Is that an issue?"

"Not at all," Omar said, his broad smile returning. "Please do enjoy
your stay."

The barrier stopping further movement of the boat slowly dropped,
and Philip's boat moved down the slight incline until it was through the
lock and we were out in the city.

Inaxia proper always takes me a few moments to adjust to. The sights
of the colourful houses, walls, and bridges, the smells of cooking somewhere in the distance, the sounds of a throng of people. It's a little bit

like if you'd never been to a massive city before, and one day you just found yourself in the middle of it. It's another reason why I don't like using the city access through the embers; it's just too much information for my brain to process.

There's this notion that ancient Rome and Greece were minimalist, all clean white stone and marble, but it couldn't be further from the truth. Rome was awash with colour. It adorned building walls, both inside and out, even the statues were painted, and the same was true in Inaxia. Murals covered the walls of buildings facing the river, and some enterprising— and daredevil—people even managed to paint the sides of the bridges that sat over the river.

The river in Inaxia was wide enough for four or five ships to move along it side-by-side. It narrowed out at the far end of the city, but until then, there was plenty of room for the large numbers of ships that were moving between docking stations, loading and offloading cargo.

The constructs had returned to the deck and were busy moving around it, checking for problems and keeping everything running that a crew would.

I dropped a gold coin into Philip's hand and wished him good luck. "Are you going to be okay with those soldiers out there hassling you?"

Philip let out a long sigh. "They're going to be a problem."

I took a shot at something. "You ever heard of a man called the Croupier?"

Philip shook his head. "Nope, should I?"

"He's helping the Blessed," I said. "But doing it from Earth. Or, at least, that's how it looks. There's a connection between them; they're causing trouble, hurting people. I was hoping to find out who he is and what is actually going on."

"Lots of people were starting to be suspicious of practitioners," Philip said. "These attacks aren't helping things, and we've all seen how it goes when people are given a scapegoat to be afraid of."

"Has there been a crackdown?" I asked.

"I get asked what I'm up to more," Philip said. "Every time I come to the city, an Investigator will ask me how things are going. I want to believe that's just because they're as concerned about everything as I am, but I'm not so sure."

"You think they're keeping an eye on you in case you harbour any extremist views?" I said.

Philip nodded.

"How very Orwellian," Casimir said.

I watched as several guards questioned people near the mouth of an alleyway between two buildings. Looks like there were some divisions within the city that would need addressing before it reached a tipping point.

Philip moved away to keep the boat steady as we passed several docks with larger ships moored. Despite the traffic, the water was crystal clear, and dozens of fish swam freely. Fishing from vessels was illegal in the city, although there were places further into the city where you could fish from the bank.

It was a slow journey through Inaxia, and it gave me some time to acclimatise myself to being back. Eventually, we moored up, Philip getting out to tie the boat to the long wooden dock, which already contained three identical vessels.

I stepped off the boat and looked back at Philip. "Thank you," I told him.

"Be careful, Lucas," Philip said, removing the line and pushing the boat away from the deck with his foot.

I nodded and set off along the dock, ignoring the Investigators and guards who watched me like the hawk who was currently sat on my shoulder.

"I don't think everyone is going to be as friendly as Philip," Casimir whispered.

I ignored the suspicious stares as I left the docking area and walked around to the front of the large building that overlooked the river next to the dock. The white stone building had been painted dark grey, matching the colour of the guards' uniform.

There were two dozen steps up to the columns that made up the front of the Investigators' plaza, and more than a few Investigators and guards were milling around outside. Some stopped what they were doing and watched me as I ascended the stairs.

The building itself was four storeys tall, with dozens of windows all around it. I was once told that it looked like someone had made a Roman temple, pushed the police office into it, and sort of merged them together, and since then I couldn't see it any other way. The grandiose opening leading to a huge foyer, the central lobby just beyond, the stairs encircling it always letting you look down on the polished marble, the sculptures of the Primes.

An Investigator stopped me at the top of the stairs before I could enter the building. She was a few inches taller than me, with tanned skin, long blond hair in a plait, and arms that would have put bodybuilders to shame.

"Can I help you?" she asked, her accent placing her somewhere in the southern states of America.

"I'm here to see Investigator Torres," I told her.

"And you are?" she asked, a slight edge to her tone. I wondered if my old friend had gotten into some trouble.

"Lucas Rurik," I told her.

Her eyes widened. "Lucas Rurik, you say?"

I nodded and felt my body tense; I didn't want to get into some kind of pissing contest with the local Investigators.

The Investigator slapped me on the shoulder hard enough to make me step to the side. "You know Isaac Gordon," she said.

I smiled. "He's an old friend of mine; is he here?"

The woman nodded. "Name is Rebel Dent," she said. "Wait here."

I did as she asked while Rebel disappeared further into the building.

She returned a short time later with a large man beside her. Bald with dark skin, he was a tall man and wore a set of black leather armour with blue trim. He'd also grown a beard since I'd last seen him.

"Lucas," Isaac boomed, rushing over and picking me up in a bear hug.

It was hard to stop my throat from tightening and tears coming to my eyes. "It's good to see you, old friend."

CHAPTER NINETEEN

Isaac had died several months earlier. He was a horned revenant and had been the head of the RCU for several years before someone had stabbed him with a poisoned rift blade. I'd managed to heal the poison but had been unable to save his life. He had died at home, after getting to spend his last few moments with his wife and children. It was unbelievably good to see him again.

Rebel had left Isaac and me alone, and my old friend had suggested we go for a coffee. Coffee had once been a luxury commodity in the rift, available only from Earth, and no riftborn merchant could keep up with the demand. Instead, rift farmers had started to grow their own, but it had taken time, finding the right land, growing the crop, manufacturing it, et cetera. And then about fifty years before, coffee became abundant, and coffee houses started to appear. As much as the people of Inaxia consider themselves separate from those on Earth, they sure do like similar stuff.

We stopped by a coffee shop near the riverbank and Isaac ordered two coffees. That was the only option. No latte, no shots of anything, just coffee in a cup. No milk, either. You drank it black or you didn't drink it, which was literally written word for word on the sign out front.

Isaac passed me my bright green cup and I inhaled the smell of freshly brewed rift coffee.

"The cups are edible," Isaac said.

"What are they made from?" I asked him.

Isaac shrugged. "Some plant or other. Taste like salted caramel."

I drank some of the coffee, which, despite having had no sugar put in it, was quite sweet and pleasant.

"One day, the big Earth coffee houses will pitch up shops here," Isaac said as we started to walk through the city.

"That sounds dreadful," I told him.

"If anyone ever figures out how to let humans cross through to the rift, you know someone is going to try to monetise it," Isaac told me, nodding to several people we passed by.

"You're making yourself at home," I told him.

"I miss my family," he said sadly. "Every morning, I wake up and they're not there. And I have to remember where I am, and why I'm here, and how I'm never going to see any of them ever again. And it breaks my heart."

"I'm sorry," I said.

"On the plus side, they know I'm here and I'm healthy, and I know that they're all good," Isaac said, drinking more of the coffee before snapping off a bit of mug, eating it.

"They do," I said. I'd been checking on his wife and kids since he passed away. "They're okay too. As okay as they can be, anyway."

Isaac smiled. "Glad to hear it. Now, it's good to see you, but why are you here?"

I rubbed the back of my neck. "That's some whiplash topic change," I said.

"Sorry, but let's cut to the chase. We know things weren't great on Earth when I left, and stuff has been getting strange here as well in the last few months," Isaac said as we walked through a quiet park, found a wooden bench overlooking the river, and sat down. Casimir took off, flying into the trees and disappearing from view.

"The Blessed," I hazarded a guess.

"You've heard of them?" Isaac asked.

"Yeah, so I'm looking for a friend of mine," I told him. "Necia Torres. She's an Investigator. I'm hoping she can help shed some light on what's happening."

Isaac stared at me intently. "*That* Necia?"

I sighed. "Yes."

"She's in the west side," Isaac said. "Bar by the name of The Human Head."

"I've heard of it," I said, finishing my coffee and risking a bite of the cup. It really did taste like salted caramel.

"It's run by a few revenants," Isaac said. "It's also frequented by a lot of criminal types. People who want to stay off the radar of the Primes and Investigators."

"Any idea why she's there?" I asked him.

Isaac shook his head. "No one knows. She told me because . . . well, because I know you. Your name brings quite a lot of baggage with it in certain parts of this city, some good, some bad. There are people who knew you as Neb's protege. People who knew you as a Guild member. People who knew you as the last Raven. Where's the medallion?"

"Left it on Earth," I told him. "Ji-hyun has it in case I need to get to her fast."

"Did you let Neb know you're here?" Isaac asked, finishing his cup. "The promise crystal isn't anything to mess with."

"I was going to send a runner to tell her," I said. "I'd rather not have to deal with Neb's irritation that I was here without my medallion if she tries to break the crystal."

"As your friend, I'll tell you to be careful," Isaac said. "As an Investigator, I'll tell you to get it done before you do anything else, because Neb is facing her own problems."

I knew that Neb had left the city; I knew that she'd set up her own city some distance from here, and that she wanted nothing to do with the people who ran Inaxia. She'd been one of the original Primes and had moved into an Ancient's role centuries back, and then had been replaced. "What's happened?" I asked.

"You know she left the city," Isaac said. "Some people think she abandoned it for better things, but the truth as far as I can see is that some of the other Ancients felt that she was no longer capable of maintaining a neutral outlook on the Primes."

"She fell out with someone," I said, filling in the gaps.

"No one will confirm nor deny that," Isaac said. "But the rumours are that whoever she fell out with still harbours a grudge."

"Well, I feel sorry for them, then," I said, thinking Neb was well able to take care of herself against some jumped-up Prime. "Fine, there's a runner station on the way to the bar; I'll stop off and get one sorted."

"Good," Isaac said, getting to his feet. "As for the Blessed, they're a dangerous bunch of extremists, Lucas. They're being investigated by people much higher up the food chain than I am, but if I'm honest, I'd think that maybe these Blessed have friends in high places. They killed some soldiers out at one of the garrisons."

"So I was told," I said. "I met Major Hephaestion and his people."

Isaac nodded knowingly. "His great-great-great grandson was one of the victims. The time between blood doesn't matter to people like the Major. Blood is blood."

"Shit," I said. "He wants revenge."

"I can neither confirm nor deny that," Isaac said with a smile.

"Is Necia investigating them?"

"Confirm nor deny," Isaac said.

"Yeah, I get the idea," I told him, finishing my own cup and hoping I got to have another before I left. Hell, I may make regular trips there just for my morning cup.

Isaac offered me his hand, which I shook. "Be careful, Lucas."

"You said that already," I told him.

"Be doubly careful," Isaac said, looking across the park. "You have shadows."

I carefully glanced Isaac's way as I got to my feet. Three soldiers, all keeping to the tree line, trying not to stand out, which is hard to do in gleaming steel amour.

Casimir, I thought. Riftborn and eidolon can use a form of telepathy to stay in communication in the rift. *Guards, my ten o'clock.*

On it, came the reply.

I never saw Casimir leave the tree line, but a moment later, I noticed him soaring through the sky.

Prime officers, Casimir said in my mind.

Thanks, I replied. *Stay out of sight.*

"They're Prime officers," I told Isaac. "Why would Prime officers be following us?"

"How would Prime officers know you're here?" Isaac asked.

"You know an Investigator Omar?" I asked him, trying to think of the people I'd actually met since arriving in the city. "Or Philip the boat master? What about Rebel?"

"Lots of boat masters in the city," Isaac said. "Rebel has little love for the Primes, and I've never heard of Investigator Omar. There are near on a thousand Investigators in the city; I've met maybe a hundred and fifty of them."

"Shall we see how interested they are in following me?" I asked. "Unless they're following you."

Isaac's eyes narrowed. "They can always find me without having to skulk around in the shadows. Badly."

I turned around to face the Prime officers. "Guys, you really need to not wear shiny armour if you're trying to be inconspicuous."

The soldiers all tried to look like they were there for other reasons. They moved back into the tree line and out of view.

"That was a gamble," Isaac said.

"If they'd wanted a fight, we'd have already had one," I told him. "I'm heading to the bar you told me about. Hopefully, I'll get some answers there."

"Stay safe, Lucas," Isaac said.

"You too," I said, and we grasped forearms before going our separate ways.

The second the path I was on went into the trees, I took off at a run. If the soldiers were going to continue following me, I wouldn't make it easy for them. Casimir squawked loudly so I knew he was with me.

I stopped running a few minutes later when the woods ended and the path took me down a slope back toward the river. I was soon walking down twisty alleyways, avoiding any crowds of people on the main streets as they went about their lives. If those Prime guards were still able to follow me, they bloody well deserved it.

I left one alleyway, took a second away from the river, walking under one of the large spokes, the sound of the train rumbling along it high above me. I ended up several streets over from where I'd started, next to a large shop with a red and white striped awning over the front door and large window. The word RUNNERS was written in big red letters across the window; beneath, it said FOR HIRE in much smaller black lettering.

Runners did exactly what it sounded like: they ran from city to city, delivering messages, post, whatever was needed. They were a mixture of the post office, security guards, and stagecoach workers. They had offices throughout the city, and main hubs at every city gate. Messages were taken from the offices to the hubs and then sent out with the runners. It was a dangerous job, and more than a few had stories they could tell about bandits, marauders, or the wealth of dangerous creatures that lived in the rift. But it also paid exceptionally well, and the people who did it usually loved it, as they enjoyed being away from the city and seeing what the rift had to offer.

I pushed open the office door and stepped inside. There was a small waiting room. A desk sat between two walls, completely separating the entrance from the rest of the premises. A metal mesh ensured that no one could get over the desk without going through that first. I doubted it was put there to stop people who could turn into smoke, but I wasn't about to make runners angry for no reason.

A red-headed lady stood behind the counter. "Can I help?" she asked, her accent Germanic, although I couldn't be more precise than that.

"I need a message sent to Nightvale."

"What's the message?" she asked, placing a piece of paper and a pen in front of me, a blank envelope beside them.

I wrote: *Neb, it's Lucas. I'm in the rift, no medallion. Couldn't be helped, will be back with it soon.* I wanted to put as much info as I was comfortable putting but nothing about *why* I was in the rift. She would know it came from Inaxia as it would be stamped to say that.

I placed the paper in the envelope, sealing it shut, writing: *Neb; Nightvale* on the front of it, and passed it back to the lady.

"One silver coin," the lady told me.

I removed one of the gold coins from my pocket and paused. The golden coins that Zeke had given me were the exact size and shape of a poker chip. I stared at it for several seconds. The coins all had the city they were minted in written in the middle. Inaxia stared back at me as I remembered the poker chips that the Croupier had used on his victims. Red and white, blue and white, with *VI* written in the middle of them.

"Gold coin will get it there quicker," the woman said, no doubt wondering at my hesitation.

I placed the coin on the desk, pushing it under the mesh. "Quick as possible," I told her.

She wrote a receipt, passed it under the mesh, and I took it before holding up another of the gold coins. "This is from Inaxia, right?"

"It is," the woman said, starting to look suspiciously at me.

"Where would it be from if it had *VI* written on it?" I asked.

She shrugged. "No idea."

Damn it, thought I had something there.

"Only the major named cities can mint coins," she continued.

"Does *VI* mean anything to you?" I asked. "Maybe the number six?"

"Six?" she asked, pondering the question. She shook her head. "No, should it?"

"Not a clue," I told her. "Thank you for your help."

My hand touched the door handle when she called out. "Hey, just because only the major cities are meant to mint coins doesn't mean no one else does too."

I looked back at her. "Lawless coins?"

"There are Lawless towns that have been known to put their own coins out," she said. "They're rougher than normal coins, not as perfect."

"Any of them painted red and white or blue and white?" I asked, hopeful that something was there, just out of reach.

"Not that I'm aware of." She asked. "Red and white are runner colours, but I don't know anything about people putting coins in those colours."

I thanked her again and left the building, wishing I had a photo of the poker chips or, even better, one of the actual chips on me. Maybe I was grasping at straws, but I was convinced there was a link between the chips and the coins.

I continued through the city, sure that I'd lost the Prime soldiers who were following me and hoping The Human Head was where I might find answers or at least find Necia. It took me the better part of an hour to make my way to its location. The sounds of raucous laughter carried to me when I was two streets away, that laughter you only get when people involved are drunk out of their minds.

There was a smash of a glass followed by a silence that was quickly filled with animalistic hysteria. I sighed and walked around the corner, the bar directly in front of me.

The bar was in its own little courtyard, away from a row of houses and next to a small bit of greenery that stretched all the way down to the last port on the river. I wondered how many of the dozen exceptionally drunk people outside the front of the bar had just gotten off a ship.

One of them—a large man with muscular arms and a huge beer belly—lay prone on the ground while a woman of equal stature, only without so large a belly, rubbed her knuckles. People were slapping her on the back and chanting for her to drink whatever passed for alcohol in the steel tankard she'd been passed. She quaffed it back in one, slammed the drinking vessel onto a wooden table, and everyone cheered.

"What are you looking at?" a particularly drunk man shouted at me, pointing a gnarled finger in my direction.

"Nothing. I'm just here to see a friend," I said.

"Oh," the man said. He was a little over five feet tall, with dirty blond hair that fell over his ears, pale skin, and a face that needed a wash. He had a black eye and bruising around his chin. He wore black leather trousers, a tunic that could charitably be called off-white, and half a dozen rings on each hand. A knife sat in a sheath by his hip. "Here to see a *friend*."

The group behind him slowly became interested in the newcomer and what entertainment value I might bring.

I stepped around the still-prone man on the floor and headed for the door of the bar.

"I didn't say you could go in there," the unwashed man said, and his friends laughed.

There was going to be trouble, either inside the bar or outside it, and I didn't really want to fight in either place. I turned back to the funny man. "Why do I need your permission?" I asked him.

"Because this is *my* bar," he said, which was a little surprising, as most bar owners I'd met didn't drink their profits to quite the degree that his breath suggested he did.

"Okay," I said, playing along. "What do I need to do to get your permission?"

"Buy us all a round," he said to a massive cheer.

"Done," I said, and placed my hand back on the door and stepped inside before the drunken idiots could say anything else.

I pushed the door open, but the drunken self-proclaimed *bar owner* barged past me into the bar. "This man is going to buy us all a drink," he declared at the top of his voice to the dozen people inside.

"I doubt that," the woman behind the bar said.

I grinned.

Roseline Vincent was an old friend, over six feet tall and broad, with huge arms and shoulders. She looked like someone who lifted exceptionally heavy weights for fun. She had dark skin and her hair was shaved over one half of her head. The other was long enough to touch her cheek, and bright pink. She wore a white-and-green tunic, with a leather apron over it.

"He said he would," the small man said, his voice now whiney as the rest of his friends entered the bar, blocking off the exit.

"You really going to buy these idiots drinks?" Roseline asked.

"No," I said, gaining a look of disgust from the smaller man, who had pushed by me.

The man rolled his shoulders. "Then me and you are going to fight." There was a small cheer from those at the doorway.

"Don't get blood everywhere," Roseline said.

"I'll keep him in one piece," the man told her, confident in himself.

"I wasn't talking to *you*," Roseline told him grimly.

The man looked over at me and I winked. There was an uncertainty in his expression now. Several of the people who had been inside the bar, having a quiet drink or bit of food, lifted their plates and tankards and moved to the far end of the bar.

"He doesn't look that special," the man said, trying to bolster his wavering confidence.

"Depends on what you mean by *special*," Roseline said. "He's the last surviving member of the Raven Guild."

The man's expression went from concern to full-out fear.

"I warned you to behave," Roseline said. "*Repeatedly.*"

"I just . . ." the man began as the door opened and several soldiers stepped inside, removing their plumed helmets, and carrying them under their arms.

"Lucas, I know that trouble follows wherever you go, but did you seriously bring Prime officers to my establishment?" Roseline asked me.

CHAPTER TWENTY

Lucas Rurik?" the leader of the officers asked me as the drunken man and his friends took the opportunity to sidle out of the door.

There were four officers; the one who had removed his helmet was clearly in charge, the rank buttons on his lapel making him a commander. A lanky man with pale skin with what looked like burn scars along the back of his hands. The other three were radiating attentive support, their hands on the hilts of their swords.

As was usual, none of them wore the colours of their Prime. Soldiers had been targeted in the past as a way to send a message to their Prime. So, now, the only colours any Prime soldier wore on their leather and metal armour were black and white.

Unfortunately, it meant I had no way of knowing who was having me followed. "Can I help you?" I asked.

"Prime Roberts would like to talk to you," the man said.

"I will be there as soon as I'm finished here," I told him.

"Is this business important?" he asked. "More important than following us to see a Prime?"

"I don't know yet," I told him. "Depends on how this conversation goes. If you wish, you can wait until I'm done, I'll go with you."

"That is satisfactory," the officer said. "We will wait outside to allow you to conduct your business. Should you try to flee, we will be forced to find you."

"Not fleeing," I assured him.

"My day was going well before you turned up," Roseline said, walking around to the front of the bar as the soldiers left to wait outside. "Come here." She hugged me, lifting me from my feet and kissing me on the forehead.

"How have you been?" I asked her as my feet touched the floor again.

"Good," Roseline said. "You're not here to chat, though. What's up?"

"Looking for Necia," I told her.

Roseline rolled her eyes.

"Not like that," I said, probably a little too quickly.

"Sure thing," Roseline said, not believing a word of it. "She's in the back room."

"Thank you," I told her, but she waved my words away, and I made my way behind the bar, though the door on the right, and down the snaking hallway, passing three shut doors until I reached the final one. It was painted red, although the paint was chipped, revealing white underneath. I knocked once.

"Yes," Necia said, her accent the sort of nondescript one you get when you've lived all over the place.

I opened the door, stepped inside, and closed it behind me.

The room was big enough for a large sofa and table with three chairs. Necia was sat on one of the chairs, reading through something. She looked up at me.

Necia was born to a Spanish father and Italian mother in Constantinople in the twelfth century. She was, like me, a riftborn, having been murdered when she was only twenty-eight years old. She never told me who killed her or why, but I knew it was something to do with her family.

"Lucas?" she asked, slowly getting to her feet.

She was just over five feet tall, with long dark hair, olive skin, and light blue eyes. She wore a red T-shirt, black jeans, and matching boots. A long dagger hung from a sheath on her hip, and she wore steel wrist guards on the back of each hand. A hatchet had been laid on the table. I'd seen her throw them before; she was lethal.

"It's been seven years," Necia said, taking a step toward me.

I nodded, trying to stop the memories of the last time we'd seen one another; I did not need the distraction.

"You have time to tell me why you've been away for so long?" she asked, and for the first time, there was anger in her tone.

"I will," I promised. "But right now, I need to talk to you about someone calling themselves the Croupier."

"Never heard of them," she said dismissively.

"I suspect it's something to do with a Prime," I told her. "There are officers out front waiting to take me to see Prime Roberts. I'm here because of a group called the Blessed."

Necia's eyebrows raised in shock. "Now, that *is* interesting," she said. "I'll join you."

"You don't have to," I said.

"You're right," she said as she reached me, and exhaled softly. "I'm coming because I want to."

I attempted to steady my heartbeat. Necia smelled good, and that wasn't helping. I wasn't there for any entanglements . . .

"They're waiting outside," I told her, attempting to throw some cold water on the direction of my thoughts.

"I'll get a jacket," she said, reaching around to the side of me and removing a leather jacket from beside the door, her bare arm brushing past mine.

She winked at me as she walked by, and my entire body felt the impact of it. Damn the soldiers outside. I did not want to leave the room in which I found Necia. I wanted to make excellent use of the desk and sofa inside that room. Repeatedly. Ours had always been a volatile pairing, and the last time I'd seen her had been an emotional one. I wasn't sure what to expect on seeing her again, but whatever our situation, it was damned hard trying to keep from looking at her ass in those jeans as she sauntered past me. We walked back through the bar, and she turned back to me and grinned, winking again. *Goddamn it.*

"You gonna be okay?" Roseline asked.

"Yep," Necia assured her. "I'm just going with Lucas for moral support. Also because I'm nosey."

Roseline laughed. "Take care of her," she told me.

"You've met Necia, right?" I asked. "She's hardly a damsel in distress."

"Too true," Roseline said. "But take care of her anyway."

I nodded slightly and followed Necia out to the bar, where the Prime officers were waiting for us. The commander was sat at a bench with a drink in hand, while his people stood close by.

"I'm coming with him," Necia said.

"Prime Roberts isn't going to like that," the leader of the men told her.

"Don't care," Necia said. "Prime Roberts can shove it up his ass if he doesn't like it."

"I'm not sure Prime Roberts would like that, either," one of the soldiers said.

Necia shrugged. "I've met Prime Roberts several times," she told him. "I've not given a single shit what he likes in any of those meetings."

"Before this descends into playground fisticuffs, can we just go?" I asked.

"I think that's a good idea," the commander said, replacing his helmet and standing up. He picked up the tankard and knocked back whatever it contained. "Investigator Torres, please refrain from telling Prime Roberts to 'shove' it. I do not wish to have to deal with him in a bad mood."

"Can't promise anything," Necia said with a smile that would have melted an iceberg. "But I'll do my best."

We set off with two of the four Prime officers in front of us and one behind. The commander walked beside me, with Necia on the opposite side of me.

"How long after I arrived did you get sent out to find me?" I asked.

"We were told of your arrival just after you entered the lock," the commander said. "It doesn't matter who by."

"I met some soldiers outside of the city," I told him. "Major Hephaestion. You know him?"

"There are several million people in this city alone," the commander said. "I don't know rank-and-file members of every military personnel. Not even majors."

"Ah, thought maybe you'd been informed about the Blessed attacking garrisons and Inaxia people," I said.

"The Blessed are not my concern," the commander informed us. "My concern is to protect and serve Prime Roberts."

"And you do an incredible job," Necia said, although I couldn't tell how much sarcasm she was putting in her words.

"Thank you," the commander said.

"I mean," Necia said, "you were told to follow Lucas across the city, to bring him back to Prime Roberts, I assume whether he wanted to go or not. Which, and correct me if I'm wrong here, is illegal without the writ of an Investigator. Do you have the writ of an Investigator, commander?"

The commander removed a piece of paper from his pocket and showed it to Necia.

"Investigator Omar," Necia said, passing the paper back to the commander. "Remind me to have a little conversation with him."

"Don't be hard on him," the commander said. "It's difficult to say no to such an easy request. Especially when a Prime is the one asking."

The remaining time spent walking through the city to the base of one of the huge spokes was done in silence. We waited for the elevator, which moved slowly down through the interior of the wall, where a small crowd had gathered.

The officer commandeered the elevator, which got him a few heckles and gestures as we took the lift to the top.

The commander sent the elevator back down to the people waiting below, just as the train pulled in. It looked like someone's antiquated version of what futuristic trains might look like: all gleaming chrome, with smooth, curved surfaces. It looked a lot like the Flying Scotsman, except a different colour, and with no wheels because it ran on a single track that was attached to the underside of the train.

Purple rift energy flickered inside large tubes that disappeared into where you'd expect an engine to be. There were two large windows at the front of the train, where two guards and a driver sat.

The rift energy moved through the train, bathing the interior in the same light purple glow. The commander ensured that we had one of the three carriages to ourselves.

The carriages reminded me of the time I'd been in a train in Berlin in the 1960s. There were dark wooden tables, and similar-coloured panelling next to large windows. The green-and-silver seats were all wooden but covered in soft velvet. They were designed to be comfortable and opulent. They did, after all, go to the heart of the city, and some of the Primes who worked there would accept nothing less.

The train set off with a slight jolt as I looked out of the window, down at the never-sleeping city of Inaxia. Some people called it the heart of the rift, and it was easy to see why. People from all walks of life, from all periods of history, living and working together. There were conflicts, but the city had stood all that time without anything close to a war between its people. The Primes were proud of that.

"It never gets boring, does it?" Necia said to me as she caught me watching the city below.

"No," I said.

Necia didn't like living on Earth. She'd lived there for centuries and, like all of our kind, had lived in the shadows, away from humans. Doing whatever we needed to do to keep them and us safe, without ever being allowed to be openly who we were. That had changed, but Necia hadn't been back in that time. She'd never shown any interest in doing so, even now. She was happy in Inaxia. This was her home.

"Commander," I asked. "How long have you worked for Prime Roberts?"

"One hundred and eight years," the commander told me.

"He a good man?" I asked.

"Yes," the commander said, although I wasn't entirely convinced. Most Prime soldiers were big on obeying orders—not so much on questioning them.

"Do you have a name beyond Commander?" I asked.

"Marcus Pike," he said dismissively before looking out of the window, our conversation now over.

The rest of the journey was done in silence. The trains made no noise except the whistle of air as it rushed through the carriage's open windows.

I caught sight of dark clouds rolling in from the north and hoped they'd dissipate before they reached the city. Storms in the rift are not fun and usually consist of everyone hiding somewhere safe for the few days they take to pass. I didn't have time to hide away.

The train pulled up to the station and the doors opened. Commander Pike motioned for us to leave, and I noticed that our carriage was the only one which had opened.

I looked down the steep hill where people in carts rode up and down. It was perfectly possibly to walk up the hill, but it was a bit like walking up the hills in San Francisco—hard work, and avoided unless necessary.

The entrance to the shield had the appearance of an ancient Greek temple, with high columns and huge open gateways. It was busy with people, many wearing the colours of their Prime. If you worked for a Prime, and you were in this area of the city, you wore their colours. It was the law, and wearing the colours of a Prime who wasn't yours was frowned upon. Committing a crime in the colours of a Prime you didn't work for was punishable by banishment or death, depending on the severity of the crime.

We walked by a group of several horned revenants. They towered over us, wearing long red-and-green robes that barely covered their huge bodies.

"Those Prime Roberts' people?" I asked Commander Pike.

"No," he said, showing Necia and me the way through the gateway and into a large temple that covered the circumference of the hill.

There were stairs that led up to the offices, judges' rooms, and various other workplaces above and below where we stood. Deep down inside the hill was where I would have arrived if I'd gone straight to the city.

Guards were stationed at every one of the half a dozen exits that I could see as the curve of the temple moved around.

"It's just as busy as I remember," I said.

"Yeah, a bit more heavily guarded now, though," Necia whispered to me.

Commander Pike and his people motioned to one of the security guards, who waved us through. We walked down a hallway with windows on either side to let in sunlight, and another security guard opened the double doors.

I stepped out onto the plateau of the shield. There were similar doors at two dozen locations around the area, each one with a path in front of it that led to eight plots of land, each one separated by a six-foot-high stone wall.

The centre itself was adorned with trees and flowers, and we walked around the path on the outside, past the massive houses that the Primes and their people stayed in, until we reached a house on almost the opposite side to where we'd entered.

"Anyone living in number eight at the moment?" I asked, looking around at the eight identical large mansions. The eighth house was reserved for the Ancients to stay in when they were in the city for voting. Usually, it was used as emergency residential, or neutral ground for any disputes.

Commander Pike ignored me and whispered to the guard, who opened the metal gate and ushered us through.

There were flowers along either side of the fifty-foot-long pathway to the ornate front door of the mansion. It was bigger than Ezekiel's home had been, although it had to be to house the Prime, their family, and up to a dozen members of staff.

Each Prime had their own city somewhere in the rift and only came to Inaxia for voting or because there was some matter that needed to be resolved. I was apparently a matter that needed to be resolved.

Like the Prime guards' uniforms, the houses were devoid of the colours of their Prime, but the second the door opened and a middle-aged man stepped out onto the porch, I caught a glimpse of the colour of the carpet on the floor of the hallway. The Prime's colours. Blue and white.

CHAPTER TWENTY-ONE

I had no actual proof that Prime Roberts was involved with the Croupier or even knew who he was. Even so, I was sure that the colours were relevant. The Croupier had used poker chips that were the same colour that Prime Roberts used. It might well not mean anything.

Except, somewhere in my gut, I knew it meant *something*. I just didn't know what.

We were taken through the Prime's residence to a room at the rear of the property with large bay windows that overlooked a large garden with a swimming pool. Primes get it good in Inaxia.

There were four guards in the room, which was more of a hall than something you'd find in a normal home. The guards all wore outfits that matched Commander Pike's, except they all had a blue-and-white sash across their torso.

Prime Roberts sat on an elevated throne at the far end of the hall, in between two banners in his colours that stretched from the high ceiling to the polished marble floor. If there was one thing I'd learned over my centuries of life, it was that Primes liked to consider themselves royalty.

"Prime Roberts," Commander Pike declared as he stood to attention beside me. "This is Lucas Rurik."

"And Investigator Torres," Prime Roberts said, sounding less than happy about her appearance.

Prime Roberts got to his feet, his blue-and-white cloak fastened around his neck with a golden pin in the shape of a large shield, which caught the sunlight outside. He had rings on each finger, with several of them containing precious stones, and he wore a long golden chain around his neck, the seal of the Prime—a silver hand, clutching a golden quill—hanging against his barrel chest.

He was just over five and a half feet tall, with long greying hair that fell over broad shoulders. He had a triangle-shaped torso—big at the top with a small waist—and large legs. He looked exactly like someone who spent all day in the gym lifting heavy things.

"Prime Roberts," Necia said, sounding about as happy to see him as he was to see her. "Always good to see you in your finery."

Commander Pike departed with a wave of Prime Roberts' bejewelled hand.

"So, why am I here?" I asked Prime Roberts.

"Leave us," Roberts barked to his guards, who filed out through the door at the far side of the hall, their footsteps echoing around us.

"I assume you'll be staying," Prime Roberts said to Necia when it was just the three of us.

"Good assumption," Necia told him.

"Fine," Roberts said with an irritated sigh. "Lucas, you are the last Raven Guild member. A man who was close to Neb, who fought in multiple wars on Earth and more than one in the rift. One in particular, several centuries ago, that is still spoken about here."

I nodded again. "That wasn't a war," I said. "It was just putting down fiends that came out of the Tempest causing havoc; a bunch of marauders decided to take advantage of the situation. It was a long time ago." And not a time I remembered with any fondness. I'd fought a primordial by the name of Prilias who had become consumed with rage and power and attacked a village close to the Tempest. In that fight I took its eye before managing to barely escape with my life. The creature had killed dozens of people that day. I occasionally wondered if that fiend was still up by the Tempest, just hoping for a chance at revenge.

"Even so, you are well versed in the martial," Prime Roberts said as he gazed out of the one of the large windows.

"You could say that," I told him, still unsure where this was all going.

"Why are you in my city?" Prime Roberts asked me.

"I'm looking for answers," I told him. No point in lying; I did actually want answers, and I was pretty sure that Roberts had at least a few I needed.

"Let us be open and honest," Prime Roberts said. "You are here searching for the Blessed, yes?"

"Sort of. I am here because we found a group of people on Earth calling themselves the Blessed," I corrected. "They have links to a man named the Croupier. He has murdered multiple people and is possibly in possession of an exceptionally dangerous drug created by a wanted fugitive. A fugitive I'm certain this Croupier knows the whereabouts of. I'm looking for the Croupier's identity and want to know how the Blessed might be involved with him."

"Do you know who they are?" Prime Roberts asked me.

I shook my head. "Those on Earth appear to be some kind of cult; they think they're saving practitioners. They're being fed some stories about how persecuted the practitioners are. A friend of mine was taken to a run-down fort to the north of here. He didn't know the exact location, but apparently, it's close to where earthsang moss grows, near the River of Ghosts. I'm hoping that it might hold some answers."

"I may know something that could help," Prime Roberts said.

"I would be grateful," I told him.

"Before we get to that, have you heard of the Blessed?" Prime Roberts asked Necia.

"Bits and pieces," Necia said. "I know they attacked the Primes a century ago, but I don't know much about who they were and why they did it. I know that there was a bunch of people rounded up and sent to a prison, but that's about it for what was made public. The Investigators were let in on some stuff, but the vast majority of the public who weren't around in the year or so that it happened have probably never even heard of them except in whispers."

"Then my work was done well," Prime Roberts said with a sigh. "A hundred years ago, the Blessed were a terrorist organisation who wanted to elevate practitioners to rule the city. They believed that as the only true riftborn, they should be in charge. Obviously, the Primes and Ancients disagreed."

"So I was told," I said. "Not exactly clear on all of the details, though."

"Members of the group integrated themselves within the city, working for several years to gain access to where we live, and then they tried to overthrow and kill us," Prime Roberts said. "They were unsuccessful, and they were—for the most part—taken to a prison city to the north never permitted to leave. Soldiers were placed around the town to ensure that they stayed there. All of this is public knowledge for anyone who was in Inaxia at the time. The prison is near a Lawless village, which acts as a sort of halfway destination for anyone working at, or needed to become involved with, the prison."

"Is there a fort nearby?" I asked.

"I don't know," Prime Roberts said. "I've never been up there; I'm not allowed to go. The prison is close to the mountains to the northeast. About a day's ride of here. Close to the River of Ghosts."

"You're not allowed to go to the prison?" I asked.

"The Ancients wanted to make sure that we don't," Prime Roberts said. "They were originally concerned about reprisals from ourselves, or our allies, and it just sort of stuck."

"So, the thought is that the people in the prison are getting people outside of the town to kill in their name?" Necia asked.

"That's the prevailing idea," Prime Roberts agreed. "We don't know how. The town is now the main prison for the rift and has many thousands of people living there. It's not difficult to imagine that anyone inside there might have allies outside."

"How are they communicating?" I asked.

"I'm hoping that's something you might be able to find out," Prime Roberts said.

"Why would the Blessed wait a century before attacking again?" I asked.

"No clue," Prime Roberts said. "There were whispers of their involvements in crimes over the years. Of people being killed or going missing, of robberies, attacks on serving members of the Inaxia military. But we had no proof that anyone in the prison was responsible. They were, at best, a nuisance. A decade ago, the Blessed started to be mentioned more and more. Patrols would vanish, leaving one person alive, and they'd mention the Blessed. People robbed on the roads would say that the Blessed did it. The Blessed were starting to tell their victims of their involvement."

"So, no one from Inaxia has gone to the city to question the people there?" I asked. "What about the guards stationed at the prison?"

"Also not allowed inside the prison," Prime Roberts said. "I know *prison* makes it sound like there are jailers and guards who just wander around the place, but it's not like that. It's a completely self-contained prison. We take food and medical supplies on a regular basis, but that's as far as we go. There are farms to the northwest that supply everything they need, and several parts of the city itself have been taken over by livestock and orchards. We tried to make it as self-sufficient as possible. What happens in the prison stays in the prison. The Ancients made sure of that."

"The Ancients are right," Necia said. "Sending anyone from Inaxia to strong-arm a prison city would result in deaths, but more than that, it would result in tales being spread and resentment festering."

"I agree with you," Prime Roberts said. "The soldiers stationed at the prison report back to us, but they are, for the most part, oblivious to anything happening inside."

"Who is in charge of the prison?" I asked. "Do they have a name?"

"Calls herself the Queen of Crows," Prime Roberts said. "Although *in charge* is possibly over-stretching her authority."

"How long has the Queen been *in charge*?" Necia asked.

"Nearly a hundred years," Marcus said.

"So, around the same time as the Blessed decided to stage their revolution," I said. "Was she one of them?"

Prime Roberts nodded.

"What is it you want me to do?" I asked, wondering who this Queen actually was.

"Well, I want you to go to the prison and talk to the Queen," Prime Roberts said. "You're investigating crimes on Earth, so you can tell the people there you have no interest in what happens in Inaxia. You're a Guild member, so you don't need an excuse, and finally, I hear you're actually good at your job, so I can't foresee you killing a bunch of people."

"But if I did, it wouldn't come back to you," I said.

"Correct," Prime Roberts said. "It would all be on you and your . . . lone-wolf ways."

"I'm going with him," Necia said.

"You are an investigator of Inaxia," Prime Roberts said. "You cannot be seen to have any influence or jurisdiction on Lawless problems."

"I'll leave my badge here," Necia said. "Resign my commission if needs must, but I am going with him. He tends to get people trying to kill him when I'm not around."

"And when you are around," I said.

"Fair," Necia said. "At least with me there, I can make sure no one is trying to screw you over."

Prime Roberts laughed. "You believe that I would try to . . . screw over Lucas?"

"Yes," Necia said. "You're a Prime. You have your own reasons for doing anything and everything."

"Fair," Prime Roberts said. "However, in this case, our needs intersect.

You're looking for a link from these Blessed to your criminal. And I'm pretty sure that's where you'll find it."

"How did you know that I was going to be here?" I asked.

"You were spotted by someone at the entrance to the city," Prime Roberts said. "Recognised by a worker. It turns out that Guild members who save lives are remembered for a long time. You didn't think you'd be able to get far without someone recognising you, did you?"

"Actually, yes," I said.

"When I heard you were here, I had my men go watch you, bring you back here," Prime Roberts said. "I didn't realise you were here searching for the Blessed. I was going to ask for your assistance, but it turns out our aims are intertwined."

"What are the odds?" Necia asked.

"I always liked games of chance," Prime Roberts mused. "Some days, you're luckier than others. Runnervale might be what you're looking for," Prime Roberts said. "It's near the River of Ghosts, and there's an abundance of earthsang moss there."

"Weird name for a village," I said.

"Yes, well, it used to be a stopover for runners going north," Prime Roberts said. "Story has it, people put odds on the runners leaving Inaxia to see who would make it to the city in one piece."

"What's the prison called?" Necia asked.

"The Crow's Perch," Prime Roberts said.

"What would you have done if I hadn't arrived?" I asked. "Just wait around for someone to turn up?"

"I would have had to find other means," Prime Roberts said with a sigh.

"How do these people feel about Guild members?" I asked. "People in Inaxia might be happy to see me, but what about further afield?"

"People trust the Guilds," Prime Roberts said. "You aren't controlled by the Primes, not officially, anyway. The Ancients are considered above all of this, so they don't get the brunt of the dislike that we get."

"And what do the Ancients think?" I asked.

"The usual," Prime Roberts said. "They don't get involved unless they have to, and right now they expect us to sort it. They got involved when the Blessed turned up and tried to murder us all, and I don't think having it happen again would go down well."

"Why not kill them all?" Necia asked. "Execution or exile from the rift?"

"Executed people fighting for a cause create martyrs," Prime Roberts said. "And exiling so many from the rift was . . . problematic. If we did that, who knows what trouble they'd have caused on Earth, and we don't need any more negative exposure for rift-fused."

"Really?" I said sarcastically. "You didn't exile them to Earth because you were worried they'd embarrass you."

"Yes," Prime Roberts admitted. "You have to understand, this ran deep. There were members of the Blessed who had close ties to more than one Prime. In some cases, very close. It was felt that putting them in a prison and forgetting they existed was the best option."

"Were there members of a Prime's family?" Necia asked.

"Not that I'm aware of," Prime Roberts said.

"Lovers?" I asked.

Prime Roberts said nothing, but he took a deep breath and let it out slowly.

"Right, you'd have to admit that the people who came here to overthrow you all, who bypassed your security, who lived among you in plain sight for some time, were, in fact, shagging you."

"A crude way of putting it," Prime Roberts said.

"I can put it cruder," I almost snapped.

"Yes, well, I've been designated to deal with them because . . . " Prime Roberts paused. "Well, because I wasn't . . . shagging anyone."

"You think they're trying to stage a coup again?" Necia asked.

"I think that attacking garrisons is insane," Prime Roberts said. "It's not a winning strategy, because sooner or later, we'll respond with equal force."

"Which will escalate matters," I said.

"Which might well be the whole plan," Necia said.

Prime Roberts nodded. "Yes. An excuse to launch a revolution."

"Okay, I'll go," I said. "I didn't ask earlier, but any chance you've heard of the Croupier?"

Prime Roberts stared at me for a heartbeat too long. "The name rings a bell," he said eventually. "I can't entirely place it, though. If he's working with the Blessed, that prison is the place to go."

"Anything else?" I asked.

"Commander Pike will be travelling with you," Prime Roberts said. "We have arranged transport. Commander Pike will not be entering the prison. He is aware of this."

"So, we'll be on our own?" Necia asked.

Prime Roberts nodded.

"How hostile are the prisoners liable to be?" Necia asked. "Prisons don't tend to breed happiness."

"It's a den of criminality," Prime Roberts said. "From what I hear, people go about their lives. It's not like one of the old mining prisons in the far north, but there are a lot of bad people in the Crow's Perch. I would watch your backs."

"Where are we meant to meet Commander Pike?" I asked. I wanted to get on with it. There was no way of knowing how it was back on Earth, and I didn't want to have turned anyone I worked with into an easy target for the Croupier to go after while I was here.

"Outside my home," Prime Roberts said. "He'll take you to your transport and accompany you to Runnervale."

"Are we going to have a problem with him wanting to go further?" I asked.

Prime Roberts shrugged. "The Blessed killed friends of his when they came for us. Friends of many of the guards who protect the Primes. More than one of them wanted retribution at the time, and it hasn't been long enough for those thoughts and feelings to have subsided."

"Is that why you limited knowledge of who was involved in the attack?" I asked. "In case of reprisals?"

"Sometimes, as a leader, you have to try and limit the information that gets out to the public," Prime Roberts said. "We tried to ensure that nothing got out, but that was quickly seen as pointless, considering the number of people involved in our defence."

"I'd never even heard of the Blessed until a short while ago," I said. "Apparently, I missed out on all of it."

"You weren't here," Prime Roberts said, sounding a little irritated. "They were the talk of Inaxia for a while, and then it died down after those responsible were arrested."

"I'm not criticising you," I said.

"Oh," Prime Roberts said with the first smile I'd seen. "Apparently, being Prime means you also get defensive about things. My term of two centuries ends in a few months; I would not have this over my head when my successor is *elected*."

You could practically hear the word *elected* in italics. Technically, Primes were elected, but in the same way that dictatorships have elections. The winner would already have been chosen by the previous Prime and their advisors, and everyone voted in keeping with that. Sometimes that works, and you get a strong, good leader. And sometimes it doesn't, and the Prime has to be . . . removed by their own people.

The Ides of March has nothing on rift politics.

Necia and I left the hall and found Commander Pike waiting outside. Fashion in the rift was a weird mesh of thousands of years all in one place. Some people wore tunics, and some wore jeans and T-shirts that had been brought through the rift. Commander Pike wore a pair of black trousers and a dark blue tunic, while his large black boots looked like something a pirate would wear.

"Is that your casual look, Commander Pike?" I asked him.

"No insignias, no uniforms," Commander Pike said. "And you will refer to me as Marcus Pike. I can't be called *Commander* while we're away from Inaxia on unofficial orders."

"Have you ever worn casual clothing before?" Necia asked him dubiously. "Ever?"

"To be fair, he's not going to stand out," I said. "I saw someone wearing biker leathers and Jandals earlier."

"Inaxia is eclectic," Marcus said.

"That's one way to put it," I told him as we left the estate and made our way back through to the temple.

I wondered exactly what kind of work Marcus and his guards had done in the past. Those who guard the Primes tended to be tougher and more . . . open to finding solutions to problems outside the box. Assassination, torture, making people vanish were all tools I'd known Prime guards to use in their duty. And usually with Prime backing.

Marcus walked off in front as if we were his troops who had to walk in his shadow.

"Something else is going on here," I whispered to Necia.

"I know," she said. "The whole thing stinks of political nonsense."

CHAPTER TWENTY-TWO

Because Necia couldn't just turn up at a Lawless city while carrying her Investigator ID, we made a quick detour to the Investigator plaza, where she handed it to someone she trusted while I waited outside with Marcus and his group of soldiers, who he was giving instructions to.

I sat on the steps outside of the plaza and waited until Necia returned. She hadn't changed, but she wore a rapier on her hip. It had been a present from me several decades earlier.

"Nice sword," I told her.

"I don't get to use it often," she told me with a smile. "Don't make me use it on you."

I laughed and got to my feet, following Marcus as we walked to the nearest exit and were ushered through the checkpoint, through the large stone archway, and out onto a dirt road that led away from Inaxia.

It was only a short distance before we stopped again, this time at a runners' stables. Once again, Necia and I stayed back while Marcus spoke to one of the runners there—a middle-aged gentleman with tattooed arms and an eye patch.

A carriage was brought out of the stable, big enough for six. It was pulled by two large creatures called oxforth, a mixture of oxen, camel, and horse, although bigger than any. Faster, too. Their chestnut fur kept them warm in the winter but cool in the summer, and they had two huge horns on either side of their large heads. Those four horns were capable of being used to great effect against anyone stupid enough to think that oxforth were easy pickings because of their usually docile nature.

There was a screech from above, and Casimir flew overhead, landing on the high branches of a nearby tree.

"Your eidolon," Necia said. "I wondered where he'd gotten to."

"Always nice to have eyes at your back," I told her.

A black horse the size of a shire, and looking like it would quite happily dance all over your face should you annoy it, was led out of the stables. It was already saddled, and Marcus pulled himself up onto the saddle.

"You two get the carriage," Marcus said as a driver climbed up onto the carriage seat and took the reins of the oxforth in her hands.

Necia climbed into the roomy wooden-and-steel carriage first, taking a seat on the comfortable red velvet. I followed suit and sat opposite her. The windows on either side of the carriage had thick purple curtains on them.

As the carriage set off, Necia moved to sit beside me and sighed. "Just how bad do you think this is going to be?"

"On a scale of one to ten?" I asked. "I'd be happy with a seven. If I'm honest, I'd rather not kill anyone. I'd like to be able to find out what I need and stop the Croupier before he kills anyone else. And then stop Callie Mitchell before she can make any more poison. I just want information and help, not bodies."

"Unfortunately, I don't think you're going to have a say in it," she said, sitting up. "We rarely do. You didn't bring the Talon's mask."

"No," I said. "I'm the last of my Guild and technically a Talon, but I didn't think bringing it to Inaxia would be a good idea. The last time I wore one in Inaxia, it didn't end well."

By *not ending well* I meant I'd killed a Prime. It had been a long time ago, and I'd gotten dragged into Prime political nonsense, although in that case, the Prime in question had been a psychopath who had murdered a bunch of people who tried to expose his . . . unpleasant pastimes. The other Primes had asked the Ancients for help, none of them wanting to be the one who went after one of their own, and the Ancients asked the Raven Guild.

I'd walked in on him murdering people and had ended his life quickly and efficiently. It had been several centuries back and wasn't widely known as ever having happened.

From what Neb had told me at the time, it was one of the few occasions where a Guild had been brought in to deal with trouble involving the Primes.

I looked out of the window at the increasingly fast scenery that sped by, and wondered if Casimir would have difficulty keeping up. Oxforth were hardy, strong animals and would run all night if needs must. The driver would need to sleep at some point, though, so we'd have to stop probably halfway.

"I missed you," Necia said, regaining my attention.

I turned back to her. "I missed you, too."

"Why didn't you come back here?" she asked.

"I was hurt," I said. "My Guild had been killed, I'd survived alone, and I found that hard to deal with. Spent a few years trying, and failing, and then I did something stupid and rendered myself human. Stayed that way for several years."

Necia took my hand in hers, an expression of concern on her face. "And you're okay now?"

I nodded. "Back to full strength," I said with a smile.

Necia kissed me on the lips. It was tentative at first, but whatever passion existed just under the skin for us both soon came to the fore, and we forgot that we were in the back of a carriage. All that mattered in that moment was that we were together.

Some moments later, when Nacia's jeans were on the floor behind her and mine were still wrapped around one of my legs, we sagged against one another.

Necia was straddled across my lap, her head buried in the side of my neck, occasionally kissing it and sending little waves of electricity down my back.

"Why do we always do this?" she asked eventually, getting up from my lap and starting to dress herself.

"Because we're both single, free, and we enjoy it," I said, pulling up my jeans and wondering where my one boot was. The windows were closed, so it hadn't been thrown outside in a fit of passion.

"Yes, but you won't live here, and I won't live on Earth," Necia said, fastening the belt on her jeans.

"Are you saying that you would rather we didn't do this?" I asked.

"I don't know," Necia said with a sigh. "I really do enjoy being with you. And not just the sex but the actually-being-with-you part. But the whole long-distance thing just won't work."

"Do you have a solution?" I asked. To be honest, it felt like neither of us were convinced that we'd last the whole relationship thing, anyway. We'd talked about it last time I'd been in the rift. We both liked our independence. And I loved my life on Earth. It kept the human part of me alive. At one time, that had been something I would have given up for her. Without her asking, I'd moved to the rift and lived there for decades with her. And she knew I'd do it again. Which was why she'd never asked me to. She'd seen how it had affected me. It was why I was more than a little bit in love with her.

"No," Necia said. "I love you, Lucas. Always have, always will, but I wonder if I need something more stable than what we have. It was so many years since I last saw you."

"You could have come through to Earth," I said to her. "Just to check on me, I mean."

Necia nodded. "Kept putting it off. You know I hate it there, but I also knew that if I went to see you and you were hurt, or . . . I would have stayed to help. And I would have hated that, too. I love living here. You love living there."

There was a jolt and the carriage slowed down. I opened a curtain just as Marcus Pike was about to knock on the window, which I pushed down.

"We're making good time," Marcus said. "Driver wanted me to ask if you'd like to continue on and get there late tonight, or stop and continue in the morning."

"Might as well get there tonight," I said. "I need to get back to Earth, so the quicker, the better."

"Can do," Marcus said, and I pulled up the window as he rode on.

The night came fast in the rift, but the sunset—which lasted only minutes—was always worth the time to watch. The red, orange, purple, blue, yellow, and green sky was spectacular.

Necia sat beside me as we watched the sunset be replaced with darkness. There wasn't a moon or stars in the rift, just a band of light that cut through the darkness of the sky, like someone had left a door ajar. Somewhere in the distance, there was a howl. Night-time in the rift was dangerous, and it was best to be inside a city or at least a building, but being in the back of a carriage travelling at high speed was good too, and few predators would ever attack an oxforth when there were so many easier things to eat.

I settled back into the seat, resting my head against the cool wall of the carriage.

"How do you hope to get anyone to tell you about this Croupier?" Necia asked. "I doubt brute force or just being nice are going to do the trick."

"I have no idea," I said. "The Croupier has powerful friends, but people like that will also have enemies, so I'm hoping that if I mention the Blessed and how they're helping him, someone might know something. We don't know anything about him, really, and he knows a lot about us. It puts us at a disadvantage, and I aim to remove that if possible."

"And if you can't?" Necia asked.

"At least I tried," I said. "Also, if it means I get a handle on the Blessed as a group, or why people on Earth are deciding to join their ranks, it might point me in the right direction."

I dozed on and off for the rest of the trip. It had been a long few days.

I woke up with a jolt, ready to fight, and Necia placed her hand on my leg. "It's okay," she assured me. "I think we've arrived."

"Excellent," I said with a yawn.

Necia opened the carriage door and stepped outside. Marcus was leading his horse by the reins and stopped to talk to the driver.

The River of Ghosts was close by; I could hear the water gently lapping against the bank. The earthsang moss gave off a sweet, flowery smell, strongly perfumed and distinctive.

"There's earthsang moss here," I said.

"There is," Necia said, joining me at the side of the road.

"Thank you," I called back to the driver, who raised a hand in acknowledgement before steering the carriage away to a large stable.

"This isn't a village," Necia said, looking around.

"It's a large stable, an inn, and what looks like two houses," I said. "I didn't expect a bustling city or anything, but *village* implies more than this. It's not even a hamlet. Zeke said he was taken here. To a Lawless village near the river, where that moss grows. He said a village; I think he'd have noticed if it was a huge inn and that was it."

A wooden signpost had been planted in the side of the mud pool that passed for a road. It said RUNNERVALE in big red letters.

"I'm going to talk to the innkeeper," Marcus told us. "It's not dawn for hours yet, so maybe we should all get some sleep and then you can both go on up to the prison tomorrow morning. I don't think traipsing around in the dark here is a very good idea."

Marcus had a point. There were a few dozen torches in Runnervale, illuminating the relatively small area, but I couldn't see much beyond that.

"Sleep it is," I said. "Any more villages around here? Apart from the prison?"

"There's the remains of a fort about an hour's ride to the north of here," Marcus said. "It was burned down about two years ago when bandits settled in."

"I think that's where Zeke was taken," I said.

"You're welcome to go check it out, but there's nothing there now," Marcus said. "It was utterly destroyed by the soldiers at the prison. I know because I went there to look myself."

I thanked Marcus for his help and stayed by the bottom of the stairs with Necia, while Marcus spoke to a large gentleman with a long dark beard and bald head. He passed Marcus some keys, and the Prime guard returned to us, passing us one bronze-coloured key.

"I assume you're sharing," he said.

Necia took the key and followed Marcus up the stairs, with me taking the rear.

Our room—ten—was at the far end of the hallway, with Marcus' nine directly beside us.

We entered the pleasantly decorated room with a large, comfortable-looking bed and a big window that overlooked . . . absolutely nothing that I could see.

Necia removed her boots and sword, and lay back on the bed. "I see a bath there," she said, pointing to the metal bathtub at the far end of the room.

"You think it has hot water?" I asked, picking up one of the many towels that had been provided.

"We can find out," she said.

"I'm beginning to think that this is some kind of romantic-getaway inn," I said.

"I don't think we have time for a romantic getaway," Necia said. "I think we do have time for one last night, though."

"One last night?" I asked as I ran the bathtub that was certainly big enough for two people. The water came out hot after only a few seconds.

Necia smiled, got off the bed, and unbelted her jeans, stepping out of them with a slight flourish as she got to work on her top. "We'll see tomorrow."

CHAPTER TWENTY-THREE

The bed turned out to be as comfortable as it looked, which was a good thing because by the time we'd gotten out of the tub, I needed sleep.

Sunlight poured through the large window and I blinked at the light, rolled over, and got a kiss on the forehead from an already-awake Necia. "I'm heading downstairs to find food," she said, getting out of bed and starting to dress.

"I'll just stay here all day," I told her with a yawn. "You can deal with the Blessed and Croupier stuff; just let me know how it goes."

Necia threw a boot at me.

"Now you've lost your boot," I said as Necia laughed. "You can hobble around all day."

"Don't make me hurt you," Necia warned.

"Now, we both know that's not a threat I'm going to pay a blind bit of attention to," I said with a chuckle.

Necia took a deep breath and held out her hand. I tossed over her boot and got out of bed, stretching before getting dressed.

I was just fastening my own boots when there was a knock at the door, which Necia answered, revealing Marcus with a wicker basket of pastries in his hands.

"They make them fresh," he said. "But we don't have time to sit and dine, so I thought you might both like food."

"I take back almost every horrible thing I said about you," I told him as Necia took the basket from his hands and thanked him.

"Almost every horrible thing?" Marcus asked with a smile.

"The day is young, Marcus Pike," I said with a smile of my own as Necia threw me a chocolate-filled pastry and I took a bite. "Good lord, I need to live here."

"How is this place so luxurious?" Necia asked.

"It's a runner stop-off," Marcus said. "Runners can pay the price to make sure something is run well and to the highest luxury. They call it a Lawless village because it can't be affiliated with Inaxia nor any of the Primes. The Runners are meant to be independent, after all."

I didn't like that *meant to be*.

"You ready?" Marcus asked as I devoured the pastry and selected a second one, which appeared to be filled with cherry jam.

We followed Marcus down the stairs and out into the sunlight.

"How are we getting to the prison?" I asked.

"We'll take the carriage," he said. "I don't want anyone to know we're here."

"Can we go the long way around?" I asked. "I want to check that fort."

Marcus nodded and went to talk to the carriage driver.

We were riding for only a few minutes when the fog began to blanket the plains and I could no longer see the ground out of the rear of the carriage. The further we got from the inn, the denser the fog became, until it looked like we were riding through the clouds themselves.

The carriage stopped not long after, with Marcus leaving first and Necia just after him, allowing me to bring up the rear and take a good look at our surroundings—fog notwithstanding.

The fort itself had been small, even when standing. But the stone was scattered over a large area, the rest of the fort left open for the elements to reclaim. It didn't take long to look around, find the entrance to the basement, and discover it had been collapsed. Whatever had been done down there to Zeke, it wasn't going to be done to anyone else.

I returned to the carriage, told Necia and Marcus of my lack of findings, and we continued on to the prison.

The walls to the Crow's Perch were sixty or seventy feet high and had ramparts atop them. Soldiers with spears and bows patrolled the pathway between the six towers that I could see, although I imagined there'd be that number again on the far side of the city. The entrance was a large portcullis with eight guards outside, next to a large two-storey building that I presumed served as a guard room. There were several large ballistae around the entrance, and two more buildings and a stable a short distance away. They *really* didn't want anyone to get out.

Marcus spoke to one of the guards, who wore black-and-silver leather armour with no identifying badges that I could see. He came back over to the carriage and removed two charcoal capes, both with hoods. "Wear these," he said. "Don't stand out."

"No weapons," the man barked at Necia and me as we put on the capes.

I wanted to tell him he was welcome to come take them from me, but it would have done me no good. I wanted into the prison, and if this was the way it had to be, then so be it. Besides, if I really needed a weapon, I could find one.

I removed my daggers and belt, passing them to a nearby guard as Necia removed her own knife belt and sword. Neither of us needed weapons to kill people, but I left that piece of information in my head. I also kept the rift-tempered knuckleduster in my pocket because I'm not stupid.

The guard went back to talking to Marcus, who stood and nodded as I yawned and looked back over the foggy ground. We really were in the middle of nowhere. The sounds of living drifted out of the prison, and something dawned on me.

"Where's the Queen of Crows?" I asked.

"Palace," the guard said as he and his comrades laughed.

"And where is the palace?" I asked him, not interested in playing whatever game he was playing.

The guards stopped laughing. "It's at the far end of the city," he said. "Good luck."

"How do you know who gets to leave?" I asked. "Or who causes trouble?"

"On point one," the guard began, "no one leaves. Not unless there's a decree from Inaxia, and there has never been a decree from Inaxia. On point two, not my problem. So long as they stay in there, it's up to them to sort it out. They all kill one another—that's less for us to guard. You will walk through, into the courtyard; you will remain there until the portcullis has closed."

The guard motioned for us to enter the city as the portcullis was raised, and a dozen guards stood beside it as if waiting for an onslaught of prisoners trying to escape. They left a big-enough gap for Necia and me to walk through.

We stood in an empty courtyard and waited for the portcullis to close as several guards with bows looked down on us. There were people just outside the courtyard, watching us with interest. I couldn't tell if they were interested because we were new or interested because we could be victims. Or both.

The laughter followed us down the cobbled street until we reached what appeared to be a main road. There were plenty of people there, going about their daily lives, and the smells of cooking from the multi-storey houses that loomed on either side of us.

We set off down the street at a normal walk. We didn't want to stand out, although from the looks we got from many of the people we passed, that ship had well and truly sailed.

"I think they're watching us," Necia whispered as we walked by a vendor selling some kind of sweet-smelling meat.

I took a quick look behind me to see a small crowd had gathered and were watching us. More than one of them had a weapon in their hand, and a few looked like they weren't the kinds of people you wanted to meet at any time of the day.

"You think they may believe we're new inmates?" I asked. Prime Roberts had mentioned that he'd wanted me to go to the prison because I was a Guild member, and they still had a semblance of trust surrounding them, but I got the feeling that information hadn't been relayed to the inhabitants of the city.

"If they do, that might be for the best," Necia said. "Let's just keep going."

We continued down the long road.

Casimir? I asked.

Lots of people down there, Casimir said. *Foggy too.*

The fog wasn't as dense as it had been on the grounds around the prison, but there was still a mist all around us, more so around our feet and shins, where it swirled.

Any chance it's a weird rift thing? I asked.

The fog? Casimir responded. *Yes, every chance.*

"That isn't helpful," I said out loud.

"What isn't?" Necia asked me.

"Sorry, talking to Casimir," I explained.

"He see anything we should worry about?" she asked.

I relayed the message.

Not really, he said. *I've landed on a house a bit further down from where you are. Nothing I can see out of the ordinary, although the crowd behind you is following you. I think you're making a stir.*

There was an itch on the back of my neck, and I longed to turn and look at the crowd but knew that it might just make things worse, and I could do without that.

Windows opened in the buildings on either side of us, and people peered out of them as we continued, never changing pace. I got the feeling that newcomers were often met with a similar mixture of distrust and interest.

The road opened up into a large square with a fountain in the middle, the shape of a large fish, and stalls all around the outside. Not including where we'd entered, there were four exits from the square, two in front and one on either side. The square was noisy, with large numbers of people shopping or just milling around. Directly in front of us, between the two exits, was a large bell tower.

"Any idea which way?" I asked.

Necia shook her head. "We were told to keep going forward toward the palace at the far end of the city. I assume the way forward is where we need to go."

The bell sounded.

"Better than staying around here," I said as the square emptied, people moving down the roads that left it, some moving into one of the many buildings that surrounded it.

"That can't be good," Necia said.

The door to the clock tower opened, and two men stepped outside. They both wore black cloaks, charcoal leather armour, and black masks with a red slash across from left temple to right jawline. One of them carried a long spear, and one had a curved sword. Neither of them looked like they were there for anything other than causing harm to people.

I slipped my knuckleduster onto my hand.

"Only two of them?" Necia asked. "I feel a little insulted."

The crowd that had been following us through the city felt like an oppressive weight against my back. Getting out of the square would require us to either go back through a crowd of people—and there was no way that was going to end well—or go through the two people in front of us.

Necia took a step toward the two armed men as the mist around her legs turned purple and began to twist and turn up around her body. Her power as a riftborn was to manipulate the power of the rift itself. The power wrapped itself around her arms and hands, forming thick gauntlets.

She sprinted toward the two attackers, dodging the strike of a spear and slamming a forearm down onto the wooden shaft, which was obliterated.

Behind you, Casimir said.

I turned as two more attackers pushed their way through the throng of people.

"You okay?" I asked Necia without turning back to her.

"All good," she said, accompanied by the sound of her fist meeting someone's body.

I rushed toward the two newcomers as one of them thrust their spear toward me. I turned to smoke, moved around it, and got inside their guard, turning solid as I brought my knuckleduster-wrapped fist into their stomach.

They shot back thirty feet, colliding with the wooden door of a large dark-bricked house and vanishing inside with a cacophony of noise and a plume of smoke. I couldn't do that again quickly, but the other attacker didn't know that, and judging from the fact that they backed off, they obviously didn't want to take the chance.

"Enough," someone bellowed as one of the attackers decided to take the chance and rush me, their sword sweeping up to try and catch me in the hip.

I stepped into the attack, grabbing their arm in mine and clapping one hand around their exposed ear with every bit of power I could.

The attacker spun to the ground and screamed in pain as blood flowed out of his ear. Burst eardrums suck.

"I said *enough*," someone shouted again, accompanied by a blast of air that picked up all the loose bits of sand, dirt, and brick and lobbed it at everyone in the middle of the square.

I turned to smoke and moved far enough back to avoid it as Necia ran for cover.

I looked at the newcomer. She wore a long black cloak that was cut to resemble feathers, and a hooded mask that completely covered her head. The mask was designed to look like a beak, resembling the old plague masks. She wore a silver-and-dark grey dress that stopped mid-thigh, black leggings, and black boots. She carried no obvious weapons, although I was pretty sure there would be plenty of hidden ones.

She raised a black-gloved hand toward me, one finger pointing in my direction.

"Lucas Rurik," she said. Her voice carried around the square as if she were stood on a stage with a microphone in front of her.

"I am," I said. "Your friends here decided to throw a welcoming party."

"I think we broke a few of them," Necia said as two of the people who had attacked us quietly whimpered on the ground.

"I am the Queen of Crows," the obvious leader said.

"You know who I am," I told her, walking over as half a dozen guards, all wearing matching black feather-like capes but in red-and-silver armour, exited through one of the roads next to the bell tower.

"I apologise for these . . . people," the Queen said. "They did not act upon my orders. Unfortunately, a city with so many criminals, you're bound to have a bad apple or two."

I couldn't tell if she was joking or not. "Good to hear," I told her. "How'd you know we were coming?"

"Get them out of here," the Queen snapped to one of her guards, completely ignoring my question. "I will want to talk to them later."

One of the guards nodded curtly and, with the help of the other six, began dragging our attackers to their feet, where their hands were bound. A cart with a large metal cage built onto the rear rode into the square, and the four attackers were forced inside. It was cramped and probably uncomfortable. Good.

"Go about your lives," the Queen shouted to the crowd.

Everyone did as they were told. Every politician on Earth would give their right leg for that kind of authority.

"How'd you know we were coming?" Necia asked, repeating my question from earlier.

"A friend informed us," the Queen said. "Come, let us walk to my palace."

More guards in red appeared and walked behind us at a respectful distance as the Queen, Necia, and I strolled through the city like nothing had happened. The Queen pointed out districts or places of interest, with people bowing as the Queen passed by, with more than one calling out *Long Live Queen of the Crows* and others tossing flowers in her path. She was beloved by many, although I also saw a few people spot us coming and quickly slink off into the shadows of alleyways between buildings. Loved and feared.

"It took some balls to come here," the Queen said as the large palace came into view. Surprisingly, it wasn't separated from the rest of the city, and while it was three or four times as long as the average building I'd seen, it was still only three storeys high. There were a lot of red-and-black-armoured guards, though. Red and silver. I wondered if the Croupier had been there. Maybe the white was meant to be silver . . . I sighed to myself. I was grasping at straws now.

"I'm just looking for answers," I told her. "Figured you might be able to provide them."

"We shall see," the Queen said.

The conversation was clearly over as we reached the alcove entrance to the palace. The set of double doors were ten feet tall and maybe as wide.

One of the guards opened the double doors and stepped inside for the Queen and her entourage to enter the large, open foyer beyond.

I stood beside Necia and looked at the black steel staircase as it twisted up to the balcony above. Bright artwork sat on the wall, each of the half dozen pieces depicting a scene within the rift itself. I found myself staring at the Tempest painting, the colour and sense of movement making me feel uneasy. I'd been to the Tempest, or at least as close to it as I'd dared. There hadn't been much time to marvel in the beauty of it when it was so close to crushing you with power where you stood.

The Queen's boots clicked on the black-and-red stone floor. "You coming, or what?" she asked without turning around.

Necia and I set off after the Queen.

As we went from hallway to hallway, we passed several open rooms with guards inside. I got the feeling that while those living outside the palace were prisoners, criminals, and ne'er-do-wells, those inside were something else entirely. I wondered if I'd stepped into some kind of military staging ground.

"There are a lot of armed guards here," Necia said, mirroring my own thoughts as a set of white doors with gold and silver dragons intertwined on them was pushed open, revealing a long room with a high ceiling and more guards stood beside a large throne at the end of the room. The throne was made of wood, and as we got closer, I spotted that it had been carved to look like a nest, with crows carved all over the armrests.

The Queen took her seat, her cape covering a large portion of the throne as she looked comfortable.

"Bring her in," the Queen said to one of her guards, who placed his hand on the wall, which slid open, and in walked a woman I knew very well.

"Hi, Lucas," Neb said.

"Bollocks," I said aloud.

CHAPTER TWENTY-FOUR

Why are you here?" I asked Neb, feeling more than a little confused.

"You sent a runner to tell me you were in the rift," Neb said. She wore a long dark-green gown, with black boots and a long-sword that hung from her hip. A circular shield sat on her back, and a small axe hung from her belt. She looked ready for war. But she always looked ready for war, so it was nothing new.

"How'd you know I was here?" I asked. "How'd you get into the city?" The questions tumbled out, and more were ready to follow them.

"I think you might have broken his brain," Necia said.

"I have people inside the Primes' administration," Neb said. "All of the Primes' administrations. I'm not an idiot, whether I work there anymore or not. They're all too dangerous and too powerful to be allowed to do whatever they want without oversight. My friends keep me informed. I knew you were coming here. I knew that you'd be looking for the Blessed. I knew that the Queen of Crows would allow me to see you."

"And you got into the city by magic?" Necia asked.

"There are tunnels under the city," the Queen said, getting to her feet. "Which is where we're going right now."

"Why?" I asked.

"You wanted answers," the Queen said. "Answers about the Croupier, about the Blessed. About whatever the hell is going on back on Earth. I think it would be easier to show you something than have you fire off a hundred questions. Neb is going to accompany us."

"You shouldn't have left your medallion on Earth," Neb said.

"No choice," I told her.

Neb nodded that she understood, but I knew she still thought it was stupid.

"Shall we?" the Queen asked, making her way to the gap in the wall and walking through with two guards behind her. Two more guards followed Necia and me with Neb in the middle as we walked down a short corridor, where the Queen opened the door and stepped into darkness.

When it was my turn to step inside, I saw there was dim lighting inside the tunnel. Small torches powered by rift energy were attached to the rock walls.

The steps were cut at odd angles, and some were larger than others, making the descent a tricky one, and more than once, the walls moved close enough to make it a single-file process. The fog remained the whole time, swirling around our ankles.

I had no idea how deep underground we'd gone when the steps stopped and we began a walk along a long tunnel. No one spoke, the only sounds being footsteps on rock and the rustling of clothing.

It took me a few steps to notice that we were moving up at a slight incline and then a steep rise.

The wind became stronger the further we walked, until a light came into view. It was another few minutes of walking before we reached it and discovered an exit barred with a large metal gate that looked exceptionally heavy.

The Queen removed a key, unlocked the gate, and pushed it open. It made a noise that went right through me, fingernails-on-a-chalkboard style.

Once out of the tunnel, we climbed up a set of grey rock steps, noticing the partial remains of skeletons buried in the walls. At the top, I turned around to survey where we were. The prison city stretched out below us, some distance away. The entrance to the tunnel was set into a large mound that anyone from below would never have seen.

"Come," the Queen said, leading the way across the hill to a copse of large trees that were continuously swaying in the wind.

Little sprigs of blossom, pink and orange, floated around us, and the smell as we got closer to the trees was a subtle, fruity perfume. The trees themselves were forty feet high with thick, light-brown bark, cracked in places, showing a bright orange skin beneath it. As if fire was trying to escape. Fire willows.

"I've never seen them blossom," I said, looking up at the now almost-bare tree.

"It happens only once every few years, but they're quite spectacular in full bloom," Neb said.

"Why are we here?" Necia asked.

"You came to my city for answers," the Queen said. "You have questions about the Blessed, this Croupier, and probably Callie Mitchell. I will answer what I can, but first you need to understand what happened here."

"Okay," I said.

"The Blessed were a group of people who decided that practitioners should have more say in this world," the Queen started. "They wanted their own Prime; they wanted their own lawmakers, their own say in how Inaxia was run. They were treated like second-class citizens in a world they were naturally born into. They'd had enough."

I was waiting for the moment where the Queen told me that something went wrong. Because something always goes wrong in things like this.

"It didn't take long for several of them to decide that being peaceful wasn't going to get the job done," the Queen said. "And only a slight amount of time after that, some of them decided that the best way to get noticed was to hurt people. A new leader was chosen. He was a single-minded man with views more aligned with the new aims of the Blessed. That same man was responsible for seditiously changing those views to begin with."

I sighed.

"Those who took charge of the Blessed forced out those with more-lenient views . . . including me. They drilled those remaining, turned them into extremists who'd kill for their cause. They'd already infiltrated useful positions in Inaxia, and with a little help from people in power who saw this as a way to gain more power, they worked in the shadows and prepared."

"You were in the Blessed?" I asked.

"Originally," the Queen said. "I, along with many others in leadership roles, were forced out before they decided on their more-violent methodology. I wanted to help make things better. They just wanted to help make themselves more powerful."

"What happened next?" Necia asked.

"It took years for everything to be in place, for these Blessed spies to have gained access to the Primes themselves, to their households," the Queen said. "So many rift-fused think when they come to the rift, they're going to be treated like royalty, but this world still needs menial tasks performed. No one expects to be a cleaner for a hundred years; it's why so many riftborn and revenants turn to the military or become runners. Life in the rift isn't quite like it's sold in the Church, is it?"

I shrugged. "Depends on what you want to do with that life," I said. "Depends what you did with your life on Earth, too."

"The rift values skills," the Queen said. "Ironically, many people of import on Earth become peasants here because they don't like to get their hands dirty. Well, practitioners start as peasants here because that's how the rift sees us."

"You're a practitioner?" I asked.

The Queen stroked the side of her mask. "Maybe." She chuckled to herself.

"So, what was the name of this man who led the Blessed down a path of destruction?" Necia asked.

"Alexander Petrov," she said.

"Never heard of him," I told her, and looked over at Necia, who shrugged.

"Not a surprise," the Queen said. "Anyway, the attempted revolution didn't exactly work, as you know. The Blessed were betrayed by one of their own. Those responsible were mostly killed during the attack, but then one night shortly after, all of those people who had been forced out of the Blessed well before any attacks had taken place found themselves arrested. Dragged out of the city and brought here, to a prison in the north."

"Were you among their number?" I asked.

The Queen nodded. "There were hundreds of us. All forced out of the Blessed in a power grab, having had nothing to do with the attack on the Primes but used as scapegoats. Evidence was forged; no one got to say that they were innocent. No one even had a chance."

"Who did it?" I asked.

"Prime Roberts," the Queen said. "He . . . *arranged* for everything. Arranged for us to be taken here, for this place to become a prison. The city had already been built and abandoned long ago. He had people marched from Inaxia to here and dumped in a prison without trial, without a chance to speak our innocence. Anyone who ran was executed on the spot. We learned quickly to stay silent."

"You all have powers," Necia said. "You could have fought back."

"There were two reasons no one did," the Queen said. "Firstly, we were separated from our loved ones. We were told that should we decide to fight, they would be executed first. And there were people who were killed to show that. Secondly, every one of us was made to wear black gloves. We couldn't access our power while they were on."

"Like a second skin?" I asked, remembering the suit that Callie Mitchell had forced me to wear several years earlier. It had stopped me from accessing my powers and had been something I'd hoped few others had ever been forced to experience.

The Queen nodded. "You can't take off a glove with a gloved hand, so we were all stuck. Powerless and utterly at their mercy. Or lack of. We were dumped here the first night, left alone. A day or two later, Prime Roberts arrived. He told us that for our crimes of being part of the Blessed, we were to be imprisoned here. People tried to say that we'd had nothing to do with what the Blessed had done, but I knew it was going to be no use. We were scapegoats.

"Prime Roberts couldn't keep the attack secret, but he knew he had to keep his involvement with anyone in the Blessed secret. Best way to do that is to round up everyone who might know something and execute them in secret before they could tell anyone of his involvement. Everyone else even slightly linked to the Blessed is locked away, just to show the people of Inaxia that they're tough on crime but that they want to give those responsible time to atone for their crimes. Once we were stuck here, no more details were let out, and the people of Inaxia moved on with their lives.

"There's no atonement here, just prison. Forever.

"The Primes were seen as heroes defending themselves from an attempted coup, and anyone who knew about Roberts' involvement was dead. Except me. He didn't find out about my knowledge of his crimes for some time."

"Prime Roberts was Blessed?" Necia asked.

"One of the founding members," the Queen said. "He was there when I and the rest of the leaders of the movement were removed. He was there when the Blessed became little more than criminals and thugs. He betrayed the Blessed after the attack, gave up the other leaders, but he got them exiled to Earth instead of killed."

"Why?" I asked.

"We'll get to that," the Queen said.

"Why go to all this trouble?" Necia asked. "Why not just kill everyone?"

"Several members had friends in high places," the Queen said. "The original Blessed were mostly academics, people who knew the law, people

who practised the law. We were used to be shown to the world how merci-
ful the Primes were, even against those who tried to kill them. The masses
of Inaxia don't really know the details of the coup, just that there was
an attack and it was stopped. They also saw a bunch of people deemed
responsible being punished."

"What happened to the other leaders who had been ousted when you
were?" I asked.

"We'll get to that, too," the Queen said.

"So, Prime Roberts sent us here hoping that what, the city would just
swallow us up?" I asked.

"What started as a city of several hundred academics, with very
few soldiers and guards among our numbers, quickly swelled over the
coming weeks," the Queen said. "The worst prisoners you could imagine were sent here. Murderers, thieves, rapists, anyone who had been
imprisoned within the walls of Inaxia or the cities they ally with. Thousands of them, alongside anyone else who publicly showed support for
the Blessed or asked questions about where all of these people had been
taken from. Soon, we had two groups: hardened criminals and everyone
else. Peace didn't last long. People died. A lot of people died. We had
allies who helped take off the gloves that removed our powers. Those
without gloves would take them off others, and soon were free. Of a
sort. We no longer had our gloves on, powers were allowed in the city,
so we could defend ourselves somewhat, but we had so many who had
never trained to fight, or if they had, it wasn't since they'd stopped being
human."

"What happened?" I asked.

"I stepped into the role of Queen," I said. "Not at first. At first, I just
went to the groups threatening us and manipulated them. I divided and
conquered, and those who came for me died hard. Publicly. Soon, this
city was mine. A lot of people here are bad people, who will stab you in
the neck because they're bored, but then they have to answer to me. The
Queen of Crows does not take that kind of act lightly."

"You turned yourself into something they fear," I said.

The Queen nodded, and I wondered just how much of herself she'd
had to lose in order to achieve peace.

"Prime Roberts told us that no one was exiled," Necia said.

The Queen chuckled behind her mask. "He lied. Publicly, we are the
Blessed. We were arrested and sent here for those crimes. Prime Roberts
took the glory of a victory and made sure there was no one around who

could challenge it. Even now, I'm probably the only person in the rift alive who could tell you that he was a part of the Blessed. He was there when I was there, and the second someone offering more power came along, he turned on me and the other leaders. Just like he did when the attack didn't go according to plan."

She motioned for me to follow her as she walked around the massive tree and stood in front of a brass plaque that was attached to the back of it. There were forty names written on it.

"What happened to the other leaders of the Blessed?" I asked. "Those who were taken from their beds, those who had nothing to do with the attack on Inaxia?"

"These are the names of every single person who died in that city when Prime Roberts sent in the murderers and monsters to thin out number," the Queen said. "The leaders are among them. They were killed one by one. Some taken in the night. Prime Roberts put bounties on our heads. I killed every single person responsible for what happened. Except Prime Roberts himself."

I looked over at Neb.

"I'd already left by that point," she said. "But was the final straw for my involvement in any way with Inaxia. I tried to save as many practitioners as I could, brought them to Nightvale."

"Why would Roberts send us here?" I asked. "He must have known that we weren't going to get killed by chance."

"The city is made up of gangs," the Queen said. "Dozens of them. Most either belong to a gang or they go it alone. While I preside over the city, the gangs kill one another all the time. When they kill someone not gang-affiliated . . . well, that's when I get involved. It wouldn't take much for Prime Roberts to have the guards at the city gates get word to one of the gangs. Kill the both of you and get rewarded. He's done it before. He'll do it again."

"He's tried to have you assassinated?" I asked.

"Not for a while," the Queen said. "He's concerned that if I die, certain allies of mine would be less than impressed."

I followed her gaze to Neb.

"Roberts is scared that if you die, Neb goes after him," I said.

"With good reason," Neb told me.

"The Croupier?" I asked. "Do you know him?"

"Tell me what you know," the Queen said as she motioned for me to walk with her passed more trees.

"He leaves a poker chip on those he kills," I said. "Same size as an Inaxia coin. With the letters *VI* on the back. They're in blue and white or red and white. The blue-and-white is to do with Prime Roberts; not sure why. The red-and-white is to do with runners. My guess is that the *VI* is the number of Blessed who were exiled."

"Told you he'd figure some of it out," Neb said.

"You're half right," she said. "The Croupier's name is Jacob Smythe. He was one of those in charge of getting people into the homes of the Primes. The blue and white is for Roberts, although not because of the betrayal. I'll explain in a second. The red-and-white is actually the colours of the Blessed banner. I'm not surprised you don't know it; they were all destroyed after the revolution failed. A red-and-white banner with *VI* in the middle in gold. The six members of the Blessed who took over when we were all ousted: Callie Mitchell—as you know her—Jacob Smythe, Prime Roberts, Alexander Petrov, Kame, and two more I never knew, as they were brought in by Alexander. The leaders of the Blessed wore masks to hide their identities. Whoever the other two were, they went to great lengths to ensure no one discovered them."

"So, they've spent a hundred years on Earth getting in the right positions, acquiring wealth and influence, ensuring that Callie Mitchell had whatever she needed, all for what?" I asked. "Revenge?"

"Not just revenge, no," the Queen said. "Prime Roberts betrayed the other five and sent them to exile, but he made it known to them that someone else had betrayed their vision. Me."

"My people confirmed it over the years," Neb said. "They believe that the Queen was responsible."

"So, apart from revenge, what else is it?" I asked.

"Alexander genuinely believed what he was doing was the only way," the Queen said. "His methods were monstrous, but I doubt he would give up trying to get what he wants just because he's exiled to Earth. Some will want revenge, but some want to return here and finish what they started."

"Including Callie?" I asked.

The Queen nodded.

"She's trying to create human-fiend hybrids," I said. "A lot of them."

"They have time and resources to get it right," the Queen said. "I doubt the next time they try to overthrow the Primes, it will end as well for those currently in power."

"So, why make themselves known now?" Necia asked.

"I don't think they did," I said. "At least, I don't think they were meant to be. We stumbled on to Callie because the person she was working with was an idiot who killed FBI and RCU agents. We tracked her to the Croupier, and him to the Blessed. I don't think we were meant to find any of this. I think they're meant to be in the background still, just ticking along until whatever they need to happen is going to start. We need to find the Croupier . . . Jacob."

The name *Jacob Smythe* rang a bell, although I couldn't for the life of me figure out where I'd heard it before. *Smythe* was certainly not a name I heard an awful lot.

"Why was the blue-and-white not just because of Roberts' betrayal?" Necia asked, bringing me back from my thoughts.

"Jacob is Prime Roberts' bastard son," Neb said.

I looked between Neb and the Queen. "Are you serious?"

Both nodded.

"Do all of the Primes know?" Necia asked.

"No," Neb said. "Only those who were part of the Blessed inner circle and those who did a lot of digging after the fact. I was the latter. I was always curious why Prime Roberts would betray the Blessed but then save them from execution. His son."

"Do you think his son believes that the Queen was still responsible for their betrayal?" Necia asked.

"I would assume so," the Queen said. "I knew Jacob well. He always thought himself a step ahead of everyone else, and he was easily swayed by people who didn't have the best interests of anyone but themselves. The second he started to gain more and more influence within the Blessed, he changed, or maybe he was always that way and it just brought out the worst in him. I do know that Jacob would not have adorned his poker chips with the colours of his father if his father had betrayed him. He would have written his father's name across the chip."

Lucas, we've got incoming. Just one, Casimir said. *On horse, coming your way. I've been tracking them for a while, but they're in quite the hurry.*

How close? I replied.

Pretty bloody close, Casimir said. *Turn around.*

I turned to see Commander Pike riding up the hill toward us. He was moving at a good speed, but slowed as the four guards around the queen dropped into a defensive stance, their spears at the ready.

"Wait," the Queen commanded, and the four guards stood down.

I had a lot of questions about the Queen, about how she'd actually taken her current role, and exactly who she was behind the mask, but it was pretty clear that they were questions for another time. Besides, the commander's appearance had changed the mood among the people with Necia and me. if Commander Pike was about to pick a fight with her guards, it was going to be a short one.

The commander stopped his horse fifty feet away, dismounted, and pulled a backpack from the saddle. No one moved; no one went for their weapons. There were half a dozen guards, Neb, the Queen, Necia, and me all stood there. I was pretty sure you'd have to be an idiot to think you had a chance at winning.

Commander Pike was clearly not an idiot, as he slowly removed the apple from the bag and gave it to the horse. He tipped another half dozen apples onto the ground, leaving the horse where it was and continuing on toward us as the Queen strolled through her guards' defence, placing a hand on the shoulder of each of them, visibly reassuring them as she passed.

"Necia and Lucas," Commander Pike shouted tossing the bag onto the floor beside him. "You're going to need these; we have trouble on the way."

Casimir, I asked.

On it, they said, and he took off at speed back toward the city.

"What kind of trouble?" Necia asked.

"Men on horses arrived at the inn," Commander Pike said. "I thought it best to warn you all."

"Bringing men of your own might have helped," Necia said.

"Can't trust the guards here," Pike said. "They're as likely to cut my throat before anyone else can."

Necia picked up the bag and brought it back over to me, where she opened it fully, revealing our weapons.

"Commander Pike," the Queen of Crows said. "Marcus."

Commander Pike dropped to one knee and took her hand in his, kissing the back of it. "My Queen."

CHAPTER TWENTY-FIVE

O kay, would anyone like to explain what in the name of Zeus's arse-hole is going on?" Necia asked as I picked up my daggers from the bag along with my knife belt and sheaths for my daggers and began to put them on.

"I have people in Inaxia," the Queen of Crows said as Commander Pike got back to his feet from his kneeling position.

"And so does Neb," I said. "Anyone in Inaxia not actually working as a double agent?"

"Don't be a smart ass," Neb chastised.

"At this exact moment in time," I said, "I can either be a smart ass or tell you all to fuck off, because I'm fed up with being drip-fed information that would have been helpful. Pick one."

Neb let out a snort of irritation but didn't argue further.

"Who's coming for us?" Necia asked.

"Major Hephaestion and his people," Commander Pike said.

"Why?" I asked. "Apart from he's trying to find the Blessed and wants revenge?"

"He doesn't want revenge for anything," Commander Pike said. "If he ever had family here, they died decades ago."

"Why is Hephaestion so angry about them, then?" Necia asked.

"And why have people been talking about the Blessed attacking things? People? Garrisons?" I asked. "It's been mentioned several times now."

"Prime Roberts has been using the name of the Blessed to spread fear and hate," Commander Pike said. "I believe he wants to use them as a way to get support for himself so that when he stops them, he can be the hero again. Two of the garrisons that were attacked were actually empty. I did some checking, and there are zero deaths reported from any of those attacks. Hephaestion hasn't been in charge of a garrison for ten years. He and his band had their ranks removed. They were stealing from runners who stopped at their garrison, blackmailing those who used the runners to send classified information."

"They're criminals using the Blessed as a way to keep on being criminals," I said. "Why harass the boats, then?"

"The Blessed cause problems, so there's a crackdown on practitioners," the Queen said. "Prime Roberts steps in, stops the crackdown, stops the Blessed. The people love him because he stopped another insurrection before it could start, and the practitioners love him because he saw that they were the innocent party and stepped in to help. He gets a lot of support from all sides."

"He just needs a bad guy to point the finger at," Neb said.

I turned to look at the Queen of Crows. "That's you, I assume."

"To the public, Roberts is already a hero," the Queen said. "I run the Crow's Perch, but my involvement in the Blessed is not public knowledge. He stopped trying to assassinate me a long time ago, and there was a mutually beneficial stalemate. He can't tell people I was behind everything, because he thinks I have information that would drop him very much in it."

"Do you?" I asked.

"No," she said.

"And now he's willing to test that theory," I said. "Why now, though? What's the aim here, apart from to finally get rid of someone who's annoyed him for so long? He sent Necia and me here to die, but he obviously hadn't done his homework, because that was never going to happen in a city full of two-bit thugs, no offence."

The Queen waved my words away.

Eight riders, going the long way around from the city, heading your way, Casimir said. *You've got maybe a minute.*

Thanks, I told Casimir.

"They're coming," I said to everyone else. "Eight of them."

"Okay, so, what's the plan?" Necia asked.

Fucking hell, Casimir snapped. *One of them is taking shots at me.*

"Get to safety, Casimir," I said, no longer bothering to talk to him in my head. "I'll deal with them."

"Didn't answer the question," Necia said.

"I figured we'd wing it," I said.

"That's it?" Commander Pike asked. "Our Queen needs to be escorted to safety."

"I've got to be honest with you: your Queen is surrounded by people who have been killing assholes like the ones coming our way since before you were born," I said. "Pretty sure she's perfectly safe where she is."

Commander Pike just stared at me, his mouth open.

"I'm going to go have a word with the asshole who thinks it's okay to shoot arrows at my eidolon," I said.

"I don't think they knew it was your eidolon," Commander Pike called after me.

"That's no excuse for being a twat," I told him.

I walked down the hill, toward the galloping horses. There were, just as Casimir had stated, eight of them. The horses were all pale grey and were close in size to the one that Commander Pike had ridden.

Hephaestion led the charge of his people. I stopped thinking of him as a major, considering he was nothing more than a common criminal who had been fired from his post.

The horses slowed as they got closer, stopping altogether about thirty feet from where I stood.

I looked between the eight riders. Only one had a bow. It was a short, curved bow and was slung over his shoulder; a quiver of red-feather-tipped arrows were attached to his horse's saddle. I bent down and picked up a rock.

Hephaestion looked around and for a just a moment; he looked confused, as if he hadn't been expecting so many of us to be stood there. He quickly regained his composure, though.

"Lucas Rurik," Hephaestion bellowed. "I knew you were working with the Blessed."

"One second," I said, raising a finger.

"I will . . . "

I threw the rock at the archer, striking him between the eyes with enough force to knock him back off his horse. He landed with a thud.

"You were saying," I said to a clearly shocked Hephaestion.

"You're working with the Blessed and will be brought in for interrogation," Hephaestion said after quickly regaining his composure.

"Okay, here's what's going to happen," I said. "You're going to drop this ridiculous charade; we know you're not with the Inaxia military. We know you're little more than common criminals using the Blessed as an excuse to harass people and commit crimes, blaming them for what you've done.

We also know that you're working for Prime Roberts, presumably doing all his dirty work so he can use it as evidence of a Blessed revival. You're crooks. You're expendable. And as much as I don't want to kill anyone today, if you push me on this, I'm going to bury the eight of you on this hill." I drew one of my two daggers, holding it down by my leg.

Hephaestion looked more than a little taken aback.

"I'll give you a few seconds to decide on the best course of action to not get killed," I told him.

"There are eight of us," the one I'd busted in the head with a rock said. His face was now covered in blood, and there appeared to be a large hole in his forehead. I hoped it hurt.

"He's a Guild member, boss," one of the members of Hephaestion's crew said.

"I assume Prime Roberts told you that," I said.

Hephaestion stared daggers at me. "Hand over the Queen and you will come to no harm."

I sighed. "Hephaestion. You're being used here. Roberts wants to blame stuff on the Blessed, give himself more power. When you become expendable, and you will, you'll be discarded to the wolves or buried on a hill like this one. You're a criminal, but I'd like to believe you're not a total idiot."

Hephaestion said nothing.

"Why were you sent here right now?" I asked, looking around, and noticing the entrance. "You're never getting into the city without being killed. You're never getting to the Queen. Surely, Prime Roberts knows that. There's quite literally nothing you can do . . . " The thought dawned on me and I turned back to the Queen as one of her guards drew a sword and moved to attack her. It didn't last long before his head was bouncing down the hill from where he stood.

The Queen of Crows had barely even moved when her sword had flashed out from under her cape, decapitating the guard.

The arrow struck Hephaestion in the throat, rocking him on his saddle, but he stayed upright. The ground shook beneath my feet, and I sighed as it increased in ferocity, frightening the horses, who bucked and kicked at imaginary foes as more and more arrows rained down on the criminals who were trying to dismount. It was amazing how none of the horses appeared to get hit by any of the arrows.

I turned to see four hooded revenants walk out of the tree line, each one firing arrows from war bows that shimmered blue. Rift-forged bows. The criminals who had come there to die didn't stand a chance. Even riftborn and the strongest of revenants weren't immune to being peppered with arrows.

Seeing how moving was the most dangerous of my options, and standing didn't feel that great either, I dropped down to a seated position on the cold grass, the mist flowing over me.

The blood flowed and the bodies dropped until all eight were little more than pincushions. One of them had tried to turn into their revenant form but was killed halfway through the transformation, leaving them only a horned revenant from the waist down. Another actually turned completely into their spined-revenant form, but it hadn't stopped them from the accuracy of the assassins.

The four hooded revenants strolled toward the dead and put arrows in each of their heads, just in case.

One of the supposedly dead criminals burst up from the ground, having completely transformed into their horned-revenant form. Their body was peppered with arrows, and they would almost certainly die from their injuries, but they were looking to take people out before that happened.

The revenant grabbed one of the assassins by the back of the head with one massive hand and slammed their horned head into their back, skewering them through the torso. The horned revenant stood up to its full nearly eight feet of height, the thrashing hooded revenant still attached to it. The other assassins turned and fired at the horned revenant, putting more arrows in it, but the revenant roared in defiance and tore the wooden revenant free from its horn, throwing the body of the assassin at their friends.

"Good job," I said to Neb, getting to my feet and drawing my daggers as I strolled down the hill toward the rampaging horned revenant who was busy trying to grab hold of a second assassin while attempting to draw their sword from its scabbard, despite their arm not working.

"Hey," I shouted over the din of the assassins trying to drag their seriously wounded comrade out of the way of a dying and enraged enemy.

The horned revenant turned to me. It had an arrow stuck in its eye and at least six more in its chest. I had no idea how it was even able to stand upright, let alone do anything dangerous.

"I really didn't want anyone to die today," I told the horned revenant, the words landing without recognition. The creature was dead on its feet. Its brain just didn't know it yet.

The horned revenant charged me, screaming bloody murder the whole way. I breathed out slowly and dodged to the side at the last moment, slicing one of the daggers through the thigh of the revenant. It crashed to the ground, blood pouring form the deep wound in its leg, and tried to get back to its feet, but its body decided that enough was enough and it couldn't get up.

I walked back up the hill toward the revenant as it spat and raged at me. It swiped with a huge, clawed hand, but I avoided it, stepped to the side of the revenant, and drove one of the blades into the side of its skull.

The revenant died instantly, and I removed the blade, wiping it free of blood on the tattered clothing of the revenant before putting both back in their sheaths and looking back at Neb, who was watching me with a mixture of pride and concern. Concern for my health? It was hard to say, possibly, although it wasn't something she'd admit to. Concern for me being angry with her and wanting more of a fight? Also possible. It wouldn't be the first time.

"Needless bloodshed," I said to her as I walked back up the hill.

"I have more than just Commander Pike working for Prime Roberts," the Queen of Crows said, her voice dripping with anger. "I knew what the intel said, but to actually see it with my own eyes . . ."

"I think they were meant to get here after you were dead," I said. "Plans changed because we weren't meant to be out here, having a nice afternoon jaunt. I'm sorry one of your own people betrayed you."

The other guards were on their knees, their swords laid upon the ground before them.

"You think he was alone?" Commander Pike asked.

"No," Neb and I said in unison.

"There will be a full *investigation*," the Queen said, making that word sound suspiciously a lot more painful that it was meant to.

"You brought four hooded revenants with you," I said to Neb. "The question is, did you know that Hephaestion was going to come here today? Was this all pre-planned?"

"Hephaestion was a criminal," Neb said.

"That didn't answer the question," I countered.

"We knew that Prime Roberts had gotten to one of the Queen's guard," Neb said. "We knew that they wanted her alive if possible. We knew that if we fed intel to the right people, we could find out where the guard was meant to escape with the queen. Or escape after killing her if no other option was available."

"Commander Pike," I said.

"I let the right people in Prime Roberts' employ know that the guard would bring the Queen out here through the tunnel," Commander Pike said. "We used your being here as a way to speed up proceedings without drawing concern from anyone."

"And I made sure to have my people here should things go south," Neb said.

"You still had a guard watch your back you knew was going to try and kill you," Necia said, although it held a touch of admiration.

"He had to believe that he had a chance to get away," the Queen said.

"What about the four in the city who attacked us?" I asked. "Had you known about them?"

"Yes," Neb said. "The two of you walking into this city without anyone touching you for several minutes, that would be unheard-of. No one spoke to you; no one tried to test you. We knew you were coming; let it slip that you were a Guild Talon and said that the first person to try and hurt either of you gets fed to a primordial."

"And those four were your people, yes?" Necia asked.

"Yes," Neb said. "They will be fine. There were still guards watching from the ramparts, still people in the city who would report back. There had to be an attack. Had to be a show. The guards tried to buy the allegiance of several members of a gang in the city. It turns out my allegiance is more valuable to them than the promise of a few coins."

I wasn't annoyed that they hadn't told me; I wasn't annoyed that they'd purposefully fed information that got several people killed. They were criminals... murderers. I didn't give a shit about what happened to them. I was irritated that Neb had put on a spectacle for our arrival and had let Necia and me kick seven bells out of her people to make it look good.

"I don't like being used," Necia said, pointing at Neb. "Don't let it happen again."

"What answers do you need?" the Queen of Crows asked.

"Where is Jacob?" I asked. "There are probably more, but that's the big one."

"Come walk with me," Neb said, not making it sound like I had any choice in the matter.

I looked down the hill, where three of the hooded revenants were busy helping their fallen ally. Considering he'd been skewered and almost eviscerated, he looked pretty good.

"I don't know where Jacob is," Neb said as we walked under a large tree. "I do know that he believes that his father saved his life, that he believes the Queen betrayed them all, even after she was ousted from the group, that she let her own vengeance blind her. Wherever he is, if he ever comes back here, he will try to kill her."

"I'd best make sure that doesn't happen, then," I said. "What about Prime Roberts? He's consolidating power. He's a threat to everyone in the rift."

"Yes, he is," Neb said. "But today we lessened that threat. I will make it known to Prime Roberts that I'm aware of his transgressions. Should he wish to come after the Queen again, I will be forced to intervene. I will contact some friends within the Ancients, make sure that Prime Roberts is kept on a short leash for a while. He won't be able to try this trick again."

"Get the guards at the prison changed," I said. "They work for Roberts."

"I can pull some strings," Neb said.

I stayed silent.

"I know that my . . . machinations have not always left our relationship on good terms," Neb said. "You are excellent at what you do, but playing politics isn't something you've ever wanted part of. And it's something I've always been good at."

"Can't deny that," I said. "So, I should just go back to Earth?"

"You need to find Jacob," Neb said. "Wherever he is, he will be involved in power. He craves it. Find his people. Break them, you'll get what you need."

My thoughts fell back to Eve. "We have one of his people. I'm not sure the authorities would appreciate it if I broke her."

"Would they appreciate dead bodies more?" Neb asked.

"Torture doesn't work, Neb," I said. "Never has."

"I always found fear to be an excellent motivator," Neb said. "What does Eve love?"

"Money," I said immediately. "That was the overwhelming feeling I got when I met her."

"With that information, you can find him; you can hopefully stop him and, in turn, stop Callie Mitchell," Neb said. "I do have a request, though. And in return, I will give you information the Queen does not know. Something I doubt even Necia knows."

I turned to look at Neb. "What's the request?"

"First, go say your goodbyes," Neb said. "There's a embers tear stone not far from here. Saves you having to travel all the way back to the river."

I stared at Neb for a moment before she waved me away, and I walked back to the Queen of Crows, Necia, and everyone else who watched me approach.

"Thank you for your help," I said to the Queen of Crows.

"I hope you find this Jacob Smythe and stop him from hurting more people," the Queen said. "Be careful."

"Always am," I said, immediately thinking of several dozen instances when I wasn't.

I shook Commander Pike's hand. "I guess you're staying."

"I'm not sure what I'm doing yet," Commander Pike said. "If I can be of assistance to the Queen by maintaining my cover, I will stay with Roberts. But I would like to stay here. Take care, Lucas."

"You too," I said, and walked off with Necia.

"You're off, then," she said.

I nodded. "Neb wants to ask me a favour. I already have a promise crystal, so I'm hoping it's nothing too huge."

Necia hugged me. "Don't let it be seven years again," she said.

We held each other for several seconds before breaking apart. "I won't," I said. "Please be careful with Neb. She's . . . she has her own agenda with everything."

"I know," Necia said with a smile. "Don't worry."

I gave Necia one last kiss and walked over to Neb, who had remained seated. "What's the favour?"

"When you find Callie Mitchell, whenever that might be, don't kill her." Neb's gaze remained firmly down the hill, toward the dead bodies of the criminals, who were being dragged away by the Queen of Crow's guards.

"Why?"

Neb turned to look at me. "I can't say. It's actually not for me to say; I'm just asking as a favour. Please."

It was the *please* that did it. "I want you to know you're the second person in the last few days to ask me to keep someone alive; it didn't work out so well for her. My point is, I can try, but I can't guarantee that someone or something else isn't going to kill her no matter what I do."

"That you try is all I ask," Neb said, getting to her feet. "I'll show you the tear stone."

We walked further up the hill until we were at its apex, where the stone came into view. It hummed with power as the high winds in the area whipped across the peak of the hill.

Casimir landed on my shoulder, allowing Neb to scratch them behind the ear.

"So, what's the information that you want to tell me and no one else knows?" I asked as I stepped onto the stone, and prepared to open a tear to my embers.

"Jacob Smythe," Neb said. "He was involved with a woman who's a rift-walker. The same rift-walker who took all of the leaders of the Blessed into exile on Earth. No one knows what happened to her, but her name is Helen Queen."

CHAPTER TWENTY-SIX

Neb hadn't stayed around to answer any of my follow-up questions, and I'd opened a tear, going back into my embers with my mind still reeling from what I'd been told. The Croupier was the illegitimate son of a Prime.

Prime Roberts had betrayed the Blessed, including his own son, and had told everyone that it had been the Queen of Crows the whole time. I think that gave the Croupier, Jacob, quite a lot of incentive to hate her. I wondered if maybe Jacob was doing anything that would be considered anti-rift-fused, and whether or not this Helen was aiding him in some way. If she was even still alive.

A rift-walker was a surprise. They were rare and powerful, and most rift-fused went their whole lives without ever even meeting one. They could open tears between the rift and Earth with a wave of their hands, moving between the two as easily as opening a door. They tended to be solitary or keep their powers hidden, as people liked to find them and pay them to start opening rifts all over the place. Unfortunately, every time they opened a rift, they risked it getting out of hand and creating a tear that allowed a huge amount of power to flood out of the rift. I'd met two in my entire life; one died after opening a tear and allowing so much power out of the rift that it took decades to hunt all of the fiends that were created. The other had taken themselves away where they were never seen again. It was a lonely existence to have a power craved by those who would use it for only selfish reasons.

"He's been quiet for several seconds," Maria said. They were in the form of a barn owl and sat perched on a nearby fence post as I walked through my embers.

"It's been a long day," Casimir said to Maria.

"It's been an exceptionally long day," I corrected. "Prime Roberts is not a good guy, his son is the Croupier, and I'm pretty sure there's a lot more going on here than just one crime boss wanting power and wealth."

"Which one is the crime boss?" Maria asked.

"Both," I said. "Just different types of crimes."

I sighed.

"I need to find Ji-hyun in London," I said. "I need to tell her and Ravi who the Croupier is and see if we can find him before more people die."

"The exit is this way," Maria said. "I can feel the pull of the Guild medallion. Turns out that maybe it was a smart idea to leave it with your friends."

I turned to look at Maria, who took off.

"So, you were wrong, then?" I called after them.

"I am flying above your head," Maria said. "It may not be wise to irritate me when I'm in this position."

"You're not a real bird," I said. "No pooping."

Maria looked down at me. "Spoilsport."

Casimir laughed, having turned into a horse, trotting alongside me.

"Do you have a plan?" Maria asked.

"Find Jacob, force him to tell me what I need to know, stop him from hurting anyone else ever again," I said. "In that order."

"Killing him, then," Casimir said.

"If that's what it takes," I replied. "I think enough people have died at his hands, though. And even more because of his actions. If I can do this without a large death toll, I'd take that road."

"Take care, Lucas," Casimir said.

"Thank you for your help," I told them both.

"Go do what you need to do," Maria said.

I opened the tear and stepped out of my embers and into a war zone.

It took me a fraction of a second to realise I was not somewhere safe, as bullets slammed into a tree beside my head and I was dragged to the ground behind a large Range Rover.

"Lucas?" Ji-hyun shouted at me as bullets continued to smash into the car.

"What the *fuck* is going on?" I asked.

I managed a quick check of our immediate problems. We were on a long stretch of road going through a wooded area. Ten feet in front of us was a large black Range Rover on its side, with another directly beside us at an angle, shielding us from both sides of the attack. All of the cars were peppered with bullet holes, although the one on its side had a gigantic smoking crater on the side of the SUV where the doors once would have been. Two police cars were on fire at the rear of the convoy, neither looked likely to be moved anytime soon. Another Range Rover was parked at an angle between us and the police cars; it looked to be in fairly good condition.

There was an embankment to the right of where we were crouched, with several masked attackers firing a variety of semi-automatic weaponry in our direction. More gunfire erupted from unseen assailants hidden by the dense woodland.

I counted four dead police, at least as many RCU agents lying motionless, and a never-ending stream of bullets heading our way. Our odds weren't exactly sparkling.

"We were taking Eve to a secure facility after Ravi got intel we were going to be attacked," Ji-hyun said. "So, we got attacked on the way instead. It just started, so thanks for joining in."

Ji-hyun and I were sat against the rear wheel arch of one Range Rover. "I hope these are reinforced."

"They're essentially tanks with marginally better handling," Ji-hyun said as Ravi and Nadia joined us, keeping low as they moved.

"Lucas," Nadia said with a smile.

"Where did you come from?" Ravi asked.

"Rift," I said. "Quick update, please."

"Unknown assailants," Ravi said. "Two of our own people betrayed us. Four more alive in Range Rover with Eve, Emily included. Half a dozen of the attackers were killed in the initial assault. The rest have moved to safer grounds. We've been here maybe sixty seconds."

"The Croupier's people come to rescue her?" I asked.

Ravi shook his head. "They're trying to kill her. No idea why."

More gunshots silenced any more questions I might have.

Ji-hyun tossed me my Guild medallion. "Sorry to drag you into this."

"Needed something to keep busy," I said. "They're going to flank us. Nadia and I will hit the embankment. Everyone else, get into the trees; we need them flushed out."

"On it," Ravi said without pause. "Aren't you going to need a gun?"

"I'll take one of theirs," I told him.

"Be careful," Ji-hyun said to me.

"You too," I said, and watched them both move around to the rear of the nearest Range Rover and begin firing in short bursts at the trees.

I had taken a step toward the side of the Range Rover when Nadia's eyes rolled up into her head and her body shook. I took a step back toward her, and there was a sudden blinding light. Nadia crashed into me, wrapping her chains around us as she threw us both to the side while heat radiated around us. We hit the ground, rolled down a steep bank at the edge of the woodland, and I felt her chains slack as we stopped.

My ears rang from the explosion that we'd been hit by. The second or third explosion in a few days. I was getting really tired of people trying to blow me up.

I rolled off Nadia and found that we were in the middle of a patch of thick undergrowth and large trees. Bullets sprayed in our direction, and I dragged Nadia as far back from where we'd landed as possible, sitting her up beside several large trees that almost intertwined. There were several soldiers on top of the bank, and the trees where we'd landed were hit with several rounds of gunfire.

"Nadia," I said. "Get up."

She remained motionless.

"Why'd you do that?" I said, slightly more concerned now. "You didn't need to save me. You didn't need to do that."

Nadia didn't move; her eyes remained closed, her chains limply wrapped over her.

I checked for a pulse and was relieved to find that it was strong. She wasn't bleeding, but the chains were marked with smoke damage, and some of them had little kinks where shrapnel had hit. I wasn't sure if that was the cause of her state or if the shockwave had done something to her brain.

"I'll be back for you," I told her.

I stood and looked through the trees at the soldiers stood atop the embankment. They cheered and shouted slurs about my parentage. They laughed at their jokes about having killed one of us.

They were all going to die.

I turned to smoke and flew across the clearing, moving up the embankment as fast as I could. One of the soldiers leaned over the edge of the clearing, looking down, just as I smashed into him. I spun the smoke around him, lifting him off the ground, re-formed, and slit his throat with one of my blades before turning back to smoke and flying across to the next soldier.

Bullets slammed into my smoke form, each one causing me pain, causing me to concentrate further as I hit the next soldier, re-forming and breaking his neck, throwing him into his nearest ally, and turning to smoke again.

I hit the next soldier as he unloaded his revolver right into my smoke form, hitting the soldier behind me, who was trying to get back to his feet. I re-formed, grabbed the attacker's arm, lifted it up, and stabbed him repeatedly under the armpit before kicking him over the side of the bank.

A bullet, this one having taken a charge from their rift-tempered weapons, cut through my smoke form as I moved toward my next target. It felt as though I was being burned from the inside out. It caused my smoke form to dissipate, which made me have to use more power to drag it back together again. Unfortunately for the soldier, I re-formed directly in front of him and hit him in the chest with an open-palm strike that sent him flying back into the nearest tree with the kind of noise that means they're not getting back up.

My body was screaming at me to stop, to take my time, to stay in my solid state for a while. I ignored it, pushed the pain aside, turned back to smoke, and flew toward the next target as the three remaining soldiers decided that close combat was the better option and drew knives.

At the sight of rift-tempered knives, I returned to my solid form. Rift-tempered bullets hurt me in my smoke form, made it difficult to concentrate, but cutting through the smoke with a rift-tempered blade was going to make me re-form at best and do me serious harm at worst.

I drew my own daggers as the three soldiers approached me. They kept in front of me, at a distance, so I couldn't run between them without someone cutting me. Like their dead and injured companions, they wore black tactical gear with matching balaclavas, which the three of them pulled down. Two men and a woman. All young. All presumably human, considering they'd showed no evidence of power.

They moved slow, keeping low, two with their knives out front and one in a reverse grip. My body continued to protest what I'd done. I'd ignored the pain and moved on pure adrenaline, but at some point, the adrenaline was going to fade and the pain would be back to embrace me. I didn't want to be fighting three trained soldiers when that happened.

One of the men lunged at me, and I took a slight step toward them, but they darted back—which I knew they were going to do—and their ally shot forward to try and stab me. I pushed his arm out of the way, locked his elbow, and brought my knee up into his stomach, doubling him over and kneeing him in the face. I pushed him to the ground and kicked him in his ruined face, which was already bleeding heavily.

The other two saw their opening and darted forward from either side of me. I moved to my left to intercept, parried the stab attempt, and brought my second dagger around, plunging it into the woman's ribs three times before pushing her to the floor.

I turned in time to avoid the third soldier stabbing me in the back. I kicked out at one of his knees and heard it pop, followed by his scream of pain, which echoed around the woodland. He dropped to his knees and waved the dagger at me in a futile attempt. I waited for the arc of the arm to go past me, grabbed it, and broke it at the elbow. I removed the dagger from his grip and threw it aside, walking past him to his softly gurgling friend as he continued to try and breathe through a ruined mouth and nose.

I wondered if it would have been easier to use the MP5, but with the higher ground, they would have had an advantage.

I dragged the soldier with the busted knee and arm over to his friend and left them both there, removing any weapons around them. I picked up a Smith & Wesson M&P 15 that one of the soldiers had dropped, checked the ammo, reloaded, and shot anyone alive through the head with it.

I wasn't done yet.

There were gunshots and explosions from the woods across the road. I slid down the embankment, jogged across the road with my rifle ready, and shot two soldiers who thought that was a good time to leave the woods.

I stepped over the dead bodies of two RCU agents to get into the woods as more and more shots rang out. I killed two more attackers with shots to their chests and heads as they ran toward me in a panic as my eyesight adjusted to the meagre light.

It didn't take long to mop up the rest of the attackers, and I tossed the rifle into the ruins of a Range Rover on my way out of the woods. I walked the length of the battle, nodding to Ravi and Ji-hyun as they left the trees, and continuing on until I saw Eve on her knees, her hands handcuffed behind her back. A female agent held a gun to the back of Eve's head.

"Lucas," someone called from a portion of the woodland where Nadia and I had descended into.

I jogged to the edge of the road and looked down. "Nadia okay?" I shouted.

"I think so," Emily said, emerging from behind the trees with Nadia beside her.

Relief flooded my body as Nadia waved at me.

"Do you need a hand?" Ji-hyun asked.

"I'm good," Nadia shouted.

The second Emily and Nadia reached us, the latter sat down. "My chains got dinged," she said sadly.

"You know you didn't have to save me," I said. "I wasn't going to die."

"I had to do it," Nadia said.

"The chains?" I asked.

She nodded. "If you got hurt here . . . you couldn't go on. Couldn't do whatever needs to be done next."

"And that is?" I asked.

Nadia shrugged. "No clue."

"Just stay there and rest, please," I said.

"I will do that," Nadia said, lying down on the ground. "This is nice."

"I'll keep an eye on her," Emily said.

"Thank you," I said.

Nadia put her hand in the air and gave a thumbs-up.

"Comms are still out," Ravi said, tapping his earpiece and walking away with one of his RCU agents to check for survivors.

I walked around the side of the Range Rover and looked down at Eve. "So, Jacob wants you dead," I said with a smile. "That has got to be unpleasant."

Ji-hyun stood beside me. "I would talk, Eve," she said.

Eve looked away.

"We were close," Ji-hyun said, continuing to look at Eve. "You think that the Croupier is going to stop here? You think he's not going to hunt you down?"

"So, you two were close," I said.

Ji-hyun stared at me for several seconds. "Very. She betrayed me when an assassin came to kill me. Told them what they needed, nearly got me killed in the process. Do what you need to do."

I turned to Eve. "You betrayed your love for money?" I asked, incredulous.

"I do what I need to do," Eve snapped. "And right now, I'm going to keep my mouth closed until I get a deal."

"A deal?" I asked. "What kind of deal?"

"The one where I get a new life," Eve said.

"I don't think you understand," I said. "Your options, as I see it, are either that you tell us what we want to know or I make it known that Jacob is trying to kill you because you betrayed him. I think the fee might go up a bit after that."

Eve chuckled. "Why do you think he wants me dead?"

"Clearing the decks," I said.

"Wait, you know his name," Eve said.

I nodded. "Jacob Smythe," I said. "Illegitimate son to a Prime of Inaxia. Cast out of the rift and settled here for however many years, building up his money and power base. I know a lot about him."

"Did you just say *Jacob Smythe*?" Ravi asked me as he returned to us.

"Yeah, that's the name of the Croupier," I said. "The name is familiar, but I can't place it."

Ravi removed his phone from his pocket. "Yes, got reception." He showed me a picture on his phone of a man I'd seen on the news only a short while previously.

"This is the Right Honourable Jacob Maxwell Smythe of Her Majesty's Government," Ravi said.

I looked down at Eve and knew from her expression that we'd hit the nail on the head.

The Right Honourable Jacob Maxwell Smythe of Her Majesty's Government was a murderous crime boss. I let out a huge sigh of annoyance. "Bollocks."

CHAPTER TWENTY-SEVEN

S o, Jacob Smythe is coming after you because you know who he is and he's worried you'll spill?" I asked Eve. We'd put her in the back seat of a Range Rover and set off, leaving the ruins of several other cars and lots of dead people in our wake. "You have form for it, after all."

"Not going to say a thing unless you give me some assurances," she said.

I sat beside Eve on one side with Ji-hyun on the other, Ravi in the front passenger seat, Emily driving, and Nadia taking up the last two seats of the seven-seat car. I didn't know where we were going, but Ravi did, and that was all that mattered.

"Actually, we know who he is now," Ji-hyun said. "I'm not sure we need you."

"I know *everything*," Eve said.

"I'd start sharing, then," Ravi told her. There was an edge to his tone that I hadn't heard before. "You want assurance; we need something to actually take from this deal."

Eve let out a long, exasperated sigh. "You all think it was Simon Wallace feeding you intel on what Jacob was doing. You paid him for that information. I *gave* it all to him. I fed him intel and got him to feed it to you."

"Why?" I asked.

"Because he wanted out," Eve said. "And so did I, but with me watching his back, I was certain he wouldn't get found out. And if he did get found out, he was the one with his head on the chopping block."

"How altruistic of you," Ji-hyun said.

"Simon got greedy," Eve said, completely ignoring Ji-hyun's comment. "He started telling you things he hadn't cleared with me. Simon got discovered. And by now, I'm guessing Simon got dead."

"His family?" I asked.

"Them too," she said.

"I'll call my people and get them to check out their house," Ravi said.

"We could always do a drive-by," Nadia suggested.

"Are you insane?" Eve asked. "If they see me . . ."

"They won't," I assured her. "But if his family is in danger, we can't just let that go. It's not their fault he was in bed with the devil."

"Is that me or Jacob?" Eve asked.

"I don't care," I told her.

"What's to stop us just executing you and throwing you in the river?" Nadia asked.

There was an uneasy silence. "I have detailed documents about everything Jacob was involved in," Eve said. "Every scam, every crime, every murder. Maybe not every, but close. I took notes. Video. Audio. Photos. I have enough information to bring down Jacob's entire organisation, and he knows it. I'm assuming he came after me because he went after Simon first, realised he wasn't the brains, and put two and two together."

"We could just go to the Houses of Parliament and drag the piece of shit out of there by the scruff of his neck," I said.

"We're still talking about Jacob, yes?" Nadia asked. "Because there are a few pieces of shit in that particular institution."

"We're not here to debate the current state of our government," Ravi said. "Also, no, you cannot drag a sitting Member of Parliament into the street."

"Don't see why not," Nadia said.

"For a number of reasons," Ravi said. "One, there are armed guards everywhere. Two, those said armed guards don't play games. You mess about, you get shot. Three, Jacob is a sitting Member of Parliament. You going in there and dragging him out breaks so many laws, I can't even begin to count."

"He's a practitioner," Ji-hyun said. "He's not legally allowed to hold office."

"Yes, but right now, no one else knows that," Ravi said. "A Guild member dragging out a Member of Parliament is going to be front-page news around the world. By the time everyone finds out the truth, it won't matter. A rift-fused attacked a member of a human government. A human member of government, democratically elected by other humans. That's the story that will run. Even after they find out he's lying, the story will still be *how many of our members of government aren't human?* It would set back human–rift-fused relations; it would drag the Ancients into it."

"I know," I said calmly.

"It would drag other Guilds into it," Ravi continued. "It would completely fuck up the RCU."

"Ravi, I'm not going to do it," I told him, hoping to calm his blood pressure before his head exploded.

"There's always someone to spoil our fun," Nadia said.

"How do we arrest someone we can't arrest?" Emily asked, practically deflating in the front seat as Ravi got on the radio and started talking to someone at his head office.

We all turned to Eve. "I'd start talking," Ravi said.

"Locker 174," Eve said. "It's at Lock It."

"What?" Nadia asked.

"It's a storage company in London," Eve said. "It's a ten-minute drive from Simon's home."

"Guess we're going on a road trip, then," I said.

Ji-hyun stared at Eve for several seconds. "How much did you steal from Jacob?" she asked eventually.

"What?" Eve asked.

"You were getting kickbacks from any information Simon gave to the RCU," Ji-hyun said. "But that couldn't have been a whole lot of money. So, how much did you steal from Jacob? And exactly what was it that Jacob did that made you betray him?"

"When I'm given assurances," Eve said.

"My people got killed because of Jacob," Ravi said. "You're going to talk, and if I like what I hear, I'll assure you that you won't be in a jail cell next to him when we take him."

Eve laughed.

"Talk or die," I said. "Pick one."

"You wouldn't," Eve said.

I showed her the Guild medallion. "Who's going to stop me?"

Eve's eyes darted toward Ravi, who turned away.

"You can't threaten me," Eve shouted.

"Not a threat," I told her. "You tell us everything, you walk. You don't, I'll make sure that Jacob finds you before we find him."

"Fine," Eve snapped. "I've been skimming off the profits for years, but I was happy to work with Jacob. He was a good boss, he left me to my own devices, and those who crossed him tended to end up dead alongside their friends and family. But a few years ago, he started to go on and on about the riftborn, about using them as the boogeymen to scare humans with. He'd been an MP for a while by that point and started to do more TV interviews, telling the world about how bad they were. Every time someone from the rift-fused community was caught doing something, he'd twist himself in knots trying to get the riftborn to be behind it. It was like he was obsessed.

"Anyway, it turned out that he was obsessed because a certain Dr. Callie Mitchell had figured out a way to make humans turn into fiends. I don't know the end plan with it all, but it involves going back to the rift to complete what the Blessed started before they were exiled."

"Take over Inaxia," I said.

"Maybe," Eve said with a shrug. "Like I said, I didn't get told everything. Jacob was the money man, the one who funds went to dirty and ended up clean. He worked with criminals all over the globe while publicly maintaining his Member of Parliament job."

"Why not just use his clout to get you taken somewhere safe and executed?" I asked.

"He took a big risk going for you here," Ji-hyun said.

"He's becoming unhinged," Eve said. "It's been happening for about six months now. Since he found . . . her."

"Her?" Nadia asked.

"Helen Queen," Eve said.

"The rift-walker?" I said.

Eve looked over at me. "How do you know that?"

"I have friends in high places too," I said. "She was the one who took all of the members of the Blessed out of the rift and through to Earth."

"Jacob said she betrayed them all," Eve said. "Said she was going to be their salvation."

"Salvation?" Ravi asked, sounding more like his usual self.

"I don't know," Eve said. "Callie Mitchell has this plan, and Helen is apparently a part of it. Jacob has to keep her locked up until she's needed, but Jacob hates her. Just outright *hates* her. He sits in front of her cell for hours, telling her over and over how she cost him everything. How she brought down the Blessed. You'd have thought she'd done it single-handedly, from the way Jacob talked. Anyway, it became pretty obvious that he was paying less and less attention to the running of the organisation and more to going on TV to blame riftborn for everything. He spent more time talking to people in America whose names I don't even know. They were all preparing for something to do with Callie."

"Do you know about his meeting with her in Canada?" I asked.

"Where he took a shipment of a bunch of vials?" Eve asked. "He has them locked in his manor house outside of Winchester."

"Is that where Helen is, too?" Ji-hyun asked.

Eve nodded.

"So, you betrayed Jacob because he was taking his eye off the ball?" Emily asked as we started to hit London traffic and slowed considerably.

"Not just off the ball," Eve said. "It was obvious that his endgame didn't involve anyone who had worked with him to get him to his current state. I can't go through to Inaxia; I'm a revenant. And I'm not dying to find out if I get to go to some fabled city. He was going to do something bad, and we were going to be left with the consequences."

"How do you know it's bad?" I asked.

"He had a rift-walker captive," Eve said. "I can't imagine that's for anything even close to good."

"So, you've skimmed millions," I said. "I assume it's millions off an exceptionally dangerous man, who is now becoming unhinged. I understand why you'd run and betray him."

"The second Simon got found out and went into protective custody, I knew my time was finite," Eve said. "I just needed to find an exit. Jacob failed in my death today, but he won't let that go. I want immunity from everything I was involved in; I want a new identity. I don't want your money; I just need your help."

"We can talk about that," Ravi said. "Once I've checked on Simon and his family, once we've made sure that you really do have all of this intel in a lock-up, and once I've made sure you're not going to get more of my people killed while we hunt your boss."

"Winchester," I said. "That where he is now?"

Eve nodded. "I assume so, yes."

It was raining by the time we'd gotten through the London traffic and pulled up outside of the storage facility, a massive building surrounded by twelve-foot-high mesh fencing, with what looked like barbed wire on top. There was a guard hut just outside and a barrier to stop people from just driving into the large parking area.

"Right, we're going to look at this lock-up of yours," I told Eve. "Ji-hyun, would you like to accompany us?"

"I think it's better if Emily does," Ji-hyun said.

"I agree," Eve said, putting a lot of venom into two short words.

Emily stopped the car, getting out as I followed suit, and waited for Eve to join us.

"We'll check on Simon's home and head back here after," Ravi said as Ji-hyun climbed into the driver's seat. "We've got more RCU headed there just in case. We only took a small number with us to move Eve, and that was a mistake I won't be repeating."

I watched the car pull away, and Emily and I marched Eve through the entrance and into the car park of the storage place.

"Where's the key?" I asked Eve.

"In an apartment in Berlin," Eve said with a smile.

"Are you taking the piss?" I snapped. "That might have been useful information beforehand."

"Oh, no, what a shame," Eve said. "Now you'll have to keep me around nice and safe while we sort something else out."

"You think you may have vastly overplayed your hand here?" Emily snapped.

Emily took point and was met by a rotund gentleman with a goatee who left through an exit marked OFFICE PERSONNEL ONLY. A woman joined them both, and there was a lot of gesticulating and pointing at a clipboard that the newcomer woman had brought with her. Emily nodded a lot, but I was too far away to hear.

She returned to me while the man and woman waited.

"What's wrong?" I asked.

"They won't give me a key," Emily said. "Apparently, it's a legal thing. You need a warrant."

"I do?" I asked. "Seriously?"

"Do we have time to go get one?" Eve asked sarcastically.

"No," I said.

The three of us walked back over to the two workers.

"Look," I said calmly. "Right now, there's a lady out there who has been kidnapped. Her name is Helen, and she's being held by a man who has just murdered a bunch of RCU agents and police officers in his bid to get hold of this lady here. Her name is Eve, and she's a terrible person who we'd very much like to put in a cell somewhere, but we need what's in that locker. Is there any way she can prove to you who she is and we can go unlock this storage facility?"

"Account number 8857445," Eve said.

The lady tapped some numbers on her pad. "Password," she asked.

"Pomegranate," Eve said. "They're my favourite fruit."

"I don't care," Emily snapped.

"Give them the key," the man told the women.

"I'll bring it to the locker," the woman told us, and walked away.

"Come with me," the man said.

"That was easier than expected," Emily said as we entered the front entrance behind the man, who opened the security door for us.

"Thank you," I said.

"Do what you need to do," the man told us, and shook my hand, noticeably looking away from Eve.

Emily, Eve, and I followed the arrows on the floor to the correct storage locker, where we were met by the lady who had been outside. She gave Emily the key.

"Was all of that true?" she asked. "About the RCU being killed and this woman being a criminal?"

"Yes," I said. "Every word."

Emily put the key into the lock on the side of the metal shutter and twisted until there was an audible *click*. I grabbed the handle on the shutter and pulled, revealing the contents of the hundred-square locker.

"I'll leave you to it," the woman said, walking away as I pulled on the lightbulb chain in the centre of the metal room.

There were seven black plastic tubs stacked along the far wall, a coffee table in the middle of the locker, and two comfortable-looking, dark-brown leather armchairs beside it.

"Take a seat," I said to Eve, who took up residence in one of the armchairs.

I grabbed the first box and put it on the coffee table, opening it up to reveal photos, documents, pieces of scrawled notes. The rest of the boxes had similar things, although they also contained USB drives and more than one hard drive from a computer.

The further we went through it all, the more it became apparent exactly what Eve had done there. It was a detailed and exhaustive list of crimes that Jacob Smythe had either personally engaged in or employed others to do on his behalf. There were names of people in law enforcement, political circles—both in the UK and abroad—and public figures. All of whom were either bribed or blackmailed, according to the notes.

"You need to see this," Emily said, showing me a black ledger.

"This is a summary of every single person who worked for or aided the Croupier's enterprise," I said, looking over at Eve. "Jacob thinks that Simon got all of this to use against him?"

"He does, yes," Eve said.

"You were going to feed Simon and his family to the wolves and not do a damn thing to stop it," I said.

"All's fair in riches and war," Eve said.

"He has children," I said, feeling my anger increase.

Eve shrugged.

Emily punched her in the face.

I was surprised to find I had phone reception, and called Ravi, who answered on the third ring. "We found Simon," he said. "He's dead. They tied him to a chair and tortured him for several hours. He wrote *Eve* in his own blood on the wall. That can't be a coincidence."

"His family?" I asked.

"His kids were at their grandparents' for the night," Ravi said. "With their mum. Simon and his wife were going through some stuff. Probably saved all of their lives. How goes the search?"

"There's enough here to put Jacob and a whole lot of other people away forever," I said.

"Just waiting on some backup arriving, and we'll head back to you," Ravi said. "Stay safe."

I ended the call and put my phone away. "Mum and kids were safe. Simon not so lucky."

Emily let out a sigh of relief.

"You going to apologise for punching me now?" Eve asked.

"I would just keep quiet for the moment," I said to her.

We spent some more time going through everything we could find before marching Eve back through the facility, when Ravi called to let us know he'd arrived. Two large black Audi Q7 SUVs were parked at the storage facility, with another one waiting outside, blocking the entrance and exit.

Ravi, Ji-hyun, and Nadia got out of one SUV, with another man who was wearing full tactical gear and carrying a rift-tempered MP5. No matter how many times you tell humans that rift-tempered guns are temperamental at best, they still insist on using them.

Emily and I quickly explained everything to Ravi before bundling Eve into the back of one of the cars and showing Ravi the contents of the storage locker and explaining that he was going to need to get people there *now* to catalogue everything.

"Oh, we managed to get some pictures of the interior of Jacob's Winchester manor," Ravi said as we left the facility again.

Ravi removed his pocket and tapped the screen before passing it to me.

I flicked through the photos of the house. "How'd you get these?" I asked him.

"They're online," he said. "Jacob likes to show off. He did a TV show where celebrities have to guess who lives somewhere. His house is easily fortified and has a large stone-and-brick fence surrounding it. Thick metal gates and, according to those photos, a castle turret. I think it's a replica, although either way, it's going to be a problem."

"Good sniper view," I said, zooming in on the photo of the turret. "This will be easier for a small team to get inside."

"By *small* you mean *not RCU*, I assume," Ravi said.

"How much flak do you take if you storm the place and bring in a sitting Member of Parliament?" I asked. "I know he's a crook, you know he's a crook, but before the truth comes out, just how much trouble could you be in?"

"I answer to people who work with MI5," Ravi said. "I know officially, we've been separated, but in reality, they're still my boss. The Ancients too. Don't see them often, though."

"Okay, so go to the Ancients and get what we need," I said. "Do you know how to contact them?"

"I have a phone number," Ravi said. "Never needed to use it before."

"Get them to remove Jacob's protections," I said. "Show them everything we have."

"Take photos of as much as you can," Ji-hyun said. "Back everything up. And I do mean *everything*. Multiple times, in multiple places. I doubt an Ancient is working with Jacob; it would literally mean their execution if they were discovered to have subverted human law like this, but you never can be too sure."

"You want to borrow the Audi, don't you?" Ravi asked.

"Please," I said.

"Let him have it," Ravi shouted, and the driver of the Audi—a young male agent—got out and tossed me the keys. "Please don't break it."

"No promises," Nadia said with a beaming smile as she leaned out of the car's open window.

"Helen is there with him," Emily said. "We'll need to find her as a matter of urgency. We don't know what'll happen once we hit the manor house."

"I'll ask him," I said. "Nicely."

"I can do *nicely*," Nadia said through the open car window.

"Do not let Nadia ask him," Ravi said. "I get the feeling that wouldn't end well for anyone. And do *not* kill him. We can't have a member of a Guild, or rift-fused in general, killing people who work for the government. No matter what they've done. I'm going to take a contingency of agents to Winchester; once we've got the go-ahead, we'll come in and help with the arrest. You don't take him out of the house without us."

"We need to wait for nightfall," Ji-hyun said. "That'll minimise anyone seeing us, or the chance of getting in the house and starting a gunfight."

"He won't leave the house," I assured Ravi. "Talk to the Ancients. Get Jacob's human protections removed."

I walked over to the car where Eve was sat. "One last question," I said. "I'll put in a good word for you with Ravi after."

"Go on, then," Eve said.

"The woodlands around the manor house," I said. "How many motion cameras are there?"

"The rear of the property has loads," she said. "Give me your phone."

I did as she asked and she opened the map app, finding the correct place and zooming in on it. "This here is a lay-by in the woods; no cameras, as they're not allowed here. It has too much traffic from cyclists, bird-watchers, hikers, stuff like that. He used to put cameras there, but they kept going haywire, so his security team had them removed. This is some distance from the house. You'll be safe there. And there's no need to threaten me; I want Jacob off the grid more than anyone, I promise you."

I closed the car door and returned to Ravi, telling him the news. "Keep an eye on her; she's craftier than she looks."

"Lots of my people want payback for what happened with the Eve transport," Ravi said, then offered me his hand, which I shook, and smiled. "She isn't going anywhere."

I walked over to the car, where Emily had already climbed into the driver's seat. Emily, Nadia, Ji-hyun, and me were going to go end this.

Jacob Maxwell Smythe was about to have an exceptionally bad day.

CHAPTER TWENTY-EIGHT

Emily drove the SUV while Ji-hyun dozed in the back and Nadia looked out of the window, practically bouncing out of her skin with barely contained energy.

"You okay?" I asked Nadia, looking back from the front passenger seat.

The Audi had come equipped with a siren and flashing lights, the latter of which Emily had put on the second we'd driven out of the storage-locker facility. It meant that driving at 115 mph down the motorway was much easier when everyone moved out of your way. Anyone who didn't got beeped and sworn at. I got the feeling that Emily found it therapeutic.

"I'm not so sure we should wait for nightfall," Ji-hyun said, the first words that she'd spoken since we'd set off. "He has at least one hostage we know of. We don't know how Helen is being treated, and we don't know how he's going to react when he finds out that the people he sent to kill Eve are now dead themselves. He'll know we're coming."

"I agree," I said. "Night is several hours away. We need to hit them before then. We still need to scope out the place and figure out where to make the entry."

"There's a drone in the back," Nadia said.

"That could come in handy," I said.

"Dibs," Nadia said. "Never played with a drone before."

"It doesn't have weapons on it," Emily told her.

Nadia considered this for a moment. "That's less cool now."

Even going at speed, it took the better part of an hour just to get halfway along the M3, where traffic decided it was going to form a complete jam, and we got stuck. What should have been thirty or so minutes ended up being nearly an hour before we could get off at the next junction, and then we had to take the back roads around the city of Winchester until we could go north to Kings Worthy, the closest village to where Jacob lived.

I settled into the seat, the air conditioning blowing a cool breeze over me as I wracked my brain to try and figure out why Jacob taking Helen would also involve Callie Mitchell. Something felt off about it. Whatever Callie had planned, the inclusion of rift-walkers automatically made it something we needed to stop.

More things to ask Jacob about when we got him.

The drive became more scenic the further we went, and we drove through small villages that were little more than a pub with a few houses nearby.

"Take a right up here," Ji-hyun said from the back seat.

"Ignore the satnav, then?" Emily asked.

"Yep, just here," Ji-hyun said, pointing to a small dirt road fifty feet or so in front of us.

Emily did as instructed, and we were soon bouncing down a path that could have been used as a rally-car route.

"Stop up here on the left," Ji-hyun said.

"Where are we?" I asked, looking out at the dense wood while the satnav had some kind of episode as it tried to get us to turn around, gave up, and just went silent.

"You broke her," Nadia said pointing to the screen.

Emily stopped the car in a small clearing off the road next to a large ditch. I got out of the SUV and looked around at the woodland which surrounded us. There was a decrepit wooden fence a short walk into the woods, and what appeared to be a huge field just beyond it.

"This is nice," Nadia said as she got out of the SUV. "Peaceful."

Ji-hyun exited the vehicle, still looking at her phone. "Jacob's mansion is about a kilometre and a half in that direction," she said, pointing over to where the field was. "This looks like the closest way to get to the field without being spotted."

"Eve was telling the truth; Jacob never put security here," Emily said, joining us after she'd examined the perimeter of where we'd parked. "Bit surprised, to be honest. Figured this was a pretty serious weakness in his defence."

"The amount of land he has is huge," Ji-hyun said. "There's a perimeter around the actual building. Pretty sure there are going to be cameras and motion detectors there."

I remembered the photos that Ravi showed me. "That's going to take some serious work to get by," I said.

"That's where this comes in," Nadia said, brandishing a black drone that she'd taken out of the boot of the SUV. It was smaller than I'd expected, maybe the size of football—a normal one, not American—and had several lights on it that blinked when she turned it on.

"I need to own one of these," Nadia said, passing the drone to Emily while she picked up the remote control.

"Is there a camera on it?" I asked as the drone took flight, moving between trees at speed until it was out of view.

"Yep," Nadia said, showing me the remote that had a screen on the front, which she turned on, and I suddenly felt very motion-sick.

Nadia got to grips with her new toy while I looked in the boot of the SUV and pulled open the black steel case to see what we'd brought with us. A few rift-tempered knives, a broadsword, a hand-axe, two Mossberg 500 shotguns, two MP5, and an Accuracy International L115A1 sniper rifle. All that we needed; there was enough ammo to ensure we didn't need to worry about running out unless we were about to fight a country. There were also several earpieces—each in their own case—that appeared to all run on a closed network, so we each took one for when needed.

"Got it," Nadia said with glee.

We all huddled around her and watched as the drone flew at a fairly high altitude so we could spot the number of guards within the ample grounds of Jacob's home.

"That's quite a few," Emily said.

"Lots of Range Rovers," Ji-hyun said. "This is looking like some last-stand shit."

"He has nowhere to go," I said. "Once the media find the truth and his lies are exposed, he's a wanted fugitive for murder and a man who will come under the scrutiny of the Ancients. He might not be able to ever get back to Inaxia, but I'm pretty sure someone will take his head back there as an example."

"You think they'll execute him?" Emily asked.

"Eventually," I said. "There are prisons for rift-fused on Earth if they can't get taken back to the rift itself. He'll spend a long time in one. Then in a few centuries, he'll be executed. The Ancients like to make sure the punishments are drawn out."

"Should just do it now and be done with it," Nadia said.

"Don't disagree," I said, looking back at the screen. "Pause there."

The drone stopped flying over a large red-brick wall with a grove of trees on one side and a path on the other. The path led down the side of the house.

"There's a door right there," I said, pointing at the screen.

"That's our ingress," Ji-hyun said. "Two teams of two. One team going that way, the other from the opposite side if possible."

The drone flew around the house where there was a wall and path, the same symmetry as before, although this side didn't have a grove for cover, just open field.

"That's not ideal," I said.

The drone gained altitude, revealing several small buildings a few dozen metres outside of the main compound. "They look like sheds," Nadia said.

"I think they're guard huts," I said.

"Or something very similar," Emily agreed. "There's a lot of open land there. A lot to monitor."

"So, all four of us taking the first entrance and then splitting off into two groups?" Ji-hyun asked.

"Could work," I said. "Those trees look like they give good cover."

"Sniper in the tower like we expected," Nadia said. "Still want to do this during the daytime?"

I checked my watch. "We've got two hours until nightfall. I think we're going to have to wait."

"You think Helen has that long?" Emily asked.

"I don't see why Jacob would kill her after taking her and bringing her here," Ji-hyun said.

"True," Emily agreed. "And it gives Ravi more time to get the Ancients to take the leash off."

"Why hasn't he left the country?" I asked. "He has wealth, means, motivation. He knows we're coming. He knows that his entire life is about to be turned upside down. Why not run?"

"There's something here he needs to stay for?" Ji-hyun said.

"Helen?" Emily suggested.

No one had any better suggestions. We all settled in for the next few hours of waiting for nightfall. No point getting caught out in the open in the middle of the day.

"You're all going to want to hear this," Ji-hyun said from outside of the SUV, and I left the confines of the car and stretched as I walked over. Nadia and Emily were already with her, the latter of whom had been off scouting the area, and the former had brought back her drone and was waiting for the controller to charge after linking it to a cable in the SUV.

"Everyone there?" Ravi asked.

"We're here," Emily said.

"The Ancients are looking into it," Ravi said. "We're on our way to Winchester now; it's not far from there to where you are. We can set up a staging post on one of the many privately owned pieces of land in the area. We'll say it's a training exercise if anyone asks."

"Looking into it?" Emily asked.

"That's the problem with people who live hundreds of years," Ravi said. "You have time to make decisions."

"We're lucky like that," Ji-hyun said.

"If Helen is a rift-walker, why hasn't she just opened a rift and escaped?" Ravi asked. "What's stopping her?"

"Could be a few things," I said. "Could be she can't for one reason or another. Could be she leaves for Inaxia, she'll have to stay a while before she comes back and has enemies there. She might have on those damn glove things that dampen powers, or Callie's version that was a whole skin-tight suit. Or maybe she hasn't used her power in a while, she uses it now and creates a ten-mile-wide tear she can't control."

Emily looked between me and Ji-hyun, alarm on her face. "Seriously? That can happen?"

"Has before," Ji-hyun said. "I assure you, being directly under a tear that just keeps on dumping power onto your head is not a good feeling."

"Is there a danger of that happening now?" Emily asked.

I shrugged. "No more so than any other time. There could be a rift-walker living in your apartment block, and you'd never know until they lost control of a tear and tore apart two blocks in the process."

"It destroys stuff?" Emily asked.

"An out-of-control tear will mess your day up," Nadia said. "And every-one around you."

"There have been villages in history that have just vanished in an instant because of a rift-walker who lost control," Ji-hyun said. "I know because I was in one when it happened. Luckily, I was able to get into my embers before it could pull my body apart or crush me under the weight of power, but most others weren't so lucky. And those who were lucky were merged with the power, becoming elder fiends."

"They were the lucky ones?" Emily asked.

I nodded. "I'm sure it won't happen this time."

"You're sure?" Emily asked. "How sure?"

"Ninety percent," I said.

"Eighty-five," Ji-hyun said.

"Are you serious?" Emily asked.

I smiled. "We're just messing around," I said. "The odds are about a billion to one."

Emily looked genuinely relieved. "I'm going to go walk off you both being assholes."

When Emily was far enough away, Nadia said, "You really messing about?"

"Nope," Ji-hyun said. "It's more like seventy percent not likely to happen. Depends on what's happening to Helen."

Nadia chuckled. "Always wanted to get a front-eye view of the apocalypse."

"There's always a silver lining," I said with a smile.

There was a loud beep from the SUV, and Nadia ran off to the car, practically giddy as she removed the drone and remote from inside and brought them back over as dusk began to settle in above us.

"Have fun," I said, and left her to her drone-flying. I wasn't entirely sure what else we'd be able to learn from watching the mansion, but forewarned is not getting shot in the head. Or however that phrase goes.

I'd quite literally just sat down in the passenger seat of the car when Nadia shouted, "You're gonna want to see this."

I rushed back over as Emily did the same, and Ji-hyun, who hadn't moved from where she'd been seated, leaned over slightly to take a look.

"There are vans showing up on the lawn over there," I said. "Media vans."

"What the hell is going on?"

I watched as more and more vans arrived, all parking on the large field to the left of the manor house.

"On the plus side, I know how we're getting in," Ji-hyun said.

I took out my phone and called Ravi. "The world's press are on his front garden," I told him. "Any chance you have Eve with you and can ask her why?"

There was a muffled conversation. "You're on speakerphone," Ravi said.

"Eve," I said. "Any chance you missed large parts of Jacob's plan?"

"I didn't miss anything," Eve snapped. "He always said that if he was ever cornered and had no other option, he'd show the world why they should be afraid of rift-fused."

"Any chance you can expand on that?" Emily asked.

"I don't fucking know," Eve said. "It was just Jacob sounding off and being an asshole. He's said it for years; no one ever took the idea that seriously that he'd do something stupid and invite the world to watch."

Everyone was quiet for a moment.

"He'll tell the world what he's done," Eve said. "The idea of having everything taken from him by someone else can't be allowed. He needs to still be in control. He'll get ahead of the story, doing the only thing he can."

"Why not flee the country?" I asked.

"Helen," Eve said. "She can't leave the mansion. There's stuff written on the walls of the basement she's in. I don't know what it says; I don't read whatever fucking language it is. I think he *needs* her. You'll have to ask him why."

"So, he's going to tell the world he's not human," Ji-hyun said. "And bring down the current government in the process."

"Of course," Eve said. "The prime minister—who is a moron, by the way—knew all about it. That the cabinet knew about it. That they have done for years and years, and none of them cared because it helped them."

"Jacob is going to tell the world he's a practitioner and then force Helen to open a rift," I said, and the realisation of Jacob's plan dawned on me. "He thinks the Queen is behind it all."

"Helen?" Ravi asked.

"No, the Queen of Crows," I said. "Jacob wants revenge on those who betrayed the Blessed, cast them out of Inaxia and to Earth. The person who actually betrayed them is Prime Roberts, Jacob's father, but he's made sure that everyone thinks it's the Queen of Crows. Jacob's fucked. He knows that it's just a matter of time before the sword drops down, but he also knows that he has a rift-walker with him. Someone who can give him that revenge. He's going to admit to everything he's done, open a rift, step through, and go kill the Queen. Doesn't matter after that; he's done what he's always wanted to do."

"What about Helen?" Nadia asked.

"The writing on the walls concerns me," Ji-hyun said. "I've seen practitioners use writing before to force powers to be used constantly. To make them more powerful. There's some bad shit going on there."

"Did you know Helen was going to be forced to open a rift?" I asked Eve.

"Why do you think I don't want to be anywhere near there?" Eve said. "I gave you enough information to get yourselves there. I don't need to hold your hands."

"I thought you wanted help to disappear," I snapped. "Maybe being open and honest would have been a good start."

"Fine," Eve said, sounding fed up. "I don't know how it's going to work, but I do know that Jacob always had a contingency plan if he got caught. He's been looking for a rift-walker to use for years. He found Helen, and she became his plan. Force open a rift, go through, and in his own words *assassinate a betrayer*. Never said more."

"Anything else you'd like to tell us before I have to hunt you down for getting my friends killed?" Ji-hyun asked.

"Good-bye, Ji-hyun," Eve said.

"Take care, everyone," Ravi said, and ended the call.

"So, Eve is delightful," Nadia said. "Just an absolute delight."

Dusk had now become darkness, and the lights from the manor house and multitude of press vehicles in the distance looked like people engaged at a large festival.

"Everyone get ready," I said. "Time to go do what we came here for."

"No killing Jacob," Emily said. "We need him alive, remember."

"What about everyone else?" Nadia asked.

"Anyone else gets in your way, put them down," I said.

"And make sure they don't get back up," Ji-hyun said.

When we were all ready, we stood atop the hill, looking down on our target. It was going to be a half-hour hike through the trees until we came to somewhere we could come out and cross the land to the press vehicles, using them as cover to get through to the manor house. Jacob had given us an in, although we still had a lot of work to do.

"Strike you as odd that Jacob allowed those vehicles so close to his manor?" Ji-hyun asked.

I nodded. "He's hoping they're going to make shields when the violence starts."

"Or stops the violence before it happens," Emily said.

"Well, let's not keep the man waiting," Nadia said, slinging her rifle over her shoulder and setting off into the dark woods.

CHAPTER TWENTY-NINE

We got through the woods, coming out as close to the media circus as we could. I was concerned that we might get spotted the moment we walked into the throng of trucks and people, but I needn't have bothered; the only people there were inside the trucks, doing whatever technical people did in trucks.

The vast majority of media people had moved away from the campsite to the front of Jacob's manor house.

"I think he might be starting his plan," Ji-hyun said as we set off through the media camp toward the din of noise.

Spotlights had been situated around the front entrance of the manor house, lighting up the front door as crowd grew louder and louder, a hundred people all trying to talk over one another; it was pretty obvious what was going on.

"Ladies and gentlemen of the press," Jacob said into a microphone.

The noise didn't dissipate as we walked around to the edge of the brick wall that separated Emily and me from the throng of people.

"Ladies and gentlemen," Jacob shouted, and this time there was quiet.

My phone vibrated and I took a step to the side, out of view as Jacob began his speech.

"The Ancients have removed any protections that Jacob enjoys," Ravi said. "We're on our way to you."

"How long out?" I asked.

Emily, Nadia, and Ji-hyun had stayed where they were, watching the spectacle unfold.

"Five minutes," Ravi said.

"Jacob is going to do something bad," I said. "Really bad. We're not going to be able to wait for you to get here."

"Arrest him," Ravi said. "Publicly if you have to. Just get him away from whatever he's doing and put a stop to it. Non-violently, Lucas."

The phone went dead and Ji-hyun passed me a pair of handcuffs, giving a second pair to Emily. "We're going to need these," she said.

"He's telling jokes," Emily said. "Jokes. About nonsensical rubbish. He has them eating out of his hand. They're meant to be the purveyors of truth, not his fan club."

"I read somewhere that he could be the next prime minister but he turned down the opportunity," I said. "I assume the actual prime minister owes him a few favours for that."

"Now, my distinguished guests from the press," Jacob said with a wide smile.

He wore a tailored blue suit with white shirt and no tie. He looked both casual and refined. His image was immaculate, well manicured, and utterly false. I wanted to put him headfirst through the front door of his lavish mansion.

"You have come here today not to hear me harp on about government policy or what we have planned but because there is something important I need to tell you all, and I wanted to tell it in a place of comfort for myself."

Several people asked questions all at once. There was a flicker of irritation, but it was soon absorbed back into the facade of Jacob.

"My friends," Jacob continued. "I am here today because I have something important to announce. I am resigning, effective immediately as a Member of Parliament."

Cue loud shouting.

"Before I go," Jacob continued. "I wish to say that I give the prime minister my full support and hope that he is able to maintain the course and continue to deliver the best for this country. He has had my support from day one, and I know that he is the one to take the United Kingdom forward as a global power."

"Can I arrest him now?" Emily asked.

"I'd rather not have to barge through a group of press," I said, fully aware that Helen was captive somewhere on the grounds. "Let's start to make our way toward them and hope that we can grab Jacob before he says anything too outrageous."

"You are probably wondering why I would resign in the middle of an election cycle," Jacob said. "And it is sadly because I have not been honest with my colleagues, nor the people of this great country. Resigning is the decent thing to do when you have brought shame to yourself and the role as a Member of Parliament for this county."

There was a deathly silence now as everyone waited to find out what Jacob had done.

"You see, my friends," Jacob continued, "I am not who I said I was. I was not born in the United Kingdom. I wasn't even born on this planet. I was born in Inaxia in the rift. I am a practitioner. A rift-fused. And I have committed a crime by pretending otherwise so that I could help this country move toward a more prosperous and fairer society. What I did, I did out of love for all of you, but I cannot keep this lie up. I cannot, in good conscience, continue on while my heart is burdened with the lie of who I proclaim to be."

"Did he just out himself on live TV, worldwide?" Emily whispered.

"Oh, yes," I said.

"There, now," Jacob exclaimed, pointing to me as the eyes of the press turned, several holding large cameras.

My face was being broadcast worldwide. *Shit, shit, shit, shit, shit, shit, shit,* I thought to myself.

"His name is Lucas Rurik," Jacob said, pointing at me. "And he is here to arrest me on behalf of the rift-fused. The Ancients. The Guilds. Words many of the people watching will know but not really understand. I am to be sacrificed on the altar of the immortals for breaking their laws."

"I'd give good money if he'd just shut up," Emily whispered as the crowd of press moved aside to give me a straight, uninterrupted walk toward Jacob.

"You see, ladies and gentlemen," Jacob continued, "I didn't invite you here just to tell you about my resignation, about who I really am. The latter is information that the prime minister and government of this country already know. I invited you all here because I want you to see the kinds of power people like Lucas here have. I want you to understand why you should fear the rift-fused. Why you should fear people like Lucas.

"Lucas Rurik is a member of the Raven Guild. He is the last surviving member of the Raven Guild. He is here to arrest me and haul me off for the good of this nation. To ensure that no matter how pure my intentions were, the law is followed. And the law should be followed, for without the law, we are nothing better than animals."

Jacob smiled the entire time he spoke. He'd outed who I was to the world, which was going to be a problem, seeing how the number of people who probably weren't going to be thrilled to discover the Ravens weren't quite as dead as they were meant to be. He'd ensured I had to go nice and easy on him, which was fine, as I had no intention of curb-stomping him, no matter how nice that sounded. And he'd made sure that I was forever linked with the big bad Ancients coming to arrest the little man for doing nothing more than trying to help humans become the best they could be. All of it was bullshit, obviously, but a large number of people watching this unfold didn't know that.

I walked up the steps toward where Jacob stood, smiling. "I bet you're wondering why I just did all of that. The UK government will collapse, you will be recognisable the world over, and I get to finish what I started all those years ago. If I'm going to be arrested by the likes of you, I'm going to take every single fucker down with me. You've left me no choice, Lucas. It's time for a scorched-earth approach."

"You get to be arrested and go live in a dark cell," I told him.

"I just told the media that you should fear the rift-fused," Jacob whispered, looking at his watch. "Time for a demonstration."

The manor house made a groaning noise as the ground beneath my feet shook. I took a step back, and Jacob shoved me, sprinting through the open front door as two of his people followed him, shutting it behind them.

The garden was torn open as parts of the house were shaken free and began to fall to the ground beside me. Someone screamed, someone else grabbed my arm and tried to pull me away as roof of the manor house exploded, and power flooded out. The sky above us was quickly torn open, a mixture of blue and purple power flowing down over the land around us. We were all in deep shit.

I turned to find that it had been Ji-hyun grabbing my arm as she practically dragged me back to the far edge of the lawn.

"Helen," I said to her as the garden was ripped apart, and a huge crack flowed up the side of the manor house.

A pulse of pure rift energy crashed down over the spot where the reporters had been just a moment before, turning the red-brick wall to dust.

"Nadia, Emily," I said. "Get these people out of here."

"I'm coming with you," Ji-hyun said.

I was running to the door just as it burst open and a dozen men came out, all trying to push through the door at the same time.

"Stop," I shouted.

"He's lost his damn mind," one of them said, frantic with fear.

"Jacob?"

"Yes," another said as they managed to extricate themselves from the doorway.

"Get over to the press corps," Ji-hyun shouted as the guards sprinted by us. "Hand yourselves in to any RCU agents; do not make me come look for you."

I grabbed hold of one of Jacob's men as he ran past. "Where is he?"

"Basement, end of the house," he said, the words tumbling out. "You can't miss it."

"Helen," I said, keeping hold of his arm as he tried to break free.

"In the basement," he stammered. "Let me go."

"How do we stop her from tearing everything in half?" I asked.

"I don't know; I'm just hired help," he shouted.

I released my grip and let him go, before entering the house.

Jacob's interior decorator must have been from the Roman Colosseum school of architecture, because everything inside the large hallway beyond the front door made me feel like I was transported back there. And running through the house, it was clear that was the theme. Everywhere we went were stone columns painted red, white stone statues of various deities, mosaics on the floor using tiles to make squares inside circles and vice versa. High ceilings decorated in colourful flowers of gold and orange.

Large chunks of the floor and ceilings had cracks in them, and several statues were missing limbs, so it really did feel a bit more like Rome than maybe Jacob had been going for.

The further into the house, the worse the destruction. We went down a flight of stairs that were cracked down the middle all the way up, but either side of the crack was polished so much, I could see myself in them, and at the bottom found that the ode to Roman decorating stopped and was replaced with wood-panelled walls, huge paintings of landscapes, and the heads of various animals knocked onto the floor, most being destroyed as purple and blue energy leaked through the cracks.

Ji-hyun pushed open a set of wooden double doors, although considering the state of them, they appeared to be held together by sheer willpower alone.

Beyond the doors was a large room with a high ceiling that currently had a hole in it the size of a large car. Looking up through the hole, you could see the tear in the sky. In the middle of the room was a woman with olive skin and dark red hair. She looked to be in her mid-thirties at most, although it was impossible to tell her real age. She was chained by the wrists and ankles to the hardwood floor and was on her knees, her eyes closed as the air around her shimmered purple.

There was writing all over the floor, the walls, even the ceiling. It lit up a bright turquoise.

"This is ancient Akkadian," Ji-hyun said. "And Latin, and Greek, and Chinese, and about a dozen other languages."

"Helen," I said calling out the woman's name. I wasn't sure if it was Helen, but I was hoping there wasn't a second rift-walker around the place, opening tears in space and time.

"Yes," she said.

"I need your help," I told her, taking a step forward as the entire room shook.

I fell to my knees, ignoring the pain, and got back up as more shakes occurred.

"What did they do to you?" Ji-hyun asked.

"Practitioner," Helen murmured as the entire wall in front of us was torn open, power spilling through the tear from the rift. The tear showed us images of Runnervale, of where Necia and I had stayed. Of Crow's Perch.

"Forced me to open a tear," she said. "Can't close it."

"Where did Jacob and his friends go?" I asked.

"Tear," Helen said as the tear began to grow inside, pushing up through the ceiling, which crumbled as the power leaked into it, raining down pieces of plaster and brick onto the floor near where Helen stayed.

"How do we get her to stop?" Ji-hyun asked, sounding more panicked than I'd heard from her in a long time.

"Helen," I said. "We need to stop Jacob, but I can't do that until you've shut off this tear."

"Writing," Helen said, pointing to the floor. "Chains. Forced."

The writing on the floor all around Helen was intact, even while the same writing on the walls began to crumble from the damage being done to it. There were bright yellow bits of writing on the chains, too, presumably to ensure that once Helen started using her power, she was incapable of stopping.

"Ji-hyun," I said. "Break the chains."

Ji-hyun punched a blue-flame-covered hand down onto the chains as they connected to the floor, and unleashed the power she held inside her, melting the metal chains beneath her hands. I turned to smoke, rushed up into the air, and flew back down to the ground, re-forming and striking the floor, casing a shock wave of power that tore the floor apart all around the impact.

The writing flickered once, twice, and then there was a rush of power as it all exploded outward from Helen, setting Ji-hyun and me careering off into separate parts of the room.

The tear on the wall blinked continuously, until finally the scenery of Crow's Perch vanished, leaving us all in a dark room.

"Lucas," Ji-hyun called out. "You okay?"

"Didn't feel great," I said. "You?"

"I want to hit something," she said.

She was going to get her chance sooner or later.

"Helen," I said.

"Here," she said softly. "Jacob had me captive for months. Blames me for helping to betray the Blessed. He's going to kill the Queen of Crows. He's taken his people with him. You have to stop him."

"I'm sorry to have to ask you," I said.

"Please don't," Helen said.

"Can you open another tear? We don't have the time for me to go via my embers," I asked, feeling pretty damn shitty for asking, but knowing I had no other choice. "We need to get him back here to stand trial for his crimes. I can't do that without a rift-walker."

"You just saw the damage I did," Helen said. "You want to risk that again?"

"If we don't, he gets away," I said. "And more people get hurt. I'm sorry."

"I can only take one of you through," Helen said. "And once I'm done, it's going to be a few hours before I can use it again."

"I'll stay here," Ji-hyun said. "People might need help, or Jacob might have more allies."

"I'll have to bring you back here," Helen said. "To this house. I don't think I'll have the energy to change the destination."

"It's okay," I told her. "Are you sure you can do it?"

"Do I have a choice?" Helen asked.

"Everyone has a choice," I told her softly.

"Not if it means stopping Jacob from hurting people," Helen said as she got to her feet.

"Is there a key for those?" I asked.

"Man by the name of Kurt has it," Helen said. "He's a minion of Jacob's. He went through the tear too."

"Okay, we find Kurt and get those things off you," I said.

"And then find Jacob and beat him into a coma with them," Helen interrupted.

"He needs to come back alive," I told her. "We have to show the humans that we don't just kill our problem people. Even if we want to. He committed crimes as a human; he needs to be tried for those crimes. Publicly."

"You can flog him with them if you like," Ji-hyun said. "No one's going to notice."

"I need to get out of here," Helen said. "Back outside. Please."

"Let's go out to the rear garden," I said. "Away from prying eyes."

I took Helen's arm, and she sagged against me, so I picked her up and carried her. "If there's any trouble, can you kill it?" I asked Ji-hyun as we started out of the room.

"My pleasure," Ji-hyun said, taking point.

Whatever damage had been done to the interior of the house, it was the same outside, with the back-garden steps leading up to the house cracked. The garden had a gaping wound in the middle of it that had been filled with water, presumably from a burst pipe.

I sat Helen down on the steps, and she rested her head against the metal railing. "Just a second. You're riftborn, yes? You know it's a real pain that you can't just go through, get him, and bring him back."

"I know," I said. "But one embers, one person."

"You know I can't bring him and you back together," Helen said. "I don't think I'll be strong enough."

"I'll get my own way back," I told her. "Just bring Jacob back here. You okay to wait, Ji-hyun?"

"I'm not going anywhere," Ji-hyun said. "Get the piece of shit back to me, and I'll take care of him."

Helen got to her feet, albeit wobbly. "You know this isn't going to feel good for you, don't you?"

Riftborn going through a tear opened by a rift-walker tended to have unpleasant side effects. They were usually short-lived, thankfully. "If there was a quicker way, I'd be happy to use it. The embers take too much time."

"I can't take you into a city," Helen said. "Can't use a tear stone, either. I have rules too. I'll get you as close as I can, though."

Helen held out her hands in front of her and a tear opened, revealing the entrance to Runnervale. "This will have to do."

"Let's go," I said, and stepped through the tear into the rift.

CHAPTER THIRTY

The first thing I did was throw up behind a rock. Well, not the first thing. The first thing I did was say, "Oh, no." Then I threw up behind a rock. It was neither heroic nor brave, but unfortunately, it's what happens when a riftborn enters the rift without using their embers.

I sat on the ground for a moment as the world spun around me.

"You okay?" Helen asked as the tear closed and she stood over me.

"You look worse than I do," I said with what I hoped was an approximation of a smile.

Helen sat down beside me, her body just folding up. She went from sitting to lying and made a low moaning noise. "I hurt," she said. "Everywhere."

"Are you going to be okay to move?" I asked, getting to my feet and wishing I'd gone through my embers.

Neither practitioners nor revenants had any issues with sickness going through a tear; it was one of the things that meant Jacob and his people were going to be well ahead of us.

I managed to get to my feet, felt a little better, and took a deep breath. "Helen," I said.

She waved without looking up at me, sighed, and stood. "You know, I've only just met you, but I get the feeling I'm going to regret it."

"I did save you from tearing apart the fabric of reality," I said.

"And I thank you for that," she said as we set off at a walk toward the city of Crow's Perch, which loomed ahead of us. "Do you have any idea how we're getting in?"

"I figured I'd work that bit out when we got there," I said.

There were six guards stood at the front entrance to the city; none of them appeared to be happy to see me. "I'm sorry, and you are?" one of them asked me.

I showed him the Guild medallion. "Lucas Rurik. I'm here to see the Queen. It's urgent."

The guard looked over to his friends before looking back at me. "I was under the impression the Raven Guild was extinct."

"You were wrong," I corrected. "You want to delay me further, or would you like to step aside so I can do my job?"

"No," the guard said.

I looked up at the ramparts; there were no guards patrolling them. "So, you look the other way while Jacob and his people assassinate the Queen, yes?"

"The fuck you say?" the large guard asked me. I remembered him from the last time I'd been there, along with his pack of giggling friends.

As he stepped closer to me, I drew a dagger from my belt, grabbed hold of the guard, turned him around, and moved my dagger so that the tip of it was mere millimetres away from his right eye.

"I wouldn't blink," I whispered. "Open the gate. Now."

"Open the fucking gate," the guard shouted.

"But we were told . . . " one of the other guards said.

"Open. The. *Fucking*. Gate," the guard screamed.

The gate was opened.

"Now leave," I told the guards. "I'd be quick; my arm is getting achy. When we're through, you're going to shut the gate behind us."

The guards dispersed several dozen feet, and I walked through the open gate with Helen and the very-still guard. When through, I turned and watched as the gates were closed. There were plenty of people in the Crow's Perch who deserved to be there, and I didn't want to have to hear about how they'd gotten out and hurt people.

"Ladies and gentlemen," I shouted to the crowd of people blocking our way.

A large number of the crowd turned back toward me.

"Which way did the man and his newcomer friends run?" I asked.

"Toward the palace," a young man said. "Some of the guards were with them."

I pushed the guard heavily to the ground. "How many are with him?" I asked.

"A few dozen," the guard said. "We're going to end the Queen once and for all."

"Why no guards on the ramparts?" I asked.

"Had to take them from somewhere," the guard told me. "Can't get on the ramparts toward the palace."

"Is that the head guard?" a large, muscular man with bushy white beard asked.

"I believe it is," I said.

"You spat at me when I was brought here," the man said.

"He had his people beat me with sticks," a woman shouted.

I stepped in front of the guard, who scrambled over to the side of the road. "We need to get to the palace," I said, pointing to Helen, who waved. "The Queen is in danger. Please move aside so that we can help."

"And him?" the big man asked me.

"My compliments," I said.

"Ronnie," the large man shouted. "Take these two down the dark path. It'll be empty. He's a Guild member; don't fuck about."

Ronnie, who it turned out was a skinny young man with short dirty-blond hair and looked about eighteen at most, stared at my medallion, nodded, and took off.

"Keep my boy Ronnie safe," the large man said.

I nodded and the crowd parted, allowing Helen and me to set off at a run after Ronnie, following a different pathway than I had before, when I'd arrived with Necia, as screams of pain could be heard behind us.

"They're going to kill him," Helen said.

"Yes," I said as we ran down a maze of mostly empty alleyways, at least once feeling like we were doubling back on ourselves.

Ronnie didn't slow for a moment and dodged piles of boxes, people lying in the street, and pools of liquid I didn't want to know about, as if he knew about them in advance. It was all I could do to keep up without turning to smoke.

Eventually, we came out at a small clearing with a single large tree under which were two wooden benches. I counted four alleyways that led from the clearing, and Ronnie took a second to look around.

"Everything okay?" Helen asked.

Ronnie nodded. "This way," he said, and set off again.

"I'm not sure how much more I can run," Helen said.

We'd been running for probably ten minutes, and considering what Helen had been through, I wasn't surprised she was exhausted.

"Ronnie," I shouted, and the young man stopped and turned back.

He looked over at Helen, who was looking pale. "She okay?"

"Rift-walker forced to keep a tear open," I explained. "She's exhausted. We need somewhere safe for her to rest."

"I'm good," Helen said, putting a hand against the nearest wall.

I caught her as she started to slide down the wall, her legs giving out.

"Can you carry her?" Ronnie asked. "It's not far."

I picked Helen up for the second time in a day.

"You know, this counts as being in a committed relationship," Helen said.

"I'll buy you dinner when we get back in one piece," I said.

"You'd better," Helen said as I set off. "I don't want people to think I get picked up and carried by strange men on a regular basis."

The noise of the crowds got louder and louder as we continued on through the city, and it wasn't much longer until Ronnie led us out of a thin alleyway right behind a large number of the city population.

"This way," Ronnie said, guiding us around the outskirts of the people as there were *oohs* and *ahhs* from the crowd, punctuated by the sound of metal on metal and cries of pain. Whatever they were watching was clearly entertaining them.

Ronnie found a strip of the thinning crowd and weaved through it, people moving aside as he shouted that he needed to see the Queen.

"Yeah, we all do, *girl*," a large man said as he pushed Ronnie back.

The man looked beyond Ronnie to me as I lowered Helen to her feet. He was taller and broader than me, but the second he saw the Guild medallion, he stepped aside. "Didn't know you was with the Guild, Ron," the man said.

Ronnie punched the man in the bollocks as he went by, and the larger man dropped to his knees. "I'm not your *girl*," he said.

The remaining crowd parted and we continued on to the large square where Necia and I had been taken by the Queen during our last visit. The entire square was surrounded by citizens of Crow's Perch as several of the Queen's guard were engaged in combat with a combination of Jacob's own guard and a few people from the city.

Commander Pike was using a shield and spear as he tried to fight off three men, none of whom wanted to make that first attack.

"Pike," I shouted. "Jacob's people are here for the Queen."

"She's inside," Pike shouted. "Could use a hand. Some of the gangs decided to help Jacob."

"Ronnie, please keep Helen safe," I said.

Ronnie drew a dagger from beneath the folds of his clothes. "I will."

I drew my own daggers and ran over to Commander Pike. Two of the men attacking him peeled off to face me, which gave Pike the opening to slam his spear through the throat of the nearest one and kick another in the back, sending him bouncing across the ground.

The final attacker came at me with murderous intent in his eyes, but I easily avoided the swipe of his sword and drove one of my daggers into his throat.

"Where's the Queen?" I asked Pike.

"In there," he said, motioning to the palace.

"Why is everyone just standing around, watching?" I asked.

"Some are waiting to see what side they should pick," Pike said. "And some are just here for the entertainment."

"I'll get Jacob," I told Pike, and ran into the palace, narrowly avoiding an arrow as it hit the doorframe beside me. I turned to smoke, moving across the foyer as a second arrow passed through me, and re-formed next to the bowman, who swiped at me with his bow and tried to stab me with an arrow.

I avoided the attack, drew both daggers, and slammed the blade of one into the bowman's thigh. He screamed in pain, trying to step back, but he was too close to the wall, and my second blade found a home in his temple.

I ran through the palace, finding the hallways beyond the opening foyer to have fierce fighting from a number of Jacob's people, several of whom were now in their revenant forms as they fought. A door to a kitchen was open, and there was the foot of a dead soldier that stopped it from closing. I didn't have time to help everyone and hoped that the Queen's guard would be able to hold their own as I darted into what had been the throne room.

A woman stood in the middle, with several dead bodies at her feet. She wore crimson-coloured leather armour, and as she turned to me, I saw the dark skull-like mask adorning her face. Her body changed, covering in red-and-black matter that glistened in the light of the room. Blood revenant.

There was a repeating crossbow on the floor between us. I leapt for it and fired twice at the blood revenant, the arrows slamming into the creature and disappearing inside of it, leaving only ripples on the surface of her skin.

"That isn't going to do a damn thing," she said, her voice now crackly and deep. No trace of humanity left.

I dropped the crossbow to the floor and drew one of my two rift-tempered blades as I got to my feet.

One of the blood revenant's arms grew by two feet, hardening as it moved until it was a blade of blood. Not an ideal thing to fight in the close quarters of the hallway, but then, the lack of space meant she couldn't swing it around without hitting the sides, so it wasn't all bad.

"So, where's the Queen?" I asked.

"With Jacob," the blood revenant told me. "You won't get to her in time."

She moved quickly, closing the gap between us and changing the length of the blade as she did so that it was smaller, more moveable in such tight confines. I avoided her blade and slashed across her stomach with my own, but her body flowed out of the way, the blade moving past her. She kicked me in the chest, but I was already moving back, keeping away from the blade as it came down across where my head would have been.

I wrapped smoke around one arm—from wrist to elbow—hardening it until it was like stone. Unlike when I turned to smoke, creating smoke for such matters didn't involve modifying a part of my body. Even so, it was a weird sensation.

The blood revenant sprinted toward me, and I ran forward to meet her, parrying her blade away with my own, pushing her arm to the side. I'd always expected blood revenants to have slippery or sticky skin, but it felt like normal skin, except it was cold. Like sticking your hands in a freezer to remove something. You held on too long, it started to hurt.

I let go of her arm and kicked out at her leg, but she lifted her foot, taking the blow on the thigh, before spinning away, her arm turning into a whip that flicked less than an inch from my face.

Gods, I hated fighting blood revenants.

I moved back out of the room and into the hallway. I kept moving back until I reached the door that led to the kitchen. The blood revenant stared at me as I stopped moving.

The creature snarled at me.

"We haven't got all day," I called out.

The revenant sprinted down the hallway. When she was only six feet away, she launched herself at me. I threw myself back, through the open door, landing on my back and rolling to the side as I pushed the dead foot away with my hand, and slammed the door into the blood revenant's face as she landed exactly where I'd been standing.

I scrambled to my feet, moving back across the room to the kitchen, where I stopped next to a large cooker that had a big pan of water atop the counter. I tested the water, and it was hot enough to be uncomfortable but not quite boiling. I switched the cooker on with the small lever on the side. The rack of flames burst to life on top of the cooker.

Blood revenants don't like heat, which was why Ji-hyun never really had an issue with them.

The door burst open and the blood revenant stalked into the kitchen. It watched me with evil intent as it kicked the dead body of the soldier to the side and screamed at me.

I moved away from the cooker, and the blood revenant took the bait, moving to the side of the kitchen. It swiped at me over the kitchen counter that sat in the middle of the room, and I threw a metal pot at her head, which she batted aside, making a huge amount of noise as it crashed into the floor.

I threw a second and third pot as I moved back across the kitchen toward the cooker, each one batted away, each one making more noise.

I stopped moving when I bumped up beside the cooker, feeling the heat radiate along my back.

The blood revenant came on, vaulting over the side of the kitchen counter, her hands now claws, outstretched to impale me. I threw the pot of now-close-to-boiling water at her.

I'd already turned to smoke as the boiling water hit the flesh of the blood revenant. It was not a pretty sight as it bubbled and blistered. Some of the larger blisters burst, filling the kitchen with the noxious smell of burned flesh. Where the contents touched the kitchen, it burned like acid.

I turned to smoke and moved over the kitchen counter, back into the living area, and drew the second dagger as I re-formed, walking around the kitchen counter as the thing on the floor writhed in agony, her white mask melting down her chest, showing nothing but muscle and empty eye sockets behind it. I punched one of the blades into the back of her skull and slit her throat with the other. I stepped back as black blood poured out of the wounds. It was still alive, although *alive* was a relative term. The boiling-hot water had done its job and given me an opening.

My arm hurt where the blood had splashed on it, burning through the hardened smoke. I removed the smoke along with my jacket, and the door was kicked in and several guards, including Commander Pike, entered the room.

"That a blood revenant?" Pike asked.

I nodded.

"It dead?" one of his guards asked.

Commander Pike severed the blood revenant's head from its shoulders with one swipe of his rift-tempered broadsword. "It is now," he said.

"Don't get cocky; I'd already done the hard bit," I pointed out.

There were more crashes from inside the palace.

"I'm going for the Queen," I told them, running out of the kitchen and into the throne room as I discovered that Commander Pike was beside me.

We left the throne room by the rear door and practically sprinted up the staircase beyond as the noise of fighting from upstairs echoed all around us.

We had to step over several dead people, most of whom looked like they lived in Crow's Perch.

"Gang members who betrayed the Queen," Commander Pike said.

We reached the hallway above and followed the sounds of battle, soon finding more dead, along with two destroyed constructs, one of which had been cleaved in half.

Pike and I followed the noise, bursting through a set of double doors and into a large room with wooden floors and various weapons adorning racks along two sides of the room. There were large windows running along one side, and in the centre of the room was the Queen of Crows, with two more destroyed constructs at her feet. She was covered in blood and swayed slightly as Jacob lunged for her with his sword; she pushed his arm out of the way and head-butted him, kicking him in the chest and sending him to the floor near the window.

"Come on, you fucker," the Queen shouted before staggering and falling to her knees.

Commander Pike was at the Queen's side in an instant as Jacob and I locked eyes.

"Hey, fuck-face," I said, and Jacob jumped out of the window.

"Stop him already," the Queen snarled.

My pleasure.

CHAPTER THIRTY-ONE

I turned to smoke, moved through the ruined window, and re-formed on the cobbled stone of the square outside the palace. Jacob was just getting back to his knees. There was no one else to fight for him. The crowd had stayed where they were, although they were now eerily silent.

I looked over at Ronnie, who had Helen beside him. Ronnie nodded and I gave him a thumbs-up as I shrugged off my jacket.

"You're done, Jacob," I said, picking up a one-handed broadsword from the ground. "You're going back to Earth, you're going to be tried for your crimes, and you're going to spend a long time in a deep, dank cell somewhere."

Jacob brushed himself down and drew a rapier from its scabbard, tossing the latter away.

"We're not duelling," I told him. "You either surrender or I hurt you. Pick one."

Jacob rushed me, slashing and thrusting with the sword, much quicker than I'd anticipated, although I still parried the attack. The rapier was the faster weapon and had the longer reach, but Jacob was just using anger to attack. There was no finesse or skill. Even so, getting caught with it was going to do me serious damage.

I avoided another thrust of the rapier, drew one of my daggers, and blocked a second swipe, pushing myself away to put distance between us.

Jacob roared in defiance and anger and charged me. I threw the broadsword at him. He batted it aside, but it was enough for me to close the gap, kick out his knee, grab his arm, and snap his wrist like a twig. His rapier clattered to the ground, and I kicked it away, pushing Jacob in the opposite direction.

Jacob got back to his feet and kicked out at me, but it was an easy block, and I stepped into his guard, grabbed his lapel, and threw him over my hip, landing him face first on the ground.

"Stop it," I said to Jacob as Commander Pike and the Queen appeared in the doorway of her palace.

"Never," Jacob said, getting back to his feet and charging me again.

I pushed his good arm away, stepped to his side, and buried my elbow in his sternum. Every ounce of fight left him in one rush, and he crashed to his knees.

I bent down to whisper, "You know she didn't betray you?"

"You lie," he said, looking up at me with hate in his eyes.

"No, I don't," I said. "The person who betrayed the Blessed was Prime Roberts. Your father."

"Kill him," the Queen commanded, and two guards advanced toward me, swords drawn.

"No," I told her loud enough that everyone was going to hear. "He goes back to Earth to stand trial. You want him after that, talk to the Ancients. Right now, he's leaving with Helen over there."

The entire crowd turned to look at Helen, who appeared to very much not want to be there.

The Queen of Crows crossed the square and stood before me. "He killed my people," she seethed. "He attacked me. No one gets to do that and live."

"Everyone dies eventually, Your Majesty," I said. "But his day is not today."

"You are in *my* city," she said.

"And I just helped save it," I told her. "And you."

The queen touched her arm at the shoulder. "I might have been able to hold him off for a while longer."

"Maybe," I said. "He hurt a lot of people on Earth. He knows where Callie Mitchell is; he knows what's going on. Can't get that intel out of him if he's dead."

The Queen stared at Jacob, and even behind her mask I knew her face was twisted with anger. "If I ever see him again, he dies."

"Thank you," I said.

The Queen looked at me. "A Guild member came to my rescue, putting his life on the line for their Queen. We will not forget that."

I sighed. "That's not exactly what happened."

"It's what I'm going to tell people," the Queen said. "Let them leave."

"You lie," Jacob screamed as I lifted him to his feet. "She betrayed us."

"No," the Queen said softly. "No, I didn't."

Jacob crumpled back to his knees. "She lies."

"Your father betrayed you all," I told him. "Accept it or don't; I don't care."

Helen walked over to me. "Is he ready?" she asked.

I removed my medallion and passed it to her. "Give it to Ji-hyun," I said. "It'll let me come through to England."

Helen opened a tear beside me, and I dragged Jacob to his feet as Ji-hyun came into view. I gave her a thumbs-up, a gesture she returned, and then I pushed Jacob through the tear.

Helen winced as Jacob landed by Ji-hyun's feet only to be kicked in the head and knocked out cold. He deserved it.

"I'll see you soon for that meal," Helen told me.

"You can count on it," I told her, and she stepped through the tear, which snapped shut behind her.

I turned to the Queen of Crows. "Any chance I can use that secret passage and get to the tear stone?"

"Of course," the Queen said.

I walked over to Ronnie. "Thank you for that," I said, offering a fist, which he bumped.

Ronnie stared at me for a moment before nodding, and I returned to the Queen as she stood atop the stairs to her palace, and the entire place erupted with cheers.

"Why didn't they all come to your aid?" I asked her as we entered the palace.

"That is our way," she said. "If I am not strong enough to hold this position, I do not deserve it. Should the gangs help, I would be beholden to them afterward, favours would have to be given, and other gangs would become distrustful of my allegiances. They support me, even love me, but they are neutral when I am challenged. My guards and I were enough. And you, of course."

We walked through the palace, where the wounded were being tended to, and the Queen stopped and offered her thanks more than once. Every time she did, I saw the swell of pride in the guard she'd spoken to. If the Queen ever decided to challenge the Primes in Inaxia, they might have some serious trouble.

She took me through the underground tunnel and out to where we'd fought the criminals who called themselves the Blessed.

"I will leave you here," the Queen of Crows said, offering me her hand, which I shook.

"Take care," I told her.

"You are welcome here at any time," she said. "Preferably without the fighting next time."

"You have good people on your side," I said. "They might not have taken up arms to fight for you, but I saw the devotion in their eyes."

I walked over to the tear stone, opened my embers, and stepped inside.

To say that Casimir and Maria were surprised to see me was an understatement.

"How are you feeling?" Maria asked as we walked the streets of the embers.

"Good now," I said. I hadn't realised that I was still feeling any effects from coming through the tear, but stepping into my embers had immediately made me realise I'd been somewhat fatigued after all.

"Do you have more to do in England?" Casimir asked.

"I don't know yet," I said. "I'm hoping this is done now. Jacob is locked up, and we'll find out where Callie is, but I think it's going to be more complicated than that."

"It always is," Maria said as we reached a tear back into Earth.

"See you soon, Lucas," Casimir said.

I nodded a thank-you and stepped through, ending up in a large bedroom.

The room I'd stepped into had a queen-sized bed and a smattering of furnishings. A large TV sat atop a chest of drawers at the end of the bed.

I walked to the closest door—one of two in the room—pausing at the window. I looked down on a dark city before me. Could be London; could be anywhere. It was night-time, and with only the myriad of lights from the streets below and the buildings around them, it looked like most other large cities I'd been in. I pushed open the closest bedroom door, revealing an en-suite bathroom that someone had painted midnight blue. I closed the door and opened the one on the opposite side of the bed, stepping out into a long, dark hallway.

The door at the end of the hallway opened, and Ravi appeared. "You weren't as long as I'd expected," he said.

"How long was I gone?" I asked him, following him through into a large living room where Ji-hyun, Nadia, Emily, and Helen were all seated on a large horseshoe-shaped couch.

"About six hours," Emily said.

"And Jacob?" I asked.

"Under arrest at a secure location," Ravi said. "We'll get the answers we need from him. He is not happy about the revelation that his father betrayed the Blessed."

"So, what happens now?" Emily asked.

"I'll stay here and help make sure no one tries to break him out of prison," Ji-hyun said.

"I'll stay with you," Emily said. "It's been nice, having a job to do."

"I'm going wherever you go," Nadia said, pointing finger guns in my direction.

Ravi shook my hand. "It's been a pleasure, mate. You're welcome to stay and talk to the piece of shit."

"I will," I said. "Thanks. Then maybe we can find Callie Mitchell and figure out what the hell she's doing."

"Jacob was going to hand me over to Callie," Helen said. "He kept going on about it. Don't know why, just that she needed rift-walkers."

"We'll keep you safe," I told her.

"Good, because I'm done with all of this shit for the foreseeable future," Helen said.

"We'll get her a safe house," Ravi said. "We might need evidence and testimony from you. From all of you, possibly. The Ancients have taken away any protections Jacob has, and his name and crimes have been plastered all over the news. It's probably going to bring down the UK government."

"Here's your chance to elect people who aren't in league with criminals," I said.

"Best-laid plans," Ravi said.

Ji-hyun tossed me my medallion, got up from her seat, opened a nearby cupboard, and removed half a dozen shot glasses and a bottle of bourbon.

She poured six glasses, and we all went over and picked one up, raising it. "To friends," she said. "May they always have your back."

"Hear, hear," everyone said, and took a shot.

Ji-hyun refilled the glasses and we all raised them a second time.

"To the future," Nadia said. "No matter what it brings."

We took our shots and Ji-hyun filled them again.

"Seriously?" Helen asked.

"Last one," Ji-hyun said. "You want this toast, Lucas?"

"To the rift," I said. "The reason we're all here in one form or another."

"May it at some point stop providing interesting times," Ravi said, and we all took a final shot.

Interesting times. I was pretty sure that by the time I was done stopping whatever Callie and her friends were up to, I was going to be more than ready to stop living through those.

ACKNOWLEDGEMENTS

In some ways, the second book in a new series is harder to write than the first. To me, the second book is where the reader gets to see more of the world, new characters, new interactions, and how our main character deals with this. It's a little more where the gloves come off, and the overall story arc of the series is given more shape, even if some of it is only through hints.

There are numerous people who have helped me get this book written.

My wife, Vanessa, and my daughters, Keira, Faith, and Harley. Their support can't really be measured. They're part of the reason I write; they're part of the reason I ever decided to try and get published in the first place. Thank you for everything you do.

To my parents, who have always been supportive of my writing and read every book I publish, thank you for being there all these years.

To my family, my friends, all of those people who have supported me, who have contacted me to tell me they've loved my work, who listen to me going on about ideas and complaining about how my brain won't shut up for five minutes to let me work on one thing, you're all awesome.

My agent, Paul Lucas, is a hell of a good guy and one I'm privileged to be able to call my agent and friend. Thank you for all you do.

To everyone at Podium. I've been working with Nicole, Victoria, Leah, Cole, and Kyle for a few books now. It's been a genuine pleasure to work with them all and I look forward to what the future brings.

My editor, Julie Crisp. An incredible editor who helps make my work better, and who manages to translate the sometimes word salad that is an early draft of my book. Thank you for being awesome to work with.

To Pius Bak, the artist who did the incredible cover to *The Last Raven*. Thank you for your amazing work.

And to everyone else who picks up my books, whether this is the first one or those who have followed my work for years, thank you. I hope you enjoyed this story, and that you continue to come along on the ride for future books.

ABOUT THE AUTHOR

Steve McHugh is the bestselling author of the Hellequin Chronicles. His novel *Scorched Shadows* was nominated for a David Gemmell Award for Fantasy in 2018. Born in Mexborough, South Yorkshire, McHugh currently lives with his wife and three daughters in Southampton.

DISCOVER
STORIES UNBOUND

PodiumAudio.com

Printed in the USA
CPSIA information can be obtained
at www.ICGtesting.com
JSHW022217140824
68134JS00018B/1116